LOOKING FOR PA

LOOKING FOR PA

A Civil War Journey
from Catlett to Manassas,
★1861★

GERALDINE LEE SUSI

EPM Publications, Inc.
McLean, Virginia

Library of Congress Cataloging–in–Publication Data

Susi, Geraldine Lee.
    Looking for Pa: a Civil War journey from Catlett to Manassas,
    1861 / Geraldine Lee Susi.
        p. cm
    Summary: When Ma dies, a brother and sister leave the family's
    northern Virginia farm to search for their father who has joined the
    Confederate forces at Manassas battlefield.
    ISBN 0–939009–87–0
    1. United States—History—Civil War, 1861–1865—Juvenile Fiction.
    [1. United States—History—Civil War, 1861–1865—Fiction.
    2. Brothers and sisters—Fiction. 3. Virginia—Fiction. 4. Bull
    Run, 1st Battle of, Va., 1861—Fiction.] I. Title.
    PZ7 . S96565Lo 1995
    [Fic]—dc20   95–6328
                                                                    CIP
                                                                    AC

EPM Publications, Inc.,1003 Turkey Run Road,
    McLean, Va 22101
Printed in the United States of America

Cover and book design by Tom Huestis

Illustrations by Douglas P. French

DEDICATION

To my loving family
because being a caring and loving family
is what this story is all about

May 1861

"Don't go, Pa," Jessie pleaded tearfully as she tugged on his hand. She held his large, calloused hand with her two tiny ones, pulling him desperately back towards the house.

Pa swept her up in his arms and said, "I won't be gone very long. Your Ma and Jacob understand why I'm going. You have to be brave like them, little girl." Jessie's only reply was to nestle her curly blonde head into Pa's deeply tanned neck and to wrap her feet around his waist like an ivy vine clinging around a big oak tree.

Jacob stood beside his mother. He wanted to do exactly what his sister was doing, but he knew his Pa expected him to act like a man. He bit his lower lip to fight back the tears. There was a lump in his throat that just wouldn't be swallowed. At age eleven it isn't that easy to be a man. He glanced up at his Ma and saw a tear rolling down her cheek. Pa pulled Jessie off and set her down next to Ma. He went over to Ma and put his strong arms around her. She didn't say anything either, just hugged him back.

"Annie, I'll be back as soon as this all gets taken care of. It won't take long, I'm sure, and Jacob will be able to help you tend to the farm until I'm back. I wish I didn't have to go, but this has got to be

★ ★ ★

done if we want to protect our way of life."

"I know that, Nate. But it don't really make the parting any easier. We'll be fine till you get back. We'll miss you though. Jacob will be able to help take care of the crops till you get home. We're all strong and healthy. Don't you worry none about us. You just take good care of yourself and don't get yourself into any fights you don't have to."

"You know I'll be careful. This should all be settled very soon and I'll be back before you all even have time to realize I'm gone." Pa kept one arm around Ma's waist and reached out and put his other hand on Jacob's shoulder. "Son, you got a mighty big responsibility now. I know you can do it though. It's only 'cause I know I can count on you that I'm able to go join with the other men to fight for our rights. You know what to do for the crops as well as I do. You got a good head on your shoulders. Do just what you figure I'd do and you'll be just fine. I know I can count on you to look after your Ma and your sister, too, though I'm sure your Ma don't think she needs looking after." He gave Ma a quick squeeze and winked at her with that winning grin of his.

Jacob nodded and swallowed hard at the lump that was forming in his throat again. He knew his voice would crack if he tried to speak. Pa didn't seem to notice. He was hugging Ma again and turning to hoist himself on Dramus, the mule. He checked in the reins and gave a couple of nudges with his heels and the mule started off. Pa looked back and gave a wave of his hand. Then he turned around and nudged the mule to a quicker pace.

Ma reached over and put one arm around Jacob's shoulder and waved half-heartedly with the other. Jessie locked her arms around Ma's waist and leaned her head on Ma's hip. The three of them stood there watching Pa ride down the red clay road. As he stood there, Jacob thought of the day when Pa had returned from a supply trip to Warrenton. Pa had jumped down from the wagon and thrown the mule's reins to him.

"Take the wagon on by the shed, boy, and unhitch Dramus

★ ★ ★

and water him down. I've got to talk to your Ma," and he hurried off to the house. It wouldn't be until the next day that Jacob would find out what it was that Pa'd needed to tell Ma in such a hurry. What it was would change their lives forever.

That day, after Jacob had milked Nanny, the goat, and fed the pig and the mule as he did every morning, Pa had put his big, rough hand on Jacob's shoulder and led him out toward the trees that lined the edge of their fields. Jacob knew this was going to be a serious talk because that's what his father always did when he had something he wanted to explain to him or to scold him for. He couldn't think of anything he'd done wrong, but he figured it had to do with whatever Pa and Ma had talked about yesterday because things had been mighty quiet at supper last night.

"Jacob, let's go sit under the hickory tree. I need to explain some things to you, boy, and I hope you'll be able to understand."

"Sure, Pa. You know I'll do anythin' you ask me to do. An' you know I do my best. I try mighty hard."

Nathan Harding turned his son around to face him and put a hand on each shoulder. He bent down slightly and looked the boy square in the eyes. "I know you do, son, and that's why I know I can do what I gotta do and I know I can trust you to take care of things."

"Sure, Pa?" Jacob's reply echoed the concern and uncertainty he was hearing from his father.

"Sit down, boy. I'll try to explain what's going on."

Jacob sat down next to his father in the green grass that grew so abundantly under the hickory tree. In another couple of months this spot would be the site of dozens of rambunctious squirrels scurrying around gathering and storing nuts for the winter. But, now, he knew he and his Pa had serious business to discuss. He waited patiently for him to begin.

"Son, I don't know if you heard me talkin' to your Ma about the things that have been goin' on in the South this winter. Like South Carolina choosin' to leave the Union and President

★ ★ ★

Lincoln not takin' too kindly to all that's been happenin'. Six more states left and joined up with South Carolina and they elected Mr. Jefferson Davis to be their president. Now, I thought maybe our Virginia could stay out of all this fuss and that maybe Mr. Lincoln would just leave things alone. Why even our own Governor Letcher tried to set up a peace meetin' right here in Virginia. It almost worked. That was until Mr. Lincoln took things into his own hands in the middle of April. He called for 75,000 soldiers to put down those states that were causing the uprising.

"Virginia had to take a stand. What I found out in town yesterday was that on April 17th our state delegates voted to secede; that means they don't want to be a part of the Union. So now Virginia's taken a stand with the South, and Governor Letcher's calling for volunteers to fight with the Confederate Army of the South. They need volunteers. Son, we're farmers and we ain't got much. But we got to fight for what's right and what we believe in. We ain't got industries like the North. Farming's all we know. It's all I know, and I want to keep Virginia the way it is. A lot of Virginians from this northern part are torn about what to do. There were lots of hard words and hard feelings in town. People shoutin' and arguin' about who's right and who's wrong.

"I told your Ma last night that I'm goin' to go an' enlist. I'll help you get everything in order before I go, but they need men now. Your Ma's strong and she understands. She don't like it none, but she knows I gotta do this. You and Jessie can help keep things going while I'm gone. You been helpin' me since you was old enough to follow along behind a plow. The way folks are talkin' this ain't gonna take long. I'll be back before the crops are ready to come in."

"But, Pa, why do you gotta go? Ain't there enough other men that ain't got families?"

"Son, it don't work that way. A man has to do what he thinks is right. I can't set around hoping someone else will fight my battles for me. You remember that, boy. If it's impor-

★ ★ ★

tant to you, then you gotta fight for it. The way we live is
important to me. I want it to stay this way. Do you understand
what I'm sayin' to you, boy?"

"I think so, Pa. But I'm afraid of what might happen, what
might happen to you. Will it be dangerous, Pa?"

"Whenever men get to shooting at one another it's dangerous. But maybe it won't have to come to that. We Hardings
know how to take care of ourselves. That's why I tried to teach
you everything I could as soon as you could learn it. You've
been the best right hand man a father could have and that's why
I know I can trust you to take care of the farm and help your
Ma. I've always said us Hardings don't need nobody else. We
take care of our own. We ain't beholden to nobody for nothing.
We work hard or we trade for all we got. You remember that,
too, boy. We're proud folk. We ain't got much, but we got
enough to be healthy and happy. We don't ever beg for nothin'.
You got that, boy?" Jacob nodded his head with a convincing
shake, and Pa reached out and squeezed him against his side
with his strong arms. Jacob had felt secure in his grasp.

Now, standing here with his mother's gentle hand on his
shoulder, his thoughts came back to the present. Jacob, Ma,
and Jessie kept standing together holding on to one another
until Pa was no more than a speck on the road and finally disappeared around the bend.

Only then did Ma break the spell. "Time to get going.
We've got things to do. Your Pa wouldn't take kindly to us just
standin' around like this. We'll all hafta work just a little harder to take up the slack. Ain't fair for Jacob to hafta take all the
load." She squeezed his shoulder reassuringly and the three of
them turned and headed toward the house.

Saturday, July 6, 1861

It seemed like an eternity, not just seven weeks since the day Pa had left. Things had gone just like normal for a while. Jacob had tended to the crops and the animals, Ma had tended the house and her garden, and Jessie had helped both of them. They had all worked harder than usual, but that was to be expected with three doing the work of four. But then things happened that they could not control and on this summer evening Jacob and Jessie found themselves sitting in the dusky light next to their mother's bed. They sat quietly watching her for any movement, any word. She'd been lying like this for two days now ever since the burning fever had gone away. Tonight her forehead and cheeks felt cool and clammy to Jacob when he reached out and touched her. He pulled the quilt up higher around her neck and shoulders. Jessie looked at him and whispered, "Is she gonna be all right?"

Jacob knew he couldn't say yes. He was scared, but he did not want Jessie to be afraid, too. She was only eight and didn't realize just how sick their mother was. So he said simply, "I hope so, Jess. I really hope so. Go on to bed now and get some sleep. We have lots of work to do tomorrow. I'll sit up by Ma." Jessie went over to their trundle bed and crawled under the covers. "Good night, Jacob."

"G'night, Jess."

Jacob continued to sit by his mother's side. He could hear her labored breathing, her short, fast gasps for air. He laid his head down against her arm and chest. He wanted to be near her. He could hear strange rattling noises in her chest as she

★ ★ ★

was breathing. Seeing her like this was hard for him. Ma was a small woman, but she had always been so strong. Oh, not strong like Pa, but in other ways. She was the one who always took care of him and Jessie and Pa when they were sick. And now, here he was, trying to take care of her, and Pa not even around to tell him what to do. She'd been fine when Pa left. But then she got drenched to the bone in a thunderstorm a few days later, while she was out tending her vegetable garden. Jacob remembered that soon after she began coughing, and then she seemed to get tired easily. That just wasn't like her at all, but she never complained, never said anything. Jacob just figured she was working too hard, what with Pa gone and all. Then one day she just couldn't get out of bed. She told Jacob she was sure she'd be fine if she could just rest a couple of days. Then she'd be up and working as good as new. He and Jessie did everything then, everything their Ma asked them to do and more. But it wasn't enough. Soon Ma wasn't asking anymore. She was just lying there, like now. They needed Pa. How he wished Pa were here to hold all of them now. He would know what to do to help Ma. Pa had said, "Do what you think I would've done." But Jacob had never had to deal with such sickness before. He thought to himself, Pa'd be mighty disappointed if he were here. He, Jacob, had not done a good job. He had let Ma get sick and now what were they going to do?

Jacob lifted his head and reached over to readjust Ma's quilt. Something wasn't quite right. He sat quietly in the dark straining to hear. Then he realized what was wrong. He couldn't hear the sound of her labored breathing anymore. She was so still. He touched her face and put his cheek by her nose and mouth. He couldn't feel any air going in or out. He put his ear to her chest. No more rattling noises. No faint thumpety thump. It couldn't be. It just couldn't be. She must be sleeping soundly. She'd be all right in the morning. She had to be. He laid his face down on the covers and cried softly until he fell asleep.

★ ★ ★

Sunday, July 7, 1861

The first soft light of morning came through the window. Jacob lifted his head. Jessie was standing silently beside him, her big grey-blue eyes watching over the older brother she adored. There had been other brothers and sisters, but two had died at birth and another, John, had died of a fever when he was about a year old. Jacob remembered this baby, but Jessie had been too young to remember. So there had really only been the two of them as far as she was concerned. They always got along well. Living out so far, they had only each other for company and that made the bond between them even stronger.

Jacob tried to clear the sleep cobwebs from his brain. He looked into Jessie's eyes which were just like Ma's and then he remembered what was lurking in the recesses of his mind, but he knew that he didn't want to face it. Reluctantly he turned his gaze to look at his mother's face. She looked so peaceful just like she was sleeping. Maybe he'd been wrong last night. Maybe...? He stood up and touched her cheek. It was cool. He felt her neck searching for a pulse, but he couldn't find one. He felt her wrist. Surely he could find her pulse there. Nothing. He let go of her arm and it dropped heavily to the quilt and then slid off the side of the bed hanging lifelessly next to his leg. Jacob lifted her arm and laid it gently across her chest.

Jacob turned away and looked at Jessie. She was staring at Ma. He took her by the hand and led her over to the table and

★ ★ ★

pulled out the bench for them to sit on.

"Jessie..." but he couldn't finish what he had to say. Big tears began to roll down his cheeks.

Jessie stood up in front of him and wiped away the tears. "It's okay, ain't it, Jacob? Ma's gonna be all right and we'll all take care of each other, right? And then Pa will be home soon? Please, Jacob? Tell me it's okay."

Jacob looked at those pleading, trusting eyes. He wished for her sake he could make everything all right, but that wasn't in his power. Forcing himself to look into her eyes, he whispered, "That's just it, Jessie. Ma ain't gonna be all right. It's just you and me now. "

Jessie still hadn't realized what he was trying to tell her. How could he do this to her? He took both of her hands in his and said in a trembling voice, "Ma is dead, Jessie. She died last night. She just wasn't strong enough to do it all. The sickness got the best of her. We did everything we could, but it wasn't enough. Jessie, you and me, we gotta take care of each other now. Jess, Ma is gone."

Jessie stared at him blankly for what seemed like forever and then she started to cry. He held her in his arms stroking her mass of curls. He was crying, too. They stayed there together, the two of them, holding one another and sobbing until the tears wouldn't come anymore. He held her for a while longer waiting for her sobs to stop.

"Jessie, I know how bad you feel 'cause I feel bad, too. I don't know what we're gonna do now. I know we gotta take care of the farm just like Pa told us to do. We gotta take care of Ma, too. We have to keep goin' and doin' things like always. Right now I want you to stay here and watch over Ma. I've gotta go outside to feed the animals and milk Nanny. Milkin' just don't wait for anything. When I get done we'll have somethin' to eat and we'll try to figure out what we have to do. Okay? Can you do that?"

Jessie nodded her head, her eyes red and swollen. She watched silently as Jacob went out the door.

★ ★ ★

The Harding farm was not a big one. In fact, by most standards it was rather small. It had afforded their family a way to
eke out a living and had provided enough for them to eat and
still have some left over for bartering. There was Dramus, the
mule, Squealer, the pig, and Nanny, the goat. Pa had traded
Nanny's twin kids, born early this spring, for Squealer and
some seed for planting. Nanny would provide them with milk
for almost a year. There were some chickens, but they weren't
much bother because they scratched and pecked all around the
farm, laid a few eggs, and occasionally ended up in Ma's stew
pot. There was one other animal and that was a present Pa
brought back for Jessie's birthday when he went to Warrenton
that last time for supplies. It was a tiny grey kitten that Pa res-
cued at the feed warehouse and brought home in the box of
supplies. It had been so little that Jessie had had to feed it
Nanny's milk dripped from the corner of a rag. There was
something special between Jessie and that cat. It went everywhere that Jessie went from morning till night.

When Pa had asked Jessie what she would name it, she had
replied in her most grown-up voice, " I think Cat. Just plain
Cat." And that's what it was.

Jacob finished his feeding chores and carried the bucket of
goat milk into the house. Jessie was sitting on the chair next to
Ma's bed rocking herself back and forth and Cat was sleeping
in her lap. It was one of those rare moments when Cat was
asleep instead of scampering about playing as she usually did
most of the day.

"Come on, Jessie. Come drink some milk and have some
ham and leftover biscuits for breakfast." They sat at the table
each thinking his own thoughts. Finally Jacob said, "Jessie,
it's gonna be hard for us for a while, but I think we can still
take care of things. I'm gonna need all your help though. Do
you think you can do it?"

Jessie nodded her head, but the look in her eyes was not at
all convincing. She was small for her age and there was only
so much you could expect her to do. Jacob knew he would

★ ★ ★

have to do most of the work now.

"I think the first thing we should do is to take care of Ma."
He remembered how Pa always took care of anything that died
on the farm right away. Pa said that was real important. Jacob
continued in a soft voice, "I remember when little baby John
died. Pa told Ma he'd make him a right fittin' burial place. I
reckon that's where we ought to put Ma, too. I know that's
where she'd want to be. Right next to John and the other two
little babies. That special place behind the house at the top of
the little knoll where the dogwoods and the redbuds grow so
pretty. I 'spect that's why Pa chose it. We're gonna have to
make a nice place there for Ma, too. Do you think you're
strong enough to help me dig?"

Jessie nodded her head. As they went out he picked up two
shovels by the shed. He trudged up to the knoll followed by
Jessie who in turn was followed by Cat. It was a somber pro-
cession since even the normally scampering kitten seemed to
sense that such actions would not be appropriate. She crept up
the hill with her grey head down and her tail trailing low.

Jacob marked off an area to the right of the three tiny wood-
en crosses already on the knoll. Although the ground was fairly soft from the spring rains, Jacob quickly realized that this
task was going to take them a lot longer than he'd ever imagined and once the hole got a little deeper, there was only room
for one person to stand in it and dig. Jacob told Jessie that she
could take Cat and go on back to the house if she wanted to,
but the frightened look in her eyes let him know that she wanted to stay right by him. So she sat off to the side under a dogwood tree.

It was almost dusk when the hole was as deep as Jacob felt
he could make it. He was already having to reach above his
shoulders to throw the dirt out of the hole. He remembered,
too, that he still had to milk Nanny before he could rest, even
though he was so tired. They would have to wait until morning
for the burial. The two trudged wearily back to the shed, hand
in hand, with Cat bouncing along behind them. Jessie stood

★ ★ ★

and watched as Jacob did the milking. In spite of his weariness he couldn't resist squirting a stream or two of milk at Cat which she then licked off her face and off the ground. It even brought a hint of a smile to Jessie's somber face.

After milking the goat they each had a long drink of milk, shared some more with Cat and fed the rest to Squealer mixed in with his feed. The pig grunted ecstatically at this unexpected treat. The children walked wearily up to the house and collapsed fully clothed and covered with dirt, side by side on their trundle. Exhausted by the emotion and the work of the day, they slumbered without care, unmindful of the death that shared their room.

★ ★ ★

Monday, July 8, 1861

When morning came, Jacob woke with every muscle in his body aching and his stomach rumbling with hunger. Even though he was used to working hard he'd never had to dig so long and intensely before. He forced himself to get up and go out to feed the animals and milk the goat. The blisters on his hands hurt as he milked. Even though he used only his thumbs and fingers to strip her of her milk, it was still painful. He knew that if he didn't milk her well she wouldn't produce as much milk. Pa had always told him that. Pa had taught him lots of things, but Pa hadn't prepared him for this. He was on his own now. He had to take care of everything, the animals, the farm, and Jessie.

Now he had to figure out how they could carry Ma's body up to the knoll. Ma was a small woman and he was big for his age, but even a grown man would find such a task taxing and Jacob wanted to be able to treat his Ma's body gently. It was the least he could do. And he also wanted to be able to tell Pa they'd done their best for Ma, just like Pa would have done. He was already wondering if Pa would blame him for not taking better care of Ma.

Once in the house, he fixed breakfast for himself and Jessie. Nanny's milk was warm and tasty as always and he made up some mush. As hungry as they both were, anything tasted good. While he was eating, Jacob decided that they could wrap Ma carefully in Granma's quilt and tie each end securely. But how could they get her up to the knoll? His eyes fell on the

★ ★ ★

trundle bed and the little wheels Pa had fitted to it so it could be rolled easily under their parents' bed during the day. If he and Jessie pulled it they could probably haul the trundle up the knoll like a cart. He could also hitch Nanny to the trundle. With her help they could probably do it easily.

And that was exactly what they did. Nanny wasn't any too happy about being forced to work like that, but with a little coaxing and the lure of some tender greens from the garden, she helped them pull the makeshift bier up the hill. Jacob carefully slid their Ma's quilt-wrapped body into the grave. Then he had said the Lord's prayer because that was the only prayer their Ma had ever taught them and Jacob knew you should pray for the dead. Next he took out his small knife and cut off two dogwood branches which he tied together to form a cross. He laid it on the ground and began to shovel the dirt. At the first sounds of earth thudding on top of the quilt, Jessie bolted away running down the hill. He knew this part was hard, but he couldn't take the time right now to go soothe her fears.

He had just finished mounding the earth over Ma's grave and had placed the cross at one end, when he was surprised to feel someone tapping him on his back. He turned and saw Jessie looking up at him with tears streaking her dirty face. In her hand she held out a scraggly bouquet of daisies, black-eyed Susans, and Queen Anne's lace.

"That's real nice, Jess. Ma would have liked them a lot. She always liked it when you brought her flowers. You put them on there. That will make it special."

Jessie bent down and laid the flowers on top of the earthen mound and then stepped back and curled her small hand around Jacob's. The two of them stood there silently, knowing that when they left this place they would have to face the reality of what it all meant. Nanny began to bleat, trying desperately to get away from the trundle to which she was still tied. She had eaten all the sweet grass that was within her reach and she wanted more. Besides, Jacob realized, it was milking time again.

★ ★ ★

Tuesday, July 9, 1861

Last night had been the first night they were truly alone. They had lain on their trundle, and the silence and the darkness had seemed more intense than ever before. The dark had never bothered him, but this time it was different. He had reached out and held Jessie's hand as if that would make the feelings of helplessness, of abandonment, go away. Jessie had squeezed his hand so tightly that he realized she must be feeling the same way, too. They had stayed that way for a long time, silent and unable to fall asleep and unable to do anything about it. Now after that restless night, Jacob was considering their options.

"Jess, I know Pa told us to take care of the farm and wait for him to come home. But we really don't know how long that might be. And besides he didn't know Ma would get sick. I know that we gotta let him know about Ma. I'm scared to tell him. I tried my best, but I just didn't know what else to do for her. But Pa's gotta know. I keep thinkin' about it. We know that he went to Warrenton to sign up. Surely someone there could tell us where he is and how to get word to him. We could walk there and it should only take us a day or so. Pa always could go to and from town in one day when he rode on Dramus. It shouldn't take us much longer than that to walk. Once we get word to Pa, we can come back home and wait for him. Why maybe he'll still be close by to town and we'll be able to talk to him ourselves and bring him home. Whaddaya think,

★ ★ ★

Jess? We could bring him home ourselves. Wouldn't that be great? That wouldn't be hard. We could do it. You could walk to town with me, couldn't you, Jess?"

Jessie had perked up as her brother spoke. The mere mention of Pa had brought a sparkle to her eyes. She nodded her head as she stroked Cat curled in her lap. She seemed to be thinking quietly for a minute, then she tapped Jacob's arm and pointed at Cat with a questioning look on her face.

"Sure, Cat can come with us. Would you like that?"

As Jessie nodded her response, Jacob became sickeningly aware that he had not heard her utter a word since... since he had told her that Ma was dead. He looked at her with disbelief in his eyes. He could read in her face the concern his look was causing her.

"Jessie, what's my name?" He said it as gently as he could, but inside his stomach was sick with anticipation. He was afraid. Afraid because he just didn't think he could deal with any more problems. "Jessie, say my name." Now his tone was getting almost angry as if he could force her to answer. Then he reached out and shook her, yelling "Say my name! Say anything, Jessie!" And with that she began to cry, huge sobs shaking her body. Jacob just stared at her with disbelief and then finally cradled her in his arms and rocked her back and forth. He'd never had to face anything like this before in his life. He wondered what else could go wrong. He was uncertain about what to do. Her death was a terrible shock, but could death make someone stop talking? He didn't know what he should do. He continued to hold her and rock her. He murmured, "It's okay, Jess. It's okay. We're gonna go find Pa. He'll take care of us. He'll know what to do. Pa will know what to do."

And with that declaration, Jacob made up his mind to look for Pa. Until that moment, Jacob hadn't really known what he should do. But talking to Jessie he knew that they had to get Pa and bring him home. They needed him now more than any army ever did.

The rest of that day, Jacob went through his chores mechan-

★ ★ ★

ically. His brain was trying to figure all the things he should do or not do. That night as he lay in the trundle beside Jessie, he could tell by her rhythmical breathing that she was sleeping peacefully. At least one of them was getting some rest. He lay there putting together a plan for how they could find Pa. What should they take? How long would it take? Would Jessie be strong enough? Would he be strong enough? Could an eleven-year-old do all that he had to do? Question after question raced through his brain until he thought his head would explode. Eventually he fell into an exhausted sleep.

★ ★ ★

Wednesday, July 10, 1861

Jacob awoke with a start. Jessie had already gotten up and had begun to make some breakfast for them. When she noticed that he was awake, she walked over and handed him the milk bucket. He knew that she was telling him in her way that she was going to do all that she could to help and that she was ready to go find their Pa. He gave her a hug and then headed out the door for the shed.

After chores and breakfast, Jacob began to go about the farm collecting whatever he thought they might need for their journey. Although he was hoping that they would only have to go to Warrenton, he realized that his Pa had already been gone for over a month and a half. It had been mid May when he rode out, and it was now the beginning of July. He could have been sent anywhere in that time. But Jacob preferred to think that Pa could still be as close as town. However, he decided that they should prepare for a longer journey. In addition to Jessie and Cat, he'd already decided to take Nanny and Squealer, too. Nanny had to come because she had to be milked twice every day and her milk would help feed them each day. Squealer, on the other hand, couldn't do much for them, but he had to be fed and Jacob just couldn't figure out how he would explain to Pa that he had lost so much in the short time Pa had been gone and he couldn't add Squealer to that list. He decided that the chickens could fend for themselves and the crops and the house would wait for their return. He was sure they would be back in no time at all.

He took some time to make rope harnesses for Nanny and for Squealer. He also rigged up two burlap sacks so they could be draped over Nanny's back. She could be their miniature mule. He didn't want to take too much stuff, thereby slowing down their travel time, but by the same token, he wanted to be able to take care of all the members of his strange little caravan. If all went well he hoped they could be ready to leave tomorrow. The sooner they were on their way, the sooner they'd be back.

In the house that evening, Jacob had Jessie help him make a larger than normal batch of biscuits. Even stale they would be easy to eat along the way. He checked through their provisions in the springhouse and in the smokehouse and took some corn meal, and some bacon and ham. He added in a tin of lucifers, matches, in case they needed to start a fire. His sling shot and his knife would also be handy. He figured he could always get an occasional rabbit or possum if they really got hungry. Pa'd always said he had a wicked aim with that slingshot. He included a tin plate, a cup and a spoon. He also had an old canteen that he and Pa used whenever they were working out in the fields. That and Nanny's milk should be all they would need. He went to sleep that night dreaming of meeting up with Pa. He slept soundly.

★ ★ ★

Thursday, July 11, 1861

Jacob was up at the crack of dawn. He gave the animals extra feed because he knew they would have to graze and root for food along the way and at least they'd have full bellies before they started. He and Jessie had a good meal, too. They gathered together all the things they planned to take and packed them in the two burlap sacks. They rolled up their two quilts and tied them with twine. They were almost ready.

Jacob spotted Ma's hairbrush on the washstand and in a sudden impulse, he took it and began to brush Jessie's golden blond curls which were always so unruly. Pa said that they made her look like a little angel. Jacob awkwardly plaited them into one braid at the back of her head.

"There, Jess. That'll be cooler for you. It don't look as nice as when Ma does it, but Pa will like it. An' don't forget your bonnet to keep the sun off your head." He ran the brush through his own straight sandy hair and then put it back on the table. Ma had always kept his hair neatly trimmed with her shears.

As he got to the door, he turned and took one last look around the room to be sure everything was in order. Was he forgetting anything? He pulled the door shut behind him. He knew that things would never again be the same. He thought to himself, "Bye, Ma. We'll be home soon with Pa."

They walked up to the shed. There he harnessed the goat

★ ★ ★

and placed the two sacks across her back fastening them and the blanket rolls to the harness. Then, while Jessie held Nanny's lead, he set about to harness Squealer. This task was not as easy as he'd anticipated. Squealer had no intention of having a rope around his neck and chest. And because he was still a young and agile pig, he managed to slip through Jacob's grip several times before the boy finally straddled him and worked the harness onto him. Once he realized he'd been outwitted, Squealer became a model traveler, at least for the present time.

The milk bucket was the last thing attached to Nanny's harness. Jacob led the ladened goat, while Jessie held Squealer's lead, and Cat followed along. They were certainly a strange sight to behold and in their youthful innocence they were ready to go anywhere to find their Pa. Yet in their wildest imaginations, they could never have imagined all that lay ahead of them as they set off on their journey.

The rolling Virginia countryside was a patchwork of woods and fields divided by small streams or runs, by stone and split rail fences, and dotted by an occasional pond. The softer greens and myriad colors of spring had given way to the deep greens of summer. The July heat was making the roads hard and dry, and the little group of five kicked up a small cloud of dust behind them.

The brilliant cardinals and their not so brilliant mates flitted in and out of the trees as the group trod along. Everything was going quite smoothly and the boy was thinking to himself that they would get to town in good time at this pace when Squealer, their "model" traveler, decided it was time to have a snack. He took off with a lurch for a little stream at the side of the road, dragging the unsuspecting and speechless Jessie with him. Squealer was about ten or twelve weeks of age and weighed about fifty or sixty pounds and when a growing shoat decides it's mealtime, there's not much you can do to convince him otherwise. Jacob yelled out, "Hold on tight, Jess. He'll probably stop when he gets to the water. I'm coming right

★ ★ ★

★ ★ ★

behind you." However such advice was unnecessary, because Jessie was doing just that and trying desperately to keep her feet beneath her. She was running as fast as her little legs would carry her. Nanny up to this point was minding her own business and ambling along politely, but when she saw the pig head for the weeds and water, she didn't want to be left out of anything good that might be down there for the taking. So there they were, both youngsters hanging on to their rope leads for all they were worth, and grateful that the stream was only a short distance away. Cat, frightened by the initial commotion, darted up the nearest tree and sat in the fork of it mewling piti- fully. Once the pig and goat reached the creek, they stepped right in and drank noisily. Jacob decided it was easier not to fight them, so he tied each animal to a nearby sapling.

"Are you all right?" He looked at Jessie and inspected her from top to bottom to make sure she hadn't been hurt. Her hands had chafed some from holding on to the coarse rope lead and she was covered with road dust, but otherwise she seemed okay. "You did just fine, Jess. You didn't let him get away. I'm proud of you."

As Jacob brushed the red clay dust off her, she became aware of the high pitched meowing of Cat and ran frantically up the hill towards the sound to see what had happened to her pet. Jacob followed along found Jessie wildly trying to jump up to reach Cat in the crook of the tree. It wasn't that high, but Cat hadn't yet learned that if she could get up a tree she could also get down. Jacob climbed up and picked up the frightened, clawing, little grey mass of fluff and handed it to his sister. She cradled the kitten in her arms and soothed it into a gentle purr. They all returned to the creek.

Her thirst quenched, Nanny was contentedly grazing on the poison ivy vines that were abundant on the trees and banks. This was one of her most favorite treats. In fact, Ma had said because Nanny ate so many of those shiny green leaves that it made her milk special, and that drinking it kept their family immune from the plant's poison. It made sense since none of

★ ★ ★

them seemed to get that awful rash that Pa said so many other folks got, and working on the farm they were all exposed to plenty of it.

Jacob looked around following the sound of contented grunts and snuffing, and there was Squealer, his pink barrel-shaped body knee deep in the muddy bank, rooting with his mud-covered blunt nose for the tender plant roots he enjoyed so much. The young boy shook his head with dismay as he began to sense that this journey was going to be a bit more complicated than he'd anticipated.

He could just see his sister at the top of the rise. She had put Cat in her bonnet which had fallen off her head and now hung in front of her and she was nonchalantly picking some ripe berries. In total exasperation, Jacob flopped down in a shady clearing and folded his arms over his face. If you can't lick them, you might as well join them, he thought, as he closed his eyes for a brief rest.

Jacob awoke with a start to find Jessie sitting beside him, watching him as a mother would watch a sleeping infant. He sat up and saw that she had spread her apron between them and on it were two biscuits and a mound of fresh berrries. She had been waiting patiently for him to wake up.

"Jessie, you mustn't ever let me fall asleep like that again." His accusing tone hurt her feelings, and he realized quickly that she had thought she was doing the right thing to let him sleep. So he gently added, "You have to wake me up if I go to sleep unless I tell you different, okay? Otherwise, we'll never get to Pa."

She nodded her head, reached down and offered him a biscuit as her way of apologizing. She was so trusting and so innocent, he couldn't ever hurt her on purpose. He felt this overpowering need to protect her from everything. Losing Ma had made him realize how delicate life really was. You could not just think everything would stay the same forever. He was learning life's lessons the hard way.

They munched on the biscuits and berries and shared drinks

★ ★ ★

of water from his canteen. He'd refill it with fresh water before they started out again.

Jacob rounded up the animals. Nanny came willingly, having eaten and drunk her fill, but Squealer, in typical pig style, was never quite full. If left to his own devices, he'd be content to root and eat all day long. That's probably why, by November, he'd weigh a whopping two hundred pounds and when butchered would provide the family with smoked meats for the whole year. So Jacob pulled and tugged, and got the mud-coated rascal back on the road and ready to travel. Meanwhile Jessie re-tied her apron around her waist with a bright reddish-purple berry splotch right in the center. This time she led the goat, while Jacob firmly and convincingly controlled Squealer's lead. Cat purred contentedly from her queenly perch inside Jessie's bonnet. Obviously, Cat had done the best job of figuring out the safest and easiest way to make this journey.

Jacob had only made this trip into town once or twice with Pa. So he couldn't remember exactly how far they had to go. Besides riding on a wagon pulled by a mule gives you a whole different perspective on the world. So they would just have to press on until they reached their destination.

Squealer was behaving a little better, partly because the mud had dried into a crusty coating on his delicate pink skin thereby affording him some protection from the hot afternoon sun as well as now having Jacob's firm grip on his lead. Whenever they could, they walked in the shade of the trees along the side of the road instead of on the road itself. They all felt the heat. Frequent stops for water were in order for all of them whenever a little run or pond appeared on their way and the animals grazed here and there as they went along. Now, however, the children kept their leads more closely in check to avoid a repeat of the morning's stampede. Jacob glanced at his sister and saw that Nanny was leading her more than she was leading Nanny. She was plodding along forcing one foot in front of the other, yet she had a determined look on her face as if she were compelling herself to go on.

★ ★ ★

Jacob was anxious to keep going, but he suggested, "How about if we rest for a bit and let the animals feed awhile? It's too hot for all of us. Later I'll milk Nanny, and we'll all have something to eat and drink. When it's a little cooler we can walk a bit farther." He could tell from Jessie's grateful look and vigorous nod that she liked that idea a lot.

The long days of summer would afford them extra travel time in the evening when it wasn't quite so hot. All of them enjoyed this rest period. Eventually, Jacob milked Nanny and all except the goat shared in her liquid bounty. The children scooped out cupsful with the tin cup they'd brought along. Jessie poured a portion in the tin plate for Cat. The remaining milk was mixed with a bit of meal in the bucket for the pig. Nanny, relieved by the milking, was happily munching the vines and plants within her tether's reach.

As the sun sank into its final arc and the temperatures abated some, the group resumed its trek along the road. Now they did stay on the road, stirring up a trail of dust. The animals, milked and fed, were willing to follow the children without any fuss.

Feeling they were finally making some good headway, Jacob began to scan the hills and gulleys for a place to camp for the night. Obviously they weren't going to get to Warrenton by dark, and he had no idea how far they'd gone or how far they still had to go. Even with all their stops, they must have gone quite a way. Jessie had walked as quickly as her little legs would carry her and, though Jacob knew he wouldn't hear any verbal complaints from her, he hadn't been aware of any non-verbal ones either. He knew that she was as eager as he was to find Pa. Perhaps even more eager, since she was the apple of Pa's eye and there was no denying that. Oh, Jacob knew his Pa loved him, too, but there was something that lit up in his Pa's eyes when his tiny golden curled angel crawled into his lap at the end of a hard day. She'd kiss his cheek and giggle with joy as he'd tickle her ribs. Jacob and Ma would laugh right along with them since watching those two together was

★ ★ ★

a pleasure in itself. Yep, Jacob thought, Pa was going to be thrilled to see them tomorrow.

Just ahead he saw a stand of oak trees and what looked like a small creek. That would be their home for tonight. They tethered each animal to a tree after allowing them to drink, and then the two children unrolled their quilts and spread them on the ground. As they snuggled down together in the dark, they were aware of all the usual night sounds of cicadas and peepers and an occasional whippoorwill. They were also aware of sounds they weren't so sure of, like mournful owl hoots and the rustling sounds of nocturnal creatures out scouring their territory for food. He felt Jessie inch closer to him. It was strange and eerie to be in the middle of nowhere. Somehow all the sounds seemed amplified. Jacob felt a tapping on his shoulder and in the dark he could barely see Jessie pointing out towards the clearing. There, all along the edges of the oaks and across the fields, were millions of tiny little lights blinking on and off creating a magical fairy land. The fireflies, in the peak of their mating ritual, reassured the two children that they weren't alone and that everything would be just fine.

"Ain't it beautiful, Jess? It's like it's not real. Let's see how many we can count before we fall asleep." And that's the way they drifted into slumber their first night out.

★ ★ ★

Friday, July 12, 1861

Jacob rolled over in those last sweet moments of sleep before waking. He felt soft lips caressing his cheek and he murmured, "Ma? That you, Ma?" She always liked to wake him with a kiss on his cheek like this whenever he'd sleep late. That was one of the things he liked so much about her. The gentle nuzzling continued and he snuggled down into the cover. Then he felt a sharp nibble on his ear and he sat bolt upright only to look right into a pair of golden eyes with horizontal black slits in them. With her long hairy muzzle, the goat nibbled his cheek and he realized he'd only been dreaming about Ma. He was here in the woods and Nanny was trying to tell him she needed milking.

"How'd you get over here, you troublemaker?" gasped Jacob. Then he saw the slack rope dragging on the ground. He whipped his head around to where he had tied Squealer and was relieved to see the pig was still attached to his tree and contentedly rooting in the ground. Jacob would have to be more careful when tying the animals at night. He got up and began his morning ritual of chores. They were always the same, only now the place was different. Jessie woke and after a bite to eat, they were anxious to get on their way.

"Today's the day, Jess. Won't be long before we find Pa. He'll be glad to see us. We'll tell him everything that's happened. Then we'll go back home together. Aren't you excited?" Jessie nodded her head and smiled up at her brother.

★ ★ ★

A short while later, the children could see occasional clouds of dust in the distance. At first, they were puzzled, and then Jacob realized excitedly, "That's got to be the Alexandria Turnpike. Pa told me about it the last time I went to town with him. It's the main road that all the farmers and travelers use to go from Warrenton to Alexandria. You have to pay money to travel on it if you're going to go very far, but we don't have to worry because meeting up with that road means we're almost there!" As if in anticipation, the five of them picked up their pace.

As they approached the turnpike, Jessie scooped Cat back into her bonnet. That would be a much safer place to be. The children held onto their animals and kept to the side of the road to avoid the wagons that passed by them going in each direction. Having always kept to themselves with Ma and Pa out on their farm, this was at once exhilarating and frightening to them. Jessie had never been to town and Jacob had only been twice and never alone like this. Up ahead they could see houses and buildings. The turnpike went right through the center of Warrenton and right up to the old courthouse door. Jess stayed real close to Jacob while taking in all the amazing sights and sounds of a bustling town. Many of the buildings were draped with red, white and blue bunting. Jacob looked around while trying to decide where to start asking about Pa and realized that this must be left from the Independence Day celebration. Pa had told them that some day, he would take them all to town to see the whooping and hollering and special things that went on in town on this holiday. Just then he spotted the blacksmith's shop and right across from it was the feed and grain store Pa always went to. Jacob decided that the owner there might remember him and Pa and maybe he would know where Pa was.

"Jess, can you stay with the animals, while I go in and ask about Pa?"

Jessie, still staring with awe at everything around her, looked apprehensive at being left alone. "I won't be long. I just have to ask about Pa, so we'll know where to find him. I'll

★ ★ ★

be right inside." Jacob glanced around and spotted a small tree beside the feedstore where he could tie the animals. "Okay, Jessie? Just stay by them so they won't get into trouble or nothin', okay? I'll come right back. I promise."

Jess nodded agreement, fascinated and frightened by all that was going on around her, and wanting desparately to find out where her Pa was. Jacob walked around and entered the feed store. He approached the counter with some apprehension. He had never been here without Pa. There were a few men standing around talking amongst themselves, but he walked up to the man he'd seen his Pa do business with. The man behind the counter saw Jacob and said brusquely, "No, I don't need no help around here. You'll have to look elsewhere."

Jacob stammered, "I... I ain't looking for work, sir. I...I'm lookin' for my Pa." The other men in the store stopped their conversations and turned to see who was talking. Jacob continued tentatively, "My Pa's Nathan Harding. He...he used to come in here for...for supplies? We're tryin' to find out if... if you know where he is? He came in to sign on with the army."

The storeowner's expression softened somewhat and he replied, "Of course, I know your Pa. You shoulda said so right on. But he ain't been in for supplies in a while. How long ago did he come in to sign up?"

Before Jacob could reply, one of the other men in the store stepped forward. "I was here the day your Pa came in to sign up, boy. But he ain't here now."

Jacob's stomach turned at the sound of those last words. That was exactly what he hadn't wanted to hear. "C..can you tell me where he went? Do you know what unit he signed on with? It's important that..that my sister and me find him." And for some reason as he looked around at the faces of those men staring down at him he decided not to tell the whole truth. "Our Ma's sick and...and we need to let him know."

The tall fellow with the reddish beard who had spoken before, said, "The day your Pa came into town to sign up there was a whole bunch a' fella's talkin' about the war and one of

★ ★ ★

'em spoke about a new company of sharpshooters formin' up in Rectortown. Them fellas all considered themselves somethin' of a good shot, and they decided then and there to ride up to Rectortown together and get in the same regiment. I believe they were talkin' about the 8th Virginia Infantry. That was about the middle of May, I reckon. I know your Pa and I'm sure he was one of 'em."

Jacob knew that would have been just about the right time that his Pa had come this way. He had left home about a week after Jessie's birthday which was May eighth. He thought to himself, "Well, we've come this far. We can't go back without Pa. We gotta keep looking for him. We need him. So he responded to the red-bearded man, "T..thank you, sir. Could you tell me how...how far Rectortown is from here?"

"It's about fifteen or twenty miles north of here, son, depending on which road you take."

Jacob's stomach turned at that news. That was a long way for Jessie and the rest of his flock to travel. For a brief minute, he wished he'd been able to travel alone, but then he knew he couldn't ever leave his sister behind. He was about to ask which way to go when he was interrupted by a gruff voice.

"That your goat, pig and sister waitin' out to the side there, boy?" A fat old man with a gnarly greyish beard and piercing grey eyes loomed over him. He had stepped outside the store while Jacob was talking to the other man and had just come back in. He leered at the boy waiting for an answer.

"Y...y...yessir."

"Well, you young'uns are in luck 'cause I just happen to be headin' toward Rectortown and I got room in my wagon to give you a lift part of the way," he rasped. "I'm leavin' soon's I conclude my business with this here fella." It was more a command than a request and Jacob noticed the other men glancing at one another, but the red bearded man sort of shrugged his shoulders at the others. Nobody said anything and Jacob realized they were waiting for him to respond. Jacob knew that it would take them forever to walk that distance by themselves

★ ★ ★

themselves and they didn't even know which way to go. They really had no choice.

He gulped and replied, "That...that'd be right kindly of you. My sister and I would be real grateful." Then Jacob remembered the words of his Pa,'We ain't beholden to no one, boy' and he added, "We'll work to earn our way, sir."

The old man responded, "That won't be necessary, boy. Believe me, it won't be necessary." And Jacob saw him glance out the door in the direction of his sister and the animals. The owner started to say something to the boy and then changed his mind as the old man walked up to him to settle his accounts.

"Wait for me outside, boy," the old man growled. "I'll be right out."

Jacob ran outside to tell Jessie the bad news and the good news. No, they hadn't found Pa. But, yes, he had found out where Pa went and someone who would take them there.

Later, as he bounced on the buckboard seat headed northward on the road towards Pa, Jacob thought about their first encounter with the old man. He was still feeling very lucky that they'd found this ride, but Jessie hadn't been at all convinced they ought to go with him. Jacob had seen the fearful look in her eyes as the old man had introduced himself to her. He had squeezed her tiny hand and whispered raspily, "My name's Vergil Turner, and we're gonna be good friends." Jessie had pulled away sharply and hidden her hands behind her back. "That's no way to be friendly, girlie. What's the matter with you?"

Jacob had quickly interceded, not wanting to lose this chance for a ride, saying, "She's just real shy. And she don't talk much either 'cause she's so shy. She just has to get to know folks to be friendly."

"I'm sure we're going to have plenty of time to get to know each other. I can wait." Then Vergil turned around and ran his fingers and hands over Squealer's round, firm and growing body. "A right solid shoat you have here. He's gonna grow

★ ★ ★

into fine ham and bacon." He lifted the squealing pig into the wagon and tied him securely. Next he hefted Nanny onto the wagon, and tied her securely. As the old man swung the goat up, Jacob realized he was pretty strong for an old man. "How much milk you get from her?" demanded Vergil.

"Almost a bucket full twice every day," Jacob responded proudly.

"Humph," was the old man's brusque reply. "You young'uns can sit up on the seat by me. We'll put the girl between us. It's safer that way." Reluctantly, Jessie had allowed the old man to lift her onto the wagon. At that moment, he had seen her clutching Cat, who up to now had been sleeping peacefully in her bonnet. "What! A cat, too! No cat! The cat has to stay behind. I won't have no cat around me," he bellowed. Jessie squirmed to be put down, and refused to let go of Cat. She looked beseechingly at Jacob and began to cry.

As much as he hated to, Jacob had blurted out, "If her cat can't go, then we'll just have to find another way to Rectortown. Thank you anyway."

Old Vergil looked longingly from the pig, to the goat, to the girl. "Forget what I said. The cat can come. Just don't let it give me any problems, you hear?"

"Yessir. I mean, no, sir."

And with that inauspicious start they began their journey with Vergil Turner. Even now as they rolled along, Jacob could feel Jessie pressing herself as close to him as possible and as far away from the old man as she could. She was clutching Cat protectively against her chest. He was sorry Jessie was so frightened of the old man. He thought it was probably because she'd been so sheltered from people by living out on their farm all her life. He pushed his own feelings of uneasiness with this man out of his mind. It was probably that raspy voice of his that made Vergil seem so rough and mean. He had offered them a ride. Now that was neighborly, wasn't it? Jacob tried to overcome his own misgivings.

★ ★ ★

They'd been riding for a while now and no one had said anything. Bouncing along on a hard wooden seat on a dusty narrow road just wide enough for one wagon was really not conducive to idle chatter, but Jacob thought he'd try to find out a little about this man and where they could expect to be going.

"How much farther is Rectortown from here, Mr. Turner?"

The old man grunted as if he'd been far away in thoughts of his own. "What?"

"How far is Rectortown from here?"

"I reckon it's about ten or twelve miles from here due north."

"How long do you think it'll take us to get there?"

"I wouldn't know, boy. I ain't goin' that far, remember. I just said I was goin' part way. My place'll be comin' up here about another hour's ride. We'll get there just in time for milkin' that goat of yours. You can spend the night and then start out again in the mornin' if that's what you've really got your heart set on. Frankly, I think you're wasting your time runnin' around the countryside after your Pa. He's too busy to worry about two kids like you. Soldiers ain't got time for kids. He's likely to be anywhere by now. You might never find him."

Jacob didn't like the tone of Vergil's voice. There was something about it that just made him feel uncomfortable. He was beginning to understand how Jessie felt. "If it's all the same to you, we still need to try to find our Pa. Until we leave, I'd like for you to have all of our goat's milk in trade for this ride. It ain't much, but it's all we've got."

"Humph. We'll see," snapped Vergil as he hied the mules into a quicker pace. Obviously, he was through talking. Jacob sat back and decided that he and his little troop would leave Vergil's place as soon as he finished milking the goat. He did not intend to subject Jessie or himself to anymore of this old man's rudeness.

Eventually they turned into a narrower road almost grown over with weeds. Up ahead they could see a most depressing ramshackle house. When they reached the clearing in front of

★ ★ ★

the house Vergil pulled up the mules. "This is home," he announced.

As Vergil climbed down from his side of the wagon, Jacob jumped off on his side and quickly helped Jessie to the ground. She stayed glued to his side with Cat cradled in her arms.

"Hey, boy? You know how to unhitch a team?"

"Yessir," replied Jacob.

"Then get these here mules unhitched and watered over there at that trough," he demanded.

Jacob grabbed at the reins and began undoing the rigging. He figured that if he helped the old man get unloaded quickly, he could milk Nanny and they could get on their way. Jessie was still by his side not daring to move.

"Tell that girlie of yours to get over here and fetch this goat and hog and tie 'em up in the pen," he snarled as he lifted them down from the wagon.

"We'd best do what he says, Jessie," he whispered. He saw the frightened look on her face and tried to reassure her. "We'll be on our way as soon as we do what we can to pay for our ride and not a minute longer. Remember, we Hardings ain't beholden to no one." He watched as she reluctantly went to the back of the wagon to retrieve the leads of the two animals. As she put one hand out to take the ropes from him, Vergil grabbed it and pulled her to him. "Come on, girlie, Vergil ain't that bad , is he?" As Jessie pulled away from him with all her might, he let go of her hand and she fell back hard into the dirt landing on her bottom. The kitten that had been clutched with her other arm, went rolling across the dirt meowing. Vergil sneered with an ugly smirk on his face, "See, girlie, if you were nice you wouldn't get hurt." Jessie spun around, grabbed Cat, got up and raced towards Jacob. Her face was white with fear and she was covered with red clay dust. Jacob dropped the mules' reins and darted over and grabbed the ropes from Vergil. "I can take care of them," he said. "Just let my sister be. She's little and you're scaring her." His voice was quavering, but Jacob surprised himself with his bravado. He wanted to hurry

★ ★ ★

with these chores and get out of there and away from this horrible old man before someone got hurt.

The old man lifted his box of supplies out of the wagon and
took it into the house. As he was walking away, Jacob went to
the wagon and retrieved Nanny's burlap bags and their blanket
rolls that the old man had tucked in the corner as they left Warrenton. He pulled out the bucket and knelt down to milk
Nanny where she was tied. Jessie stood on the other side of
Nanny so she could keep an eye on the old man with as much
distance as possible between him and her.

Vergil re-emerged from the shack. "Hurry up, boy. Ain't
you done with that milkin' yet? You're slow as molasses. I
wanna eat now."

Jacob hadn't stripped her dry yet, but he didn't want to give
the old man any more cause than necessary to be angry, so he
patted the goat on her haunch and whispered, "I'll do a better
job later, old girl, I promise." He squirted a bit of milk at Cat to
keep her satisfied for a while. Then he picked up the bucket in
one hand and reached out to Jessie with the other. They
approached the doorway where Vergil was leaning against the
frame. "Here's the bucket of milk I promised you, Mr. Turner.
You can have it all. We'll be on our way now if you don't
mind. Thank you for the ride. We gotta go find our Pa."

Before either of them knew what had happened, the old man
reached out and grabbed Jessie whipping her into the house
behind him. Gripping her arm tightly, he reached out with the
other hand and seized the bucket of milk. "You two ain't goin'
no where 'til ole Verg says you go. Understand, boy?" he
snarled through crooked yellow teeth.

Seeing his sister absolutely petrified and a virtual prisoner
of this crazy man, Jacob had no other recourse than to whisper
fearfully, "Yessir."

Old Vergil was crazy. Jacob was convinced of that as they
sat on the floor in a corner of the squalid shack while the old
man ate. The shack was one small room and bare except for a
bed, a crude table and a bench. Wooden boxes piled with junk

★ ★ ★

were scattered around the edges. A small lighted oil lamp on the table cast eerie shadows around the room. As Jacob watched the old man, he remembered the look the men in town had given each other after Vergil had offered him the ride. Had they known that Vergil was crazy? Had they even suspected? Why hadn't they said something to him? Well, all of this wasn't going to help him now. He glanced around the room. There was nothing that could help him and Jess. The best they could do was to stay quiet and hope the old man would ignore them. Maybe later when he went to sleep, if he went to sleep, they could sneak out. Just then Jacob's attention was drawn to the doorway. In the flickering lamplight he noticed a little grey paw reaching in and out through a crack at the bottom of the door. Cat was outside playing with a little moth that had been attracted to the light. As Jacob's eye moved up the door frame he noticed that the door was not latched. In fact, it was slightly ajar. It would be easy for them to slip out later.

Vergil pulled a brown jug out of the box he'd brought in from the wagon and set it on the table. The old man ate and drank. He offered them nothing. They watched as he chewed on some hard dry biscuits dunking them in the bucket of milk. Crumbs and milk dribbled down his beard. Jessie had been too scared to cry, and her arm still bore a fiery red handprint where the old man had grabbed her. He had flung her into the corner and then shoved Jacob on top of her. He warned them not to move or else. They hadn't. He uncorked the jug and took a long gulping drink and wiped his mouth with his arm. Just then they heard Cat meowing outside the door. Jessie trembled and he knew they were both thinking the same thing. "If he hears that he'll probably kill the cat." Cat meowed again and Jacob thought "Please, Cat, please be quiet. Go away. This old man is dangerous." Vergil took another drink and another. His face was gnarly and red and his eyes were glassy. He had not heard Cat or if he had, he hadn't reacted. The children both sighed quietly with relief. Then, as if he suddenly remembered that they were there, Vergil turned and looked at them.

★ ★ ★

"C'mere, girlie, and clean up this table!" he slurred. Jacob squeezed Jessie's hand to let her know she shouldn't move. "C'mere, I said!" he bellowed and started to get up from the bench by the table. He clumsily got one leg over the bench and was trying to swing the other around. For an instant, his back was towards them. Jacob darted across the room, dragging Jessie with him and they burst out of the front door before the drunken old man was able to get his feet underneath him. Jessie, half tripping and stumbling, had enough presence of mind to scoop up the astonished cat as they ran headlong into the darkness.

They ran and ran not daring to stop They didn't know if the pounding in their ears was Vergil's footsteps behind them or just their own racing heartbeats. They could hear the old man roaring, "And don't think I couldn't getcha if I had a mind to. Good riddance to ya. Don't ever let me catch sight of you two brats around here ever again or you'll know what it's like to be hunted animals." They turned around long enough to see his huge silhouette in the doorway. Then he slammed the door shut leaving them in total darkness.

They collapsed in a heap, Jessie sobbing on Jacob's chest, and Jacob shaking all over. He tried to console Jessie, but he couldn't even control himself. Only the cat, glad to be back with Jess, was contentedly purring and kneading Jacob's stomach with her paws. They stayed in the dark for what seemed like forever, not daring to move or make a sound. Jacob lay there, holding Jessie and stroking her head. Now he had really gotten them into a mess. They had nothing but each other and Cat. And they hadn't had anything to eat since morning. Their biscuits, their blankets, all their supplies were down at that crazy man's house. Their goat and their pig were there, too. His heart was beating more slowly now, but just the thought of Vergil frightened him all over again.

"Jessie?" he whispered.

She lifted her head from his chest.

"Jessie, we gotta do something. We can't stay here. Who

★ ★ ★

knows what that crazy old man might decide to do." Just then he heard her stomach rumbling. He realized she was as hungry as he was. That made him mad. "Who does that Vergil Turner think he is?" he said out loud surprising even himself. "He's got all of our stuff. All of our food. And he's got Nanny and Squealer, too. Jess, I'm gonna try sneakin' back down there. I know where our bags are 'cause I took them down off the wagon. If I don't hear anythin', I'm gonna get them and bring them back for us. At least we've got some old biscuits in there that we can chew on. You wait here with Cat. I know how much that old man scares you." And he thought to himself, and I know how much he scares me! "Okay, Jess?"

The sky was filled with a million stars, but only the merest sliver of a moon. It gave them just enough light to see by; Jacob stood up and he felt Jessie right by his side. When she slid her hand into his, he knew she was going to go back with him.

They crept slowly through the weeds. Even the flickering fireflies were not reassuring this night. Low branches brushed across their faces giving them a momentary fright. It was a slow, agonizing trip. At any moment they expected Vergil to jump out and grab them. But everything remained quiet.

When they reached the edge of the clearing in front of the shack, Jacob whispered, "You stay right here. Don't move. I'll be right back as soon as I get our bags. I don't want you anywhere near that madman." Jessie squeezed his hand and let go. Jacob inched his way towards the shack. He crept up to the right side of the building out of sight of the door. He sat there for a minute with his back against the wall, his heart pounding like a drum. He listened intently for any sound from within. Nothing. Then he began his slow crawl, towards the front door. To his immense relief, he could hear low rumbling snores coming from inside. Old Vergil must be sound asleep. At that, Jacob picked up his pace a little and scurried to where he thought he had dropped the burlap sacks. Success! There they were. He gently gathered them up so that the objects inside

★ ★ ★

wouldn't clatter. He ran in a semi-crouched position back to where he'd left Jessie at the edge of the clearing. She was still there. He dropped down with his treasures.

"Here, Jessie, hold these bags. Old man Vergil is asleep and snoring like bees in a hive. I'm going back to get Nanny and Squealer."

Again, Jacob scurried across the clearing. This time he went directly to the pen where the two animals were tied up. He gently patted Nanny and untied her lead. The two mules started to snicker from inside the fence. Jacob stood still for a second in case Vergil heard them. Everything was still quiet. So he inched towards Squealer. The pig's rope was tied so tight that he had to drop Nanny's lead to use two hands to work at the knot. He struggled to unloosen it. There! He almost had it.

An ear piercing, "JA..A..A..COB!" shattered the dark night air.

He spun around as a gun butt smashed down with a resounding thud right where he had been standing. There stood crazy old Vergil, gunbarrel in hand, ready to lift and try again. Before Jacob could react or move out of harm's way, something propelled the old man forward throwing him off his feet and cracked his head into the fence. Jacob, in a state of shock, couldn't move. Just then Jessie ran up to him, grabbed Nanny's lead, and yelled, "Jacob, he almost killed you. Nanny smashed him a good one in the rear and saved your life. Come on, we gotta hurry before he wakes up." Jacob snapped out of his stupor and pulled hard on Squealer's lead, while Jessie held onto the goat. They could hear the old man on the ground starting to moan.

"Here, quick, hold Squealer a second, too, Jess." Jacob darted into the house and came out carrying the milk bucket. He threw the remaining milk onto the ground. "We need the pail. Let's go! Where'd you leave the bags?"

"Over by the bushes," she replied.

Jacob snatched up the bags and threw them over his shoul-

★ ★ ★

★ ★ ★

der. "Keep moving, Jessie. He's probably going to wake up any second and come after us."

They moved through the weeds running as fast as they could with the animals. Briars seemed to reach out and grab their legs and arms, but they kept going. Sticks snapped under their feet and the pig kept snorting and squealing. Finally, out of breath and totally exhausted, Jacob plopped on the ground. Jessie plopped beside him. Even the pig and goat seemed relieved to rest. "What in the world," Jacob gasped, "was that awful yell? I thought you couldn't talk anymore."

"I thought so, too, but when you took so long to get the animals, I started to creep towards the house to try an' see what was taking you so long. Just then I saw that awful old man come out of the house with his gun and go towards the pen. And then I saw you, and he was going to kill you, and I just opened my mouth and screamed. I guess I scared Nanny, too, 'cause she just reared back, bent her head down and hit him in the bottom with all of her might. And...and...and then you saw me and we ran."

Jacob was dumbfounded. "For a girl who couldn't talk two hours ago, you sure have a lot to say now." Then he added, "I love you, Jess. I'm sure glad you found a reason to want to talk again. It was getting lonely without you to talk with." And he hugged her against him, and they fell back laughing on the ground. A loud meow came from somewhere between them. "Jessie, where's Cat?"

"Don't worry. I wasn't taking any chances that old Vergil might get her." She reached down and unbuttoned a couple of buttons on the front of her dress and pulled the kitten out. "She liked it in there. She knew she was safe."

"Come on, Jess. Let me finish that milking I promised Nanny a while ago and we'll all have something to eat and drink."

So the little group tied up there for the night, had a bite to eat, rolled out their blankets, and called it a day. A very exciting day that they wouldn't soon forget.

★ ★ ★

Saturday, July 13, 1861

Jacob did not sleep well that night. He woke at the least sound fully expecting to see Vergil Turner standing over them with his gun. Dawn finally came, and they were still safe and alone—-but with no idea of where they were. Jacob wanted to get moving as soon as they milked Nanny. They could chew on a biscuit along the way. He remembered old Vergil saying that Rectortown was ten or twelve miles due north from where they were yesterday. He had no idea what direction they had run last night. But he decided that they should head north, figuring that it would take them farther away from Vergil and hoping that it would bring them closer to Pa.

The terrain was more hilly here and the traveling was slower. They didn't have any roads or paths to follow. They just tried to keep heading north using the sun as their compass. The animals liked this better since there were more plants for them to nibble on along the way. That, too, made the going slower.

Since they had seen several rabbits scamper away in the fields, Jacob decided to see if he still had a steady aim with his slingshot. If he could get a rabbit, they'd build a small fire and have a real meal for a change.

"Jess, you rest here and keep an eye on the animals. I'm going to see if I can catch us some dinner."

"Don't go far, Jacob. I don't want to be alone out here."

"Don't worry. I'm just going to sneak out into that field over there. You'll probably still be able to see me from here.

★ ★ ★

And look, there's some more berries right next to those rocks. You pick some of those and we'll really have a feast tonight." He dug into the burlap bag pulling out his slingshot and his small knife. He headed out into the field picking up some small stones as he went and stuffing them into his pockets.

As his Pa had said, his aim was true, and after a brief wait behind an outcropping of rocks, he got a large hare. He carefully cleaned and skinned it there and hurriedly buried the head, pelt and innards. Some scavenger animal would uncover those later . He always dressed his catch like this before heading home because Jessie didn't like to see any little creature that had been hurt. Once dressed and ready for the fire, it didn't seem to bother her as much. On his way back, he used the knife again to cut three sturdy green branches to make a spit for roasting.

Meanwhile Jessie had filled the tin plate to overflowing with lots of succulent blackberries. Her fingers were purple from picking them. She looked up and saw Jacob trotting in, holding up the skinned, beheaded rabbit, and calling out, "We've got us a treat, Jessie. Help me gather some firewood." She carefully set down her tin of berries, and within a few minutes they had each collected an armful of fallen branches and sticks.

All of a sudden, Jessie screeched, "No, you don't, you selfish pig!" and dropped her firewood in a heap. Squealer, enticed by the aroma of the berries, had stretched to the end of his lead and was just allowing himself the luxury of rooting into the tin of berries. Jessie's scream caused him to glance up momentarily, displaying a berry-coated purple snout that contrasted starkly with his pink jowls. Jessie snatched the plate, leaving him standing there with a bewildered look. "You naughty, naughty pig. You are just one big troublemaker. I don't know why we ever brought you along."

Jacob wanted to laugh out loud at his dirty faced, blond little sister scolding her pig, but he thought better of it. He put down his load of firewood, grabbed Squealer's lead, and dragged him away from the clearing to another tree where he

★ ★ ★

tied him securely . "You better mind yourself, Squealer, or you're gonna be bacon before you know it."

The two youngsters quickly prepared a fire. Jacob was glad he'd brought the lucifers along. He struck one and got the fire started. That was much faster than striking a flint. Then they spitted the rabbit and hung it across the fire on two forked sticks. They sat on their blanket, listening to the sizzles as the juices bounced into the fire. The smell of the roasting meat made their mouths water.

As he waited, Jacob thought to himself that they had learned a lot in the three days that they had been on the road. The most important lesson was that you had to be careful with people. You couldn't trust them all. They had never had a reason not to trust anyone. Their life had been a very sheltered one, but they were learning—-the hard way. They'd be more careful whom they talked to and whom they went with from now on. He found out, too, that Jessie was stronger than he thought she might be. She was strong like Ma. He looked at her now sitting quietly on the blanket, petting Cat, who lay curled and purring in her lap. Gazing on this peaceful scene, who would have believed the predicament they'd been in yesterday?

That night they feasted on roast rabbit, fresh blackberries and milk. Their bellies full, they lay down and slept soundly.

★ ★ ★

Sunday, July 14, 1861

The next morning was overcast, and as a result they slept a little longer than Jacob had planned. The cloudy skies made the day less warm, but the air was humid and heavy. They took care of the animals, fed themselves, packed up their gear and were on their way. They were establishing a sort of routine, each of them assuming certain responsibilities.

Since they had no idea where they were, or how far they had gone, they kept moving north, or what Jacob felt was north. Without the sun, Jacob relied on instinct to tell him where to go. The terrain was still very hilly, and wooded with oaks and pines and hickories. Rock outcroppings appeared here and there as if the earth had sent up hard grey bubbles from beneath the green fields. Occasional streams wound their way between the hills.

At one such refreshing stream they had all been drinking when Jessie tapped Jacob on the shoulder and pointed silently. There, in a little clearing on the opposite bank, an amber colored deer stood staring at them. Her moist black nose was sniffing, her ears twitching and turning to catch every sound. Her tail swished from side to side ready to snap up like a white flag to signal danger if necessary. They stood immobile staring at each other before the deer finally meandered away, apparently deciding that they were not a threat to her. Secure in their little company, the boy and the girl, and the goat, pig and cat pressed on. They could take care of each other. They

★ ★ ★

knew that they would find Pa. They were committed to that goal, and nothing could stop them.

As they walked, they began to see fences of stone and split rail, which meant there must be farms around. They weren't anxious to meet up with any people after their encounter with Vergil, but at least they felt as if they might be headed in the right direction and perhaps Rectortown was not too far off. They came upon a road which seemed to be leading in a northerly direction. They decided to follow it.

The skies, which had been overcast this morning, were now filling with threatening thunderheads. Jacob scanned the horizon, searching for a place that might protect them if it rained. These late afternoon summer storms could pass by with only the rumbling threat of rain, or they could catch you off guard and pound you with sheets of rain, as well as hailstones and wild wind. It had been just such an unexpected downpour that had drenched Ma out in the field and started her sickness. They picked up their pace a little. Jessie seemed to sense the concern that Jacob was feeling even though no words had been spoken. The thunder rumbled louder and the clouds darkened. Just up ahead Jacob thought he saw a small bridge crossing a gulley. That would surely be a stroke of luck. He was glad to see it for two reasons. They could hide beneath it to avoid the wrath of the storm. And it meant that this must be a pretty well traveled road if it had a bridge.

"Jessie! Look up ahead. Don't that look like a bridge to you?"

Jessie strained her eyes to focus. "Yes, I think so," she agreed.

"Let's try to get to it before the rain comes. We may be able to stand under it and keep a little bit dry. This storm looks like a big one and we can't hide under a tree with all this lightning. We better run if we're gonna make it in time." They hurried the animals and got to the bridge just as the rain began to pelt down. There was a narrow little path descending to the creek along the right side of the bridge. They carefully led the

★ ★ ★

animals down and found a small rock shelf to stand on under the bridge.

"That was close, Jessie. We'll wait out the storm down here, and as soon as it passes we'll find a spot to make camp for the night. Tomorrow we'll head on and see what we can find out about Pa's unit." A couple of strikes of lightning hit close by, judging from the immediate booms of thunder that followed. The animals began to get restless. It was now very dark. Jessie calmed Nanny with reassuring words and by stroking her back and head. Jacob had a harder time with Squealer who was snorting and pawing and pulling at his lead, trying to run back up the bank to the road. The rain by now was pouring down so heavily you couldn't see ten feet away. It made two waterfalls running off the sides of the bridge.

Under the bridge there was barely enough room on the small rock shelf for the five of them to stand together. But it was dry and seemed a perfect resting place. The only way they could go back up would be by the same path that they had followed down. From past experience, Jacob knew these explosive storms usually stopped as quickly as they began. The water in the creek was beginning to rise, but they still had plenty of dry space. Nanny was tugging and rearing, and Jessie was having a time trying to control her. It was not like Nanny to act like this. Jacob wanted to help Jess, but his hands were more than full with Squealer who was wrapping the lead around Jacob's legs in a vain struggle to go past him to get up and out.

Intent on calming the animals, the two were caught off guard by a rapidly approaching roar. Looking at each other, they realized the sound was coming at them fast. "Run, Jess, run!" Jacob yelled above the roar. "The rain must have flooded the creek bed. Let Nanny pull you up the hill! Hurry! I'm right behind you."

Jessie slipped and slid on the now muddy path, holding desperately to Nanny's lead. The goat's sharp little hooves gripped in pulling the two of them up to the road just in time for Jessie to see a wall of water careening down the gulley

★ ★ ★

towards the bridge. Jacob was behind her on the path, still
struggling with Squealer's lead.

"Jacob, let him go! Get up here! The water's coming," she
screamed as she ran to help him.

"I can't, Jessie. I'm tangled in the rope." His frantic cries
mingled with the ear piercing squeals of the pig. Before Jessie
could reach out to him, the swirling waters engulfed the boy
and pig and carried them pell-mell down the stream. Jessie
screamed and ran wildly after them looking for a way to get to
her brother.

Jacob, pulled under by the initial surge of water, bobbed to
the surface holding onto Squealer's neck. Squealer may not
have been good for much, but at least, with all his fat, he was
able to float. The two of them rode the raging stream, striving
instinctively to keep their heads above the water. Jacob hung
on to the floating pig, reaching out as he was carried along to
catch at a branch, at anything that might stop this crazy, dizzy-
ing ride. The few branches he did grab, snapped right off with
the sheer force of the waterflow and their weight. He felt as if

★ ★ ★

he were part of a wild nightmare. This couldn't be happening to him. What if he never saw Jessie again? What if he never saw Pa again? As everything flashed past him, he saw visions of his mother's face. She was trying to help him. If only he could reach out to her.

Then just ahead of him he spied a tree trunk leaning over the water. With one arm up as high as he could reach, Jacob grabbed hold of the trunk as he was about to pass beneath it. Squealer, released from his grasp at that moment, kept on going downstream. With two arms Jacob pulled himself up across the trunk, just as the pig's lead, still tangled around his leg, snagged tight. Jacob held on, inching himself over the trunk until he could grasp at the rope which was digging painfully into his ankle. He finally managed to grab it and untangle it, and, hand over hand, pulled in the floundering pig. Holding the rope to keep the pig's head out of the water, Jacob hung suspended until he could catch his breath and get enough energy to move again. He continued inching his way along the trunk, dragging the half-floating pig, until they reached the bank. Once there, Jacob rolled onto the wet, grassy bank, drenched and panting and totally spent. At his side lay an equally exhausted, but clean, pig. And that's the way they were when Jessie finally caught up with them.

"Jacob! Jacob!" she cried. She dropped down beside him and pulled his head onto her lap. Tears of fear turned into tears of joy as she realized that he was alive. Cat poked her head out of Jessie's dress and began to lick the water off Jacob's face. Nanny came trotting up through the trees dragging her lead behind her as if to say, "Hey, we're all in this together. Wait for me."

In the calm after the storm, flickering rays of sunlight filtered through the trees, and raindrops hung from the leaftips like crystals from a chandelier. This would have been an idyllic scene, except for the dark raging waters still churning beside them. These violent torrents of water explained why many of the streams were called "runs" in this part of the country. In

★ ★ ★

dry weather, they were sluggish waterflows, even nonexistent at times. But when the rain fell in vast amounts over a short time as it had this day, it collected and converged in the runs to form devastating, unstoppable walls of water.

Jessie cradled her brother's head on her lap. With sobs still wracking her body, she whispered, "I thought you were gone, Jacob. I was so afraid. I ran and ran and I couldn't see you anywhere. I thought I was all alone. I was afraid to ever stop running."

"I won't ever leave you, Jessie. I promise. I kept seeing your face as I was rushing down the river, but I couldn't get to you." He paused and then continued, "I saw Ma's face, too. I felt like she was trying to help me, and that's when I saw the tree trunk. It was all so weird, Jessie. I can't explain it, but I felt like she was really there."

"I miss Ma so much, Jacob," she sobbed. "And I miss Pa, too."

"I know, Jessie. I know."

Later, Jacob, stripped of his drenched clothing, sat wrapped in the quilt. Jessie hung all his clothes on bushes and tree limbs to dry. He was still trembling, more from fear than from cold, and a fire would have felt good. But everything was still too wet after the torrential rain and there would be no dry wood. Fortunately it was July and even after the rain, it was still quite warm. His ankle was raw and bleeding where the rope had twisted around it. His arms were scratched and bruised where he had caught the trunk. He just wanted to stay still and not move. He hurt all over. Squealer had recovered sufficiently from his ordeal and was rooting and foraging for food as always. Nanny chewed contentedly on some poison ivy vines. The burlap bags of gear had survived intact since Nanny had managed to get herself and Jessie out of harm's way so quickly. It had stopped raining shortly after Jessie had started to run after Jacob. So the blankets were almost totally dry. Jessie had the bucket and was attempting to milk Nanny. She had tried once or twice in the past and knew how, but she did

★ ★ ★

not like doing it. Besides it was Jacob's job. This time she must have been doing a fairly decent job of it, since Nanny wasn't protesting at all. Jacob wasn't protesting either. He thought a good long warm drink of milk would taste mighty good right now. Obviously that was what Jessie thought, too, because she brought the bucket and tin cup directly to Jacob. He dipped the cup and took a long warm drink. What would they have done without Nanny? She was worth her weight in gold, as Pa would say.

Jessie sat down next to Jacob. She had taken out a chunk of the cured ham they'd packed in the bags. She pulled off pieces for each of them. She was very quiet. Jacob looked at her dirt streaked face. Her apron was stained with berry juice and mud. Her dress was more the color of red clay than the blue it was supposed to be. Her hands and face were all scratched. Her hair was tangled and matted with mud. She was a pitiful sight and although he was tired and sore from his river escapade, he realized it had cleaned and refreshed him. He reached his arm around her and said, "Tomorrow we're gonna get you cleaned up, too, Jess. You wanna look nice if you're gonna see Pa. We'll take some time in the morning to wash up. You'll feel better, too. Besides we need some time to rest a little. It'll make us both feel better."

★ ★ ★

Monday, July 15, 1861

Jacob's body rebelled at any thought of movement in the morning. He hurt everywhere. He rolled over and remembered he was naked. All his clothes were hanging out to dry. He slipped out from under the covers, crouched down and headed for his underdrawers. As he stood up to step into them, he heard a giggle from behind him. He struggled to get his drawers pulled over his bare white bottom, and turned around to see Jessie peeping out from under the quilt at him. He laughed and said, "Just you wait. Your turn is coming. Then we'll see who laughs." He snatched his trousers off the tree and pulled them on, and then his shirt. He felt his shoes and they were still quite wet. He left them in a sunny spot to continue drying.

They had milk and the last of their ham for breakfast. They still had some cornmeal and a chunk of bacon, but their supplies were getting low. He hoped Rectortown and Pa were just across the bridge.

"Okay, Jessie. Let's look for a spot along the creek where you can wash yourself and your clothes. We'll sit and rest until they dry. They walked down to the site of yesterday's raging river. By this morning, the flattened plants and muddy paths were the only signs that anything unusual had occurred. The creek, though still high, had settled down to a respectable flow. They found a place that was not too deep and Jacob said, "Just

★ ★ ★

take off your shoes, Jess, and jump in. You can wash your clothes the way I did mine. Still wearin' 'em. Works real good."

Jessie wasn't too sure she wanted to get anywhere near that creek. "Jacob, what if it carries me away, like you?"

"Don't worry. It's going a lot slower today than it was yesterday. I'll be right here. I wouldn't let anything happen to you. I wouldn't tell you to do it if I thought it wasn't safe."

Removing her leather high top shoes, she put one foot tentatively into the water. She pulled back and was about to turn around, when Jacob gave her a shove and she found herself flopping around in waist deep water. "You're not fair! You're mean! I'm not going to talk to you anymore!" she bawled indignantly from the middle of the stream. She was about to cry when she realized her brother was sitting on the grass and rolling back and forth with laughter. It caught her off guard and instead of crying she started laughing, too.

"Oh, Jess. What a sight you are! But you'll look beautiful later when Pa sees you. Untie your braid, and wash all the mud and burrs out of your hair. And swish up and down so all of your dress gets washed. See it isn't so bad, is it? You can swim and play and get clean all at once." Jacob thought to himself that Ma probably wouldn't have liked his cleaning methods, but then what did he know about washing clothes anyway? After he figured Jessie had soaked long enough, he extended a hand to her and helped her up on the bank. She looked like a pitiful little drenched kitten. She stood for a minute, her clothes clinging to her body and little rivulets of water dripping from her hair and her fingers and her skirt.

"C'mon, Jessie. I've got your shoes. Let's get back to the camp and get you wrapped in the quilt. I'll twist out your clothes and spread them in the sun so they can dry.

The animals were contentedly grazing and rooting, happy for a little peace and quiet. Jacob and Jessie sat in a sunny spot so her hair could dry. Jacob tried to comb through her curls with his fingers. It was next to impossible. Jessie was petting

★ ★ ★

Cat who was curled at her feet. She had conveniently disappeared during the washing episode. No bathtime for that cat. As Jessie stroked Cat she whispered, "Tell me things you 'member about Ma, Jacob."

Jacob continued untangling her hair and thought a minute. "I don't know," he murmured. "There's so many things. I 'member her cool hand on my head when I was sick. I 'member her working so hard all the time. An' the way she used to laugh. It was such a happy sound you couldn't help but laugh with her, too. Just like when you laugh. I 'member how sad she looked the day Pa rode away, too. I wanted to make her feel better, but I knew I couldn't. Only Pa could. Jess, do you think she died 'cause she missed Pa?"

"I don't know, Jacob. I know she wasn't happy any more after he went away. Her eyes didn't smile the way they used to. That made me sad, too. I miss her. I wish Pa had never gone away. The army took Pa and made Ma get sick and die. It's not fair. Why'd he have to go?"

Jacob realized his sister was voicing a lot of the same thoughts he had. It was true. Everything was just fine before Pa left. What could be so important that the army had to take their Pa away from them? He couldn't think of a thing and he couldn't think of any answers to his sister's questions. "That's why we're going to find him, Jess. He'll understand and he'll tell that old army that he has to come home with us. You'll see. It won't be long now."

They lay in the warm morning sun feeling its warmth like gentle arms embracing them in their time of need. They soaked up the calm and quiet, renewing their bodies as well as their spirits. For two children who'd never been far from their farm in Catlett, they had come a long way. They didn't know how much farther they would have to go, but they wouldn't stop until they found their father.

By noon, Jessie's clothes were dry enough for them to get on their way. Jacob's shoes were still wet, but they would have to dry as he walked down the road wearing them. Jacob had

★ ★ ★

tied Jessie's hair at the back of her neck with a piece of string. They were basically clean and their clothes were at least presentable now.

They found their way back to the road. They had gone a lot farther down the river than they thought, but eventually they saw the bridge. As they crossed over it they had the feeling that this was a good sign for them. There were cornfields on both sides of the road standing tall and straight. Like soldiers all in a row, Jacob thought to himself. Like green soldiers with golden tassels on their hats. Off in the distance he saw a house, then several houses. As they came closer, he also saw a railroad and one of the houses appeared to be a station. Jacob stopped beside a field with a small grove of trees.

"Jessie, I think it might be best if you stay here with the animals hidden in this grove of trees while I go see what I can find out in town. I'll come right back to get you as soon as I find out where Pa is. We just don't know who might be there."

Jessie didn't argue. The memory of old Vergil was still fresh in her mind and she knew exactly what her brother was implying. They had learned quickly that all people could not be trusted. You had to be careful whom you talked to and what you said to them. "Just be careful, Jacob. And hurry. I'll try not to be too scared. Besides, Cat will keep me company."

With Jessie settled in the little grove, Jacob trotted on down the road certain that Pa could not be far off now. This had to be Rectortown. And Rectortown was where the red-bearded man said Pa had gone. The largest building was of weatherworn board with white letters painted above a platform. He strained his eyes to try to read what it said. It looked like Salem. Salem Station. As he got closer he could see someone sitting on the platform. He slowed to a walk now. He didn't want to seem too eager. Things seemed very quiet. The man was leaning against a large beam supporting the roof of the platform. He appeared to be sleeping or at least resting with his cap pulled down over his eyes. Jacob approached warily. He wondered if this man could be trusted; if this man would know the answers

★ ★ ★

to any of his questions. Jacob walked over to the other end of the platform and sat with his legs dangling over the edge. The old fellow pushed his cap back on his white hair and measured Jacob carefully with his eyes. Jacob thought that the old man looked friendly enough. His blue eyes had a sparkle to them and the corners crinkled in an agreeable sort of way.

"Afternoon, young fella. Waiting on the train, are ya?'

"Not really, sir. I was on my way to Rectortown to get my Pa. I kinda thought this might be Rectortown."

"Sonny, did ya read them letters up there on this here station? They say, "Salem". This here is Salem, Virginia. Right on the Manassas Gap Railroad line. Rectortown is the next stop north on this line a couple of miles. You're one stop too soon."

"I'm not taking the train. I'm walking. My Pa went to join up with the army in Rectortown about two months ago. My Ma is sick and I'm trying to find him to let him know."

"Lookin' for your Pa, huh? Say he signed up in Rectortown about two months ago? That was about the time Captain Carter was signin' on folks to form Company B of the Eighth Virginia Infantry Regiment. That was on May 17th if my memory serves me rightly. Lotta fellas passed through here headin' up that way. Piedmont Rifles they called themselves. They's all a bunch a' sharpshooters. Looked to make a mighty fine unit."

Jacob's heart began to pound. That was what the man at Warrenton had said. Could his Pa actually be just a couple of miles up the road? It was too much to hope for. This old man seemed friendly enough and he certainly knew a lot about the army. At least his Pa's army. "Could you tell me if Company B is still at Rectortown? Could I find my Pa there?" he asked holding his breath in anticipation.

"Nope. That whole regiment went on up to Leesburg to drill and guard the crossings at the Potomac River. They been gone more than a month now."

The disappointment on Jacob's face was obvious. "How

★ ★ ★

far away is that? Leesburg, I mean?"

"Young fella," the old man continued kindly, "Leesburg's a mighty far walk. But let me tell you, I sit here day after day watching all the comin's and goin's on this train line. I hear all the news that the folks traveling in these here parts got to tell and there's many a soldier's been traveling on these trains. They're sayin' that most of the troops are getting ready to head toward Manassas Junction. They say that's where the action's gonna take place. If you wanta find your Pa, that's where I'd head to look. By the time you'd get to Leesburg on foot, they'd be long gone. You could head them off. Your Ma must be mighty sick to get you walkin' such a piece after your Pa. Where'd you start from, boy?"

Jacob hesitated a minute then decided to answer truthfully. This man seemed honest and friendly. "We...I started from near Catlett, south of Warrenton. Been walkin' about a week."

"You oughta be right tired then I reckon. When'd you last have something hot to eat?"

"Couple a days ago, we had a rabbit I got with my sling-shot."

"Who else is with you, boy? You go fetch your friend and I'll serve us all some of my special stew and cornbread. After you get somethin' substantial in your belly, then you can get on your way and find your Pa. But I can't let you go without a decent meal."

Jacob hesitated, trying to think of an excuse to leave and not come back. As if reading his mind, the old man said, "Look, son, my name's John Lanham. You can just call me John. I got my own personal stake in Company B. My youngest boy went an' signed on with that unit. That's how come I know so much about 'em. I'd be pleased to share a meal with folks that also got kin in the same company. You don't have to fear from me, son. I don't mean no harm. Things are mighty quiet around here today and I could do with a bit of good company. Whadda ya say?"

Again Jacob hesitated and then he said, "Will you tell us

★ ★ ★

more about Company B?"

"Nothin' would pleasure me more. I'll go set out some plates. What did ya say your name was, son?"

Jacob had already jumped down and started to cross back over the tracks. "Jacob. Jacob Harding," he yelled over his shoulder.

He ran all the way back to the grove of trees. Jessie was waiting impatiently for him. "What took you so long? I was ready to come after you again. I figured you got in trouble again."

"No trouble," he panted. "I met a man who knows about Pa's unit. He's got a son in the same company. He offered us a hot meal and he'll tell us more about Company B." He saw the look that Jessie shot at him and he quickly added, "Jess, he seems real nice. If you don't like him, we won't stay. I promise."

"I'm not so sure about this, Jacob. How can we be sure he doesn't just want our goat or pig."

"Because he doesn't even know we have a goat or a pig. He doesn't even know you're a girl. He thinks I have a friend here. He sure will be surprised when we come back together."

"Okay. But only if we leave if I think it ain't safe."

So the children untied the animals and headed for Salem Station and John Lanham's place. John was nowhere to be seen as they approached the tracks, and Jacob could see that Jessie was hesitant about this meeting. "You wait here, Jess, by the side of the platform. I'll go get John, and if you don't like him after you meet him, we'll just keep on walking. Okay?"

She nodded and Jacob climbed the steps of the platform. Something smelled absolutely wonderful. He entered the station door. John was stirring a large pot of stew on the iron stove. He noticed Jacob by the door. "Well, what do ya think, Jacob? Smell good enough to eat? Where's your friend? Or do you have more than one?"

"Well, yes and no. My friend is outside. But there's more than one. But only one that'll join us for dinner." John, curi-

★ ★ ★

ous now, followed Jacob out the door. His right leg was lame and he limped after the boy. Jacob stopped and pointed to the end of the platform. "That there's my sister, Jessie. And that's our pig and our goat, too."

"Well, I'll be. And just when I thought I'd seen everything. You young'uns are somethin' else. Well, little Miss Jessie, I'd be right honored to have you and your brother join me for dinner." And he smiled a big crinkly smile from ear to ear and his blue eyes sparkled with delight. Jacob watched his sister for some sign as to what she wanted to do.

"Jacob, what should I do with the animals?" was her reply, and Jacob knew she, too, sensed that John could be trusted.

John showed them a place to tie the animals near a water trough out behind the building. Jacob slipped the burlap sacks off Nanny, and the children followed John inside. "Well, folks, this here's where I live and work. I run the station and live in the rooms back here. It's very handy for an old fella like me. Have a seat at the table and I'll fetch us up a very special dinner."

The children sat and John served them stew and hot cornbread with honey. They thought it was the best meal they'd ever tasted. They dug right in and didn't say anything until they'd finished. John offered them more but they didn't have room.

"All I have is coffee for an old man to drink. Would you like some?"

"Oh, no, sir. I forgot all about Nanny. I can go milk her and we'll have plenty of fresh milk to drink. Nanny's milk has kept us going all these days we've been traveling," said Jacob.

"Sounds like you two have had quite a journey. Care to tell an old man all about it?"

And as if needing to release it all and take a great burden off their minds, the two children took turns recounting all the things that had happened to them. When they finished, John drew in a deep breath and let it out very slowly and deliberately. He leaned back in his chair and lit his pipe. "You two

★ ★ ★

young'uns have been through an awful lot. Now I understand why you weren't too sure about stayin' with me. And why the little lady here wanted to check me out. I'm glad I passed your inspection. Gets lonesome around here at times, and an old man enjoys a little company. But I ain't no Vergil Turner. Don't you worry none about that."

"You said you'd tell us more about Company B," reminded Jacob. "Jessie ain't heard none of it yet."

"That's right I did, didn't I?" John puffed on his pipe a couple of times and then began in a low voice, "Company B is just one part of the Eighth Virginia Infantry. The fellas who signed on with Company B pretty much all signed on at Rectortown on May 17th. My boy was one of 'em. He considered himself right handy with a rifle and couldn't wait to run off and sign up. Heard that group called ther'selves the Piedmont Rifles. A pack of sharpshooters they were. Captain Richard Carter did the recruitin'. After a couple of days, my boy rode back down to let me know they was headed for Leesburg to meet up with the rest of the units that was to make up the Eighth. There they was gonna drill and practice to be soldiers. Some were gonna help guard the crossings at the Potomac. That was the last news I had from them."

"But if they ain't fightin' yet, why'd our Pa have to go? Did they really need him?" Jacob asked.

"Son, I wish I knew. But there has been fightin'. Some in South Carolina. Heard we did right well there. Federals surrendered the fort and nobody was killed. A few other skirmishes here and there. But there's talk that something's brewin' for Manassas Junction. That's where this railroad, the Manassas Gap Line, and the Orange and Alexandria Railroad meet. Folks figure the Federals want to take over that position."

"But why are people fightin' anyway?" interrupted Jessie.

"That's a good question, young lady. A very good question. And even wiser and older men than me aren't sure of the answer. How old did you two say you was?"

★ ★ ★

"I'm eleven. Almost twelve. Be twelve in September,"
responded Jacob. "Jessie just turned eight in May."
John puffed on his pipe again, gazing off as if collecting his
thoughts. "Well, those are two good ages. But let me see if I
can find some answers for you that you can understand. I'm
not sure I even know where to start. I find it hard to understand myself. In fact, folks are saying that Mr. Lincoln ain't
even sure about the reasons for this war. One minute, he's
sayin' it's 'cause he wants to keep the union together and the
next minute it's 'cause he says owning slaves ain't right."

"But we ain't even got any slaves," Jacob said with a bewildered look on his face.

"It ain't fair. Why'd our Pa have to go away to fight for
that?" Jessie added with a pout.

"Well, there's lots of other reasons folks are talkin' about
besides 'secesh' and slaves. Like whether the big factories in
the North aren't tryin' to put the farmers in the South out of
business. Many of the soldiers fightin' for us don't own slaves,
but just try to earn an honest livin' by farmin' and your Pa's a
farmer, right? I reckon that's why he up and joined the army. I
can't imagine what else would be important enough to take him
away from you young'uns and your Ma. Your Pa musta done
what he thought was right for his family and the way you've
always lived. He couldn't a knowed that your Ma would take
sick. From what you said it sounds to me like she done caught
pneumonia. There wasn't much you two young'uns could a
done. It wasn't your fault." Hearing that made Jacob feel a little better. He'd always had this nagging worry in the back of
his mind that he had been responsible for what happened to his
Ma. He wondered if John had sensed his feelings. John continued, "But all those who joined up ain't got the same good
reasons for fightin'. There's a good many just fightin' for fightin's sake. Some young fellas couldn't enlist fast enough.
They's afraid the war would be over before they got there. It
was like they was going to a big picnic or celebration instead of
to fightin' and killin'. But you don't want to hear about that.

★ ★ ★

Let's hope that what folks is sayin' is right and this war will be over before we know it."

They all sat there quietly for a few minutes, John puffing on his pipe, and the children trying to make some sense out of things that seemed so foreign to them and their little world on the farm. They were having to come face to face with the harsh realities of life. It wasn't easy when you were only eight and eleven. Then a startled, "Oh, my gosh, I forgot about Nanny," broke everyone's silent thoughts. "I gotta go milk her before it gets much later." Jacob jumped up and headed for the front door where he had set down the blankets, bags, and bucket.

"Before you go out, son, how about if you two spend the night here. I reckon you ain't slept in a real bed in a week. My boy's bed is empty back there and he'd be pleased to know that the family of someone else in Company B slept in it. In the morning I'll fix up a hearty breakfast to send you two on your way after your Pa. If I wasn't so old and so lame, I might even think about goin' with you. But my travelin' days are over. What do you two say?"

Jacob looked at Jessie, then said, "That would be real neighborly of you. I reckon we'd both like that. And in no time at all I'll be back with some of the best goat's milk around. You'll see."

As Jacob went out, John slowly got up from his chair and gently massaged his bad leg. "Well, Miss Jessie, I'll clean up this dinner stuff. Then we'll get your bed set. I sure am glad to have such good company. It gets lonely when you get old. People don't have time to bother with old folk."

Jessie ran over to the pile of quilts and the bags by the door. She reached down and picked up Cat who had been nestling contentedly in the middle. "You need one of these to keep you company. This is Cat. She's my best friend. Except for Jacob, of course."

John looked over and burst out laughing. "And what other little critters do you have hidden away in those bags?"

"No more. This is it. Just Jacob, and me, and Cat, and

★ ★ ★

Nanny, and Squealer," she replied innocently.

"And they all have names, too. It must be a wonderful sight to see you all trotting along down the road." He reached out and scratched the kitten's neck.

By the time Jacob returned with the bucket of milk, John was just finishing up with Jessie's help. Jacob said, "I fed some of the milk to Squealer for a treat, but I saved enough for us. I'll get us a whole new bucket in the morning for breakfast." All three of them had a cupful of fresh, warm goat's milk and Jessie saved out a little to share with Cat.

John showed the children to the spare bed. He looked at Jacob's raw ankles and coated them gently with a healing salve that he fetched from his cupboard. Then with stomachs full of stew and goat's milk and their hearts and minds unburdened by the evening's conversation, the two children sank into the luxury of a real mattress, and were quickly sound asleep. Even the loud and erratic snoring of the old man in the bed nearby was not enough to disturb these weary travelers.

★ ★ ★

Tuesday, July 16, 1861

The tantalizing aroma of sizzling bacon and fresh brewed coffee drifted into their bedroom. The children were snuggled comfortably in the bed left empty by John's son. Jacob turned over and murmured something in his sleep, but he was too content in bed to succumb to the urgings of his stomach. Eventually though, the smells wafting in from the kitchen won out, and he woke Jessie.

"Smells just like home, don't it, Jess? John sure is mighty nice. He can cook good, too. I better get out and milk Nanny so we can have some fresh milk. I reckon John would like it, too. Maybe you can help John till I get back."

They hustled out of bed, put on their shoes and entered the kitchen. "Good mornin'," they chimed together.

"Well, I see a good bed agreed with you young'uns. Just set a spell and this here breakfast will be ready." John looked wide awake and was busy cooking in several pans on the iron stove.

"Jessie'll stay and help if you need it, but I gotta go milk our goat."

"You go milk that goat of yours now and breakfast ought to be about ready when you come back in."

That morning's meal was the best Jacob thought he'd ever eaten in his life. There was bacon, some fried potatoes, grits with honey, and fresh biscuits ready to be topped with home-made peach preserves. Along with their fresh goat milk, they

★ ★ ★

ate until they thought they'd burst.

"John, I think this is the best meal I ever had. And I ain't just sayin' that to make you feel good. It's true. Ain't that true, Jessie?" Jacob mumbled between bites of biscuit and peach jam. Jessie nodded her head vigorously, her mouth too full to say anything.

As Jacob spread jam on another biscuit, he remembered the words of his Pa. "We Hardings ain't beholden to no one. We work or trade for whatever we get." He put down the knife and said, "John, we gotta work to pay for all this fine food you've shared with us and for the bed you let us use. Our Pa always said to work for what you get. And I aim to try to do what he told me."

John looked across the table at the boy. Jacob was so young and yet he was so old. John wanted to say, "Nothin', son. Do nothin'." He knew their company had made him feel happy and spry and glad to be alive again. But he also knew there was a sense of pride and duty in that young voice. So he said, "I know what you mean, Jacob, and I'll oblige the best I can. First off, we'll count the milk from last night and then all of this morning's bucket as starters. Then, if Miss Jessie here will help me to clean up from breakfast, you can fetch me in some firewood to fill my firebox. This stove needs wood to cook this fine food and my legs don't work as well as they used to. Does that sound like a fair trade to you?"

"Yessir. Yessir." And he finished eating, thoroughly enjoying every bite knowing he would do his part to earn it.

A short while later the children had completed their chores and were anxious to get on their way. John had prepared an extra large batch of biscuits that morning and tucked some of them into the burlap sack. "These'll make sure that you don't go hungry till you find your Pa." He also added another chunk of ham and some dried apples. They still had a little cornmeal left, but John refilled that, too. "This'll make sure that pig of yours keeps growin' so you'll have a full larder this winter. And you can also fix some for yourself, too. And to pay for

★ ★ ★

all this food, I have somethin' special that I need you to do for me." He reached into his vest pocket and pulled out an envelope. "When you find your Pa, would you get this letter to my boy for me? I wrote it after you two went to sleep last night. I've put his name on the outside here. I'd be right grateful."

Jacob took the letter. He folded it and put it in his pocket. "I'd be honored to take this letter to your boy. Maybe it won't be so long and he'll be back with you."

John shook his head. "You don't understand, son. My boy and I had hard words about his goin' off to fight in this here war, when I felt I needed him here with me. Talkin' with you two young'uns made me realize that I was bein' a selfish old man. I want my boy to know that, in case somethin' happens to him 'fore I see him again to tell him myself."

"I'm sure your boy knows that. I always know that my Pa cares even when he gets mad at me. It's the same thing."

John gave the boy a hug, and Jacob felt a little embarrassed. But he understood. The hug was meant for John's son, too.

"Now you young'uns just follow these tracks. They'll take you through the gap in the Bull Run Mountains and bring you to the Warrenton-Alexandria Turnpike. Head east following the turnpike to Bull Run. You'll find your Pa and my boy there for sure."

The children thanked John and hated to go. He had made them feel happy and secure. But the thought that their father was not far off spurred them on. They waved as they walked along the tracks, until they could no longer see him. The five of them were on their way again.

Following the tracks made the traveling easier for them. There was no guessing as to what direction to take. Although the terrain all around them was hilly and wooded, the right of way for the tracks eased through the mountains at the point of least resistance. What they didn't know was that in just five days these very same tracks would be bringing Confederate troops by the thousands through this mountain pass to deliver

★ ★ ★

them to the junction at Manassas.

Because there were long stretches of uncultivated wood-lands and forests, they were astounded to come upon a vast orchard with apple and peach trees as far as they could see. The apples were still small, firm and green, but the peaches were at their peak. In fact, they were probably past their peak judging from the amount of fallen fruit beneath the trees. Squealer's large triangular ears began to wiggle and his nose lifted in the air as he caught the scent of that ripe fruit. At the nearest peach tree, Squealer began to gorge with delight on the soft, ripe fruit. The pig didn't know which way to turn. All this food and no one telling him to stop. He just grunted and snorted as he gobbled down peaches with a voracious appetite. Jacob tied him to a tree with lots of slack. Nanny was enjoying a peach or two as well as the leaves from the trees, so Jacob decided this was as good a place as any to stay for the night. They spread their quilts under a nearby oak tree and feasted on John's biscuits and Nanny's milk. As they lay back they could still hear the pig munching. Jacob said, "Jessie, if that pig eats much more, I allow as how we're gonna wake up in the mornin' and find he's done blowed hisself up."

Jessie giggled, and Jacob did, too, at the vision of a huge ballooning pig in a million pieces. They fell asleep listening to the forest sounds at night. The chirping and scratching and whirring and peeping. It was amazing how many sounds there were. The lonesome sound of a whippoorwill finally lulled them to sleep.

★ ★ ★

Wednesday, July 17, 1861

Grunts, squeals and snorts roused Jacob from his sleep. That lazy, fat old pig, thought Jacob. All he does is eat and get in trouble! The snorts grew louder now. They were not snorts of contentment though. Mingled with the snorts was a sort of growl, followed by several more growls. Jacob rolled over slowly under the quilt and peered out toward where he had tied Squealer last night. There he saw a small black bear cub approaching the pig. It shuffled along, randomly taking bites from the peaches lying on the ground. Squealer snorted and charged at the cub for daring to invade his fruit-filled territory. He lunged at the cub full force, sending the little ball of fur rolling down the hill and yelping with fright. At that very moment, a very large, very angry and protective mother bear appeared on the scene. Her roar let everyone know that no one was going to trifle with her cub.

Jacob shook Jessie. "Wake up," he whispered.

"What should we do?" she whispered back, her eyes wide with fright.

"Just move back slowly, Jess. Stay right by me. Don't make any noise. I think that bear's mad at Squealer and she hasn't seen us yet."

As the two children inched backwards, their eyes were glued in terror on the scene before them. Squealer, standing his

★ ★ ★

ground to protect his new found food supply, had placed himself squarely between the mother and her yowling cub. Not only was this pig greedy and troublesome, but Jacob decided he was incredibly stupid, too.

Low rumbling growls came from the mother as she lumbered toward this fat, round pink threat to her baby. Squealer flapped his large triangular ears, fluttered his eyelashes, and, too late, thought better of what he had done. As he turned to run, the mother bear picked up speed and caught up to him just as he reached the end of his rope. The bear gave the pig one big, powerful swipe with her paw sending him end over end toward the tree. At that instant, with the high piercing screeches of the pig and the roaring growls of the bear echoing in their ears, the two children stood up together and ran. They ran not daring to turn around to look even when the squeals suddenly stopped. They finally stood panting in a small thicket, ready to run at the slightest sight or sound of bear. The kitten had caught up with them and was rubbing against Jessie's skirt.

"Jacob, what about Nanny?"

"I don't know. I didn't even have a chance to see where she was. I do know that Squealer finally did one stupid thing too many. That pig was bound and determined to get us all killed one way or another. I guess we're lucky we got away. We just oughta wait here for a while though. When things have stayed quiet and I think the bears have gone, I'll head back up there and see if Nanny is still tied to her tree. All the rest of our stuff is up there. Everything. We have to wait and try to get it back. At least you still have Cat, and we still have each other. I hope the bears will leave us something to eat for breakfast."

They waited, listening for any growl or snapping of brush that might indicate the approach of bears.

Jacob eventually cautioned, "Let's head back slowly. If we hear anything, run as fast as you can. Okay?"

Jessie nodded her head and held her brother's hand in a death grip. When they got to where they could almost see their blankets, Jacob said, "You stay here. I don't know what's

★ ★ ★

gonna be up there and I don't want you to see things that might make you feel bad. Okay? You'll be able to see me from here. I think that bear's gone off with her young'un, but you yell real loud if you see or hear anything."

"Okay, Jacob. You be careful. I'll be watchin' real good. Don't you worry." She stood next to a small maple and held Cat tightly in her arms.

Jacob walked cautiously up the hill. The slightest sound and he was ready to hightail it out of there. Their quilts lay on the ground as they left them. But neither Nanny nor Squealer was anywhere to be seen. His heart sank. Squealer had been nothing but trouble. He deserved what he got. But Nanny! She'd saved his life at ole Vergil's, and her milk was what was keeping them going on this whole journey. He was really gonna miss her. He hesitated, then began to walk to where Squealer's lead had been. The pig was gone. Only a dark red stain on the ground and a severed piece of rope tied around a peach tree remained. Jacob turned slowly away and went to gather their meager and dwindling belongings. He bent down to roll up the blankets. He could see Jessie in the distance watching his every move. He threw the bags and the blankets over his shoulder and trudged sadheartedly down the hill.

Jessie clutched Cat in her arms. They fell into step side by side, following the railroad tracks again. Jessie waited for Jacob to say something. He looked so tired and sad. She didn't know what to say and she didn't want to ask about Nanny or Squealer for fear the answers would be more than she could bear. She was hungry, too, but was afraid to disturb her brother in his present state. Eventually, unable to contain herself any longer, she said in a meek voice, "Are you okay, Jacob?"

Jacob just kept walking straight ahead. He didn't answer or even act as though he had heard. He had the bags slung over one shoulder and the quilts over the other and the bucket in one hand. His shoulders sagged, but not from the weight of his physical burdens. It was the burdens of his mind that were weighing heaviest on him. How could he be such a failure?

★ ★ ★

First he'd lost Ma, and now Squealer and Nanny. He'd subjected his little sister to all sorts of dangers. How could he possibly face his father with all of this bad news? His pace slowed
even more and he began to dread the moment when he would
have to own up to all these failures. Should they have stayed
on the farm and never gone to look for their Pa? How could a
boy like him know what to do? What was best? He hated this
war. It just wasn't fair.

They continued walking in silence. The only sound was the
clop of their footsteps on the stones. Clop, clop, clop. It had a
kind of rhythm. Clop, clop, clop. Then an echoing clip, clip,
clip. The sounds interrupted his thoughts. Clop, clop, clop.
Clip, clip, clip. He listened to them again. Then he slowly
turned his head. Following along, several yards behind, was
Nanny dragging her rope lead. Jacob dropped his bundles and
ran back to her. He dropped to his knees and threw his arms
around the goat's neck. "Oh, Nanny. I missed you. I thought
we had lost you, too." And he buried his sobbing face in the
goat's coarse tan fur while scratching her neck and ears. Jessie
stood off to the side, snuggling Cat. She knew her brother
wouldn't want her to see his tears. She could wait.

"You poor, poor baby. How long have you been following
us? How did you get loose? Are you hurt?" he murmured as
he searched her body for claw marks or tooth marks. She
seemed fine, except for a pair of milk-laden teats. "You need
to be milked, old girl. You're long overdue. You must be
hurtin'. I'll be real gentle." Fetching the bucket, he led her
over to a tree, tied her up and gently, but firmly, milked her till
she was dry. "There, that ought to feel much better."

Without Squealer to share their milk, there was much more
than the children and the kitten could begin to finish. As much
as he hated to waste the milk, Jacob decided that it would be
too burdensome to carry. Besides they would have more when
he milked Nanny that evening. So he emptied the bucket
beside the tracks.

After the commotion of the morning, the rest of the day

★ ★ ★

seemed calm by comparison. Without Squealer, the little troop should have been able to pick up their pace. But Jacob just plodded along listlessly. It was a slow, somber day for the two youngsters despite the return of Nanny.

It was early evening when Jacob observed, "Look, Jessie. Can you see the houses and buildings way up ahead?"

"What is it, Jacob? Are we going there?" Jessie asked.

"If what John told us is right, that must be Gainesville. That's where the railroad crosses the Alexandria Turnpike. That road will take us to Manassas Junction, where Pa's company is supposed to be going. I sure hope John is right about that."

"It's got to be right, Jacob. I just know we're gonna see Pa real soon." "I wish I could be as sure as you are, little sister, 'cause I'm getting mighty down. I keep thinkin'maybe we shouldn't have tried to make this trip at all."

"Don't say that, Jacob. We had to do it. You'll see. Everything will seem much better as soon as we find Pa." She looked at him with such devotion and trust. He knew he could count on her to follow him anywhere.

He thought to himself, "But what if we don't find Pa? What do we do then?" He didn't dare crush her innocent hopes. However, in truth, he was becoming more cynical. "I think we ought to wait until tomorrow to go through town. We can spend the night here, and we'll be rested when we reach town in the morning," he said to Jessie. Actually, he was worried about what news they might hear in town, and he couldn't bear any more bad news today. Also, he didn't want to take the chance of encountering another Vergil Turner.

They found a small grove of trees, and prepared for the night. They hoped they'd left the bears behind in the hillside orchards. As he settled in beside Jessie, the warm sultry air bore the scent of honeysuckle and the smell made Jacob homesick for the first time since they'd been on the road. He prayed that tomorrow would be a better day.

★ ★ ★

Thursday, July 18, 1861

Gainesville was a small town built at the intersection of the Manassas Gap Railroad and the Warrenton-Alexandria Turnpike. As the children walked through the town, catching snatches of conversation here and there, they realized that something here had put the people on edge. With only Nanny to lead, and Cat tucked safely away in Jessie's bonnet, the children did not attract the attention they had when Squealer was also with them. As they passed by one of the general stores, they heard a group of older men talking loudly. The children slowed down and Jacob pretended to adjust the baggage on Nanny's back while he listened.

"I heard Federal troops are moving towards Centreville at this very minute," said one.

"Well, I hear there's about 35,000 of 'em and they left Washington a couple of days ago. There's even congressmen and ladies comin' along in their buggies to watch the show," groused another.

"Somethin's a brewin' down by Bull Run. Confederate troops been marchin' in from all around for weeks now."

Hearing that, Jacob began to hope again. His Pa had to be among those troops at Bull Run. Jacob started walking again before anyone questioned what they were doing there. But just then, they heard a raspy voice shout loudly, "Hey, you! Stop right there !" They froze in their tracks. They would never forget that rasping voice. It was Vergil. Where could they go? Where could they hide? Jacob slowly turned his head, and there was Vergil as big as life. He was sitting astride one of his mules, red faced, sweating and wobbling from side to side. He had a piece of white cloth wrapped around his head like a bandage. Jacob was getting ready to grab Jessie and run when he heard Vergil bellow, "Stop, you stupid mule! I said stop!" and he realized that the old man hadn't yet spotted them and was only shouting at his mule. Relief flooded through Jacob's mind, but he also realized that if they stood there any longer, Vergil might notice them. He didn't want to find out what that crazy old man would do if he saw them.

Jacob whispered to Jessie, "Follow me. Let's get off this street fast." Jacob ducked down the first little alley he saw and the two of them collapsed again the wall of the building, taking in big breaths and feeling their hearts pound against their chests. "That was close, Jessie. Too close. We gotta get out of here and find Pa fast. Did ya hear what those first guys said, Jess? They said the troops are all headin' to Manassas Junction and Bull Run. Pa's gotta be there, too."

Jessie caught her breath and gasped, "How far do you think we have to go now, Jacob? How far is Bull Run?"

"Not far. Not far at all." Jacob didn't know, but he hoped he was right. He was anxious to get going. He had no way of knowing though that at that very moment, their Pa was on his way south from Leesburg. The Eighth Virginia Infantry had been ordered to Bull Run to prepare for a possible battle. The Hardings were all headed toward the same place.

The children decided to travel alongside the turnpike even though they had no money if they had to pay a fare. As they walked, they kept glancing over their shoulders. They were not going to let Vergil creep up behind them again if they could help it.

The countryside here was mostly wooded and was graced with gently rolling hills. Occasionally the woods were inter-

★ ★ ★

spersed with fields of cattle grazing, or fields of tall green corn just reaching maturity. The road was covered with crushed rocks and stones to fill the inevitable ruts that developed on such a busy road. It made for dusty traveling.

The children passed through the small village of Groveton. It was nice to see a few more houses, but they were anxious to keep going. They passed over several small creeks, some dry or almost dry with the summer heat. Up on the left, they saw a sign at the entrance to a large estate that said, "Rosefield". It was a prosperous looking farm surrounded by peach orchards and cornfields.

A little farther down the road they came upon another major intersection. They would later learn that this crossroad was the Manassas-Sudley Road. But for now their eyes were drawn to a large red stone house situated right at the corner of these two roads. It was only two stories high, but to the two children it seemed to tower into the sky like a grand castle. It had a large chimney on each end constructed of the same red stone.

It was now late afternoon and Jacob said, "Let's see if we can get a drink from the well here and maybe find out where we are." He also wanted a chance to get a closer look at this fine house.

"Look, Jacob, the front door is open. You can ask there for a drink."

Jacob looked at the front door with several steps leading up to it. "Jessie, hold Nanny and I'll be right back." He walked across the grass and hesitated at the bottom step. A woman appeared at the door.

"Well. Well. What have we here? What can I do for you, son?"

"We...we wondered if you'd mind if we had a...a drink from your well, ma'am?" stammered Jacob.

"Help yourself, son. Most folks ain't even polite enough to ask. They just walks up and takes." She added, "Are they with you?" nodding towards Jessie and Nanny.

"Yes'm. That's my sister with our goat."

★ ★ ★

"What are you young'uns doin' here alone or are your folks somewhere's nearby?" she asked with concern in her voice.

"Our folks ain't with us. We're looking for our Pa. Could you tell me where this crossroad goes? And how far is Bull Run?"

"Son, this road goes north to Sudley and south to Manassas Junction. And Bull Run meanders all through these woods to the east of us and the stone bridge crosses it a mile or so down the pike. But there's soldiers camping all along the run now. It ain't any place for a young boy and girl to be, especially alone," she warned.

"Ma'am, we been walkin' a long ways tryin' to find our Pa. Our Ma took sick and we got to let him know. We was told he was headed to Manassas Junction and so we came, too. Have you heard anythin' about the Eighth Virginia Infantry at all? About Company B? They were comin' from Leesburg?" Jacob watched her face anxiously, hoping for a sign of recognition. Of good news.

"Son, we just happen to live here. We see folks come and go down this turnpike and sometimes we hear things. We've seen a lot of troops movin' in and we've even heard today that the Federals have been arriving on the other side of Bull Run at Centreville. General Beauregard's got his Confederate troops all over along Bull Run. I wouldn't have the slightest idea if one of those groups is the one your Pa is in. But I know I wouldn't want no young'uns of mine runnin' through the woods tryin' to find out. It ain't safe. Soldiers has got itchy trigger fingers these days what with all this waitin' they been doin'. You best find a place to set a spell and I'll see if anyone inside has any news for you." She sounded pretty determined and Jacob thought he better not argue. Besides maybe she could find out about Company B for him.

"I'd be grateful for any news you might get, ma'am. Me and my sister are real anxious to find our Pa."

"You go out by your sister and I'll bring you two a bite to eat. Let me see if anyone knows anythin' about the Eighth. I'll

★ ★ ★

be right back." And she bustled off.

Jacob went back to Jessie and began to pull up the bucket from the well. They each drank a dipper full and Jacob put a couple of scoops into their bucket for Nanny. As they were doing this, he told Jessie what the lady said to him.

"But Jacob, Pa can't be far now. She said the soldiers are all around here. Pa must be here, too." Her eyes were bright with excitement and anticipation. He wished he could be as sure as she was.

"Let's just wait and see what news she brings us. Then we'll decide." And they sat in the shade of a nearby tree and waited. A brilliant red ball of sun was approaching the horizon to the west. They watched as it moved behind the rich rolling hills of Rosefield, the beautiful farm they had passed earlier that day. Jacob dreamed out loud, "Maybe someday we can have a farm like that, or a stone house like this one. Wouldn't that be nice, Jessie?"

Jessie was just dozing off, but opened her eyes at his question and murmured, "Uh huh." And then the lady that Jacob spoke with approached them with two plates. "Here you go, young'uns. I'd have you come in, but it's really cooler out here. Actually it ain't cool anywhere these days, but you don't mind. My name's Matthews, Jane Matthews. We provide food and drink for those passin' through on the turnpike. It's been busy with all the activity goin' on around here."

The children accepted the plates, murmuring thanks. The woman was plump and had a jovial face. Her rosy cheeks and easy smile made the children feel at ease. Her reddish-brown hair was pinned in a knot at the back of her head and several stray wisps had escaped and were plastered to her neck with sweat. She had on a plain brown dress and an apron soiled on each side where she wiped her hands. Jacob asked hopefully, "Did anyone know about the Eighth Virginia infantry?"

"Son, there's been lots of troops arriving. Nobody's heard nuthin' about your Pa's unit. I'm sorry I couldn't be more help. But tell me now, what would your names be and where are you

★ ★ ★

from?"

"We're Jacob and Jessie Harding," he replied, "and we're from near Catlett. That's south of Warrenton. Our Pa's Nathan Harding."

"I've heard of Catlett. Glad to meet you both. You're brave ones to be out lookin' for your Pa like this. He oughta be right proud of you two. But I tell you, right now I think you young'uns oughta stay here tonight. I hear there's some big rainclouds heading this way. There's room in the shed and at least you'll have a roof over your head. Tomorrow, we can see if anyone knows anythin' about your Pa. All right?"

At the moment Jacob couldn't think of what else to do, and at least here was someone who was willing to try to find some news of his Pa. And he really didn't want to spend the night sleeping in the rain. "Yes'm, that would be right nice of you. And we could pay you by giving you our goat's milk from tonight and tomorrow morning, if that's okay. Our Pa taught us never to be beholden to no one."

"That's a deal," she said jovially. "It just so happens I love goat's milk. It'll make a fine addition to our table. Now go find yourself a spot in the shed and a place in there to tie your goat. There's plenty of hay to sleep on and plenty to feed the goat. Make yourself to home." And she was off in a flurry and back inside before they knew what happened.

"She seems real nice, Jacob," Jessie offered. "And maybe she'll be able to find out somethin' for us."

"I think you're right, Jessie. Let's go tie Nanny up inside and I'll milk her. Then we'll bring the bucket of milk to Mrs. Matthews. She sounded real happy to have Nanny's milk. Then we'll sit out front here and see if we see any soldiers passing by who might know about Pa."

From the shed they noticed a side door to the house. It was built into a stone entryway. After milking Nanny, they gave a small cup of milk to Cat and left the animals in the shed. They carried the bucket to the house and knocked at the open front door. Mrs. Matthews appeared and gushed, "Why you sweet

★ ★ ★

things. I am going to put this milk to good use. There is nothin' better than fresh goat cheese. Take this around to the side door and tell Tizzie to take it to the springhouse." And she bustled off inside.

They went around to the side door and knocked. A young black girl came up the stairs. "Yassir? Whut you be needin'?"

"Mrs. Matthews said for us to give you this bucket of goat's milk to take to the springhouse. She's goin' to make goat cheese with it," responded Jacob.

The girl took the bucket from Jacob and started to go out to the springhouse without a word. Then she turned around and yelled, "You be needin' this bucket back?"

"Yes'm. It's my bucket."

Without another word she turned around and walked away. The children looked at each other. Then Jacob said, "She must be Mrs. Matthew's help....her slave, maybe. Part of what this war's about. But I can't see why they'd be fightin' about that."

Jessie watched the girl walk away. "Why is she a slave? What does that mean?"

"She belongs to the Matthews just like Nanny belongs to us. Don't seem right that people can own people, but that's how it is. Maybe it's 'cause they are a different color. Maybe that makes them different."

Jessie thought about that. "I guess I just ain't old enough to understand. I just didn't understand everything John was tellin' us."

They sat watching as traffic on the road began to lessen with the approach of evening. They could see the rainclouds Mrs. Matthews had predicted sitting on the horizon. As they went into the shed they spotted their bucket by the door. Tizzie must have set it there. They went inside and snuggled into the hay to sleep.

★ ★ ★

Friday, July 19, 1861

"**G**ood mornin', young'uns. Time to rise and shine." Mrs. Matthews bustled into the shed with a basket of eggs on her arm. "Time to milk that goat of yours, and this mornin' you can drink some of my cow's milk instead. I'll keep your goat's milk for making cheese. And, Jessie, I sure could use a young lady's help in the kitchen this mornin', if you're willin'?"

Jessie jumped up and began brushing the hay off her dress. "I'd be happy to, ma'am." And she scurried off trying to keep up with the bustling pace of Mrs. Matthews. She tucked the cat into her bonnet as she followed.

Jacob milked Nanny as quickly as possible and then tied her out in the yard where she could graze for a while. He couldn't wait to bring that bucket of milk into Mrs. Matthews' kitchen. He could already smell the bacon and coffee aromas drifting through the morning air. He went up the five big stone steps to the front door. There were two small rooms on his right that looked to be bedrooms. Straight ahead was a stairway leading to the second floor. He wondered what was up there. To his left was a door to a very large serving room. The walls were all whitewashed and there were cupboards full of mugs and crockery. The far wall was taken up by an immense stone fireplace. Mrs. Matthews was standing behind a tall bar

★ ★ ★

to the right of the fireplace and Jessie was putting two bowls of oatmeal on the table.

"Folks coming through will be wanting a bite to eat. Keeps a soul busy tryin' to keep up with it all. Soon as Jessie finishes settin' out that oatmeal, you two set down to eat. Tizzie, take this boy's bucket of goat milk to the springhouse and put it with what he gave us last night. Today you can make the goat cheese. Bring back a bit of cream from the top of our milk for their cereal. Hurry, girl. Don't be slow." Jacob wondered where Mr. Matthews was. As if she could read his thoughts, she added, "My husband is out checking the fields early this mornin'. Says it's gonna be scorchin' hot the next couple of days. The rain last night just made things more sticky than ever. You see, he takes care of the farm and fields while I take care of the tavern."

"Yes'm," Jacob responded. "Can I help, ma'am?"

"Just have a seat, boy. I want you young'uns fed and out of the way before any other guests arrive."

Tizzie came back in and quietly set a small pottery creamer on the table near Jacob as well as a pot of honey. Then she went back outside. The two children ate quickly. The cereal was filling and the cream was as rich as anything they'd ever tasted. Tizzie seemed to appear out of nowhere to take their bowls and spoons away. Mrs. Matthews turned around in time to notice their puzzled faces. She laughed. "That's her job. She takes the dishes and washes them so they'll be ready for the next guest. I couldn't manage without her. Now scoot. I have a lot to do. Stay out of trouble and when I get a chance I'll see if there's any word about your Pa."

They went outside quickly. They didn't want to upset Mrs. Matthews although it appeared her good humor was hard to disturb. Right outside the door was their milk bucket where Tizzie had apparently set it. They sat down under the tree and watched for wagons to come by.

"Jacob, how long you reckon to stay here and wait?"

"Don't you like it here? Don't you like Mrs. Matthews?"

★ ★ ★

"It ain't that, Jacob. It's just that I want to be going to Pa. Where do you think he is?"

"I ain't sure, Jess. John Lanham said they were goin' to Manassas Junction. This ain't Manassas Junction, but I think it's close. This sure is where lots of Confederate soldiers are, and one of 'em might be Pa. We'll wait a while and then if we ain't heard nothin' we'll decide which direction to go and move on again. Okay? Meanwhile we'll keep a watch out for any soldiers who might be able to tell us something." Jessie nodded.

They didn't have to wait too long. A couple of men wearing long grey jackets, grey pants and knee high brown boots rode up to the stone house and tied their horses out front. As they dismounted, Jacob noticed the long curving swords and pistols strapped to their belts. The men hurried inside.

"Jacob, did you see that? Do you think Pa has a uniform like that? Do you think he has a long knife and a gun, too?" She was so excited she was out of breath.

"Shhh. They'll hear you. I don't know. And besides they call that a sword, not a long knife. Let's wait over by their horses till they come back out and we'll ask them about Pa."

The children could hear Mrs. Matthews' hearty laugh and the men's deep guffaws. Then it was quiet. Jacob guessed they must be eating. It seemed like they waited forever, and the sun was getting hotter by the minute. Eventually, the two men reappeared, adjusting their belts and laughing together.

Jacob stood up quickly and untied the horses and handed the reins to the men. "Well, what have we here? A new service from the Matthews? Thank you, boy."

"S..sir. I...I was wonderin' if I c...could ask you a question?" Jacob addressed the man who had spoken to him.

"Well, I may not know the answer, but go ahead." He smiled at the other soldier as if sharing a secret. The two men were aides to General Beauregard, but Jacob had no way of knowing that.

"S...sir, me and my sister are lookin' for our Pa. He joined

★ ★ ★

up with the Eighth Virginia Infantry. He's in Company B from Rectortown. They're called the Piedmont Rifles. W..we heard they was comin' here. But we don't know where to look. Have you heard anythin' about them?"

The man looked at his friend questioningly and then back at Jacob. He thought for a few minutes and then responded, "Son, I know a lot of the troops that are here, but I haven't heard that the Eighth is encamped yet. Could be that they are on their way. Of course, your Pa could be among those camped at Manassas Junction. That's about all I can tell you. Sorry, son, that I can't be of more help."

Jacob was crushed. Somehow in his naive mind he thought all soldiers knew where all other soldiers were. Kind of like one big family. He had been so sure that they would be able to answer his question. The soldier saw the crestfallen look on Jacob's face. "What do you need to find your Pa for, son?"

Jacob was too disappointed to lie. He whispered, "Our Ma's dead and we gotta find him to let him know."

The soldier had to lean down to hear what he said. He glanced at Jessie and seemed truly sorry. "Look, son, I'd like to help. But our troops are spread all over. And even if I knew I wouldn't send you children in there. Things are getting tense now that McDowell's troops are at Centreville. There was already some fighting at Blackburn's Crossing yesterday and several men were killed or wounded. This is not a good place to be. You young'uns better find a place to stay until you can get some definite word on where your father is. We've got to get back to headquarters now before we're missed. Stay out of trouble and stay out of the way." With that, he mounted his horse and the two men rode south along the Manassas road. A cloud of dust followed them up the hill. Jacob watched until they disappeared over the crest.

Jessie came up beside him and reached out and held his hand. "Don't worry, Jacob. We'll find Pa."

He pulled his hand away angrily. "How are we going to find him when his own soldiers don't know where he is?" he

★ ★ ★

snapped at her. He stalked off towards the shed.

Jessie ran after him. He threw himself down in the hay on his stomach and buried his face in his arms. "Jacob. Jacob. We can go to Manassas Junction. That's the way those men went. Maybe that's where Pa went, too."

Jacob rolled over and looked up at her innocent face. Cat scampered up and jumped on his stomach. He sat up and stroked the kitten. He realized that getting mad at his sister wasn't going to help. "I'm sorry, Jessie. Okay, let's go. It makes as much sense as sitting here. At least we'll be movin'. C'mon, let's get Nanny. We'll say goodbye to Mrs. Matthews."

Mrs. Matthews wasn't any too keen about their leaving. Apparently the two officers had told her enough during breakfast to let her know that something could happen at any time. She was worried about what might happen to them. When they told her the direction they planned to go, she whistled through her teeth and then said, "Well, if you must, you must. I ain't got no hold on you. But when you go up the hill, would you stop by Spring Hill. That's old Mrs. Henry's house. I'd like to send her up some honey and preserves. Mrs. Henry's taken to bed most of the time now, but you can give it to her girl, Lucy. Tell her I sent it. Now, be off with you before I change my mind and try to make you stay."

Jacob and Jessie headed up the road, one on each side of the goat. Jessie carried the kitten to protect her from the dust. They looked back and saw Mrs. Matthews who was waving her apron cheerily from her doorway. And then she was gone. Probably back to the bustle of her duties.

Sudley-Manassas Road rose up steeply from the turnpike intersection. It was such an incline that the children did not see the house at Spring Hill until they reached the top. These hills and sloping inclines would prove to be the downfall or the salvation of the men who would fight here. The key was to be who was going up or who was going down.

The children cut across the field passing the springhouse in the middle of a small grove of hickory and locust trees. The

★ ★ ★

fields were knee deep in timothy grass and weeds. The house and the grounds around it looked equally unkempt. The grapevines were so overgrown on the arbor that it appeared to be one massive bush instead of an arbor. The roses were in sad need of trimming, too. Jacob remembered Mrs. Matthews saying that old Mrs. Henry was sick in bed. But wasn't there anyone to care for her fields and garden for her?

The children approached the house. It was small from the outside, perhaps one floor with a loft. It needed repairs. They knocked.

A small black woman opened the door. She put her finger to her lips to tell them to be quiet. She came outside and pulled the door shut behind her. "They's all restin' inside. What you chil'uns want here?"

"Mrs. Matthews sent some honey and preserves for Mrs. Henry. We told her we'd bring it by," Jacob explained.

"That's right nice of her. She knows Miz Henry been ailin' a long spell. Let me fetch a drink for you chil'uns. You wait here." She slipped back into the house closing the door behind her. She came back out with a pitcher of water and glasses.

"Tain't nothin' but water, but it'll taste good on such a hot day. That's why the folks inside is restin'. When you is old, the heat hits real bad." She poured water for each of them.

"How long has Mrs. Henry been sick?" asked Jessie. She always worried about anyone who wasn't well.

"Chile, that woman is nigh on 85 years. She ain't been well for some time. And then there's Mr. Hugh. He's her son. He ain't never been well. They say somethin's wrong, but no doctor could ever tell what. Miz Ellen's her daughter and I reckon the heat's got to her. But they's all gettin' on. And me, I got to do all the fixin' and carin'." She sighed a deep sigh. "What you chil'uns doin' 'round here? Don't you know soldiers crawlin' all over this countryside?"

"We're lookin' for our Pa. He joined the army and then our Ma took sick and died. And we have to find our Pa and tell him, so he can come home with us," explained Jacob.

★ ★ ★

"And how you be expectin' to find your Pa out here?" she fussed.

"We just keep walkin' and askin'. And we keep hopin' someone will know. We know he's comin' round here somewheres. We just gotta keep lookin'."

"Well, you best be goin' now before Miz Henry wakes up. She don't like to be disturbed none. I best be in the house if she calls." She turned to go inside taking the glasses and pitcher. Then she turned around and asked, "I knows I shouldn't be askin' this..."

"What?" replied Jacob.

"Everythin' 'round this place is fallin' down. But there's a bunch of old peach trees. Ain't been cared for, but they's got peaches this year. I cain't never find time to pick them, what with carin' for all the sick folk. If you chil'uns could pick a bunch for me, I'll fix a plate of dinner for you. And I'll tell you a place to go where you might find some news about your Pa."

Jacob's ears perked up. What could this woman know about finding his Pa? But then who else had known anything? "We can pick your peaches," he replied, "but we'll need some baskets or buckets though. Just show us where the old trees are."

"They's old buckets down by the springhouse. You'll see the trees from there. Bring'em by the house when you finish, but don't knock. I'll keep a eye out for you. Those ol' folks gonna love peach pie and peach butter." She actually looked happy as she went inside.

The children tied Nanny to a tree and ran down to the springhouse to collect the baskets. Cat scampered behind them. The trees were definitely uncared for. Many branches were dead or broken off, but there were some peaches. They started to pick the ripe fruit. "Jacob, I can't help but think about dumb old Squealer whenever I see peaches. I sure hope there are no bears here."

"I don't think we need to worry about that. I'll climb up and get the ones up high and you get ones that are low. Okay? It

★ ★ ★

shouldn't take us long to fill these buckets. Lucy seemed pleased that she finally had someone to help her. I hope she wasn't teasing us about knowin' someone who could help us find Pa though."

"I sure hope so too."

The children trudged up the hill as soon as they filled the buckets. They set them by the door of the house and then went to sit under the shade of a tree. It was hot and sticky as Mrs. Matthews had said it would be. Cat curled up in Jessie's lap. The door opened and the young black woman came out.

"You done good. I hated to see those peaches rottin' on the trees. Like I promised I'll fix some food. Then I'll send you to Mr. Robinson's house on the next hill. Folks round here call him "Gentleman Jim". He's been watchin' all the comin's and goin's 'round here for a long time. He might be able to help you. You just tell him Lucy sent you. Gentleman Jim, he be special. He a freedman. He's no more slave." Jacob and Jessie looked at each other. Lately they were seeing and hearing more about slaves than they'd learned in their whole life. "You chil'uns wait here and rest. I'll be out shortly with a plate for you."

"You don't need to do that, Miss Lucy. If you just show us the way to go, we'll be on our way to Mr. Robinson's. It was our pleasure to help with the peaches," said Jacob. He was anxious to find his Pa.

"Bless you, chil'uns. You just head right north there across that field. You can almost see his house from here. They be right nice folk."

Jacob untied Nanny and Jessie held Cat as they started across the field to the Robinson's house.

"Jacob, do you suppose Lucy is a slave? Her skin is dark and she does all the work."

"I don't know. I never thought much about it before. John said slavery was one of the reasons why Pa was fightin' this war. But if she was a slave she seemed happy enough and she was nice to us." Then he added, changing the subject, "Let's

★ ★ ★

run across the field. I feel happy. I think we're gonna find Pa soon." He couldn't think about slaves now.

As they were scampering across the field, unbeknownst to them, the Eighth Virginia Infantry was just arriving south of them near Lewis Ford on Bull Run. The regiment would make camp there that night on Holkum's Branch. The Hardings had just missed each other by minutes.

As the children crossed the crest of the hill, they could look down and see Mrs. Matthews' stone house. From up here on the hill it had a cold, forlorn look to it. It gave each of them a strange feeling. It would have been hard for them to understand how those warm, friendly rooms they had just shared would soon be filled with the misery of dead and dying Federal soldiers as the house and its rooms were turned into a temporary hospital.

The children turned and scampered on down the hill. The wrinkles that Mother Nature carved into the earth made little valleys and ridges for them to traverse. Down in the valley, a stand of oaks and beech trees blocked the stone house from view. It seemed to vanish from their sight as if it had never been there. They ran up the other side of the hill through a field overgrown with timothy grass, honeysuckle and clover. They were just barely able to see the peak of the Robinsons' roof. As they ran closer, they could see a rail fence all around the small white house they were headed for. When they got to the fence, they could climb over it, but poor Nanny wasn't able to. That was the problem with a milk producing goat. Normally goats loved nothing more than to jump and leap. But Nanny, her udder filled with milk, could not jump over. So the children began to skirt along the edge of the fence, hoping to find a break in it somewhere. Eventually, to the rear of the house, they found a little pass-through. As they walked toward the back of the house they saw several dark-skinned girls working in a large vegetable garden. They looked up at Jacob and Jessie, but said nothing and continued working. Jacob wondered if they were slaves of Mr. Robinson. They walked

★ ★ ★

around and approached the front door which was sheltered by a small porch that held a wooden bench. Jacob handed the rope lead to his sister.

"Jess, you hold Nanny and I'll go see if anyone is home." But before he took two steps, an old black man came out of the house.

"What brings you two chil'uns up here?" He had a deep, serious voice and that, coupled with his dark skin, frightened the children.

"M...miss L...lucy sent us. She said M...mr. R..obinson might be able t...to help us find our Pa," stammered Jacob. He found himself taking a step backwards as the man approached him.

"Ah's Mr. Robinson. Gentleman Jim is what folks call me. What makes you think I can help you?"

Jacob was surprised. Somehow he didn't think Mr. Robinson would be black. But Lucy had said he was a freed slave. "I...I don't know. M...miss L...lucy th...thought you knew where some of the t...troops were."

"Your Pa a soldier? What side?" His questions were short and curt. Jessie had nestled the kitten into her bonnet and had sidled up to Jacob by now. He felt some safety in their closeness.

"M...my Pa joined the Eighth V...virginia Infantry. C...company B. They're Confederate troops. I h...heard th...they was headed th...this way."

"Why you lookin' for him?"

The man's curt questions kept Jacob on edge. He couldn't think straight. He stammered, "Our M...ma's dead. W...we gotta find our P...pa and tell him. We ain't got n...no one else." He felt tears welling up in his eyes, but he didn't want to cry. What would this man think?

"Well, why didn't you say so in the first place. No chil'uns gonna be alone in this house." And he displayed a broad grin of white teeth that lit up his whole face. "You chil'uns c'mon by the house. We'll see what we can do to help you. You jest

★ ★ ★

set a spell on the front porch. Tie that old goat to the maple tree." Jessie's tenseness faded. This dark man was a friend. The children did what he said and soon found themselves seated on the porch with a cool drink, and they explained who they were and told their whole story to this old man. He listened patiently, nodding his head and looking very concerned as they spoke of Vergil, and the incident with the bear. Then he said, "You chil'uns had a tough time. Ole Gentleman Jim here's gonna see what he can do for you. First off, you heard right. Lots of troops been comin' in here for weeks now. I know some of 'em 'cause I been selling some of my extra vegetables and stuff to them. I run a drover's tavern here, too, so I get word from the folks driving through. The closest troops to here are Evans' Brigade down by the stone bridge. There's boys there from Louisiana and some from South Carolina and even some cavalry from Virginia. But you said your Pa was infantry, right, Jacob?"

"Yes sir," he replied.

"Well, I tell you what. Soon's my girls come in with today's pickins from the garden, I'll take you with me when I go down to sell them. We'll see if any folks down there know about your Pa. How's that sound to you?"

"I'd be mighty grateful, sir. We sure would like to find him. Jess and me are getting tired of walking around. We'd sure like to go back home."

"Well, you wait here and I'll go out back and check on the girls."

As he walked off, Jessie nudged Jacob. "Is he a slave, too?"

"I don't think so. Remember Miss Lucy said he was free."

"How'd he get free. Jacob?"

"I don't know, Jessie. I reckon we'll just have to ask him." While they talked and waited, they heard thunder rumbling in the distance. A few minutes later, rain began to fall. Mr. Robinson and his girls came running in from the garden carrying several large baskets of tomatoes, squash, beans, and greens. They ducked in under the porch, just as the rain really

★ ★ ★

started to come down.

"Son, it looks like we're gonna have to wait 'til tomorrow to go down and ask around about your Pa. I don't like to go peddling in this rain. That old red clay gets slick and mucky. You chil'uns come join our family for dinner and we'll find a dry spot for you to sleep tonight. Your Pa'll still be there tomorrow."

Jacob and Jessie must have shown their disappointment, because he said, "Now, we'll have no sad faces in this house. We all got to enjoy life and what the good Lord's seen fit to give us. Let's see a smile." And he gave Jacob a reassuring pat on the shoulder.

Jacob smiled a feeble smile. "I'll try, sir. Now I reckon I'd best go milk Nanny and we can all share some fresh goat milk."

"That sounds mighty good to me. Take her to the shed out back and tie her in there. She can stay there for the night. And little Miss Jessie and her kitty can come on in and help the girls."

They joined the family for dinner. They never before had shared a meal with a black family. There were lots of questions they wanted to ask about slaves and freedmen, but for a while everyone was asking questions about them and their travels. They enjoyed this warm hospitality. Finally, as the women began to clear the table, Jacob got a chance to ask his questions. "Miss Lucy told us that you were a freedman. What does that mean?"

James Robinson looked at the boy to see if he was joking, but he realized Jacob truly didn't know. "I was once the slave of Mr. Carter. In fact, Miz Henry on the hill across the way is one of his kin. I was a good and faithful servant to that man and on his deathbed he said I was to be free. He gave me a bit of land right here to build me a cabin."

"But how can one man own another man?" Jacob looked puzzled.

"That's just how it got to be. Mr. Carter, he owned me and

★　★　★

my wife and my children. He set me free, but he still owned my family."

Jacob looked around the room at the people there. "But you have your family here now."

"That's because I worked hard to make money on this place and I saved every penny to buy back my family one by one. First I bought my wife, Susan. We have six children, but I have only been able to buy back three of them, two girls and a boy. My two other sons, Alfred and James, are stonemasons and very good ones. Folks with more money than I had bought them at an auction at the stone house and took them off someplace far away. I ain't seen them since."

"But that don't seem right to sell a man's family. Is that what this war is about?"

"I hear that's part of it, son. I sure would like to see my sons be able to come back home free men some day."

Jacob looked at the old man. "Are you hopin' that the Federals will win this war then?"

"I don't like to see no war and no killin' and I'm too old to be a soldier even if they would take me. But if it might mean my family will be free, then, yes, I hope it's the Federals that wins. I don't mean no harm to your Pa, but you can understand what I mean, right, son?"

Jacob nodded his head. Things were getting more confused and more complicated. He'd never thought about all of this before. He'd always thought his Pa was right. But after listening to Mr. Jim, maybe that wasn't true. It was difficult to sort out who was right and who was wrong. As soon as they found Pa, Jacob was gonna have to talk to him about these things.   That night Jacob and Jessie slept on blankets on the floor of Jim's house. Tomorrow would be another day. Tomorrow they would find Pa.

★ ★ ★

Saturday, July 20, 1861

The day dawned clear and stifling hot. The rain from the night before made the sultry air feel like it was pressing down on their bodies. Even breathing was hard. Jacob got up and rolled up his blanket and tiptoed out to milk the goat. Jessie and the other girls were still asleep. He went outside and old Jim was already up, too.

"You're up early, son. Too sticky hot for you, too? These kind of days a body don't hardly want to do nothin'."

"Yessir. But Nanny doesn't care what kind of day it is. She still wants to be milked."

"Your old goat is waitin' for you in the shed. C'mon back inside when you finish. By then the rest of the family will be awake and we'll have a bite to eat."

"What time you reckon to go down to the troops today?" Jacob inquired hopefully.

"I got several chores I got to get done this morning before this heat gets the best of me. If'n I don't go down the first thing in the morning, then I just wait until late afternoon. He saw Jacob's disappointment again at the thought of waiting. "But I don't see any reason why you shouldn't be able to walk down to the camps by yourself to ask your questions. You don't need to wait for an old man like me. You done told me

★ ★ ★

about enough adventures to let me know you can take care of yourself. Now go milk your goat and then have a bite. Then I'll tell you how to get there.

Jacob was excited. He'd finally be talkin' to a whole regiment of soldiers. He was sure he could find out about his father. He milked Nanny and hummed as he did. His journey was nearing its end.

After breakfast, old Jim spoke to Jacob. "Son, you best go down by yourself. A soldiers' camp ain't no place for a little lady. Your sister can stay here with her kitten and the goat. They'll be fine here while you go askin' your questions. Besides you'll be able to go faster by yourself. My farm road leads right out to the turnpike that you just traveled on. Follow the turnpike to the east until just before the stone bridge. You can't miss Evans' boys. They're spread out all over this side of the bridge. Just tell them ole Gentleman Jim sent you. And tell them what you told me about your Pa. Then come back here and let us know what you find out. Okay?"

Jacob nodded. Jessie followed Jacob outside. She stared up at him with a hurt look in her eyes. "But, Jess, you heard what Mr. Robinson said," he tried to explain. "It ain't a good place for a girl to go. I'll be comin' right back as soon as I find out anythin'. I promise. I won't go to Pa without you." Those last words seemed to put her a little more at ease.

"But, Jacob. It's just that we ain't been apart since Pa left and I'm afraid to be without you. I'm so afraid somethin' might happen to you and I won't be able to help you. I'm afraid that I won't see you again." She wrapped her arms around him and hugged him tight. He reached out and hugged her back, stroking her tangled golden curls.

"Jessie, you don't ever have to worry about me. I'll always be here for you. I'm just going down and see if anyone knows about the Eighth Virginia and as soon as I find out anythin' I'll come back. I won't stay long. You'll see."

She let go of her brother and stepped back. Cat scampered up to her feet. She picked up the kitten and held it out to Jacob.

★ ★ ★

"Promise Cat that you'll come right back, too. Then I'll believe you."

"Okay." He took the kitten and looked in its little grey face and said solemnly in a deep voice, "Cat, I promise to come right back when I find out about Pa." As he handed the cat back to Jessie, they both laughed.

Before he left, he filled his canteen with spring water. On such a hot day, even a short trip could be wearing. The girls gave him a couple of corn muffins to take along. He walked down the short farm road. At the turnpike he turned and waved to Jessie and then headed east.

The road was hot and the dust kicked up in spite of yesterday's rain. You could see people coming long before they arrived by the dust cloud that preceded them. Jacob felt strange traveling by himself. Whenever he'd seen anything interesting before, he'd always had Jessie to share it with. Now he just had himself. He decided he didn't like being alone. He hurried off anxious to find the soldiers' camps. He crossed a large field. A small hill rose at the other side. When he finally crested the hill and looked down, he saw the tents of hundreds of soldiers. He was amazed at how many there were. He would have to remember just what everything looked like so he could explain it to Jessie. He slowly started down the other side of the hill, gradually getting closer and closer to the men. Some were lying down in the shade or in their tents. Some were cleaning and polishing their long rifles. The metal gleamed and the wooden stocks shone. Some had their bayonets affixed and those too were glistening in the sunlight. Jacob thought how frightful they looked, for a rifle topped with a bayonet was as tall as a man. Some men were fixing food over campfires. He saw large stew pots and coffee pots and the food smelled good. Other soldiers sat around in small groups playing cards. Jacob approached the first group he saw. As he got closer he noticed their uniforms were far different from any others he had seen or heard about. The men were wearing baggy blue and white striped pants and brown

★ ★ ★

jackets. Some had on maroon hats shaped like upside down flower pots. Several were talking and he couldn't understand what they were saying. It didn't sound like any words he'd ever heard before.

A young soldier, sitting on the ground sharpenening his bayonet, pointed at Jacob. He laughed and said something that Jacob didn't understand.

Another soldier said, "Eh, boy. What you want?" His words had a funny accent.

Jacob replied, "I'm looking for my Pa, sir. I came down from Gentleman Jim's just up the road a ways. He said someone here might be able to help me."

"Ah, Monsieur Jim, I know heem. Your Pa, who he ees? "His name is Nathan Harding. He's with the Eighth Virginia Infantry, Company B. The Piedmont Rifles. Have you heard of them?"

"No. We are ze Louisiane Tigers. We speek French. Over ze road you find ze men from Virginia. Zey answer you questions, yes?"

Jacob thanked the soldier and headed across the turnpike. He wondered where these strange speaking men were from and why they were fighting in this war. As he walked across the field, he could see that this group of men were busy grooming and caring for their horses. Saddles and bridles were being polished. Some men were checking their horses' hooves. He noticed that most of the horses were black. Jacob saw one man off by himself brushing his horse, and he approached him.

"Sir. I'm looking for the Eighth Virginia Infantry. My Pa's in that unit and I need to find him. Have you heard anythin' about them?"

The man looked up, surprised to be interrupted by such a young voice. "Who are you?" he asked.

"My name's Jacob Harding. My Pa is Nathan Harding," replied the boy.

"Well, it just so happens that they passed through yesterday heading downstream. They were gonna set up camp along the

★ ★ ★

Bull Run somewhere. If you let me finish grooming my horse, we'll go find one of the other men, who may know where they went. But while you're waiting, I could use a helper to fetch me a bucket of water from the creek for my horse. Think you could manage that?"

"Yessir!" Jacob replied, ecstatic with the news that his father had actually been near here yesterday. He couldn't be far away at all now. Jessie would be so excited, too.

Jacob discovered that the walk to get the water was a lot farther than he'd expected. He could see why the man had asked him to do it. Jacob had to ask several times for directions to the creek as he went. Finally he got to what must be the famous Bull Run that he had been hearing so much about. It wasn't very impressive at all. It was just a shallow muddy creek. However, he found out that there were not many easy places to get down to the water to fill a bucket. The banks were rather steep and slippery. He found a place to scoot down, filled the bucket and headed back. He hoped he'd remember which way he had come. He finally saw his soldier and began to hurry only to have to slow down again to avoid spilling all the water he had just fetched.

"Well done, son! You'll make a fine soldier someday." Jacob didn't think he ever wanted to be a soldier, but he didn't say so. He sat down in the grass under a tree and had a drink from his canteen. He was glad he brought it. He wished the man would hurry up. It had taken him a long time to get the water and now he was anxious to find out where his Pa's unit was.

"All right, Lightning. That ought to have you ready for whatever may lie ahead of us." He placed the bucket of water where the horse could get it and then beckoned to Jacob. "Let's go, Jacob Harding, and see what we can find out about The Eighth."

The man walked with a long stride and Jacob had to take two steps to every one of his. They approached a tent in among the trees. "You wait out here and I'll see if anyone inside has

★ ★ ★

heard where the Eighth set up camp."

Jacob waited impatiently outside, shifting from one foot to the other. The man was gone a long time. Jacob could hear talking inside the tent, but he couldn't make out what they were saying. Didn't they know how long he'd been waiting to find out this news about his father? Didn't they know he had a little sister waiting for him to come back with this news? Hurry, mister, hurry. But obviously the soldier had other things on his mind. He was still talking, and Jacob knew he would just have to be patient. This was the closest he had come to actually finding his father. This was someone who knew his Pa's regiment was in the area. He could wait a few more minutes.

A few yards away, a young soldier sat in front of a tent, playing a dulcimer on his lap. As he played he sang. All the words were hard to catch, but it seemed to be about a soldier leaving his girl friend behind. Jacob began to hum along with the chorus as the soldier played it over and over between the verses,

> *"I'll throw my knapsack on my back,*
> *My rifle on my shoulder,*
> *I'll go marching down to town,*
> *Enlist and be a soldier."*

As Jacob hummed along, the words reminded him of the day his Pa left to enlist with his rifle, knapsack and mule. It seemed like a very long time ago now.

Finally, the soldier re-emerged from the tent. He almost walked right past Jacob. He had forgotten all about him. "Oh, you," he said absent-mindedly as he headed back towards his horse. Jacob looked at him expectantly, waiting for word on his Pa. He had to run to keep up with the man. The man was lost in his own thoughts.

Jacob prodded, "The Eighth, sir, the Eighth? Do you know where they are?" He held his breath, waiting for the reply.

"Yes," the man said without really thinking. "They're at Lewis Ford near Holkums Branch. Word came in today." Then

★ ★ ★

as if something clicked in his brain, he spun around and grabbed the boy's shoulders. "Look, son. I know you want to find your Pa, but my advice to you is to get back to the Robinson house and to find a safe place to hide. Things are reaching a dangerous level here. This is not a time for a boy to be out wandering around. Mark my word. Things will be over fast once they start. Then you'll be able to find your Pa and go home. But right now GO! Get someplace safe! Do you understand?"

"Y...yessir. Th..thank you, sir." And Jacob turned and ran across the field to the crest of the hill that would lead him back to old Jim's house. Something in the way that man spoke to him, in the way that he was preoccupied, scared Jacob. That man learned something in that tent. Something that he hadn't known before. And that something had frightened him, and he had tried to convey that fear to Jacob.

Jacob ran most of the way back. Anxiety and fear and a sense of uncertainty raged in his head. He ran stumbling, struggling to concentrate on placing one foot in front of the other. It was hot, and he was sweating all over. His hair was dripping wet. He wanted to get back to the house and to Jessie. He would tell them what he had found out. Maybe old Jim would know where Lewis Ford was. Maybe he could help Jacob decide if it would be safe to go there. But Jacob remembered the way the soldier grabbed him and warned him to hide. He would have to think about what he should do.

He turned up the farm road to old Jim's house. He was worn out and had to force himself to keep moving up the hill.. Jessie came running down from the top. She must have been sitting there waiting for him. As she ran towards him, she yelled, "Jacob. Jacob. What did you find out? Do you know where Pa is? What took you so long? Me an' Cat have been waiting forever. Hurry up and tell me." When she got close to him she saw how tired and sweaty he was. She saw the look of concern and worry on his face. "What's wrong, Jacob? What happened? Is Pa all right?"

★ ★ ★

At the top of the hill, Jacob flopped down under a beech tree. Jessie knelt down beside him, wiping his face with her apron. He opened his canteen, took a long drink and poured the rest over his head. It felt good. Jessie waited, but anxiety was written all over her face. She knew when Jacob was in a mood like this she better not press him, but what had he found out?

Jacob took a deep breath and began. "Pa's unit got here yesterday. He's camped somewhere near here by Bull Run. I'm sure Old Jim will know where it is, but..."

"But what?" Jessie prodded urgently.

"One of the soldiers warned me not to try to find Pa right away. He said it's too dangerous. He said we should find a place to hide. I don't know what to do. Pa's so close now. I thought maybe old Jim could help us decide. Jessie, I'm afraid. If you could have seen the way that soldier looked when he told me to hide. We gotta talk to Jim. Where is he?"

"He ain't come back from his chores yet. C'mon to the back of the house. It's cooler there under the trees. I'll get you some cool water from the spring and we can wait for Mr. Jim." Jessie pulled Jacob up and they trudged hand in hand around the house. While Jacob sat down, Jessie ran to the spring, and came back with a ladle full of cool, clear water.

"Thanks, Jess." He handed the ladle back to her, and continued, "You should have seen all the soldiers down there. Hundreds and hundreds of 'em and rows and rows of tents. I never knew there were so many. Some of them spoke a funny way that I couldn't understand. Said they were from Louisiane. The man I talked to was from a group that had horses. I had to fetch water for his horse. That's partly what took me so long. I got to go down to Bull Run. It ain't much of a creek. Don't know why everybody talks about it so much."

Jessie looked towards the back door of the house. One of Jim's grown daughters was calling to her. "I gotta go help with the vegetables. I said I would after you got back. I'll come

★ ★ ★

back here in a little bit. You rest some."

She bent down and kissed his wet head and left.

Jacob leaned back and closed his eyes. Thoughts flooded his brain. He remembered Pa's words before he left. He thought about John Lanham's feelings on war. He quickly felt his pocket to be sure John's letter was still there. Then he thought about his conversation with Gentleman Jim last night. He thought about Jim's children and Lucy and Tizzie. Pa said you had to fight for what you thought was right. And Pa went off to fight with the Confederates for Virginia. John Lanham hadn't wanted his boy to go to war, but it sounded like his boy couldn't wait to be a Confederate soldier and go off and fight. But Jim's family's freedom depended on this war and Jim was hoping the Federals would win. They couldn't all be right, could they? They couldn't all win. His head hurt thinking about it. All he wanted was to find his Pa and bring him home. Things were so much simpler on their farm. He hadn't known about all these people and their troubles. He had never thought about who was right or who was wrong. But he was so tired. It was too much to think about.

"Jacob. Jacob. Wake up, chile. It's time to eat. You been sleepin' like a baby out here. No one wanted to wake you." It was old Jim shaking and prodding the boy. Jacob awoke with a start. He had to think for a minute to remember where he was. Jim saw the frightened look on the boy's face, "It's all right, son. You're right here at my house. No one's gonna hurt you."

Jacob blurted out, "But I wanted to find Pa. Pa's nearby. You shouldn't let me sleep so long. Pa's near Lewis Ford. I gotta go to him. Can you help me?"

"Whoa, boy, whoa. Not so fast. Slow down," Jim said, patting Jacob's shoulder. "Tell me again where your Pa's at?"

Jacob took a deep breath, "They're at Lewis Ford near Holkum's Branch. They got there yesterday. Can you take me there or tell me which way to go?"

"I know right where it is, son, but..."

★ ★ ★

"But what? I gotta find my Pa!"

"Hold on a minute. Listen to me. I been riding around today. All the troops are preparing for something big soon. I been told by all my soldier friends to find a safe place for me and my family for a day or so. They weren't foolin' none." Jacob thought of the soldier's words this morning and of the look on his face. But how could he wait when Pa was so close. "Come have a bite to eat, Jacob. Tomorrow if things seem quiet enough I'll get you to your Pa. Will you settle for that?"

Jacob thought a minute. Another day. He didn't want to wait, but he felt he had no choice. He could go on his own right now, but he didn't know where to go. If he waited till tomorrow, old Jim would take him directly there. "Okay," he said with resignation. "Tomorrow."

The house was ominously quiet that night and Jacob had difficulty going to sleep. A bright moon shone through the window, casting eerie shadows on the planked floor. Thoughts of his father kept marching through his mind, but eventually he fell into a fitful sleep.

★ ★ ★

Sunday, July 21, 1861

K A-BOOM! The whole house shook and everything rattled. Jacob and Jessie sat bolt upright where they were sleeping on the floor. Old Jim and his wife came running out from their room pulling on their clothes. The rest of the family appeared. Everyone was wide-eyed even though seconds before they had all been sound asleep.

"What was that?" whispered Jessie, clutching onto Jacob's arm.

"I don't know," Jacob replied.

KA-BOOM! A second roar and within a few seconds a resounding third ka-boom.

Old Jim surveyed the faces of the assembled group. "It's started, I reckon. That was cannon. The fightin' and killin' is underway." Jim looked at Jacob. "That's what they was tryin' to tell us yesterday." Everybody just kept standing and staring at one another, until Jim ordered, "We best get some things together and go down to the food cellar. That's probably the safest place to be. Let's go. Everybody move."

Then as if they'd been snapped out of a trance, each person scurried off in one direction or another collecting blankets and pots and whatever they thought they would need.

Jacob walked over to Jim and whispered with fear, "What do you think will happen to my Pa?"

The old man put his hand on the boy's shoulder and shook his head. "I don't know, Jacob. I don't know. But I promise

★ ★ ★

you that as soon as it's safe enough, I'll help you find your Pa. And Gentleman Jim don't never go back on his word. Okay, boy?"

Jacob nodded his head. Until now, the war had only been a spoken word. But the roar of the cannons brought the reality of that word into focus in an instant. "You best go quickly and milk your goat. If it sounds like gunfire nearby, head to the cellar door in a hurry, milk or no," the old man warned. With all the commotion, Jacob had completely forgotten about Nanny. It was good old Jim had his wits about him. Jacob went out to the shed. It was very early and the sun was just rising to the east over Bull Run.

Jacob carried the bucket of milk back to the house. He could hear gun shots, but they sounded far off. Jim called out from the porch, "Bring that milk in here. We're gonna have somethin' to eat before we head to the cellar. The gunfire sounds like it's far enough away that we'll have time to run and hide if we need to."

Everyone ate in silence. They were all listening for any sounds that would indicate that soldiers were headed this direction. Jessie sat close to her brother. She looked very frightened. Jacob wanted to reassure her, but how could he when he was scared to death himself? Mostly he was sick with worry about Pa and where he was in this fighting.

Throughout the morning hours, they sat on the front porch. From their vantage point on the hill, they could see and hear a great deal. There was sporadic gunfire and an occasional cannon roar. In the far distance to the north they saw dust clouds on the horizon. Old Jim guessed that it was probably Union troops on the march. At midmorning, the noise of gunfire made it obvious that a major battle was taking place across the turnpike. Jim said that was the Matthews' farm property. He said there was a sweeping hill north of the stone house and the smoke and noise seemed to be coming from that direction. Jacob hoped Mrs. Matthews was in a safe place. Then old Jim told the ladies that he thought it best that they go down to the

★ ★ ★

root cellar. He and his son and Jacob remained on the porch to
watch what was happening.

It wasn't long before Jacob yelled, "Look! Over there by
Miz Henry's. There's soldiers moving toward the stone house."
As the group watched, column after column of infantry moved
across the ridge, and down the hillside toward the turnpike.
Because of the trees they lost sight of the troops, but assumed
they were going to reinforce the Confederate line behind the
stone house. From the position of the sun they could tell it was
close to noon.

From that point on Jacob lost track of time. Before they
knew what was happening, they saw groups of soldiers retreating back across the hill between the stone house and Mrs.
Henry's house. Some were dragging wounded men between
them. They were scattered, not at all like the orderly columns
they had observed moments earlier going the other direction.
Some were occupying the hills and gulleys right in front of Old
Jim's house. Jacob was transfixed. What if one of those men
was his Pa?

The old man said, "Let's go, son. Fightin's gettin' too close
to stay out here anymore. Time for us to go to the cellar." The
Robinson men got up to go. But Jacob couldn't hide now. His
father might be right out there. Old Jim tried to take hold of his
arm to pull him along. Jacob wrenched free and darted across
the yard toward the split rail fence. Jacob could just barely
hear the old man saying, "Crazy boy, he'll get hisself kilt that
way. He'll come in as soon's the first shot passes by him."
And the two black men went down to the cellar.

Jacob huddled against the fence in the far back corner of
the yard. He tried to make himself as small as he could. But
he had to keep looking. He had to watch for his Pa. As he
watched, the men continued to find refuge in the same wrinkles in the terrain that he and Jessie had crossed only two days
ago. There were troops appearing and forming all around on
the hillsides from the Robinson house across to the Henry
house and beyond. Jacob saw cannons and limbers loaded with

★ ★ ★

ammunition and pulled by horses being placed in position on the hill. There was sporadic gunfire as the Confederate troops continued to pull back to this side of the turnpike. Men on horseback rode up and down the line shouting to the men. Then everything went quiet. It was an eerie quiet because Jacob from his vantage point could still see many soldiers all around. It was as if someone had called out, "Lunch time." But it wasn't lunch time at all.

Jacob was dripping wet with sweat. His hair was wet. His shirt stuck to his back. He was out in the full sun and too afraid to run or hide anyplace else for fear he'd be discovered and shot. He couldn't imagine how those men could run and shoot with wool uniforms and blanket rolls and leather straps crisscrossing their chests in this intense heat. He lay quietly watching and looking. He wished he had his canteen. He was so thirsty. It seemed like an eternity, but in fact it was only about an hour that he lay there. Suddenly, the entire line of soldiers began to move and fire their guns.

Jacob tried to remember all that happened from then on. It seemed as though soldiers appeared on the hill from everywhere. The tree line behind old Jim's house burst alive with line after line of men. Uniforms and flags of grey, blue, red, and white formed a kaleidoscope of color on the field. It was impossible to tell which side was which. Bayonets glistened in the sun. The drummers beat a steady rhythm that echoed in his head. The cannons roared from all sides and his stomach reverberated with the noise. Smoke hung like a dense fog across the field. It formed a veil of sorrow over the wounded and dying below. Sharp cracks of resounding rifles came from every direction. Horses were shot out from under their riders and lay dying in the blistering sun. The screaming yells of each new rank of soldiers that appeared created a cacophony that made Jacob cup his hands over his ears. He wanted to shout for them to stop, to be quiet. Stop shooting and killing. But that was when he saw a familiar head of curly blond hair just like Jessie's moving forward across the hill. It was Pa! He

★ ★ ★

knew it was! He was just about to yell out to him, when he saw his father reel backward with his arms outstretched, his gun falling from his hands. Then, as he watched, his Pa fell to the ground.

Jacob stood up. He leaped over the fence and raced towards his father. He was racing through a silent world and felt as if he were running on air. He was suspended in a vacuum of time and space. Nothing else existed for him at that moment, except for his Pa lying on the field. A dull thud resounded in his head and a high pitched ringing filled his brain. It was as though he were running in slow motion and couldn't move any faster. His legs were moving as fast as they could go, but he didn't seem to be getting anywhere. Finally, after an eternity, he reached his Pa and dropped down on the ground beside him.

His heart was pounding and his head ached. When he saw the blood all over the front of his father's shirt he thought he was going to be sick. People were still shooting all around him. He had to help his Pa. He slipped his shirt over his head and wadded it up. He pushed it inside Pa's jacket and held it against the wound to stop the bleeding. He pressed and pressed. He thought he felt a heart beat, but it could just have been his own pulse echoing in his head. It was hard to tell. He tried to yell out, "Pa! Pa! You can't die. We need you. Jessie and me, we need you." But the noise of the battlefield drowned out any cries he made. He realized, too, that only wracking sobs were coming from his mouth. He had to save Pa. He had to win this time. He wasn't going to lose his Pa like he had his Ma. At least not if he could help it. He felt for his father's canteen on the ground between them. He worked the strap around his father's shoulder until he could open the top and pour out water to wipe his father's face. He looked around and it seemed that the soldiers were going backwards again. Back towards the trees and the woods. Retreating. The cannons were as loud as ever. He couldn't tell who was Confederate and who was Federal. He was afraid to cry out for fear someone would shoot him or his Pa. The flags all looked the same.

★ ★ ★

Red, white and blue. Which was the Stars and Stripes and which was the Stars and Bars? The flies began to hover and he tried to keep them away from his father. The low moaning and groaning of men and beasts wasted on the field could be heard between the crack of gunfire and the roar of cannon. He held his hand against the wound until it was numb. His back burned in the sun. He pressed himself against his Pa as if to be invisible, as if to give him strength. Would this day never end? Was this what war was about? The two old men he had met had both warned against this fighting and killing. What could be worth the horrors that Jacob saw all around him at this moment? Pa, why did you have to go fight? Pa, was it really worth fighting for? Pa, please don't die. It just ain't fair. Pa, I need you.

Suddenly bugles rang out and men surged forward again toward the turnpike and the stone house. They were screaming and yelling in victorious madness. They were coming from everywhere and racing past him. Commanders on horseback charged and led the way across the ridge. Soon the gunfire seemed to be getting farther away. He could see men running down the road, running down the turnpike towards the stone bridge. Would they be coming back or was it finally over? He hoped so. He truly hoped so.

Jacob slowly raised his head. He shifted himself around so he could pull his father's head onto his lap. He held the bloody shirt in place over the wound trying desperately to hold his Pa together. With his other hand he poured more water on his Pa's forehead. He saw some men with pull carts coming across the field.

"Help!" he yelled. "Please, help my Pa!"

The men came running. "He's just a boy. What you doin' here boy?"

"Please. My Pa's shot bad. Don't let him die."

"Don't worry, boy. We'll take care of him now." They lifted Pa gently onto the cart. Then one of the men looked at Jacob. "Why, boy, you been hit, too. Didn't you feel that nick

★ ★ ★

on your head? You better let the doc have a look at you, too."
And they lifted him into the cart beside his father. Jacob
reached up and felt his head and then looked at his hand. It
was covered with his own blood. He felt a ringing in his ears
and then everything went black.

When Jacob came to he was lying on a blanket in a tent.
He felt his head and there was a bandage around it. He tried to
sit up, but someone said that he should lie back down.

"But my Pa. Where's my Pa?"

"The doctor's with your Pa. He's very weak, but I think
he'll be okay. Right now there's somebody here waiting to see
you."

Jacob looked around. Jessie came running over and hugged
him. She was crying and couldn't say anything. He rubbed
her curly head. "How did you find me?" he asked.

She sniffed her nose and wiped her eyes. "Old Jim saw
them put you on the cart. He followed you and Pa here. Then
he came back and got me. He knew I thought you were both
dead. You've been layin' here for a long time. I thought you'd
never wake up. Pa's been hurt real bad, Jacob. Jim's been
stayin' by him in case there's anythin' to be done. The doctor
told Jim we just have to wait and pray a lot. The doctor let me
stay here by you. He said you were a brave boy. That you
probably saved Pa's life."

Jacob held his sister's hand. "We finally found Pa, Jessie.
We had to look for a long time and go a long ways. God
wouldn't let us travel all that way just to watch him die. He's
gonna be all right. You'll see. Everythin' will be all right."

★ ★ ★

After the Battle

July 22 was a rainy, dreary day. It matched the mood of those left to tend to the wounded and bury the dead on the battle-field at Manassas. The Confederates had claimed victory that day. But, between them and the Union troops, over 800 men were dead, 2,700 were wounded and almost 2,000 were missing. It was a costly victory, if in fact, it could be called a victory. The stone house of the Matthews was used as a temporary hospital for the Union soldiers. A Union cannon, fired at the home of Mrs. Henry during the battle, had killed the old woman and wounded her servant, Lucy Griffith. Fortunately, Gentleman Jim, his family and their house were untouched.

As with most of the wounded, Nathan Harding was cared for at one of the nearby makeshift hospitals. The bullet in his chest had missed his heart, but had seriously injured his lungs. Jacob and Jessie sat somberly beside their father's cot. Jacob worried about how he would be able to tell his father all of their bad news. It seemed like they waited forever before Nathan Harding finally opened his eyes and saw them.

"Pa, oh, Pa," Jacob blurted. "We looked everywhere for you, Pa. But I let you down. I couldn't do what you wanted me to do and now it's too late. Pa, it's...it's... about Ma. Ma's..."

But before Jacob could finish, Nathan Harding reached out his arm to his son. "It's all right, son. I know about Ma. Ole

★ ★ ★

Jim was sittin' with me late last night when I first woke up. He told me that you were both here and some of what had happened. He knew I should know, and he knew that it was gonna be hard for you to tell me. But it wasn't your fault, son. You did everything that you could. I should never have left the three of you alone. You needed me and I wasn't there. If anyone is to blame, it's me."

"But, Pa. Squealer's gone, too. The bears got him and we..."

"Jacob, you did everything you could. I am so proud of you. It takes a man to do what you did. You and Jessie had a lot of courage to come and find me. This has been so hard for the two of you. But I promise that as soon as I'm strong enough, we're gonna go back home. Back home together! And I won't ever leave you again."

Nathan Harding hugged his two children and they cried quietly together, finally able to share the grief that they had not been able to share before. Although he was very weak, the sight of his children at his side gave him renewed strength and a reason to survive. Because of the seriousness of his injury, he was granted a medical discharge and allowed to return home.

The Eighth Virginia remained along Bull Run for only a few days after the battle. Jacob made sure the letter he had carried from Salem was delivered to John Lanham's son, also a survivor. The commander of the Eighth, Colonel Eppa Hunton reporting on the battle that day, wrote, "... the Eighth made a most gallant and impetuous charge, routing the enemy, and losing in killed, wounded, and missing thirty-three soldiers (6 killed, 26 wounded, and 1 missing)." Those who survived would go on to fight in many more battles before the war was over.

Jacob and Jessie stayed with the Robinsons near their father until he was strong enough to travel. Dramus, the mule, had remained at the campsite of the Eighth during the battle. So when it was time to go, the mule pulled them home in a small cart lent to them by Gentleman Jim. They headed down the

★ ★ ★

turnpike together: Pa, Jacob, Jessie, Nanny and Cat.

Jacob realized as they rumbled down the road that day, that their lives would never be the same. He had so many things to sort out in his mind. It was obvious now that this war would not be over as quickly as everyone had at first predicted. How long would it go on? How many more men would die for a cause that wasn't entirely understood by most of those doing the fighting? So many of his father's soldier friends had told Jacob how brave he had been and what a fine soldier he would make. But how could he ever be a soldier when he couldn't decide which side was the right side? He would think about that on another day, at another time.

But now, he looked around at Pa and Jessie sitting beside him on the wagon. This was all he wanted to think about. Their search was over. They were together and they were going home to their farm in Catlett. They were really going home.

★ ★ ★

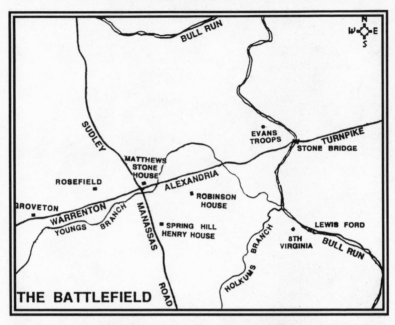

THE BATTLEFIELD

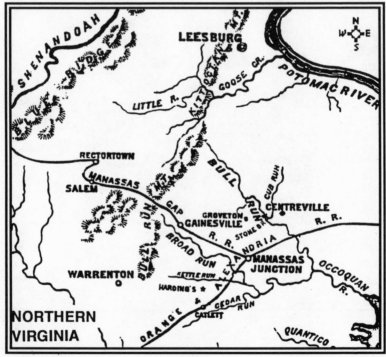

NORTHERN
VIRGINIA

★ ★ ★

Many thanks to Chris Bryce
of the Manassas Battlefield National Park
and Dave Purschwitz of the Manassas Museum
for their assistance in checking out the
historical accuracy of the story

★ ★ ★

MR. LINCOLN'S CITY by Richard M. Lee

An Illustrated Guide to the Civil War Sites of Washington

While standing on a downtown street corner with this pictorial history and guide in hand, you can imagine Washington as it was between 1861–65. The book brings back to life 80 sites, many of which still exist, and vividly recalls through fascinating wartime photos and drawings and engaging text those that have passed from the scene. Meant to be visited on foot or by car, each site is accompanied by one or more of 130 photos, some heretofore unpublished. **$17.95**

GENERAL LEE'S CITY by Richard M. Lee

An Illustrated Guide to the Historic Sites of Confederate Richmond

In this companion to MR. LINCOLN'S CITY, General Lee takes us back in dramatic detail to the turbulent, heroic and ultimately tragic life of the capital of the Confederacy. Organized into five driving tours covering 106 historic sites and featuring photos, drawings, maps and first-hand accounts, this guide virtually reconstructs Richmond under siege. **$16.95**

THE CIVIL WAR DIARY OF ANNE S. FROBEL

While their neighbors' homes were searched, plundered and all contents sent north, Anne and Lizzie Frobel persevered to save their farm, Wilton Hill, in Fairfax, VA. Marauding soldiers raided their chicken coops, wiped out gardens, robbed bee hives, killed cows, stole horses and burned fence posts. With passion and outrage, Anne recorded their trials even as occupying forces moved into the house. Her diary covers the war along the Potomac and its aftermath to 1879. An inspiring account of honor and nobility during even the darkest days, it is proof that forgiveness and understanding can transform hostility and fear into healing. **$14.95**

BICYCLING THROUGH CIVIL WAR HISTORY by Kurt B. Detwiler

In Maryland, Pennsylvania, West Virginia and Virginia

This is the first Mid-Atlantic guidebook that combines bicycle routes around 25 Civil War sites with gripping history lessons. All descriptions include at least one map, clear directions, mile markers, suggested reading and photos.

Detwiler believes that the bicycle is the best means of transportation through battlefields. Bicyclists can easily read interpretive marker and with the geography of the land literally at their feet, they can better understand the physical demands on soldiers who fought the war on foot and horse. Bicycles, moreover, offer a non-polluting, quiet way of exploring sacred battlefields. 216 pp. **$14.95**

RECOLLECTIONS OF 92 YEARS 1824–1916 by Elizabeth Avery
Meriwether

As the wife of a Confederate officer, Elizabeth Meriwether was banned
from her home in Memphis by Union General William T. Sherman.
Seven months pregnant, she fled with her two boys, aged three and five,
on a "Rockaway" pulled by a mule. On Christmas night in 1862, and in a
stranger's home, she gave birth to her third son. For the next two years,
she wandered from place to place in search of food and shelter.
    Returned at last to her home and husband, she devoted herself to
rearing their boys, editing her own newsletter, writing novels and speaking out for women's suffrage. Her crusade for women continued until her
death in 1916–the same year the Republican and Democratic parties
promised to support a Constitutional amendment giving women the vote.
$14.95

RANGER MOSBY by Virgil Carrington Jones

The definitive biography of the crafty, flamboyant Civil War fighter, John
S. Mosby, takes you deep inside Union lines where he spanked a general
in his bed, emptied $172,000 from a federal payroll train and raised havoc
with his enemies' plans. Nearly all of Loudoun County was burned in an
effort to trap him; however, he repeatedly frustrated his pursuers. The
bounty on Mosby's head was never claimed. **$14.95**

GRAY GHOSTS AND REBEL RAIDERS by Virgil Carrington Jones

This first quality-paperback edition of the 1956 bestseller tells the story of
the Confederate guerrillas who, without ever fighting a major battle,
prolonged the Civil War many months through their daring, unpredictable
attacks behind enemy lines. They rode off with supply wagons, horses
and guns, destroyed bridges and railroads, and intercepted secret mes-
sages. **$14.95**

BALL'S BLUFF: *A Small Battle and Its Long Shadow*
by Byron Farwell

On October 21, 1861, Confederate troops scored what was probably the
most complete victory by either side in the Civil War at Ball's Bluff, 35
miles above Washington on the Virginia bank of the Potomac. Although
the two armies totaled only about 33,000, the effects of this encounter
were enormous. Southerners accorded the battle too much importance,
boosting hopes for an ultimate triumph. Northerners were crushed, and so
spectacular was their defeat that many refused to accept it. In a shameful
investigation, Union politicians sought and found a scapegoat. **$12.95**

TO ORDER OR REQUEST A CATALOG: Call (703)442-7810
or (800)289-2339

About the Author

GERALDINE (Jeri) SUSI was born in New York and grew up moving between Westchester County and California. Her marriage to an Air Force pilot kept her moving even more. She and her husband, Ronald, have visited every state on the continent and resided in eight of them.

Even when she was rearing their own four children, Mrs. Susi was teaching reading to intermediate and elementary school students. She received a Bachelor of Science in Lubbock, Texas and her Masters in Troy, Alabama. She has worked on her Doctorate at George Mason University.

Shortly after settling in Virginia she was nominated for Fairfax County Teacher of the Year in 1982 and since that time the School Board has commended her for professional excellence. Though she writes articles for leading professional journals, this children's novel is her first book.

Since his retirement from the Air Force Colonel Susi has joined his wife as a Fairfax County teacher. He teaches fourth grade at Virginia Run School and she is a reading specialist at Lees Corner School. Their home in Catlett, Virginia is near where Jessie and Jacob begin their harrowing adventure described in LOOKING FOR PA.

Peace, War, and Terrorism

DENNIS OKERSTROM
Park University

Property of
VTLCI

PEARSON
Longman

New York   San Francisco   Boston
London   Toronto   Sydney   Tokyo   Singapore   Madrid
Mexico City   Munich   Paris   Cape Town   Hong Kong   Montreal

For Chase Haakon Okerstrom,
b. June 14, 2004. Flag Day

Born in a year of war and violence,
may you grow into a world at peace

Publisher: Joseph Opiela
Marketing Manager: Wendy Albert
Production Coordinator: Shafiena Ghani
Project Coordination, Text Design, and Electronic Page Makeup:
    Sunflower Publishing Services
Cover Design Manager: Wendy Ann Fredericks
Cover Photo: Raslon Rahmant/AFP/Getty Images
Manufacturing Manager: Mary Fischer
Printer and Binder: RR Donnelley and Sons Company/Harrisonburg
Cover Printer: Coral Graphics Services

For permission to use copyrighted material, grateful acknowledg-
ment is made to the copyright holders on pages 243–244, which are
hereby made part of this copyright page.

Library of Congress Cataloging-in-Publication Data

Okerstrom, Dennis.
    Peace, war, and terrorism / Dennis Okerstrom.
        p. cm. — (A Longman topics reader)
    ISBN 0-321-29230-8
        1. War. 2. Terrorism. 3. War on Terrorism, 2001– 4. Peace.
    I. Title. II. Longman

JZ6385.O38 2005
303.6′25—dc22   2004063127

Please visit our website at http://www.ablongman.com

ISBN 0-321-29230-8

    3 4 5 6 7 8 9 10—DOH—08 07 06

Preface   v

CHAPTER 1   The New Face of War   1

Osama bin Laden, Jihad Against Jews and Crusaders   3
George W. Bush, President's Radio Address   6
Peter Simpson, The War on Terrorism: Its Moral
    Justification and Limits   9
Daniel Benjamin, Two Years After 9/11: A Balance Sheet   24
Richard Engel, Inside Al-Qaeda: A Window into the
    World of Militant Islam and the Afghani Alumni   31
Michael Meacher, This War on Terrorism Is Bogus   39
Bin Ladin Determined to Strike in U.S.   45
United Nations Security Council Resolution 1377   47
Other Journeys: Suggestions for Further Writing and Research   49

CHAPTER 2   Pre-emptive War   51

Condoleezza Rice, A Balance of Power That Favors Freedom   52
William Galston, Perils of Preemptive War   59
Richard F. Grimmett, U.S. Use of Preemptive
    Military Force: The Historical Record   66
William P. Saunders, Possible War with Iraq   72
Arthur Schlesinger, Jr., The Immorality of Preemptive War   76
Steven R. Weisman, Doctrine of Preemptive
    War Has Its Roots in Early 1990s   78
Steven C. Welsh, Preemptive War and International Law   82
Ulrich Arnswald, Preventive War or Preemptive War   92
Other Journeys: Suggestions for Further Writing and Research   94

CHAPTER 3   The Homefront and Terrorism   95

John Ashcroft, USA Patriot Act "Honors"
    Liberty and Freedom   96
Susan Herman, The USA Patriot Act and the U.S.
    Department of Justice: Losing Our Balances?   103
David Tell, John Ashcroft, Maligned Again   110
Stephen Gale and Lawrence Husick, From MAD
    (Mutual Assured Destruction) to MUD (Multilateral
    Unconstrained Disruption): Dealing with the
    New Terrorism   113

Robert L. Hutchings, Terrorism and Economic Security   121
Jim Hightower, In a Time of Terror, Protest Is Patriotism   135
Tim Weiner, U.S. Law Puts World Ports on Notice   143
John R. Macarthur, The Unchallenged "Evidence"
     for War   147
Other Journeys: Suggestions for Further Writing and Research   152

CHAPTER 4   Weapons and Terror   **153**

George W. Bush, New Measures to Counter
     the Threat of WMD   154
Owen Bowcott and Richard Norton-Taylor, War
     on Terror Fuels Small Arms Trade   163
The Associated Press, Al-Qaida Leader Says
     They Have Briefcase Nukes   166
Paul Wilkinson, Overview of the Terrorist Threat
     to International Peace and Security   168
Joyce M. Davis, Mission of Suicide Bombers Is
     Martyrdom, Retribution   175
Scott Peterson, "Smarter" Bombs Still Hit Civilians   179
John R. Bolton, The International Aspects of
     Terrorism and Weapons of Mass Destruction   183
Other Journeys: Suggestions for Further Writing and Research   190

CHAPTER 5   Ethics, Peace, and Tomorrow   **192**

Alberto R. Gonzales, Memorandum for the President   193
Martin L. Cook, Ethical Issues in Counterterrorism
     Warfare   199
Human Rights Watch, The Road to Abu Ghraib:
     A Policy to Evade International Law   204
Geneva Convention Relative to the Treatment of
     Prisoners of War   216
E. Thomas McClanahan, White House Should
     Clarify Torture Policy   219
Abdulaziz Sachedina, From Defensive to Offensive
     Warfare: The Use and Abuse of Jihad in the
     Muslim World   222
Mary Ellen McNish, A Second Moment of Hope   235
4th Global Summit of Nobel Peace Laureates, Ethics
     and Policy   239
Other Journeys: Suggestions for Further Writing and Research   242

Credits   243

After September 11, 2001, it's a whole new world.

Or is it?

Following the attacks on the World Trade Center and the Pentagon, Americans were roused to righteous anger by the deaths of nearly 3,000 persons. The President and Congress were clearly united in their determination to wage war on terrorism: the Patriot Act was quickly passed; the department of Homeland Security was established; the military was alerted for a mission against al-Qaida in Afghanistan. Nations around the globe, many with no history of admiration for the United States, expressed sympathy and vowed in a UN resolution to fight the scourge of terrorism. Americans were determined to grin and bear it over increased security measures at airports. We snickered a bit self-consciously over the threat-level color codes issued periodically from Washington. Many of us prepared to sacrifice some of our comforts in a long and costly war that seemed the only response to the attacks.

Much has changed in the few short years since what everyone now calls 9/11.

At the time of this writing, the United States finds itself deeply embroiled in fierce combat in Iraq, continuing military action in Afghanistan, and facing charges of torturing prisoners at Abu Ghraib prison. Instead of reeling in retreat, terrorists seem to be ubiquitous, determined, and growing in numbers. A report from the International Institute of Strategic Studies in London in May 2004 estimated that al-Qaida, the best known of the terrorist organizations, had more than 18,000 members and was still growing in response to the war in Iraq. Across the globe, new targets for terrorists have emerged: nearly two hundred died in the bombing of commuter trains in Madrid; the ghastly casualties on both sides continue with mind-numbing regularity in the Gaza Strip and Israel; more than two hundred Australian tourists were killed in a nightclub bombing in Bali. Suicide bombers in Israel and in Iraq have added a new, and for Americans, unfathomable, dimension to the violence.

America finds herself isolated, condemned for the war in Iraq, and awash in a series of hearings determined to learn about intelligence failures, planning deficiencies, leadership lapses, and morality debacles. Will we ever know peace again?

Most of us know that peace is a prize not easily obtained, and Americans commonly think of peace as a lack of state-sponsored violence in one's own region. But seldom if ever has there been a time when everywhere on the planet was at peace. Perhaps when Americans speak of a new world, we really mean that things have changed for *us*, that terrorism (more about that term later) has come to *our* shores, killed *our* citizens, destroyed *our* buildings, and disrupted *our* lives in ways large and small. For other parts of the globe, it is business as usual. Terrorism has been a weapon of the stateless for decades, perhaps centuries. For most Americans, though, it has been something "over there," seemingly random and mindless violence in other regions.

But for much of the world, terrorism was already all too well known before America's baptism by jet fuel. In Ireland and England, republicanism had taken hundreds of lives in decades of violence, and a separatist Basque movement in Spain has been simmering, occasionally boiling over, for years. Extreme leftist ideology led to bombings and murders by the Red Army Faction in Germany in the 1970s and 1980s, the Red Brigades in Italy, and Direct Action and the Combatant Communist Cells in France and Belgium. In Peru, the Maoist organization Shining Path has used terror as a weapon since the 1980s, and the Middle East has been decimated by tit-for-tat violence for more than 50 years.

Terrorism is a Hydra-haired foe. One first must define the term, and that is not easy. To some, terrorists are freedom fighters, akin to Shakespeare's rose. The U.S. State Department offers up the view that terrorism is violence directed against noncombatants. It might be related to religious fundamentalism, or it might be state-sponsored with a political and economic imperative. It could be the result of ethnic strife, such as the situation the world tried to ignore in Rwanda in the 1990s, or Bosnia where NATO intervened, or the Darfur region of the Sudan in 2004. But several factors in the last decade have ramped up the potential threat of terrorism past immediate proximity to the discontent. One is access to weapons of mass destruction (an unwieldy name, and a bit deceiving: a pistol can be a weapon of mass destruction). Since the breakup of the Soviet Union in the early 1990s, there has been much concern over the security of nuclear weapons. Biological and chemical weapons have proliferated, and are cheap and relatively easy to produce. Second, the use of the internet, cell phones, and global positioning systems have greatly aided all of us—including terrorists. Finally, cheap and easy international travel allows individuals to carry their campaigns to regions they view as the ultimate source of their discontent.

A decade ago, following the first Gulf War, I published a textbook (with Sarah Morgan) titled *Peace and War: Readings for Writers* (Allyn & Bacon, 1993). That text outlined some of the issues not ordinarily considered in debates about war: the causes of war, the evolution of weapons, who actually fights, the killing of civilians, and the odds for peace. With the onset of more military action in Afghanistan and Iraq and the increasing emphasis on homeland security, I thought the time had come to update that text, perhaps add a few new essays and a new section on terrorism. It quickly became apparent, however, that a revision would be inadequate to explore the new issues that have arisen since the first Gulf War. Concepts of pre-emptive war, WMD, the Patriot Act, prisoners at Guantanamo and Abu Ghraib, Geneva Conventions, exit strategies—all these and more have infused themselves into public debate since September 11, 2001.

This book will explore some of those issues. It is not intended as a single, comprehensive source of information about a broad and complicated subject. It is, instead, one step in exploring these important and vital topics, and I offer the information included here in an attempt at balance. I have my own views on this war and others; I'll let you form your own after you have researched the various issues.

World War II is often touted as the last "good war," a conflict between the forces of good and evil. For those of my generation, our fathers and uncles and even mothers and aunts were the heroes of that largest and most destructive of all wars. For many of you, they will be your grandfathers and great uncles, grandmothers and great aunts, perhaps even an additional "great." They were the members of what Tom Brokaw has termed "the greatest generation." My father served in the Eighth Air Force, based in England, where he met and married my mother, an apple-cheeked Shropshire girl. I grew up hearing the stories of my family in the fight against Hitler: Uncle Bert Nicholls, British Army, captured at Dunkirk, France, May, 1940; Uncle Leonard Nicholls, killed at Tobruk, Libya, November, 1941; Uncle Stan Nicholls, wounded, 1943, North Africa; my dad's brother Tage, a navigator on a B-17 when he was 19 years old. Later, I heard the stories of my wife's father, Lynn Johnston, who flew 63 missions in a B-29.

For the British, French, Belgians, Czechs, Poles, and much of the rest of Europe, the war started more than two years before Pearl Harbor, a fact we Americans tend to forget. And a student from Russia in one of my graduate courses recently asserted to me that it was Russian blood, not American machinery, that had won World War II. Those who have studied that war in even the most cursory way are familiar with the Holocaust, the Rape of Nanking, the Bataan Death March, the siege of Leningrad—the cost in human terms was staggering. World War II has been the subject of thousands of articles, books, and documentaries, and will continue to be as we realize that those who fought it are dying at the rate of 1,000 a day. There has been a virtual stampede in the past five years or so to record their individual stories while they still can be told.

But even that last "good war" is not free from controversy. Historians today continue to debate the necessity for dropping the atomic bomb on the Japanese cities of Hiroshima and Nagasaki, or the efficacy as well as the morality of the bombing campaign against Germany, where firebombs killed perhaps 100,000 Germans—mainly civilians—in a single 1,000-bomber raid on Dresden, and another on Hamburg.

There is little debate, however, on whether it was a war—and when it started and ended. World War II was a huge, destructive, classic war in the sense that nation states declared war on other nation states, and the winners and losers eventually signed treaties ending the hostilities. The war—at least from the point of view of this American professor—was largely a war of machines. David Kennedy, in his Pulitzer Prize–winning *Freedom from Fear*, argues that Americans were determined to fight that war with overwhelming numbers of weapons and machines: Some 300,000 airplanes, 88,000 tanks, 634,569 jeeps, 40 billion bullets—and, of course, The Bomb.

There followed a very short period of relative peace, with the United States in sole control of atomic weapons. Other nations were not convinced that the United States was to be trusted as the only nuclear power, and the race was on to develop their own bomb. Mutual suspicion contributed to the Cold War, a 45-year-long period of bellicosity, paranoia, and stark fear. Many times during my tenure in the service near the end of that "war," I found myself in somber discussions with other young men and women in uniform about where we might end up, as rumors flew about overseas deployments in response to perceived threats by the Soviets. All the while, both camps were building and storing up unfathomable stockpiles of weapons—nuclear, biological, and chemical.

And of course, there were numerous sparks and hot spots during the plunging diplomatic temperatures of the Cold War—starting with Korea in 1950, then the Cuban missile crisis of 1962, and proceeding into Vietnam in the 1960s. Some of these were in response to U.S. foreign policy—containment—in effect at the time. Others were reactions against perceived aggression, and an effort to thwart the falling row of dominoes, the political trope of the day. But even as horrible as those wars (or "police actions") were, and as inconclusive as the cessation of hostilities often seemed, they were still in the context of traditional wars. Most were fought between nations which had diplomatic relations with each other, however strained, using uniformed soldiers and airmen and seamen, using conventional weapons and observing certain international laws or agreements. Even guerilla wars, which made use of citizen-soldiers who were hard to detect, were in essence still conventional conflicts in that the combatants used military hardware against recognizable and discrete foes.

We may be kidding ourselves, but the current global violence seems vastly different than previous incidents, wars, and resistance movements. For Americans, the involvement of the U.S. military brings a bewildering array of images, of questions, of debates, hearings, and recriminations, of pride, sorrow, and humiliation, and of angst and hubris.

We still have the semblance of conventional war, replete with armor, circling helicopters, precision- and carpet-bombing strikes, mines, RPGs, and camouflaged soldiers with automatic weapons. In both Afghanistan and Iraq, soldiers and civilians are dying daily, and flag-draped coffins are coming back to Dover—and the question of whether to show images of those coffins has itself become an issue. The difference, however, between other wars in other places at other times and the current violence is less of image and more of substance. Substantive questions arise about the reasons for war, the possibility of peace, the explosion of terrorism. And the technology of mass destruction, developed so ably during World War II and the Cold War, leads to the nightmare of terrorists obtaining those weapons.

Following the attack on the World Trade Center and the Pentagon, a shadowy group called al-Qaida—Arabic for "the base"—claimed responsibility, and vowed more attacks on a decadent Western culture dominated by the United States. Founded in the late 1980s by Osama bin Laden, a wealthy Saudi who fought the

Russians in Afghanistan, al-Qaida has claimed responsibility for the bombing of the U.S. embassies in Kenya and Tanzania in 1998 that killed more than 300; for the bombing of the USS Cole in the port of Aden, Yemen, in 2000, in which 17 sailors died; the bombing of a tourist hotel in Mombasa, Kenya, in which 15 persons lost their lives; and numerous other acts of violence. Training camps were pinpointed in Afghanistan and President George W. Bush ordered U.S. troops into that nation to root out al-Qaida and capture bin Laden in late 2001. Some 20,000 troops are still there at this writing, and although the repressive Taliban government has been overthrown and many al-Qaida killed or captured, bin Laden remains on the loose.

What followed the invasion of Afghanistan, though, is the source of much debate.

The armed intervention in Afghanistan was widely viewed, here and abroad, as a reasonable response to the attacks of September 11th. The party claiming responsibility was sheltered there, and the Taliban government was uncooperative with diplomatic efforts to quash al-Qaida. But soon after the Taliban were overthrown, and many members of al-Qaida killed or captured, the United States began building a case for invading Iraq. In sessions before the United Nations, Secretary of State Colin Powell (A four-star general during the Gulf War) presented photographs and other data that he said were solid and irrefutable evidence that Saddam Hussein was building an inventory of weapons of mass destruction, including biological and chemical weapons, and was developing a nuclear weapons capability. Major allies in the 1991 Gulf War, with the exception of Great Britain, failed to support the new campaign to invade Iraq, overthrow Hussein, and seize the weapons of mass destruction, now commonly known as WMD.

The United States, with the aid of Britain and a few detachments from smaller nations, invaded Iraq in March 2003 in a swift campaign of tanks and air strikes. The war was over quickly—by April that year President Bush flew out to the carrier USS Abraham Lincoln and announced that the "major combat is over." No WMD were found, and the purpose of the war was said to be the freeing of Iraq, with the goal of establishing democracy there and stabilizing the region.

But a year of occupation led to increased violence—IED became a new household acronym as improvised explosive devices were detonated with deadly efficiency across Iraq, killing both American troops and Iraqi civilians. The horrors of war were manifested in heart-wrenching stories of young soldiers killed, in images of Iraqis bleeding and maimed in car bombings, in photos of Iraqi detainees at Abu Ghraib prison being abused and humiliated by smiling American troops, of hideous videotapes of the beheading of kidnapped civilians by hooded assassins.

For some, the war against terror seems relatively simple to understand: often it is cited as a "war against Islamist extremists," and the now-familiar word "jihad" is frequently trotted out as evidence that Muslims are fundamentally opposed to the West, and viscerally committed to our destruction (or, presumably, our conversion.) But this seems monumentally unfair to millions of Muslims of good will and peaceful intent. In October 2002, with the war in Afghanistan underway and the drums beating for an invasion of Iraq, my wife and I traveled widely throughout Senegal, which is 95 percent Muslim. Everywhere, we were greeted with enthusiasm and warmth. Professionals, tourist industry workers, and educators all wanted to talk about the state of the world, and were eager to discuss Islam, the concept of jihad, and the war against terrorism. At no time did we ever feel threatened, insecure, or even vaguely uneasy. Thus, as part of the focus of this text, I have included essays that address basic Islamic beliefs to dispel misconceptions about that religion.

Each war brings its own atrocities, its own stories of valor, its high and low points, its own debate over issues. The current war on terror—including the war in Iraq—brings to the classroom, the barroom, the barbershop, and the shopping mall the anxious search for answers by ordinary citizens caught up once more in events not of their choosing. This text is an effort to bring some sense of order to the impassioned arguments over the need for a war, the direction and effects of the battle itself, and of the bewildering array of issues and information available. I have attempted to be balanced, to present the words of the proponents of all sides of various issues, and to suggest sources for additional study so that students can arrive at their own decisions. My students over the years have heard me say—often to gasps of dismay—that I do not care about their opinions. Some are mollified when I explain: Opinions are beliefs not founded on research, they echo old views or articulate responses without truly knowing the facts: "Fords are better than Chevys." Conclusions, however, are reached after research into the topic. They might be the same as a previously held opinion, but now the speaker can cite her or his reasons for reaching that conclusion.

Peace, War, and Terrorism is arranged topically, with opposing views opening each chapter, followed by three to five essays or articles that provide additional information. I have attempted to include both primary and secondary sources for students to access including, where appropriate, government or organization documents. A short essay introduces each chapter, providing some background and posing essential questions for the topic, and each reading is followed by a set of questions to help students in their use of the text. Finally, at the end of each chapter suggestions for further investigation into the issues are provided.

It is my hope that this book will spur students to study with open minds and in the true spirit of academic inquiry the issues that face us in the new wars. Failure to understand those issues could be catastrophic for the futures of ourselves, our children, and our grandchildren.

A note about spelling. Various names from Arabic and perhaps other language groups appear throughout this text, often spelled in very different ways according to the translators. This is one of the issues anyone faces in researching and writing about multi-ethnic and multi-linguistic topics. In the sections of this text that I have written, I have adopted the style of the Associated Press in the spelling of Osama bin Laden, al-Qaida, and certain other names. However, I have chosen to retain as written other spellings in reprinted articles to preserve their basic integrity. I trust this will not be confusing; it is an issue students and readers will face as they go beyond this text in their research.

DENNIS OKERSTROM

The New Face
of War

It is one of those moments frozen in our collective memories.

Everyone, it seems, knows where they were, whom they were with, what they were doing on the morning of September 11, 2001.

For most of us, the emergence of the Islamic fundamentalist group known as al-Qaida came as something of a shock as we watched, transfixed, the horrifying and surreal images of airliners crashing into the twin towers of the World Trade Center. News footage of bodies hurtling through space as workers threw themselves out of windows 70 or 80 stories high to escape the flames still horrify us. The billowing, acrid clouds of smoke, ash, and debris as the towers themselves collapsed still seem to clog our nostrils, permeate our skin, burn our eyes. Old photographs of the New York City skyline, the towers dominating the scene as they thrust proudly into the sky, still evoke a sense of disbelief that they could be gone, so quickly, with so much loss of life.

Why? The most basic answers seemed beyond the ability of anyone to articulate. America attacked. By whom? For what purpose? To what end?

There were those, of course, for whom this cataclysmic event was not quite so surprising. Those who had studied the increasing use of terror in the modern world, who had traced the increasing ability of individuals and groups to obtain ever more dangerous weapons, who had followed the rise of individuals and groups in regions of the world that appeared headed toward dangerous polarities. These people, while not knowing of specific plans, knew that the United States in particular—because of its high profile in a global economy, because of its relatively open society, and perhaps even for perceived inequities in its foreign policy—would be an easy target for someone dedicated to destruction and willing to sacrifice themselves in the process.

While the United States has known a great deal of violence in its past, and—let's be honest—has inflicted grievous violence on a variety of minority groups here and abroad, we have been largely spared the carnage of 20th century warfare that has ravaged parts of Europe and Asia. We did not endure the blitz of bombers nightly pounding our cities, nor did we suffer the indignity of foreign armies occupying our lands, and the ignominy of defeat in our homeland. This is not to say that we did not sacrifice during World War II, but it is to make a distinction among the degrees of damage suffered by the various nations involved. Following that horrendous war, the United States emerged as a world leader, with an economy stronger than before the war, and a confidence in its own abilities. In the more than 60 years since the end of that global conflict, many nations have seen their economies grow, the standards of living of their citizens rise, and found ways other than war to settle international disputes.

But not everyone has felt blessed by this apparent change. Nor have some even sought an invitation to the table.

Terrorism can be roughly divided into two groups based on the goals of the organization involved: Those who seek inclusion in the global economy, representing overlooked and underprivileged peoples and cultures, and those who reject the direction, goals, and values of an increasingly Westernized world. It is also possible that there may be various shades in between.

In this chapter, you will read several essays and articles that present differing views of this conflict we call the War on Terrorism. Osama bin Laden first called for *jihad* ("Holy War") against "Jews and Crusaders" in 1998, and spelled out his grievances in a *fatwa* ("religious ruling"). Included here is the translated text of that call to arms. President George W. Bush on several occasions has detailed the dangers and sought responses to the continuing threat of terrorism. A transcript of his radio address from February 2004 is representative of numerous appeals by the President for support of the War on Terror. Daniel Benjamin, writing for the United States Institute of Peace, presented in October 2003 an analysis of the progress to that point of actions against terrorism, and Richard Engle provides an inside view of the individuals within the al-Qaida network. A dissenting view of American intentions, written by a British Member of Parliament, is included. Peter Simpson, a philosopher, considers the moral elements of the War on Terror. Much has been made of possible intelligence failures by organizations within the U.S.

government, and the declassified Presidential Daily Briefing of August 6, 2001, is presented. The briefing discusses bin Laden specifically, and includes references to terrorist strikes in the United States and the hijacking of aircraft. And finally, United Nations Resolution 1377 is detailed, which declares that "acts of international terrorism constitute one of the most serious threats to international peace and security in the twenty-first century" and calls for specific efforts to combat terrorism.

The war in Iraq and the debate over preemptive war is treated separately in Chapter Two, not as a political decision but simply as an organizational issue.

As you read Chapter One, consider these questions:

- Was this conflict resulting in the war on terror inevitable? Was it a preventable clash of cultures, religions, and values?
- Is the War on Terror winnable, in the classic sense of, say, World War II? Or is it akin to the war on crime or the war on drugs?
- What should be the role of educated members of a society when its country goes to war?
- How should we attempt to change the conditions that breed international terrorism?
- What are the primary causes of terrorism? Is it possible to "profile" a terrorist?

Jihad Against Jews and Crusaders
OSAMA BIN LADIN

On February 23, 1998, Osama bin Ladin issued a fatwa, or religious ruling, that called on Muslims everywhere to kill Americans, both civilian and military. The document included here, available on the website of the Federation of American Scientists, in Washington, D.C., is translated from the original Arabic; an Arabic text is also available at the FAS website (http://www.fas.org). You may wish to read this in conjunction with the explication of "just war" theory by William P. Saunders ("Possible War With Iraq") found in Chapter Two, and an exploration of jihad in the article by Abdulaziz Sachedina in Chapter Five.

———————— ✦ ————————

23 February 1998

> Shaykh Usamah Bin-Muhammad Bin-Ladin
>
> Ayman al-Zawahiri, amir of the Jihad Group in Egypt
>
> Abu-Yasir Rifa'i Ahmad Taha, Egyptian Islamic Group
>
> Shaykh Mir Hamzah, secretary of the Jamiat-ul-Ulema-e-Pakistan
>
> Fazlur Rahman, amir of the Jihad Movement in Bangladesh

Praise be to Allah, who revealed the Book, controls the clouds, defeats factionalism, and says in His Book: "But when the forbidden months are past, then fight and slay the pagans wherever ye find them, seize them, beleaguer them, and lie in wait for them in every stratagem (of war)"; and peace be upon our Prophet, Muhammad Bin-Abdallah, who said: I have been sent with the sword between my hands to ensure that no one but Allah is worshipped, Allah who put my livelihood under the shadow of my spear and who inflicts humiliation and scorn on those who disobey my orders.

The Arabian Peninsula has never—since Allah made it flat, created its desert, and encircled it with seas—been stormed by any forces like the crusader armies spreading in it like locusts, eating its riches and wiping out its plantations. All this is happening at a time in which nations are attacking Muslims like people fighting over a plate of food. In the light of the grave situation and the lack of support, we and you are obliged to discuss current events, and we should all agree on how to settle the matter.

No one argues today about three facts that are known to everyone; we will list them, in order to remind everyone:

> First, for over seven years the United States has been occupying the lands of Islam in the holiest of places, the Arabian Peninsula, plundering its riches, dictating to its rulers, humiliating its people, terrorizing its neighbors, and turning its bases in the Peninsula into a spearhead through which to fight the neighboring Muslim peoples.
>
> If some people have in the past argued about the fact of the occupation, all the people of the Peninsula have now acknowledged it. The best proof of this is the Americans' continuing aggression against the Iraqi people using the Peninsula as a staging post, even though all its rulers are against their territories being used to that end, but they are helpless.

Second, despite the great devastation inflicted on the Iraqi people by the crusader-Zionist alliance, and despite the huge number of those killed, which has exceeded 1 million ... despite all this, the Americans are once again trying to repeat the horrific massacres, as though they are not content with the protracted blockade imposed after the ferocious war or the fragmentation and devastation.

So here they come to annihilate what is left of this people and to humiliate their Muslim neighbors.

Third, if the Americans' aims behind these wars are religious and economic, the aim is also to serve the Jews' petty state and divert attention from its occupation of Jerusalem and murder of Muslims there. The best proof of this is their eagerness to destroy Iraq, the strongest neighboring Arab state, and their endeavor to fragment all the states of the region such as Iraq, Saudi Arabia, Egypt, and Sudan into paper statelets and through their disunion and weakness to guarantee Israel's survival and the continuation of the brutal crusade occupation of the Peninsula.

All these crimes and sins committed by the Americans are a clear declaration of war on Allah, his messenger, and Muslims. And ulema have throughout Islamic history unanimously agreed that the jihad is an individual duty if the enemy destroys the Muslim countries. This was revealed by Imam Bin-Qadamah in "Al-Mughni," Imam al-Kisa'i in "Al-Bada'i," al-Qurtubi in his interpretation, and the shaykh of al-Islam in his books, where he said: "As for the fighting to repulse [an enemy], it is aimed at defending sanctity and religion, and it is a duty as agreed [by the ulema]. Nothing is more sacred than belief except repulsing an enemy who is attacking religion and life."

On that basis, and in compliance with Allah's order, we issue   5
the following fatwa to all Muslims:

The ruling to kill the Americans and their allies—civilians and military—is an individual duty for every Muslim who can do it in any country in which it is possible to do it, in order to liberate the al-Aqsa Mosque and the holy mosque [Mecca] from their grip, and in order for their armies to move out of all the lands of Islam, defeated and unable to threaten any Muslim. This is in accordance with the words of Almighty Allah, "and fight the pagans all together as they fight you all together," and "fight them until there is no more tumult or oppression, and there prevail justice and faith in Allah."

This is in addition to the words of Almighty Allah: "And why should ye not fight in the cause of Allah and of those who, being weak, are ill-treated (and oppressed)?—women and children, whose cry is: 'Our Lord, rescue us from this town, whose people are oppressors; and raise for us from thee one who will help!' "

We—with Allah's help—call on every Muslim who believes in Allah and wishes to be rewarded to comply with Allah's order to kill the Americans and plunder their money wherever and whenever they find it. We also call on Muslim ulema, leaders, youths, and soldiers to launch the raid on Satan's U.S. troops and the devil's supporters allying with them, and to displace those who are behind them so that they may learn a lesson.

Almighty Allah said: "O ye who believe, give your response to Allah and His Apostle, when He calleth you to that which will give you life. And know that Allah cometh between a man and his heart, and that it is He to whom ye shall all be gathered."

10   Almighty Allah also says: "O ye who believe, what is the matter with you, that when ye are asked to go forth in the cause of Allah, ye cling so heavily to the earth! Do ye prefer the life of this world to the hereafter? But little is the comfort of this life, as compared with the hereafter. Unless ye go forth, He will punish you with a grievous penalty, and put others in your place; but Him ye would not harm in the least. For Allah hath power over all things."

Almighty Allah also says: "So lose no heart, nor fall into despair. For ye must gain mastery if ye are true in faith."

Starting Points

1. Bin Laden cites three issues regarding American imperialism in Islamic lands, and calls for killing Americans everywhere based on these "facts." Consider very carefully these three points, and attempt to discern where facts end and interpretation begins.
2. Assume the perspective of a resident of the region. How compelling is bin Laden's argument?
3. What is the tone of bin Laden's statement? Do his frequent references to religious sources add to the authority of his statement? How would you frame a response to bin Laden?

President's Radio Address
GEORGE W. BUSH

President George W. Bush has made numerous speeches and radio addresses regarding the war on terror. This one, delivered on February 14, 2004, calls for closing loopholes in the Nuclear Non-

Proliferation Treaty and other steps for dealing with the possibility
of terrorists gaining nuclear weapons. Because this address was to
the American public, assume you know as little or as much as the
next listener regarding nuclear weapons. Is his language and are the
explanations he offers suitable for a general audience?

———————————— ✦ ————————————

Good morning. On September the 11th, 2001, America and the
world saw the great harm that terrorists could inflict upon
our country, armed with box cutters, mace and 19 airline tickets.

Those attacks also raised the prospect of even worse dangers,
of terrorists armed with chemical, biological, radiological and nuclear weapons. The possibility of secret and sudden attack with
weapons of mass destruction is the greatest threat before humanity today.

America is confronting this danger with open eyes and unbending purpose. America faces the possibility of catastrophic attack from ballistic missiles armed with weapons of mass destruction, so we are developing and deploying missile defenses to
guard our people. The best intelligence is necessary to win the
war on terror and to stop proliferation. So we are improving and
adapting our intelligence capabilities for new and emerging
threats. We are using every means of diplomacy to confront the
regimes that develop deadly weapons. We are cooperating with
more than a dozen nations under the Proliferation Security Initiative, to interdict lethal materials transported by land, sea or air.
And we have shown our willingness to use force when force is required. No one can now doubt the determination of America to
oppose and to end these threats to our security.

We are aggressively pursuing another dangerous source of proliferation: black-market operatives who sell equipment and expertise related to weapons of mass destruction. The world recently
learned of the network led by A.Q. Khan, the former head of Pakistan's nuclear weapons program. Khan and his associates sold nuclear technology and know-how to rogue regimes around the
world, such as Iran and North Korea. Thanks to the tireless work
of intelligence officers from the United States and the United Kingdom and other nations, the Khan network is being dismantled.

This week, I proposed a series of new, ambitious steps to   5
build on our recent success against proliferation. We must expand the international cooperation of law enforcement organizations to act against proliferation networks, to shut down their

labs, to seize their materials, to freeze their assets and to bring their members to justice.

We must strengthen laws and international controls that fight proliferation. Last fall at the United Nations I proposed a new Security Council resolution requiring all states to criminalize proliferation, enact strict export controls and secure all sensitive materials within their borders. I urge the Council to pass these measures quickly.

The Nuclear Non-Proliferation Treaty, one of the most important tools for preventing the spread of nuclear weapons, is undermined by a loophole that allows countries to seek nuclear weapons under the cover of civilian nuclear power programs. I propose that the world's leading nuclear exporters close that loophole. The Nuclear Suppliers Group should refuse to sell enrichment and reprocessing equipment and technologies to any state that does not already possess full scale, functioning enrichment and reprocessing plants.

For international rules and laws to be effective, they must be enforced. We must ensure that the International Atomic Energy Agency [IAEA] is fully capable of exposing and reporting banned nuclear activity. Every nation should sign what is called the Additional Protocol, which would allow the IAEA to make broader inspections of nuclear sites. We should also establish a special IAEA committee to focus on safeguards and verification. And no nation under investigation for proliferation violations should be able to serve on this committee or on the governing board of the IAEA. Governments breaking the rules should not be trusted with enforcing the rules.

Terrorists and terrorist states are in a race for weapons of mass murder, a race they must lose. They are resourceful—we must be more resourceful. They are determined—we must be more determined. We will never lose focus or resolve. We will be unrelenting in the defense of free nations, and rise to the hard demands of our dangerous time.

Starting Points

1. Part of a president's job is reassuring the public in times of disquiet. Is this address reassuring or alarming? Specifically, what parts are alarming? Which are reassuring, and why?
2. Inevitably, charges of politics are raised each time any sitting president delivers a speech. Carefully re-read each paragraph, and evaluate whether you believe this is a self-serving text, a factual, informational text, or a text that contains elements of each.

3. The Proliferation Security Initiative (paragraph 3) aims at preventing the spread of nuclear weapons. From the perspective of nations that have nuclear weapons, this of course seems like a good idea. How do you think other nations—that is, those who do not possess such weapons—feel about the prohibition and prevention of their ever possessing such weapons? Is this a variation on the right-to-carry concealed weapons arguments in many states, that an armed society is a polite society? Would other nations feel more secure—resulting in fewer violent incidents—if each nation possessed such weapons of mass destruction as a retaliatory threat?

The War on Terrorism: Its Moral Justification and Limits
PETER SIMPSON

In this reading, Peter Simpson, professor of philosophy and classics at the Graduate Center, City University of New York, considers the war on terrorism from a philosophical and moral perspective. The author received his Ph.D. from Victoria University of Manchester, and has published widely on classical philosophy. His most recent book is Vices, Virtues, and Consequences *(Catholic University of America Press, 2000). This essay is from the web site Ethics Updates, founded by Lawrence W. Hinman, University of San Diego. It was written while the author was in Beijing, China, in 2001–2002.*

◆

THE EVIL OF TERRORISM

The first thing to say about terrorism, and to say with all the firmness that one can command, is that it is an evil, a heinous crime, an attack on civilized life and on peace. I say this because there has been a tendency in some parts of the media and among some commentators, including not a few philosophers, to excuse the terrorists who attacked the U.S. on September 11th on the grounds that the U.S. brought these attacks on itself by its own foreign policy, and in particular by its policy in the Middle East. But however plausible these claims may be (a point I shall return to), we should not let them blind us to clear and manifest truths. We must state the truth and state it clearly and without hesitation. The attacks on the U.S. were evil deeds and those who planned and carried them out were evil men. So much is elementary. To doubt this, as some who ought to know better have done, is to betray a certain confusion if not corruption of mind. Surely we all know, surely we have all known from our earliest youth, that two wrongs do not make a right. Let it be, if you will, that the terrorists had grievances, even legitimate grievances, against the U.S. These grievances could never justify their deeds. An evil deed can never be justified. An evil deed is precisely that, an evil deed. No grievance or pretext, however strong, can ever make it not to be an evil deed. Mr. Bin Laden, however, who if not behind the attacks on September 11th certainly applauds them, is able to give no other excuse for them than random accusations against U.S. policy. But Mr. Bin Laden clearly has a corrupt mind. We should not expect better from him.

I do not mean by these remarks that we should pay no attention to the grievances alleged by Mr. Bin Laden and others. Nor do I mean that, because the evil of their deeds is so obvious, we should not discuss or explain the evil or say in what it consists. On the contrary we should do both, and I will endeavor to do both in what follows. What I mean is that, whatever else we say or discuss, at no point should we say, or allow others to say without challenge, that terrorists attacks are not evil. Their evil is the first and most undeniable fact about them. If we are to have any hope of understanding the phenomenon of terrorism or of how to deal with it, we must all start there. It is the beginning of wisdom. Thankfully, this is not a point on which our political leaders have any doubt. For them it is as clear as day that terrorism is an evil and an evil of great wickedness. Commentators in the media and some philosophers may hesitate and even doubt. But our leaders at least have not lost their grip on such basic common sense. As evidence I can do no better in the present context than quote the words of the Chinese permanent representative to the United Nations: "Terrorism, which endangers innocent lives, causes losses of social wealth and jeopardizes state security, constitutes a serious challenge to human civilization and dignity as well as a serious threat to international peace and security" (*China Daily*, Friday, October 5, 2001).

But grasping this truth, vital though it be, is only the beginning. We must, for the sake of clarity of understanding, carry our reflections further. The first step to take in this regard would seem to be to lay down some basic definition of terrorism so that we know in universal terms, and not just with reference to particular and manifest cases, what it is we are talking about. One problem, however, that arises here and that has, I think, caused no little confusion, is what has been called **state terrorism**. Those who use this term typically have in mind acts of violence used by governments and government forces against parts of their own people or against other peoples. The attacks by Israeli forces, for instance, against segments of the Palestinian population have sometimes been described as state terrorism, and so have some of the actions of the U.S. in Central and South America. Indeed the Taliban have themselves described the recent U.S. and British attacks on terrorist camps and government buildings in Afghanistan as acts of terrorism.

I will not comment at present on the justice or injustice of any of these attacks. I will only say that, if one wishes to condemn them as wrong, understanding is ill served by using the word *terrorism* to do so. We have other words to describe the unjust assaults of governments, among which are tyranny, despotism, imperialist aggression, police brutality, and the like. Terrorism, however, at least in its primary and typical use (and certainly in its use in the phrase "the war on terrorism"), refers to acts of private individuals or groups of private individuals and not to governments, even if these individuals receive support and succor from governments. I think we should also distinguish terrorism in this its primary sense from the acts, often destructive and sometimes wicked too, of rebels and revolutionaries against existing governments and peoples. By rebels and revolutionaries we mean typically people who belong to the country whose government they are attacking and whose aim is to overthrow that government and to replace it with another. As such rebels and revolutionaries are not so much a grouping of private individuals as a rival government in waiting. But terrorists as typically understood are not a rival government nor are they seeking to overthrow the existing government, even if they would not be sorry if that happened. The terrorists who attacked the U.S. on September 11th, for instance, were not Americans seeking to overthrow the U.S. government and replace it with another one.

There is something else also that needs to be noted about terrorism if we are to be clear about what it is. For the violence of terrorists is typically directed at civilians and civilian institutions, albeit civilians of the country against which the terrorists have a grievance, and is and is meant to be indiscriminate. It is from this

5

feature, indeed, that terrorism gets its name. For such indiscriminate and violent acts are designed to cause terror among the people at large, and it is by means of such terror that terrorists seek to attain their goals and force the hand of governments. Such indiscriminate violence can also be a feature of the acts of certain government officials and of certain rebel groups. Members of the police force in some parts of the world engage in random acts of violence against the civilian population as part of a policy of terrorizing the people into subservience. I think in particular of Guatemala. Again, some rebel groups, devoted to overthrowing the existing government, may also engage in similar acts of random violence against the civilian population. I think here of the Basque group ETA and the IRA. Such groups have also, of course, engaged in attacks on military installations and personnel, including assassination. I would nevertheless want to call these acts of police force and rebels acts of terrorism. The members of police forces who engage in random acts of violence are doing so clandestinely and when off duty, as it were, even if with the connivance and encouragement of their superiors. Were they to do so openly and in their capacity as police officers I would say their acts were acts of tyranny and government oppression. Again, in the case of ETA and the IRA, I would say that their attacks on military installations and government agencies could be acts of rebellion (though they need not be) while their attacks on civilians would have to be acts of terrorism. This is because attacks on civilians cannot be construed as attacks on the existing government so as to overthrow it, and hence cannot be construed as attacks by a would-be rival government in its capacity as a would-be rival government. They can only be construed as attacks by certain persons, who may indeed belong to a group that wishes to overthrow the government, but who in this case are operating as individuals to sow terror among the population at large. And I would say the same was true of attacks on military personnel if the aim here too was to sow terror and was not part of an act of defense against or an attack on an armed force that was hostile and threatening (so the attack on the USS Cole, for instance, would be terrorism and not rebellion).

But perhaps I need not insist on all these distinctions for my present purposes. Let it be sufficient then if we characterize terrorism as acts of violence committed by private individuals or groups of individuals, having no political authority or pretense of political authority, and directed indiscriminately against civilian or at least non-hostile populations and institutions so as to spread fear and terror there in order to achieve some limited goal short of the immediate overthrow of the existing government. This definition may need some further clarification and correction, but I think we are more likely, with its help, to get a clearer grasp of the phenomenon of terrorism as we ordinarily speak of terrorism, and certainly as we are speaking of terrorism in the present context of the war on terrorism. (Other phenomena, which may be close to it but are not really part of it, such as what is called state terrorism, can thus be set aside—not indeed so as to be ignored, but so as to be dealt with more clearly in their own place and in their own terms.)

At all events, with this definition of terrorism, we can see at once why terrorism is and must be evil and unjust. Note first that the evil and injustice of terrorism is not part of the definition of terrorism. I have not defined terrorism as unjust or evil acts of violence. I have defined it by reference to certain acts of violence, to be sure, but without mention of good or bad. The injustice of terrorism does, nevertheless, immediately follow from this definition when we add to it the further proposition that deliberate and intentional attacks on the innocent are unjust. That it is unjust to attack the innocent is something of a self-evident proposition. Justice is fundamentally a matter of giving each their due, but the deliberate infliction of harm or injury is not due to the innocent who, precisely as innocent, are owed peace and protection, not violence. That civilian populations and also non-hostile military personnel, who are the objects of terrorist attacks, are innocent in this sense is also obvious. This is not to say that all those who suffer in terrorist attacks are innocent of every crime whatever. Some might indeed happen to be criminals. But it is to say that they are innocent in the precise respect in which they are attacked. For they are attacked simply in their capacity as civilians or non-hostile military going about their ordinary tasks (a warship in a friendly port, for instance, is not a hostile presence about to inflict death or injury). Such tasks are not attacks or threats against anyone, least of all against the terrorists. They cannot, taken precisely as such, be construed as in any way deserving of attack or injury or death. They are innocent tasks. But it is against people engaged in such innocent tasks that terrorists launch their attacks. Terrorist attacks are therefore attacks on innocents and so cannot be anything but evil and unjust.

It matters not here what grievances the terrorists may have or what accusations they level against those countries whose people they attack. An evil deed is an evil deed and nothing can make it to be a good deed. Not even religion, not even the Muslim religion, can make it to be a good deed. Those who say it can, or who claim the support of Islam for their terrorist attacks (as we know from private letters that the hijackers did on September 11th), are simply abusing religion and Islam. Do not take my argument alone for this. Take rather the words of one of the Taliban themselves, the Taliban ambassador to Pakistan, who said of the attack on the U.S.: "This action is terrorist action. We know this was not Islamic and was a very dangerous action, and we condemn that" (*China Daily*, Thursday, October 4, 2001). Mr. Bin Laden has, of course, said the exact opposite. He has praised the attacks on the U.S. and on civilians, and said that Islam expressly requires Muslims to engage in such attacks. But if even the Taliban deny that this is what Islam teaches, one wonders what sort of Islam Mr. Bin Laden is following or whether he is really following Islam at all rather than his own corrupt inventions. At all events decent Muslims have good reason to repudiate, and to repudiate openly and loudly, the Islam preached by Mr. Bin Laden. We can be grateful, therefore, to those Islamic countries that have done so, among whom Saudi Arabia should be mentioned. Saudi Arabia severed relations with the Taliban on the grounds that the Taliban had brought Islam into disrepute which, with their support for Mr. Bin Laden, must, even by the Taliban's own admission, be true.

RESPONDING TO THE EVIL OF TERRORISM

Terrorism then is an evil, and an evil of a particularly vicious kind which constitutes, as the Chinese permanent representative to the UN said, "a serious challenge to human civilization and dignity as well as a serious threat to international peace and security." Those countries, therefore, which love peace and care for the good of mankind must do something to rid the world of this evil. Not to do so would be a dereliction of duty. It is everyone's duty to do good (pursuing good and avoiding evil is an elementary injunction of reason), and among the good things to be done is the removal of evils, especially grave evils—to the extent, at any rate, that this is possible. Here, however, we must be careful, for in opposing evil it is all too easy to fall into evil oneself. We are all doubtless aware, even from our youth, of how easy it is, when someone has injured or insulted us, to respond with hatred and fury and to inflict, or try to inflict, worse injury than we first suffered. We may in this way satisfy our lust for revenge but we do not in this way remove evil or make the world a better place. On the contrary we simply add to the evil in the world, for we add

our own evil to the evil of the other. One cannot defeat evil with
evil. That is simply contradictory. To use evil against evil is not to
defeat evil but to be defeated by it and to become evil, or even
more evil, in one's own turn. This is a truth that Mr. Bin Laden
has altogether failed to grasp. But we, who profess to be opposing
Mr. Bin Laden and his ilk, must not sink to his level. We must not
become terrorists and mass murderers ourselves. For we cannot
on the one hand condemn terrorism and set out to destroy it,
while on the other hand commit acts of terrorism of our own. As I
have already said, two wrongs do not make a right and evil cannot be defeated by evil. Only right can make a right, and only
good can defeat evil.

Now it is a striking fact that in all the build-up to the war on   10
terrorism, beginning from President Bush's first declaration immediately after September 11th, there have been repeated and
persistent declarations from all sides that the war should be conducted with great prudence and caution, that it should only target
the guilty, that it should not result in collateral damage or as little
such damage as possible, and so forth. These declarations came
first from the American Government itself. They were then repeated by almost all countries round the world, whether friendly
or hostile to the U.S. The hostile countries, among which we
should particularly mention Taliban-controlled Afghanistan,
made these declarations with a certain indignation and even with
fear (springing, perhaps, from secret guilt). But it is a tribute to
the U.S. that they made these declarations at all. The declarations
were an admission that it made sense to appeal to justice when
talking to the U.S.; that one could reasonably expect the U.S. to
be sensitive to the claims of justice when deciding what to do;
that one had some hope, indeed, of getting the U.S. to change its
mind if its policies could be shown not to accord with justice. I do
not mean to imply by this that the U.S. always acts with justice,
that none of its policies has been unjust, or that none of its officers has behaved unjustly. That would be too much to expect of
any country or government. We are human, all too human. We
make mistakes, sometimes deliberately. We regret only after the
event and not before. But at least we can regret; at least we can
acknowledge the claims of justice against us; at least we can be
restrained by appeals to what is good. Certainly the world, including the Taliban, think that is true of the U.S., for otherwise why
make appeals to justice?

But consider the contrast here. Has the world thought it
worth appealing to justice with the Taliban or with Mr. Bin

Laden? Has the world beaten a path to Mr. Bin Laden's door appealing to him to follow justice and prudence in his decisions of who and what to attack? Has the world appealed to him, in the name of justice, to give himself up to a court of law to prove his innocence or to admit his guilt? Some appeal was indeed made to the Taliban in the name of justice to hand Mr. Bin Laden over, but we know how little regard they paid to that appeal. Again, to change focus slightly, has anyone appealed to Mr. Saddam Hussein in the name of justice to stop the tyranny and oppression of his people, to abide by UN resolutions, to apologize and make reparation for his aggression against Iran and Kuwait? To my knowledge this has not happened, at least not on the same scale as appeals to justice have been made in the case of the U.S. and the war on terrorism. But why the difference? Surely because no one believes that Mr. Bin Laden, the Taliban, Mr. Saddam Hussein have a sufficient sense of justice to make such appeals worthwhile. We have all learned that these people are too far gone in evil to be sensitive to the principles of good. Only force could bring home to them the error of their ways and there is no guarantee of success even then. Let us, therefore, give tribute and blame where tribute and blame are due: tribute to the U.S. because we all see that the U.S. has not lost its sensitivity to justice, blame to Mr. Bin Laden and the Taliban and Mr. Saddam Hussein because we all see that they have.

Let it be agreed then that we must resist evil and resist it with good. Our particular question, however, concerns the evil of terrorism and how to resist it with good. The short answer is that we should resist it with all the good at our command. In all our actions, in all our lives, we should be doing the most good we can and encouraging our neighbors to do the same. For the evil of terrorism springs from many sources, and in particular it springs from the injustices, real or apparent, committed by others against what the terrorists hold dear. Such injustices give no excuse, of course, to the evil deeds of terrorists as I have already several times remarked, but if we can, each in our own way and in our own place, reduce the injustice around us, we will be doing our part to reduce the emergence of more terrorists in the future, as well as making the world a better place in general. But such an answer, while vital and in need of frequent repetition, is not enough. Our concern is the more specific question of whether force, in particular the force of war, is a just response to terrorism. If it is not we ought not to engage in it; but if it is we need to know what sort of force, under what conditions, subject to what limits, and so forth.

The first thing to note here is that *force* is a neutral term. It does not by itself connote something either good or bad. The same is true, for instance, of tolerance. That too connotes something neither good nor bad in itself. Everything depends on what is tolerated and why. Tolerating the murder of infants would clearly be bad; tolerating the expression of different opinions in the course of philosophical debate would clearly be good. That is why those who praise tolerance as a virtue are speaking too simply. Tolerance as such is not a virtue, nor is intolerance as such a vice. We need to know tolerance or intolerance of what, by whom, when, how. That is also why those who condemn force as a vice, such as pacifists, are speaking too simply as well. Is all use of force always and everywhere wrong? Is the force used by parents to discipline children wrong? Is the force used by police forces to arrest criminals wrong? Is the force used to defend oneself against attackers wrong? It seems patent that to answer yes to all these questions is absurd. Some uses of force are clearly right and just. The only interesting question to ask is which uses are so.

Since force is in itself neutral, it can only be just or unjust according to the way it is used, that is say for what goals or ends, in what amount or kind, against and by whom, when and where, with what likely consequences, and so forth. Of these several features, the goal or end of force would seem to be the first and most important. No amount of force, used by anyone on any occasion, could be just if the end aimed at were not just. So what are the just aims for which force may be used? Well ultimately, since we are talking of the use of force by men against men, the goals must be the good of men. Only if force has as its goal the promotion of the human good could it be good. The human good is clearly a complex whole consisting of many parts, from material and physical goods, to external goods, to cultural, educational, and spiritual goods. There is no need to spell these out in detail or explain their connections and relative subordination to each other. It is enough to note them in their general outline. For our concern is less about what the human good is than about what uses of force are justified with relation to it. In particular, since the war on terrorism is directed against resisting an evil, the evil of attacks on innocent life and limb, on habitations and property, on economic and social structures, the question is what determines the legitimate use of force in resistance to evil.

The operative idea here is clearly that of self-defense. Since the human good is the object of pursuit, whatever attacks that good or hinders that pursuit may be resisted and repulsed sufficiently to make the pursuit of the good possible again. Suppose,

15

however, that force is the only, or only reasonable, way to preserve and promote the good. Are we justified in having recourse to it? The answer would seem to be an unambiguous yes in the case of ordinary criminals who threaten us from within our own communities. One could hardly conceive of a community, at least a decent community, that did not protect itself and its members, using force if need be, against such criminal activities. Since such activities serve to undermine any community and threaten its viability, and the more so the more they are left to grow unchecked, a community that does not undertake to defend itself against them has, to all intents and purposes, given up the desire to survive as a community at all. By parity of reasoning, the same should hold in the case of enemies and terrorists who attack the community from without and in more violent and destructive ways. In other words, the justification for armies and wars is of the same sort as the justification for policemen and prisons.

There is, however, a paradox here, a paradox that lends considerable support to the case of pacifists. For any use of force seems always to be an attack on the good as well as a defense of it. Policemen have sometimes lost their lives in the attempt to arrest criminals by force and their families and friends have suffered all the grief of bereavement as a result. If such harm arises in these cases, how much more does it do so in time of war? Not only are more people maimed and killed in war (and in more awful ways), and more families tortured with grief, but the potential loss of civilian life, the destruction of property, the suspension of peacetime activities, the disruption of the economy and so forth make the damage to the human good so great as to render war unacceptable.

This paradox admits of an answer and an answer that points to the true place of force in human affairs, namely that it is a last resort, to be undertaken reluctantly and only because no other reasonable course of action is available. A situation where force is necessary is something regrettable, which one would avoid if possible, because it is a situation where one is unable to preserve all the goods one would wish to preserve. Some have to be sacrificed for the sake of others more important. That it is right to sacrifice some goods for the sake of others when harsh fate compels such a choice would be conceded by most of us, because it is conceded by most of us in many other cases besides war and the use of force. We consider it right to amputate a diseased limb to save the whole body or to cast overboard precious cargo to save the ship from sinking. One must look at the war on terrorism in the same way. Regrettable though it is, it is yet the only sensible way forward in some circumstances.

Force, then, is necessary for the pursuit of the good, but only as a last resort and only as long as force is necessary. As soon as it becomes possible to pursue the good again without recourse to the use of force we should do so. Now it is clear that in the case of the current war against terrorism the U.S. and its allies are following the logic of this argument. Before any force was used as many appeals were made as possible and through as many channels as possible to get the Taliban to give up the terrorists within their midst and to close down the camps where these terrorists trained. The Taliban have refused and since the terrorists have also refused to give themselves up voluntarily both groups have effectively declared themselves at war with the civilized world. For any part of the civilized world is a potential object of their attacks. The civilized world, therefore, has been driven by them into the last resort of using force against them.

A clarification is needed at this point, however, because of certain confusions that have appeared in the media. The use of force is sanctioned under the idea of self-defense. It is because the pursuit of the good requires us to defend ourselves against attack that we are permitted, in extreme cases and as a last resort, to use force. But acts of self-defense, even acts that are themselves attacks on offending countries, are not as such acts of retaliation or revenge (contrary to what some of the media have implied). In fact, self-defense cannot and does not justify retaliation or revenge. It justifies only self-defense. Once sufficient force has been used to secure such defense there can be no justification for further use of force. To continue force beyond that point would be to engage in unjust aggression oneself and so to become guilty of the injustice that one was condemning in one's enemy. As has been said before, one cannot defeat evil with evil. Retaliation and revenge, however, clearly go beyond the requirements of self-defense and even if, in a given case, they do not, they cannot be justified by appeal to the human good. Retaliation and revenge are the infliction on another of suffering and loss because he has first inflicted suffering and loss on us. Such retaliation and revenge may simply consist in making the other suffer as much as he made us suffer, but more often than not the lust for revenge makes us inflict more suffering than we suffered. But how does the infliction of such suffering help us to defend ourselves against attack or help us to continue the pursuit of the good without fear and in peace? Take the concrete case of the attacks on New York.

Over 6,000 people were killed in those attacks and billions of dollars worth of damage was caused. Are we to continue attacks on terrorists in Afghanistan until we have killed over 6,000 of them and until we have inflicted on them billions of dollars worth of damage? The very thought is ridiculous. Apart from the fact that there are probably not 6,000 terrorists in Afghanistan and that the country is too desperately poor to have assets totaling billions of dollars, the idea that inflicting such damage is the only way to defend ourselves against terrorist attacks only needs to be stated to be dismissed.

20   No, the war on terrorism cannot be about revenge; it is about self-defense. This point has been made very clear by the U.S. and allied governments, and indeed by civilized governments all over the world, including China. Indeed the way the war is being talked about, the way everyone has insisted that only the guilty be pursued and only those countries that support them attacked, that collateral damage be kept to an absolute minimum, all demonstrate this fact. Of course, we must all remain vigilant that this goal is not in any way perverted. But such vigilance has been made all the easier by the fact that the U.S. and its allies have tried to get the whole civilized world behind the war on terrorism. We may be sure that many countries will be watching the war with care and will not be slow to protest if it oversteps its stated limits. At the present time Pakistan is clearly exercising such vigilance and we can be fairly confident that the concerns of Pakistan are being carefully listened to and that they are having their effect on the conduct of attacks on Afghanistan. If the attacks have to be extended further afield we can be equally sure that other countries will exercise similar vigilance.

This vigilance must concern not only the aim of the war—defense against terrorist attacks—but the means used to achieve it and their likely effects. For clearly the means must be measured by the goal and must not exceed it. Once defense has been secured, say by destruction of terrorist training camps and safe havens, and once the power of the Taliban in particular to support and foster terrorism has been destroyed, there is no need to continue the attacks. Any such continuation would not fall under the needs of defense but under revenge or retaliation or something of the sort and so would clearly be unjust. Further, if the attacks, despite not fully achieving their aim, start becoming counterproductive and cause more damage, especially collateral damage, than they are meant to cure, then they should cease. The war is justified by self-defense which is justified by the human good. But if the war starts causing more damage to that good than it could possibly remove, it has itself become an attack on the good and not a defense of it.

So much should, I think, be sufficient to show the basic justice of the war on terrorism and what its goals are and what its limits should be. There remains only the question of whether and to what extent the U.S. may have brought terrorist attacks on itself by its own misguided policies. The policies in question, if we go by the remarks of Mr. Bin Laden himself, are the keeping of U.S. troops in Saudi Arabia and U.S. support for Israel. As regards the former, one can hardly see what the problem is, especially since U.S. forces are there at the invitation and pleasure of the Saudis. If Mr. Bin Laden wants the U.S. forces gone then he only has to persuade the Saudis to withdraw the invitation. Why has he not done that or why has he not taken his complaint, and his terrorism, to Saudi Arabia? Actually Mr. Bin Laden wants the U.S. forces gone because they are infidels in the land of the Prophet. But why do the Saudis, who are the protectors of that land and of the holy places of Islam, not agree with him? Is Mr. Bin Laden the only true interpreter of what is and is not tolerable to Islam? Must all Muslims bow to Mr. Bin Laden's authority or else face his terrorist wrath? It is beginning to look as if Mr. Bin Laden is more your typical tyrant than your typical Muslim. At all events we may dismiss this complaint of his as frivolous. The presence of U.S. forces in Saudi Arabia is not unjust and not un-Islamic, whatever Mr. Bin Laden may say.

As regards the other complaint, U.S. support of Israel, it is again difficult to see what the problem is. That Israel has the right to exist, and therefore also the right of self-defense, is conceded by the whole civilized world, including the Arab world, and is expressly guaranteed by UN resolutions. Even the Palestinians under Mr. Arafat concede this. Now some Arabs of course do not concede it, including the terrorist organization Hamas and including Mr. Bin Laden. But then Mr. Bin Laden has set himself, not only against the whole civilized world, but against the whole Arab world. Must the Arab world again bow down to him and follow only his judgment about what Muslims should believe and do about the state of Israel? Is Mr. Bin Laden the new prophet, the new voice of God?

We may dismiss this complaint then as frivolous too. U.S. support for the existence and defense of the state of Israel is only what the whole civilized world concedes. We may, however, raise another point which no doubt lies behind Mr. Bin Laden's anger as it also lies behind the worries of many Arabs and Arab states. I mean, not the right of Israel to exist and defend itself, but the particular acts that Israel carries out in the name of self-defense. I have in mind the periodic incursions of Israeli military into Palestinian areas, the destruction of property, the resulting deaths of Palestinian protesters, the targeted killings, or assassinations, of specific individuals. The first thing to note here is that the U.S. has itself been at the forefront of those criticizing and condemning Israel for these kinds of attacks. Israel certainly has the right to defend itself, particularly against the frequent terrorist attacks within Israeli territory, but not the right to go beyond that. I am inclined to think, in fact, that Israel has fallen into the error of confusing retaliation with self-defense. As I said earlier, the two are not the same and the second does not justify the first. Yet Israel typically describes its incursions into Palestinian areas as reprisals and these incursions also typically come after some terrorist attack. Such incursions cannot be justified, or they cannot be justified like this. They, or some of them, could, however, be justified as acts of self-defense, but only if they take that form. For instance, the terrorist attacks on Israel are planned and carried out by terrorist groups, such as Hamas, that deny the right of Israel to exist. They do not come from the PLO, the organization headed by Mr. Arafat. What Israel may legitimately do, therefore, is to go after Hamas, arrest their personnel and destroy their training camps and weapons (not unlike, indeed, what the U.S. is trying to do in Afghanistan). This might require incursions into Palestinian territory of a greater nature than Israel currently undertakes for acts of reprisal. Moreover such acts could be done in concert with the PLO. Indeed the PLO is itself partly to blame here. It should be their responsibility to suppress terrorism within their territory, as Israel has often and legitimately complained. But the PLO are seemingly incapable of doing so. Since the PLO agree that Israel has a right to exist, that Hamas and similar organizations are wrong and engaged in acts of terrorism, why do they not call upon Israeli help to rid Palestine of such people? Israeli fire power and PLO intelligence should together be enough to do the job. Palestine is not a big place. There are not many places for terrorists to hide.

25   Well, that is one suggestion. Perhaps it is a good one, perhaps it is not. I do not know enough, I'm afraid, to be able to judge. But what I can and will say is that the U.S. cannot in any sense be blamed for its policy in the Middle East. The U.S. is upholding, in a way that few other countries have been willing to do, the basic

right of Israel to exist. That is an important, necessary, and fundamentally just act. The U.S. has nevertheless recognized the right
of the Palestinians to a homeland and to a peaceful homeland. Indeed the U.S. has recently recognized the desirability of there being an independent Palestinian state. The U.S. has also condemned many Israeli acts of reprisal, particularly the targeted
killings or assassinations. Moreover the U.S. has tried time out of
number to broker a workable peace in Israel. The Camp David accords, which secured the basic peace between Israel and her Arab
neighbors, go back to the presidency of Jimmy Carter in the late
'70s. Every president since has tried to build on those accords and
bring final peace to a troubled land. That success has still not
been reached cannot, I think, be put down to lack of will on the
part of the U.S. I don't think, therefore, that U.S. policy in the
Middle East can be blamed in any fundamental way. Perhaps mistakes have been made, but if so they are the mistakes to which human nature is only too prone. They do not spring from malice, or
hatred of Islam, or indifference to Palestinian rights. In short, a
fair minded assessment of U.S. policy cannot, I think, accuse it of
being a cause of terrorist attacks. Terrorists may allege U.S. policy
as a cause but then it is they who are at fault for having an unjust
approach to the Israeli question in the first place. They want Israel to cease to exist and that can in no way be conceded to them,
as the whole civilized world, including the Arab world, agrees.

In short, whatever were the motives that drove the terrorists
to their attacks on the U.S., the blame cannot be put on the U.S.
The terrorists and they alone must bear the responsibility for
their deeds.

Starting Points

1. In defining terrorism, Peter Simpson makes distinctions among a variety of
   acts of violence (paragraphs 3–5). In collaborative groups, formulate your
   own definition of terrorism. Do you agree or disagree with Simpson's categories regarding police violence, state-sponsored aggression, and tyranny?
   Do such definitions and exclusions create distinctions without a difference,
   or are they necessary to understanding complex and multi-faceted issues?
2. The author in the first paragraph says that the perpetrators of the attacks of
   September 11th might have had grievances against the United States, but
   there is never a justification for evil. In the context of war and terrorism,
   consider whether in your own personal value system there are immutable
   categories such as good and evil, love and hate, right and wrong. Does war
   change them? Does terrorism?

3. In paragraph 13, Simpson writes that "force" is a neutral term, as is "tolerance." Consider other words that by themselves carry no value judgments but that we often use in particular ways, ways that may tend to confuse issues. For example, we tend to think of "discriminate" as pejorative, yet we all discriminate in our choice of food, what movies to watch, the clothes we purchase. Stress is another: without stress, our ancestors would never have outrun the carnivores.

Two Years After 9/11: A Balance Sheet
DANIEL BENJAMIN

Daniel Benjamin is a senior fellow at the Center for Strategic and International Studies, former director for counter-terrorism at the National Security Council, and former senior fellow at the U.S. Institute of Peace. He is the author, with Steven Simon, of The Age of Sacred Terror *(Random House, 2002). In October 2003, he analyzed the status of the war on terror for a special report of the Institute of Peace.*

━━━━━━━━━━ ✦ ━━━━━━━━━━

Some two years after the September 11 attacks, an accounting of how the United States is faring in the war on terror reveals a mixed record. In some areas, American counter-terrorism efforts are performing substantially better than we had any right to expect in the aftermath of the catastrophic events of 2001. In others, Washington has been slow to take necessary steps to ensure the nation's long-term security. Though we may have won a short-term hiatus—as demonstrated by absence of a catastrophic attack against U.S. interests in the last two years—it would be delusory to believe that America's experience with radical Islamist terror will be anything but long and difficult.

WHAT WE'RE DOING RIGHT

Undoubtedly, the success story of the last two years has been the ability of the U.S intelligence community and its foreign partners to disrupt al Qaeda cells and apprehend operatives, including a significant number from the group's top tier. There were a number of noteworthy accomplishments: On September 11, 2002, Ramzi bin al-Shibh, a Yemeni leader of the team behind the attacks of the previous year, was captured in Karachi. Two months later, Qaed Senyan al-Harthi, a high-level al Qaeda official, was killed with five others in a remote area of Yemen by a missile fired from a Predator drone. Also in November, Abd al-Rahim al-Nashiri, a Saudi who served as operations chief on the Arabian Peninsula, was apprehended in the Persian Gulf region. In 2003, Walid Baattash, another operative involved in the World Trade Center/Pentagon attacks, was arrested in Karachi.

The pinnacle of this campaign was the apprehension of Khalid Sheikh Mohammed, who was arrested in a predawn operation on March 1, 2003 in Rawalpindi. He had collaborated with his nephew, Ramzi Yousef, in a conspiracy to blow up a dozen U.S. 747 airplanes over the Pacific in 1995 and was an architect of the September 11 attacks. Mohammed had eluded capture for almost a decade, and he was an important reason why al Qaeda had emerged as the most tactically imaginative terrorist group in history.

There have been advances in other areas as well: Government officials, speaking on background, say there have been quiet but real improvements in cutting off the flow of funds to terrorists, especially those that course through Saudi Arabia's large charities and non-governmental organizations (NGOs). These improvements have occurred more through tactical intelligence cooperation than through permanent reforms, and they have been complicated by continuing turf wars within the Washington bureaucracy. Nonetheless, the progress is significant.

NO LICENSE FOR TRIUMPHALISM

The record is by no means one of unchallenged American victories. On the contrary—and despite creeping notes of overconfidence in some official U.S. pronouncements—the terrorists of al Qaeda and affiliated groups have continued to be extremely active, frequently to disastrous effect. The litany of attacks is long: The August 2003 bombing of the Jakarta Marriott suggests that Jemaah Islamiya, the Indonesian jihadist group with close ties to al Qaeda, remains a potent threat 10 months after the October 2002 bombing of two nightclubs on Bali, which killed more than 200 people. (By any measure except that of September 11, Bali was a terrorist attack of major proportions.) In the same month as the Bali attack, Chechen rebels led by Movsar Basayev, a protégé of bin Laden's closest associate in the Caucasus, took some

5

800 theatergoers hostage in Moscow and threatened to blow up the building. A two-day standoff ended tragically when Russian special forces used an opiate gas to render the terrorists unconscious before storming the building. The gas was too potent and killed as many as 128 of the hostages; the 41 hostage-takers were either killed by the gas or shot. There is a tendency to write off Chechen violence as a problem of the dissolution of the Soviet/Russian empire, but the increasingly spectacular methodology of some Chechen terrorists and the increasingly Islamist tone of their rhetoric cannot be discounted.

In November 2002, al Qaeda's resourcefulness was displayed again in Mombasa, Kenya. The organization had a cell there from the early 1990s, and it had been thought to be cleaned out after the August 1998 bombing of the American embassies in Nairobi and Dar es Salaam. That belief was discredited when suicide operatives crashed a bomb-laden sport utility vehicle into a hotel owned by and catering to Israelis. Ten Kenyan workers and three Israeli tourists were killed. Almost simultaneously, terrorists launched two Soviet-made Strela shoulder-fired missiles at an Israeli charter jet that had just taken off from the local airport for Tel Aviv. The missiles narrowly missed the aircraft. Al Qaeda had been known to have Stinger-type missiles, but the attack demonstrated its willingness to use them in offensive operations out of the Afghanistan theater. It also confirmed the group's ever-increasing desire to attack Israeli targets and thereby establish its bona fides as the champion of the Palestinian cause and broaden its appeal in the Islamic world.

These were the largest attacks, but there were many other less spectacular ones, including the bombing of a French oil tanker off the coast of Yemen, the shootings of American servicemen in the Persian Gulf, the assassination of an American diplomat in Jordan, and a string of bombings in the Philippines. While we should be relieved that there has been no second 9/11, we should not lose sight of the magnitude of these events. In the last half century, no other terrorist organization has carried out or supported so much killing in a comparable period of time. That includes Hezbollah, which in 1983 bombed the barracks of U.S. Marines and French forces as well as the U.S. embassy in Beirut.

THE STATE OF AL QAEDA

Intelligence operations and the war in Afghanistan have led to the death or capture of a dozen or so top al Qaeda officials and the incarceration of some 3000 lower-level members of the group. Undoubtedly, these losses and eviction from the sanctuary in Afghanistan have led to the degradation of the organization's capabilities. Looking at the other side of the coin, though, there are still about a dozen high-level operatives with the skill and authority to carry out a major attack. Western intelligence services have consistently underestimated the group's overall strength. Some services now estimate the number of members in the group to be in the range of 25,000–70,000. Some care needs to be taken in viewing even these imprecise figures. Too often, terrorist organizations are likened to armies. And while the removal of large numbers of operatives is undoubtedly for the good, a group like al Qaeda needs only a small number of intact cells to carry out an operation—even a major one. Decapitation of the leadership also will not suffice for a group that is so ideologically driven and whose ideology is spreading fast.

SHAPING THE ENVIRONMENT?

A central goal of combat with any foe is to shape the environment to one's advantage. Here, one can question whether the United States is doing an effective job. This has been the year of Phase Two in the war on terror, the year of regime change in Iraq. While no one can overlook the long-term potential benefits for the Iraqi people of removing Saddam Hussein, so far as the battle against al Qaeda is concerned, the invasion of Iraq was a non sequitur. No convincing evidence of a substantive link between the Baghdad regime and Osama bin Laden's organization has ever been presented, and, in fact, the intelligence record of the last decade suggests that while contacts may have occurred and terrorist operatives may have crossed through Iraq, no collaborative efforts of note have occurred between the arch-secularist Baath regime and the radical fundamentalists of al Qaeda.

For the war on terrorism in the broadest sense, the invasion of Iraq brought two important advantages: A state sponsor of terrorism, albeit a rather inactive one, has been removed, and the demonstration of military might in toppling Saddam Hussein's regime has given the United States more leverage against the outstanding state sponsors of terrorism—Iran and Syria. (Both, it should be added, appear to be behaving somewhat better, although the jury will remain out for some time on Iranian activity within the borders of neighboring Iraq and Afghanistan.) But as a threat to U.S. interests, the state sponsors are of relatively minor

10

consequence compared to the non-state actors such as al Qaeda—which may in fact benefit from the American occupation of Iraq.

COSTS OF IRAQ

How does al Qaeda benefit? The greatest windfall for bin Laden's forces comes in the realm of propaganda, not a small issue for a movement that views establishing itself as the undisputed champion of Islam as a primary goal. By occupying Iraq, the United States has given al Qaeda a major opportunity to drive home its argument that the "leader of world infidelity" seeks to destroy Islam and subjugate its believers. This has been at the very core of al Qaeda's message throughout its existence, and the group is now using the example of Iraq to reap gains in the areas of recruitment and fundraising. Independent polling by groups such as the Pew Foundation and others has established that conditions are ripe for this message since there has been a massive turn in public opinion against America in the last two years. The data suggest that the long slow erosion of positive feelings about the United States has given way to a landslide during the period of the war on terror, and especially during the run-up to the invasion of Iraq. A long-term U.S. presence in Iraq, a central country within the historic realm of Islam and a longtime seat of the caliphate, will make it difficult to reverse these impressions. Positive perceptions about the reconstruction of Iraq may help, but they will have to be strong ones, widely affirmed by Iraqis themselves, to reverse this trend.

The occupation of Iraq presents other, related dangers in the war on terrorism. First, it seems highly likely that Iraq itself will become a central theater for Islamists seeking to attack the United States. Some may argue that this is preferable to having them attack the United States elsewhere, including at home. But the argument is false since there is no suggestion that one area of activity will affect the other. Iraq will attract those fighters who are prepared to carry on classic guerrilla warfare—as many of the trainees of the Afghan camps are capable of—while those with specific terrorist training will continue to focus on U.S. and Western interests elsewhere. (These fighters will feel honor-bound to attack American forces in Iraq since the Islamists' credibility will be on the line.) The potential cost to the reconstruction effort is considerable: Until U.S. forces can concentrate more on supporting the rebuilding and less on force protection, we will be challenged to deliver the kind of future that Iraqis expect, and that, in turn, will affect U.S. standing throughout the region. There are also further threats, such as proliferation of weapons and other dangerous materials. In the worst-case scenario, weapons of mass destruction material may have been privatized by regime adherents who know their future in an American-guided Iraq is unpromising. Additionally, weapons such as shoulder-fired anti-aircraft missiles, of which Iraq had many, may have fallen into terrorist hands—a possibility that has been voiced by senior U.S. military officials.

ELSEWHERE

A number of other developments suggest additional problems that require greater attention by the United States and its allies. Perhaps the outstanding one is the deterioration of conditions in Afghanistan. Both Taliban and al Qaeda fighters are showing increasing signs of activity, and, with the ambit of Hamid Karzai's government essentially restricted to Kabul, the possibility of another round of warlordism is growing. In the past, terrorists have found safe haven in the territory of these regional strongmen, and this could well happen again, giving the terrorists a greater level of security as they plot and train. Additionally, some experts see the geographic base of Islamist terror shifting to the Caucasus, where camps are said to have been established. Russian and other forces may be able to destroy these camps, but without a comprehensive settlement in Chechnya and the broader region, terrorists will move from camp to camp and remain a problem.

Another growing issue is the radicalization of Europe's Muslim population. Just the last year witnessed the first suicide bombing in Israel carried out by Muslims who were British citizens. The incident was unique but it bespoke a deeper reality. As polling demonstrates, a growing and dangerous alienation of young, European-born Muslims has taken root, and, as the French scholar Olivier Roy has observed, this cohort increasingly embraces an alternative, pan-Islamic identity that is often radical and occasionally violent. This could emerge as a considerable security challenge for Europe and the West in general.

WHAT'S MISSING

Success in intelligence operations has led to an overemphasis on this prong of strategy at the expense of all others. Washington continues to focus too heavily on state sponsors of terror, and to   15 ignore what Daniel Byman has rightly called the global insurgency now underway from the Pacific Rim to the Maghreb and Europe. The conflict we face is not just one against a single, determined group but against a fast-spreading, profoundly hostile ideology. Our record at disrupting cells and conspiracies is impressive, but it offers no promise that the next round of major terrorist attacks will be less dramatic than those of 9/11.

What is to be done? There is no magic bullet, of course, but the United States must begin to focus on the wider circle of Muslims who may be tempted by the al Qaeda message. We must not relax our efforts in intelligence and law enforcement in any way—indeed, this should be a period of constant innovation, particularly because other nations have come to share our threat assessment, which was not the case before September 2001. But we must also develop a foreign policy that addresses the tendency to radicalization in the Muslim world.

Core elements of such a policy would include greater emphasis on a number of fronts:

- *Democratization.* Only democracies can hope to contain some of the dissent developing in Muslim countries. Yet support for democratization must be tempered by gradualism and an effort to join with existing regimes—whose assistance in counter-terrorism remains essential—to encourage a new openness. Too abrupt a shift in U.S. policy risks bringing to power militants who would be inimical to American interests.
- *Improvement of regional educational systems.* The widespread decay of state schools in the region has given many parents no option but to enroll their children in religious schools that inculcate radical ideology and do not prepare the young for the modern economy.
- *Economic liberalization.* The countries of the Muslim world face enormous demographic and economic stresses. None of them is likely to produce the number of jobs necessary for their exploding populations. The primary hope for ameliorating some of the hardships is economic growth, which has long been stunted by the failure of economic reform.
- *Curbing incitement.* Too many of the region's authoritarian regimes have sought to deflect criticism away from themselves and onto an external enemy—Israel, the United States, the West in general. U.S. leaders have long decried this tendency but have seldom put real pressure on these regimes to stop the incitement. To end the cultivation of radicalism,

Muslim leaders must be shown that this practice will not be tolerated.

Making real progress on these fronts will require both diplomatic energy and money. The United States has taken a step in the right direction with the State Department's Middle East Partnership Initiative, which encourages democratization at the grassroots, and supports groups that have hitherto had little voice in their countries' affairs. But it will take much more to make a lasting impact—and a great deal of political capital has already been spent to buy support, or at least quiet, on the issue of Iraq. Historically, the United States has given the region's authoritarian regimes great leeway to do what they like domestically so long as they support our policies regarding the Middle East peace process and Persian Gulf security. But so long as many of these countries are incubators for radicals, we can no longer afford to turn a blind eye to what goes on within their borders.

Starting Points

1. After a close reading of Daniel Benjamin's article, do you think the title is accurate? Has Benjamin attempted a balanced analysis, or do you believe he has an agenda?
2. Is Benjamin's depiction accurate when he describes the current campaign as a war opposing "radical Islamist terror"? Is it Islamist, or is Islam being used by some individuals for their own ends?
3. Consider the points that Benjamin declares are necessary—and currently absent—if the war on terrorism is to succeed. Which of the four do you consider most important? Which of the points have the best chances for success?

Inside Al-Qaeda: A Window into the World of Militant Islam and the Afghani Alumni
RICHARD ENGEL

Jane's *is a world-wide publisher of technical data and analyses of* *military hardware and capabilities. Richard Engel,* Jane's *corre-* *spondent in Cairo and Amman, offers a view inside the secretive*

*world of Al-Qaeda, and the inner circle that arose out of the resist-
ance to the Soviet invasion of Afghanistan.*

---------------- ✦ ----------------

Sitting on a rooftop in a poor Cairo neighbourhood, 38-year-old Ibrahim recalled when he first met Osama bin Laden. It was 1983 and Ibrahim was one of the leaders of the Gamaa Islamiya (Islamic Group), one of Egypt's two main Islamic militant organizations centred largely in southern Egypt around the town of Assiout.

"I was one of the emirs [commanders] of the Gamaa Islamiya in southern Egypt at the time in Assiout. I was at the university of Assiout, the heart of the Islamic activism," said Ibrahim, who asked not to be further identified. Ibrahim had spent several months at one of Bin Laden's guerrilla training camps in Sudan learning how to use Kalashnikov assault rifles and other light weapons.

Now that his training was complete, it was time for Ibrahim to meet his benefactor, Bin Laden. He travelled to the Saudi Arabian capital, Riyadh, with a group of Islamic activists, most of them fellow university students.

"We met Osama ibn bin Laden on an Islamic pilgrimage to Saudi Arabia," said Ibrahim, using the traditional Islamic form of the Saudi exile's name. "He was a devoted young man who, like any young man, loved his religion. Then he changed and wanted there to be Islamic movements all over the world, and he fled Saudi Arabia and they stripped him of his citizenship." In a rare move, the Saudi government revoked Bin Laden's nationality in April 1994, despite the prominence of his wealthy family. His family, originally from the southern Yemeni province of Hadhramaut, also publicly disavowed him.

5   Ibrahim says he remembers Bin Laden as both polite and well educated. Bin Laden talked a lot, Ibrahim says, and although he was prosperous, he dressed humbly and kept the company of people with no money.

"Osama bin Laden would help any Islamic group, in Sudan, in any Arab country. God blessed him with money, so he gave to Islamic groups," said Ibrahim.

As Ibrahim and the other students were leaving Saudi Arabia, Bin Laden gave him a bag stuffed with Egyptian currency.

Ibrahim would not say how much, but it was clear that the idea was to use it to try to make Egypt an Islamic regime. He wanted to set up a military camp in the hills near Assiout, Ibrahim says. That's when Ibrahim lost his nerve.

"I saw my friends being arrested and being tortured and I didn't want to end up like them. So I made a plea bargain with the police and turned the money over to them," he said. Ibrahim served only one year in prison for his activities with the Gamaa Islamiya. He continues to be monitored by the Egyptian security authorities.

Ibrahim's story is typical of how Bin Laden has tried to align with local militant groups with country-specific grievances to increase his reach and influence. Bin Laden's methods and connections with local militant cells have expanded and become more sophisticated over the years, as exemplified by the case of confessed Jordanian militant Raed Hijazi.

Thirty-two-year-old Hijazi, a former Boston taxi driver and a U.S. citizen, is on trial in Jordan for plotting to blow up a fully booked, 400-room Jordanian hotel and two Christian tourist sites on the border with Israel on the eve of the millennium in December 1999. He faces the death penalty and prosecutors say the Jordanian militant cell Hijazi helped create worked in co-ordination with Bin Laden. Hijazi and other members of the Jordan militant group have confessed to many of the prosecution's accusations, but Hijazi's lawyers say he gave information under torture.

Speaking outside the state security court in Amman where Hijazi is being re-tried—he was already sentenced to death in absentia—his father Mohammed says his son is innocent. "No, he has no relation with Bin Laden at all. First of all he is poor. He has no funds. He lives on very little money and his apartment is a very little apartment near Amman. If you belong to Bin Laden you have to have some money," said Mohammed, an engineer of Palestinian origin.

Born in San Jose, California, to relative privilege, Raed Hijazi grew up travelling between the United States, Saudi Arabia and Jordan. In 1986, he enrolled in California State University in Sacramento to study business administration, according to his father. Prosecutors say it was in the United States that he got his first taste of radical Islamic teaching.

A Fijian cleric at a Muslim prayer group near the university convinced Hijazi to travel to Afghanistan to join the mujahideen

(Islamic fighters), who had been battling the Soviet Union since 1979. In addition to learning to use mortars and small arms in Afghanistan, Hijazi also formed alliances he would later allegedly use to build his own Jordanian terror cell, according to prosecutors. Hijazi was especially adept with mortars and earned the noms de guerre "Abu Ahmed the Mortarman" and "Abu Ahmed the American." After the beleaguered Soviet troops pulled out of Afghanistan following a decade of fighting, many mujahideen became convinced that a force of devoted Muslim believers could defeat any army, even one belonging to a superpower like the Soviet Union. Some mujahideen made it their goal to bring their holy war from the mountains of Afghanistan to their home countries.

THE AFGHAN ALUMNI

While not all saw combat, some 5,000 Saudis, 3,000 Yemenis, 2,800 Algerians, 2,000 Egyptians, 400 Tunisians, 350 Iraqis, 200 Libyans and dozens of Jordanians served alongside the Afghani mujahideen in the war. Between 1,000 and 1,500 of them returned to Algeria and formed the backbone of the Islamic radicals who are continuing to fight against the government in what has been a nine-year civil war that has claimed more than 100,000 lives. Those who returned to Egypt became valued members of the Gamaa Islamiya and the Gihad group, but their success was severely limited by arrest campaigns and several mass trials in the 1990s under the title of "the returnees from Afghanistan." Some Egyptians, who saw that they would be imprisoned if they returned home, remained in Afghanistan or took refuge wherever they could. U.S. authorities have said that as many as 200 Afghan alumni settled in the New York/New Jersey area, some of them congregating around the New Jersey mosque where Omar Abdel Rahman preached.

15   Largely at the request of Egypt and Algeria, Pakistan has cracked down on its Afghan veterans. Some so-called "Afghani Arabs" also headed to Asia and joined up in the Philippines with the Abu Sayyaf group—named for a famous Afghan mujahid. Other Afghani Arabs continued to fight the Russians in Tajikistan while still others continued to participate in other conflicts where Muslims were involved, mainly participating in the wars in Bosnia and Chechnya.

Raed Hijazi was one of the Jordanian Afghan returnees who wanted to bring his battle home, according to the prosecution. In 1996, Hijazi met Hader Abu Hoshar, a fellow Afghan veteran who was also of Palestinian origin. Abu Hoshar was a longtime enemy of Jordan and, according to statements given to the court, it was during this meeting at a Palestinian refugee camp in Syria that the plot to carryout a massive attack against foreigners in Jordan was born.

After the plot was set, Hijazi moved back to the United States and worked for the Boston Cab Company. According to prosecutors, he used the job to send some $13,000 to his growing Jordanian terror cell. The group also raised money by selling false documents.

U.S. federal investigators are currently examining a possible link between Hijazi and two of the suspected hijackers who boarded planes in Boston on 11 September and hijacked them for the attacks on the World Trade Center and the Pentagon. Investigations say Hijazi is linked to suspects Ahmed Alghamdi and Satam al-Suqami. If proven, it would be a concrete link between the attacks against the United States and Bin Laden.

Jordanian court officials say Hijazi's cell contacted Bin Laden's group Al-Qaeda ("The Base") in 1998, asking for help in explosives training. Through a key Al-Qaeda operative known as Abu Zubayida, Bin Laden's group arranged for four people, including Hijazi, to travel through Turkey to a training camp in Afghanistan. Hijazi, prosecutors say, learned to use explosives and remote-controlled triggering devices there.

Abu Zubayida is one of the men Washington has listed as 20 wanted after the terror attacks in New York and Washington. He is believed to function as Al-Qaeda's foreign minister, setting up connections and maintaining relations with Islamic militant cells around the world.

By December 1999, Hijazi's Jordanian cell—now in co-operation with Al-Qaeda, which helped approve targets and coordinate timing—had stockpiled enough nitric and sulphuric acid to make a bomb equivalent to 16-tons of TNT. Jordanian police, who foiled the millennium attack, found the chemicals stockpiled in plastic barrels in a pit dug underneath a house outside of Jordan. A Jordanian intelligence official testifying against Hijazi said that authorities only learned by accident of the terror plot just weeks before it was set to take place.

Western diplomats have said the failed Jordanian plot is a blueprint of how Bin Laden currently operates, using a loosely tied network of local militant groups that operate with his blessing and support, but which cannot be easily traced directly back to him. It is also this loose structure that makes it so difficult for intelligence and police agencies to disrupt the network.

A former Egyptian militant interviewed described the structure of radical Islamic groups as having been modelled after "a bunch of grapes." "Each group operates independently with its members not knowing who the others are. That way, if one member of the group is plucked off by police, the others remain unaffected," he said.

MAJOR PLAYERS

While there were many heroes and martyrs in the Afghan war, which was supported by U.S. intelligence as part of its battle against communism, many of the mujahideen rallied around three main people: charismatic Saudi financier Osama Bin Laden, blind cleric Sheih Omar Abdel Rahman and intelligent technocrat Dr Ayman al-Zawahari.

25   Egyptian-born Sheih Omar Abdel Rahman is currently serving a life sentence in a Minnesota prison after being convicted of conspiring with a group of his followers to destroy the World Trade Center and New York City bridges and tunnels in 1993.

Abdel Rahman's son, Abdullah, says there are both similarities and differences between Bin Laden and his father, the blind imam of Muslim guerrillas. "Sheikh Omar and Osama Bin Laden are both Muslims and involved in the Afghani cause and followed the path of the mujahideen in Afghanistan," said Abdullah, who is studying like his father at Cairo's al-Azhar university, the world's oldest centre of Muslim teaching. "Osama Bin Laden also donated much of his money to the Afghani cause. The differences between the two are in the level of religious study. Sheikh Omar Abdel Rahman is a man who all of his life was dedicated to Islamic study. He was a graduate of al-Azhar University and also holds a doctorate, which he received with highest honours in Koranic studies. He is an Islamic cleric able to issue fatwas (Islamic rulings) saying what is a sin and what is a blessing. On the other hand, Osama bin Laden's education was in engineering and he is a military person with expertise in military training," said Abdullah.

Sheikh Omar Abdel Rahman continues to be revered by radical Muslims around the world who view him as their spiritual leader. Both Bin Laden and al-Zawahari, who is now his deputy, have vowed to take revenge against the United States if Abdel Rahman, a diabetic, dies while in a U.S. jail.

Ayman al-Zawahari, 50, has more experience in radical Islamic politics than even Bin Laden. Interpol has listed al-Zawahari among its most wanted men. He is described by Western officials as Bin Laden's right-hand man and heir apparent to his organisation. Hailing from a long line of prominent politicians, doctors and religious leaders, his full name is Ayman Mohammed Rabie al-Zawahari, although he has used the code names Abu Mohammed and Abu Fatima.

A surgeon, al-Zawahari has been described as a private, intelligent and vindictive person. "He was first arrested in 1966 when he was just 15 years old for belonging to the then-outlawed Muslim Brotherhood, Egypt's oldest radical Islamic group. During the 1970s, al-Zawahari remained involved with militant Islamic organisations and emerged as a leader of Egypt's Gihad group, which, in conjunction with the Gamaa Islamiya, carried out the 1981 assassination of Egyptian President Anwar Sadat.

After Sadat's murder, al-Zawahari was arrested, but police were never able to tie him directly to the assassination. Instead, al-Zawahari was sentenced to three years in prison on a weapons charge. A former friend suggests that al-Zawahari was set up by an enemy who threw an assault rifle into the garden of his family's villa in the affluent Maadi district of Cairo. It was during his incarceration, says the friend, that al-Zawahari snapped, the torture he was subjected to in prison sending him over the edge. 30

After his release from prison in 1984, al-Zawahari left Egypt for good. Mamoun Hodeibi, the deputy leader of the Muslim Brotherhood, says many members of his organisation went to Afghanistan. "Some of them went there to be doctors. Others worked for charities and Islamic societies," said Hodeibi at the Muslim Brotherhood's Cairo office.

Al-Zawahari was one of these and supported the mujahideen's medical personnel. After the war, al-Zawahari moved to Europe, residing in Switzerland and Denmark, according to Egyptian security officials. Al-Zawahari supposedly carries Egyptian, French, Swiss and Dutch passports, although Switzerland denies he was ever issued a Swiss passport. Egyptian officials say his French and Swiss passports are under the name Amin Othman and that his Dutch passport, number 513116, is in the name Sami Mahmoud.

By the 1990s, al-Zawahari had emerged as the leader of the military wing of the Egyptian Gihad group, known as the Vanguards of Conquest. In the mid-1990s, he returned to Afghanistan to join forces with Bin Laden: a move that caused a rift in his Gihad group.

Diaa Rashwan, a senior researcher of Islamic militant groups at Egypt's al-Ahram centre for strategic studies, says al-Zawahari and Bin Laden have become very close since the announcement in 1998 of the formation of the World Islamic Front for Jihad against Jews and Crusaders. Other key members of the front are Egyptians Mustafa Hamza, 43, and Rifie Ahmed Taha, 47, as well as Mohammed Islambouli, 46, the brother of Khaled Islambouli, Sadat's assassin. Egyptian intelligence officials say Mohammed Islambouli holds two Egyptian passports, a Qatari passport and an Algerian passport in the name Mahmoud Youssef.

35   "Ayman al-Zawahari from the beginning was as all the other ordinary Islamists," said Rashwan. "He had his own project to establish an Islamic state here in Egypt, but over the last three years, he has gone closer to the Osama Bin Laden theory. It means to fight the enemies of Islam, the Americans and Israelis, but not to build an Islamic state."

Until two weeks ago [September 28, 2001], rhetoric from men like Ayman al-Zawahari about fighting the enemies of Islam wasn't taken as seriously as it is today. Now, Washington is presumably re-examining statements from al-Zawahari that it may previously have considered bluster. Two years ago, for example, his Gihad group said it had chemical and biological weapons that it intended to use against the United States and Israel.

DEFINING THE TERRORISTS

In 1998, the 22-member Arab League gave its approval to a pan-Arab counter-terrorism treaty. Since then, the nations have in varying degrees been co-operating to extradite and crack down on militants in the Middle East. The Arab pact requires countries to deny support to groups that launch attacks on other nations in the region, share intelligence and extradite suspects. Extraditions between Arab states, which have been frequent but rarely made public, operate according to bilateral treaties: a condition that has been problematic because extradition accords do not exist between all of the Arab League's member nations. Opponents of the treaty also fear that undemocratic Arab governments could use anti-terrorism legislation to target political dissidents.

Since the 11 September attacks against the United States, Egypt's President Hosni Mubarak has renewed a call he has consistently made since the late 1990s to hold an international conference against terrorism. While the conference may be vital to close loopholes that allow militant groups to operate in Europe and the United States under the guise of human rights organisa-

tions or charities, the overall effectiveness of such a global conference is questionable.

As evidenced from statements made at the Arab League's inte-
rior and justice ministers' meetings that established the Arab
wide anti-terrorism treaty, there is a deep desire in the Arab world
for Israel to be sanctioned for what Arab nations consider its
"state terrorism" against the Palestinians. Furthermore, Arab
states do not consider groups like the Lebanese Hizbollah or
Palestinian Hamas to be terrorist groups, although they are listed
as such by the U.S. State Department. Therefore, one of the
toughest steps in battling terrorists, like the vast array of Afghani
alumni who operate across borders, may be coming to terms with
the age-old question of who is a terrorist.

Starting Points

1. How important to defeating terrorism is an understanding of the individuals involved and their motivation? Does this article contribute to that
   understanding?

2. Engle makes the point that members of the Arab League have long called for
   Israel to be sanctioned for "state terrorism" as an important part of a global
   campaign against terrorism. In what ways does the United States refusal to
   censure Israel contribute to global terrorism?

3. How great is the danger of a global rift between Islamic and non-Islamic
   cultures because of the call for a jihad by some terrorist groups? What is the
   view of prominent Islamic clerics regarding such a jihad?

This War on Terrorism Is Bogus
The 9/11 Attacks Gave the U.S.
an Ideal Pretext to Use Force to
Secure its Global Domination
Michael Meacher

*Michael Meacher, a Labour Member of Britain's Parliament, was
environment minister from 1997 to 2003. In this article from* The
Guardian, *Meacher decries the American-led war on terror as part
of a blueprint for global domination. The wars in Afghanistan and
Iraq, according to Meacher, have been used to further military control of the region, control that was planned before the attacks on the*

World Trade Center and the Pentagon. This article appeared Sunday, September 6, 2003.

───────────── ✦ ─────────────

Massive attention has now been given—and rightly so—to the reasons why Britain went to war against Iraq. But far too little attention has focused on why the U.S. went to war, and that throws light on British motives too. The conventional explanation is that after the Twin Towers were hit, retaliation against al-Qaida bases in Afghanistan was a natural first step in launching a global war against terrorism. Then, because Saddam Hussein was alleged by the U.S. and UK governments to retain weapons of mass destruction, the war could be extended to Iraq as well. However this theory does not fit all the facts. The truth may be a great deal murkier.

We now know that a blueprint for the creation of a global Pax Americana was drawn up for Dick Cheney (now vice-president), Donald Rumsfeld (defence secretary), Paul Wolfowitz (Rumsfeld's deputy), Jeb Bush (George Bush's younger brother) and Lewis Libby (Cheney's chief of staff). The document, entitled Rebuilding America's Defences, was written in September 2000 by the neoconservative think tank, Project for the New American Century (PNAC).

The plan shows Bush's cabinet intended to take military control of the Gulf region whether or not Saddam Hussein was in power. It says "while the unresolved conflict with Iraq provides the immediate justification, the need for a substantial American force presence in the Gulf transcends the issue of the regime of Saddam Hussein."

The PNAC blueprint supports an earlier document attributed to Wolfowitz and Libby which said the U.S. must "discourage advanced industrial nations from challenging our leadership or even aspiring to a larger regional or global role." It refers to key allies such as the UK as "the most effective and efficient means of exercising American global leadership." It describes peacekeeping missions as "demanding American political leadership rather than that of the UN." It says "even should Saddam pass from the scene," U.S. bases in Saudi Arabia and Kuwait will remain permanently . . . as "Iran may well prove as large a threat to U.S. interests as Iraq has." It spotlights China for "regime change," saying "it is time to increase the presence of American forces in SE Asia."

5   The document also calls for the creation of "U.S. space forces" to dominate space, and the total control of cyberspace to

prevent "enemies" using the internet against the U.S. It also hints that the U.S. may consider developing biological weapons "that can target specific genotypes [and] may transform biological warfare from the realm of terror to a politically useful tool."

Finally—written a year before 9/11—it pinpoints North Korea, Syria and Iran as dangerous regimes, and says their existence justifies the creation of a "worldwide command and control system." This is a blueprint for U.S. world domination. But before it is dismissed as an agenda for rightwing fantasists, it is clear it provides a much better explanation of what actually happened before, during and after 9/11 than the global war on terrorism thesis. This can be seen in several ways.

First, it is clear the U.S. authorities did little or nothing to pre-empt the events of 9/11. It is known that at least 11 countries provided advance warning to the U.S. of the 9/11 attacks. Two senior Mossad experts were sent to Washington in August 2001 to alert the CIA and FBI to a cell of 200 terrorists said to be preparing a big operation (*Daily Telegraph*, September 16, 2001). The list they provided included the names of four of the 9/11 hijackers, none of whom was arrested.

It had been known as early as 1996 that there were plans to hit Washington targets with aeroplanes. Then in 1999 a U.S. national intelligence council report noted that "al-Qaida suicide bombers could crash-land an aircraft packed with high explosives into the Pentagon, the headquarters of the CIA, or the White House."

Fifteen of the 9/11 hijackers obtained their visas in Saudi Arabia. Michael Springman, the former head of the American visa bureau in Jeddah, has stated that since 1987 the CIA had been illicitly issuing visas to unqualified applicants from the Middle East and bringing them to the U.S. for training in terrorism for the Afghan war in collaboration with Bin Laden (BBC, November 6, 2001). It seems this operation continued after the Afghan war for other purposes. It is also reported that five of the hijackers received training at secure U.S. military installations in the 1990s (*Newsweek*, September 15, 2001).

Instructive leads prior to 9/11 were not followed up. French 10 Moroccan flight student Zacarias Moussaoui (now thought to be the 20th hijacker) was arrested in August 2001 after an instructor reported he showed a suspicious interest in learning how to steer large airliners. When U.S. agents learned from French intelligence he had radical Islamist ties, they sought a warrant to search his computer, which contained clues to the September 11 mission (*Times*, November 3, 2001). But they were turned down by the FBI. One agent wrote, a month before 9/11, that Moussaoui might be planning to crash into the Twin Towers (*Newsweek*, May 20, 2002).

All of this makes it all the more astonishing—on the war on terrorism perspective—that there was such slow reaction on September 11 itself. The first hijacking was suspected at not later than 8:20 AM, and the last hijacked aircraft crashed in Pennsylvania at 10:06 AM. Not a single fighter plane was scrambled to investigate from the U.S. Andrews airforce base, just 10 miles from Washington D.C., until after the third plane had hit the Pentagon at 9:38 AM. Why not? There were standard FAA intercept procedures for hijacked aircraft before 9/11. Between September 2000 and June 2001 the U.S. military launched fighter aircraft on 67 occasions to chase suspicious aircraft (AP, August 13, 2002). It is a U.S. legal requirement that once an aircraft has moved significantly off its flight plan, fighter planes are sent up to investigate.

Was this inaction simply the result of key people disregarding, or being ignorant of, the evidence? Or could U.S. air security operations have been deliberately stood down on September 11? If so, why, and on whose authority? The former U.S. federal crimes prosecutor, John Loftus, has said: "The information provided by European intelligence services prior to 9/11 was so extensive that it is no longer possible for either the CIA or FBI to assert a defence of incompetence."

Nor is the U.S. response after 9/11 any better. No serious attempt has ever been made to catch Bin Laden. In late September and early October 2001, leaders of Pakistan's two Islamist parties negotiated Bin Laden's extradition to Pakistan to stand trial for 9/11. However, a U.S. official said, significantly, that "casting our objectives too narrowly" risked "a premature collapse of the international effort if by some lucky chance Mr. Bin Laden was captured." The U.S. chairman of the joint chiefs of staff, General Myers, went so far as to say that "the goal has never been to get Bin Laden" (AP, April 5, 2002). The whistleblowing FBI agent Robert Wright told ABC News (December 19, 2002) that FBI headquarters wanted no arrests. And in November 2001 the U.S. airforce complained it had had al-Qaida and Taliban leaders in its sights as many as 10 times over the previous six weeks, but had been unable to attack because they did not receive permission quickly enough (*Time Magazine*, May 13, 2002). None of this assembled evidence, all of which comes from sources already in the public domain, is compatible with the idea of a real, determined war on terrorism.

The catalogue of evidence does, however, fall into place when set against the PNAC blueprint. From this it seems that the so-called "war on terrorism" is being used largely as bogus cover for achieving wider U.S. strategic geopolitical objectives. Indeed Tony Blair himself hinted at this when he said to the Commons liaison committee: "To be truthful about it, there was no way we could have got the public consent to have suddenly launched a campaign on Afghanistan but for what happened on September 11" (*Times*, July 17, 2002). Similarly Rumsfeld was so determined to obtain a rationale for an attack on Iraq that on 10 separate occasions he asked the CIA to find evidence linking Iraq to 9/11; the CIA repeatedly came back empty-handed (*Time Magazine*, May 13, 2002).

In fact, 9/11 offered an extremely convenient pretext to put   15 the PNAC plan into action. The evidence again is quite clear that plans for military action against Afghanistan and Iraq were in hand well before 9/11. A report prepared for the U.S. government from the Baker Institute of Public Policy stated in April 2001 that "the U.S. remains a prisoner of its energy dilemma. Iraq remains a destabilising influence to . . . the flow of oil to international markets from the Middle East." Submitted to Vice-President Cheney's energy task group, the report recommended that because this was an unacceptable risk to the U.S., "military intervention" was necessary (*Sunday Herald*, October 6, 2002).

Similar evidence exists in regard to Afghanistan. The BBC reported (September 18, 2001) that Niaz Niak, a former Pakistan foreign secretary, was told by senior American officials at a meeting in Berlin in mid-July 2001 that "military action against Afghanistan would go ahead by the middle of October." Until July 2001 the U.S. government saw the Taliban regime as a source of stability in Central Asia that would enable the construction of hydrocarbon pipelines from the oil and gas fields in Turkmenistan, Uzbekistan, Kazakhstan, through Afghanistan and Pakistan, to the Indian Ocean. But, confronted with the Taliban's refusal to accept U.S. conditions, the U.S. representatives told them "either you accept our offer of a carpet of gold, or we bury you under a carpet of bombs" (Inter Press Service, November 15, 2001).

Given this background, it is not surprising that some have seen the U.S. failure to avert the 9/11 attacks as creating an invaluable pretext for attacking Afghanistan in a war that had clearly already been well planned in advance. There is a possible precedent for this. The U.S. national archives reveal that President Roosevelt used exactly this approach in relation to Pearl Harbor on December 7, 1941. Some advance warning of the attacks was received, but the information never reached the U.S. fleet. The ensuing national outrage persuaded a reluctant U.S. public to join the second world war. Similarly the PNAC blueprint of September 2000 states that the process of transforming the U.S. into "tomorrow's dominant force" is likely to be a long one in the absence of "some catastrophic and catalyzing event—like a new Pearl Harbor." The 9/11 attacks allowed the U.S. to press the "go" button for a strategy in accordance with the PNAC agenda which it would otherwise have been politically impossible to implement.

The overriding motivation for this political smokescreen is that the U.S. and the UK are beginning to run out of secure hydrocarbon energy supplies. By 2010 the Muslim world will control as much as 60% of the world's oil production and, even more importantly, 95% of remaining global oil export capacity. As demand is increasing, so supply is decreasing, continually since the 1960s.

This is leading to increasing dependence on foreign oil supplies for both the U.S. and the UK. The U.S., which in 1990 produced domestically 57% of its total energy demand, is predicted to produce only 39% of its needs by 2010. A DTI [Department of Trade and Industry] minister has admitted that the UK could be facing "severe" gas shortages by 2005. The UK government has confirmed that 70% of our electricity will come from gas by 2020, and 90% of that will be imported. In that context it should be noted that Iraq has 110 trillion cubic feet of gas reserves in addition to its oil.

20   A report from the commission on America's national interests in July 2000 noted that the most promising new source of world supplies was the Caspian region, and this would relieve U.S. dependence on Saudi Arabia. To diversify supply routes from the Caspian, one pipeline would run westward via Azerbaijan and Georgia to the Turkish port of Ceyhan. Another would extend eastwards through Afghanistan and Pakistan and terminate near the Indian border. This would rescue Enron's beleaguered power plant at Dabhol on India's west coast, in which Enron had sunk $3bn investment and whose economic survival was dependent on access to cheap gas.

Nor has the UK been disinterested in this scramble for the remaining world supplies of hydrocarbons, and this may partly explain British participation in U.S. military actions. Lord Browne, chief executive of BP, warned Washington not to carve up Iraq for its own oil companies in the aftermath of war (*Guardian*, October 30, 2002). And when a British foreign minister met Gadaffi in his desert tent in August 2002, it was said that "the UK does not want to lose out to other European nations already jostling for advantage when it comes to potentially lucrative oil contracts" with Libya (BBC Online, August 10, 2002).

The conclusion of all this analysis must surely be that the "global war on terrorism" has the hallmarks of a political myth propagated to pave the way for a wholly different agenda—the U.S. goal of world hegemony, built around securing by force command over the oil supplies required to drive the whole project. Is collusion in this myth and junior participation in this project really a proper aspiration for British foreign policy? If there was ever need to justify a more objective British stance, driven by our own independent goals, this whole depressing saga surely provides all the evidence needed for a radical change of course.

Starting Points

1. Michael Meacher alleges that "Rebuilding America's Defenses," a document out of the Project for the New American Century (PNAC), outlines a plan for military control of the oil regions of the Mideast prior to September 11th. Locate the document and decide whether you credit Meacher's thesis.
2. Analyze the points Meacher stresses here, rating them on a scale of absolute credibility to fantastic conspiracy theory. Consider using outside sources on which to base your conclusions.
3. Research the sources (*Time, Newsweek*, ABC News, *Daily Telegraph*, for example) that Meacher cites in this article and see if you reach similar conclusions, or if it is possible to read the same information and arrive at completely different conclusions.

Bin Ladin Determined to Strike in U.S.

Much discussion of the events of September 11th has centered on whether intelligence agencies had information about planned al-Qaida strikes in the United States, and whether President George W. Bush had been warned about such plans. Congressional hearings on 9/11 focused on a Presidential Daily Briefing (PDB) of August 6, 2001. The White House declassified and released that briefing, included here, on April 10, 2004.

———————— ✦ ————————

Clandestine, foreign government, and media reports indicate Bin Ladin since 1997 has wanted to conduct terrorist attacks in the U.S. Bin Ladin implied in U.S. television interviews in 1997 and 1998 that his followers would follow the example of World Trade Center bomber Ramzi Yousef and "bring the fighting to America."

After U.S. missile strikes on his base in Afghanistan in 1998, Bin Ladin told followers he wanted to retaliate in Washington, according to a [redacted portion] service.

An Egyptian Islamic Jihad (EIJ) operative told an [redacted portion] service at the same time that Bin Ladin was planning to exploit the operative's access to the U.S. to mount a terrorist strike.

The millennium plotting in Canada in 1999 may have been part of Bin Ladin's first serious attempt to implement a terrorist strike in the U.S. Convicted plotter Ahmed Ressam has told the FBI that he conceived the idea to attack Los Angeles International Airport himself, but that Bin Ladin lieutenant Abu Zubaydah encouraged him and helped facilitate the operation. Ressam also said that in 1998 Abu Zubaydah was planning his own U.S. attack.

5   Ressam says Bin Ladin was aware of the Los Angeles operation.

Although Bin Ladin has not succeeded, his attacks against the U.S. Embassies in Kenya and Tanzania in 1998 demonstrate that he prepares operations years in advance and is not deterred by setbacks. Bin Ladin associates surveilled our Embassies in Nairobi and Dar es Salaam as early as 1993, and some members of the Nairobi cell planning the bombings were arrested and deported in 1997.

Al-Qa'ida members—including some who are U.S. citizens—have resided in or traveled to the U.S. for years, and the group apparently maintains a support structure that could aid attacks. Two al-Qa'ida members found guilty in the conspiracy to bomb our Embassies in East Africa were U.S. citizens, and a senior EIJ member lived in California in the mid-1990s.

A clandestine source said in 1998 that a Bin Ladin cell in New York was recruiting Muslim-American youth for attacks.

We have not been able to corroborate some of the more sensational threat reporting, such as that from a [redacted portion] service in 1998 saying that Bin Ladin wanted to hijack a U.S. aircraft to gain the release of "Blind Shaykh" 'Umar' Abd al-Rahman and other U.S.-held extremists.

10   Nevertheless, FBI information since that time indicates patterns of suspicious activity in this country consistent with preparations for hijackings or other types of attacks, including recent surveillance of federal buildings in New York.

The FBI is conducting approximately 70 full field investigations throughout the U.S. that it considers Bin Ladin-related. CIA and the FBI are investigating a call to our Embassy in the UAE in

May saying that a group of Bin Ladin supporters was in the U.S. planning attacks with explosives.

Starting Points

1. What conclusions might be drawn from the briefing? Is it evident that a 9/11-style attack was imminent?
2. What limitations if any should be placed on public access to intelligence reports and briefings?
3. Was the attack on the World Trade Center and Pentagon a failure to act on intelligence or were such reports too vague for a response?

United Nations Security Council Resolution 1377

Adopted by the Security Council at its 4413th meeting, on 12 November 2001

The United Nations has adopted numerous resolutions regarding global terrorism before and after the September 11th attacks on America. In a resolution adopted by the Security Council two months after those attacks, international terrorism is called "one of the most serious to international peace and security in the twenty-first century." In addition to reaffirming an earlier resolution (1373), it underscores the necessity for member nations to deny financial support and safe haven for terrorists and those supporting them.

———————— ✦ ————————

The Security Council,

Decides to adopt the attached declaration on the global effort to combat terrorism.

2
S/RES/1377 (2001)
Annex

The Security Council,

Meeting at the Ministerial level,

Recalling its resolutions 1269 (1999) of 19 October 1999, 1368 (2001) of 12 September 2001 and 1373 (2001) of 28 September 2001,   5

Declares that acts of international terrorism constitute one of the most serious threats to international peace and security in the twenty-first century,

Further declares that acts of international terrorism constitute a challenge to all States and to all of humanity,

Reaffirms its unequivocal condemnation of all acts, methods and practices of terrorism as criminal and unjustifiable, regardless of their motivation, in all their forms and manifestations, wherever and by whomever committed,

Stresses that acts of international terrorism are contrary to the purposes and principles of the Charter of the United Nations, and that the financing, planning and preparation of as well as any other form of support for acts of international terrorism are similarly contrary to the purposes and principles of the Charter of the United Nations,

10   *Underlines* that acts of terrorism endanger innocent lives and the dignity and security of human beings everywhere, threaten the social and economic development of all States and undermine global stability and prosperity,

Affirms that a sustained, comprehensive approach involving the active participation and collaboration of all Member States of the United Nations, and in accordance with the Charter of the United Nations and international law, is essential to combat the scourge of international terrorism,

Stresses that continuing international efforts to broaden the understanding among civilizations and to address regional conflicts and the full range of global issues, including development issues, will contribute to international cooperation and collaboration, which themselves are necessary to sustain the broadest possible fight against international terrorism,

Welcomes the commitment expressed by States to fight the scourge of international terrorism, including during the General Assembly plenary debate from 1 to 5 October 2001, *calls on* all States to become parties as soon as possible to the relevant international conventions and protocols relating to terrorism, and encourages Member States to take forward work in this area,

Calls on all States to take urgent steps to implement fully resolution 1373 (2001), and to assist each other in doing so, and *underlines* the obligation on States to deny financial and all other forms of support and safe haven to terrorists and those supporting terrorism,

15   *Expresses* its determination to proceed with the implementation of that resolution in full cooperation with the whole membership of the United Nations, and *welcomes* the progress made

so far by the Counter-Terrorism Committee established by paragraph 6 of resolution 1373 (2001) to monitor implementation of that resolution,

3
S/RES/1377 (2001)

Recognizes that many States will require assistance in implementing all the requirements of resolution 1373 (2001), and *invites* States to inform the Counter-Terrorism Committee of areas in which they require such support,

   In that context, invites the Counter-Terrorism Committee to explore ways in which States can be assisted, and in particular to explore with international, regional and subregional organizations:

- the promotion of best-practice in the areas covered by resolution 1373 (2001), including the preparation of model laws as appropriate,
- the availability of existing technical, financial, regulatory, legislative or other assistance programmes which might facilitate the implementation of resolution 1373 (2001),
- the promotion of possible synergies between these assistance programmes,

   Calls on all States to intensify their efforts to eliminate the scourge of international terrorism.

Starting Points

1. Find other UN resolutions regarding the fight against international terrorism and determine whether they are consistent and specific. What steps do they spell out to end terrorism? Would these steps be effective?
2. If the war on terrorism is international, how much should any nation rely on the aid of other states in the fight? Is it possible to fight such a war alone? Would reliance on an international body result in gridlock, with no results?
3. After further reading on terrorism, what is your conclusion about the most effective means to prevent terrorism?

Other Journeys: Suggestions for Further Writing and Research

1. Hours of discussion, an avalanche of speeches, and a flood of government documents since September 11, 2001, have all centered on the

term "war." What is war, and how has it been defined in the past? Is there a legal definition? An agreed-upon international definition? Has the definition changed since 9/11? Who, in our system, has the power to declare war?

2. How many times since 1776 have American troops been placed in harm's way? How many of those were outside the borders of the United States? Research the number of times Congress declared war. What were the other occasions considered? What is the difference between a war and a "police action?" How is the present War on Terror similar to other wars? How is it different?

3. Interview a veteran of a previous war. Avoid questions such as "did you kill anyone?" and instead consider questions that center on whether the veteran viewed the war as a worthwhile cause or not, his or her relationship to other troops, his or her treatment overseas and when he or she returned home, and how combat changed his or her life. Include traumatic events such as killing or losing friends only if the veteran brings them up. If the veteran interviewed is a family member, remember that you are writing family history that future generations will read.

4. Try to recall your own response to the attacks on September 11th. What did you think? What were your remarks in conversations? Are your thoughts on the War on Terror any different now than they were then?

5. The current global terrorists have been characterized by some as "Islamic extremists." Is this accurate or a profanation of a religion? Interview an Islamic cleric or scholar, or invite one to address your class. Is the world in danger of a new century of religious wars? Does Islam encourage violence? Is a jihad a call to war? (See Abdulaziz Sachedina's article in Chapter 5.)

6. What is a "terrorist"? Does the term merely camouflage and demonize someone who has been marginalized and oppressed, or does it accurately reflect the course of action of an individual or organization? Israel refers to Palestinian fighters as terrorists, but how do Palestinians view them?

7. During World War II, American sailors faced suicide bombers in the form of kamikaze ("Divine Wind") pilots. Such willingness to die is alien to American and most Western thought. Why are so many so willing, perhaps even eager, to give their lives in the current campaign?

8. Find and study magazines and newspapers from other countries that focus on the War on Terror or the war in Iraq. If there is a difference between American coverage and coverage abroad, analyze the arguments presented. From the perspective of writers living elsewhere, does the war seem necessary? Winnable? Counterproductive?

Pre-emptive War

The issue of pre-emptive war—that is, a first-strike military force in Iraq to prevent the use of presumed weapons of mass destruction (WMD)—has proven to be a major issue in the war on terror since September 11, 2001. As it turned out, of course, no WMD were found, and the issue became a major embarrassment for the U.S. government. The focus shifted to regime change, and the need to bring freedom to the oppressed Iraqi people.

This chapter seeks to disengage from the debate over this specific war and to focus instead on the philosophy and policy of pre-emption. Long before the invasion, when President George M Bush and his team of advisors began to articulate their argument for not waiting until WMD had been deployed to act, there was considerable discussion over the wisdom of such a plan and the possible consequences, as well as the legality and morality of attacking first. Both sides have presented some compelling arguments in favor of or opposed to a pre-emptive war—that is, after all, why it is an issue.

The United States had never before in its history struck the first blow in a war, according to the Congressional Research Service, a government entity. Such an attack was likened by some to Pearl Harbor—with us cast in the role of torpedo bombers coming in low on an early Sunday morning. But did the violence of 9/11 and the willingness of some to use any potential weapons they could garner mean that a whole new paradigm was now a necessity? The argument for pre-emption was this: It makes no sense, indeed is highest folly, in an age of horrendously destructive weapons to wait until we are attacked again. Prudence and survival in the modern age dictate that a policy that "favors freedom" should be adopted, and that policy should include a first-strike proviso.

The arguments against pre-emptive war were based on ethical, moral, legal, and historical paradigms. If the United States launches a first strike against Iraq, then any nation will feel released from all obligations and consider attacking its neighbors on any pretense, went one argument. The United States would no longer have the moral authority to broker peace anywhere on the planet. International law prohibits such strikes, and to flout the law would result in international anarchy. The opponents of pre-emption were vociferous in their opposition.

Much debate still centers on concepts of "just war," a theory first articulated by St. Augustine in the Fifth century, and later adapted by St. Thomas Aquinas. Included in this chapter is an explanation of the theory by a Catholic clergyman. The theory has informed western concepts of war for nearly 1,600 years, and an understanding of it is necessary to understanding the debate. It is not intended to produce a theological skirmish, but it might be useful to read it in conjunction with the explanation of jihad as explained by Abdulaziz Sachedina, an Islamic scholar, in Chapter 5.

Perhaps only history will reveal the answers in this debate over pre-emption, just war, and jihad, a debate that promises to continue for years. Until the final verdict is in, study the issues embedded within the topics and make your own conclusions.

A Balance of Power That Favors Freedom

CONDOLEEZZA RICE

Condoleezza Rice, national security advisor to President George W. Bush, outlines the rationale and the policy implications for pre-emptive strikes against terrorists and terrorist regimes. The text here is adapted from the 2002 Wriston Lecture, delivered to the Manhattan Institute in New York City on October 1, 2002, before the start of the war in Iraq.

◆

The fall of the Berlin Wall and the fall of the World Trade Center were the bookends of a long transition period. During that period those of us who think about foreign policy for a living searched for an overarching, explanatory theory or framework that would describe the new threats and the proper response to them. Some said that nations and their militaries were no longer relevant, only global markets knitted together by new technologies. Others foresaw a future dominated by ethnic conflict. And some even thought that in the future the primary energies of America's armed forces would be devoted to managing civil conflict and humanitarian assistance.

It will take years to understand the long-term effects of September 11th [2001]. But there are certain verities that the tragedy brought home to us in the most vivid way.

Perhaps most fundamentally, 9/11 crystallized our vulnerability. It also threw into sharp relief the nature of the threats we face today. Today's threats come less from massing armies than from small, shadowy bands of terrorists—less from strong states than from weak or failed states. And after 9/11, there is no longer any doubt that today America faces an existential threat to our security—a threat as great as any we faced during the Civil War, the so-called "Good War," or the Cold War.

President Bush's new National Security Strategy offers a bold vision for protecting our nation that captures today's new realities and new opportunities.

It calls on America to use our position of unparalleled strength and influence to create a balance of power that favors freedom. As the president says in the cover letter: we seek to create the "conditions in which all nations and all societies can choose for themselves the rewards and challenges of political and economic liberty."

This strategy has three pillars:

- We will defend the peace by opposing and preventing violence by terrorists and outlaw regimes.
- We will preserve the peace by fostering an era of good relations among the world's great powers.
- And we will extend the peace by seeking to extend the benefits of freedom and prosperity across the globe.

Defending our nation from its enemies is the first and fundamental commitment of the federal government. And the United States has a special responsibility to help make the world more secure.

In fighting global terror, we will work with coalition partners on every continent, using every tool in our arsenal—from diplomacy and better defenses to law enforcement, intelligence, cutting off terrorist financing, and, if needed, military power.

We will break up terror networks, hold to account nations that harbor terrorists, and confront aggressive tyrants holding or seeking nuclear, chemical, and biological weapons that might be passed to terrorist allies. These are different faces of the same evil. Terrorists need a place to plot, train, and organize. Tyrants allied with terrorists can greatly extend the reach of their deadly mischief. Terrorists allied with tyrants can acquire technologies allowing them to murder on an ever more massive scale. Each threat magnifies the danger of the other. And the only path to safety is to effectively confront both terrorists and tyrants.

10   For these reasons, President Bush is committed to confronting the Iraqi regime, which has defied the just demands of the world for over a decade. We are on notice. The danger from Saddam Hussein's arsenal is far more clear than anything we could have foreseen prior to September 11th. And history will judge harshly any leader or nation that saw this dark cloud and sat by in complacency or indecision.

The Iraqi regime's violation of every condition set forth by the U.N. Security Council for the 1991 cease-fire fully justifies—legally and morally—the enforcement of those conditions.

It is also true that since 9/11, our nation is properly focused as never before on preventing attacks against us before they happen.

The National Security Strategy does not overturn five decades of doctrine and jettison either containment or deterrence. These strategic concepts can and will continue to be employed where appropriate. But some threats are so potentially catastrophic—and can arrive with so little warning, by means that are untraceable—that they cannot be contained. Extremists who seem to view suicide as a sacrament are unlikely to ever be deterred. And new technology requires new thinking about when a threat actually becomes "imminent." So as a matter of common sense, the United States must be prepared to take action, when necessary, before threats have fully materialized.

Preemption is not a new concept. There has never been a moral or legal requirement that a country wait to be attacked before it can address existential threats. As George Shultz recently wrote, "If there is a rattlesnake in the yard, you don't wait for it to strike before you take action in self-defense." The United States has long affirmed the right to anticipatory self-defense—from the Cuban Missile Crisis in 1962 to the crisis on the Korean peninsula in 1994.

But this approach must be treated with great caution. The 15
number of cases in which it might be justified will always be
small. It does not give a green light—to the United States or any
other nation—to act first without exhausting other means, including diplomacy. Preemptive action does not come at the beginning of a long chain of effort. The threat must be very grave. And
the risks of waiting must far outweigh the risks of action.

To support all these means of defending the peace, the United
States will build and maintain 21st century military forces that
are beyond challenge.

We will seek to dissuade any potential adversary from pursuing a military build-up in the hope of surpassing, or equaling, the
power of the United States and our allies. Some have criticized
this frankness as impolitic. But surely clarity is a virtue here. Dis-
suading military competition can prevent potential conflict and
costly global arms races. And the United States invites—indeed,
we exhort—our freedom loving allies, such as those in Europe, to
increase their military capabilities.

The burden of maintaining a balance of power that favors
freedom should be shouldered by all nations that favor freedom.
What none of us should want is the emergence of a militarily
powerful adversary who does not share our common values.

Thankfully, this possibility seems more remote today than at
any point in our lifetimes. We have an historic opportunity to
break the destructive pattern of great power rivalry that has be-
deviled the world since the rise of the nation-state in the 17th century. Today, the world's great centers of power are united by common interests, common dangers, and—increasingly—common
values. The United States will make this a key strategy for preserving the peace for many decades to come.

There is an old argument between the so-called "realistic" 20
school of foreign affairs and the "idealistic" school. To oversim-
plify, realists downplay the importance of values and the internal
structures of states, emphasizing instead the balance of power as
the key to stability and peace. Idealists emphasize the primacy of
values, such as freedom and democracy and human rights in ensuring that just political order is obtained. As a professor, I recognize that this debate has won tenure for and sustained the careers
of many generations of scholars. As a policymaker, I can tell you
that these categories obscure reality.

In real life, power and values are married completely. Power
matters in the conduct of world affairs. Great powers matter a
great deal—they have the ability to influence the lives of millions

and change history. And the values of great powers matter as well. If the Soviet Union had won the Cold War, the world would look very different today—Germany today might look like the old German Democratic Republic, or Latin America like Cuba.

Today, there is an increasing awareness—on every continent—of a paradigm of progress, founded on political and economic liberty. The United States, our NATO allies, our neighbors in the Western Hemisphere, Japan, and our other friends and allies in Asia and Africa all share a broad commitment to democracy, the rule of law, a market-based economy, and open trade.

In addition, since September 11th all the world's great powers see themselves as falling on the same side of a profound divide between the forces of chaos and order, and they are acting accordingly.

America and Europe have long shared a commitment to liberty. We also now understand that being the target of trained killers is a powerful tonic that makes disputes over other important issues look like the policy differences they are, instead of fundamental clashes of values.

25   The United States is also cooperating with India across a range of issues—even as we work closely with Pakistan.

Russia is an important partner in the war on terror and is reaching toward a future of greater democracy and economic freedom. As it does so, our relationship will continue to broaden and deepen. The passing of the ABM [1972 Anti-Ballistic Missile] Treaty and the signing of the Moscow Treaty reducing strategic arms by two-thirds make clear that the days of Russian military confrontation with the West are over.

China and the United States are cooperating on issues ranging from the fight against terror to maintaining stability on the Korean peninsula. And China's transition continues. Admittedly, in some areas, its leaders still follow practices that are abhorrent. Yet China's leaders have said that their main goal is to raise living standards for the Chinese people. They will find that reaching that goal in today's world will depend more on developing China's human capital than it will on China's natural resources or territorial possessions. And as China's populace become more educated, more free to think, and more entrepreneurial, we believe this will inevitably lead to greater political freedom. You cannot expect people to think on the job, but not at home.

This confluence of common interests and increasingly common values creates a moment of enormous opportunities. Instead of repeating the historic pattern where great power rivalry exacerbates local conflicts, we can use great power cooperation to solve conflicts, from the Middle East to Kashmir, Congo, and beyond. Great power cooperation also creates an opportunity for multilateral institutions—such as the U.N., NATO, and the WTO [World Trade Organization]—to prove their worth. That's the challenge set forth by the president to the U.N. concerning Iraq. And great power cooperation can be the basis for moving forward on problems that require multilateral solutions—from terror to the environment.

To build a balance of power that favors freedom, we must also extend the peace by extending the benefits of liberty and prosperity as broadly as possible. As the president has said, we have a responsibility to build a world that is not only safer, but better. The United States will fight poverty, disease, and oppression because it is the right thing to do—and the smart thing to do. We have seen how poor states can become weak or even failed states, vulnerable to hijacking by terrorist networks—with potentially catastrophic consequences. And in societies where legal avenues for political dissent are stifled, the temptation to speak through violence grows.

We will lead efforts to build a global trading system that is   30 growing and more free. Here in our own hemisphere, for example, we are committed to completing a Free Trade Area of the Americas by 2005. We are also starting negotiations on a free trade agreement with the Southern African Customs Union. Expanding trade is essential to the development efforts of poor nations and to the economic health of all nations.

We will continue to lead the world in efforts to combat HIV/AIDS—a pandemic which challenges our humanity and threatens whole societies.

We will seek to bring every nation into an expanding circle of development. Earlier this year the president proposed a 50 percent increase in U.S. development assistance. But he also made clear that new money means new terms. The new resources will only be available to countries that work to govern justly, invest in the health and education of their people, and encourage economic liberty.

We know from experience that corruption, bad policies, and bad practices can make aid money worse than useless. In such environments, aid props up bad policy, chasing out investment and perpetuating misery. Good policy, on the other hand, attracts private capital and expands trade. In a sound policy environment, development aid is a catalyst, not a crutch.

At the core of America's foreign policy is our resolve to stand on the side of men and women in every nation who stand for what the president has called the "non-negotiable demands of human dignity"—free speech, equal justice, respect for women, religious tolerance, and limits on the power of the state.

35   These principles are universal—and President Bush has made them part of the debate in regions where many thought that merely to raise them was imprudent or impossible. From Cairo and Ramallah to Tehran and Tashkent, the president has made clear that values must be a vital part of our relationships with other countries. In our development aid, our diplomacy, our international broadcasting, and in our educational assistance, the United States will promote moderation, tolerance, and human rights. And we look forward to one day standing for these aspirations in a free and unified Iraq.

We reject the condescending view that freedom will not grow in the soil of the Middle East—or that Muslims somehow do not share in the desire to be free. The celebrations we saw on the streets of Kabul last year proved otherwise. And in a recent U.N. report, a panel of 30 Arab intellectuals recognized that for their nations to fully join in the progress of our times will require greater political and economic freedom, the empowerment of women, and better, more modern education.

We do not seek to impose democracy on others, we seek only to help create conditions in which people can claim a freer future for themselves. We recognize as well that there is no "one size fits all" answer. Our vision of the future is not one where every person eats Big Macs and drinks Coke—or where every nation has a bicameral legislature with 535 members and a judiciary that follows the principles of Marbury vs. Madison.

Germany, Indonesia, Japan, the Philippines, South Africa, South Korea, Taiwan, and Turkey show that freedom manifests itself differently around the globe—and that new liberties can find an honored place amidst ancient traditions. In countries such as Bahrain, Jordan, Morocco, and Qatar, reform is underway, taking shape according to different local circumstances. And in Afghanistan this year, a traditional Loya Jirga assembly was the vehicle for creating the most broadly representative government in Afghan history. Because of our own history, the United States knows we must be patient—and humble. Change—even if it is for the better—is often difficult. And progress is sometimes slow. America has not always lived up to our own high standards. When the Founding Fathers said, "We, the people," they didn't mean me. Democracy is hard work. And 226 years later, we are still practicing each day to get it right.

We have the ability to forge a 21st century that lives up to our hopes and not down to our fears. But only if we go about our work with purpose and clarity. Only if we are unwavering in our refusal to live in a world governed by terror and chaos. Only if we are unwilling to ignore growing dangers from aggressive tyrants and deadly technologies. And only if we are persistent and patient in exercising our influence in the service of our ideals, and not just ourselves.

Starting Points

1. How effective is Condoleezza Rice's argument? Have events in Iraq bolstered her thesis, or contradicted it in some way?
2. Rice specifically mentions Saddam Hussein's arsenal as being particularly dangerous to the United States. Does the failure to find weapons of mass destruction in Iraq in any way negate her view, or was the intelligence information on which the assessment was based enough to mitigate her stance?
3. Some might question the phrase "balance of power." Should American foreign policy and the War on Terror be based on power or on a balance of opportunity?

Perils of Preemptive War
Why America's Place in the World Will Shift—for the Worse—If We Attack Iraq
WILLIAM GALSTON

Writing in The American Prospect, *William Galston takes issue with the concept of pre-emptive war, arguing that America will become less safe and would lose moral authority in the world. This article is from September 23, 2002, before the start of the war in Iraq.*

◆

On June 1 at West Point, President George W. Bush set forth a new doctrine for U.S. security policy. The successful strategies of the Cold War era, he declared, are ill suited to national defense in the 21st century. Deterrence means nothing against terrorist networks; containment will not thwart unbalanced dictators possessing weapons of mass destruction. We cannot afford to wait until we are attacked. In today's circumstances, Americans must be ready to take "preemptive action" to defend our lives and liberties.

On Aug. 26, Vice President Dick Cheney forcefully applied this new doctrine to Iraq. Saddam Hussein, he stated, is bolstering the country's chemical and biological capabilities and is aggressively pursuing nuclear weapons. "What we must not do in the face of a mortal threat," he declared, "is to give in to wishful thinking or willful blindness. . . . Deliverable weapons of mass destrction in the hands of a terror network or murderous dictator or the two working together constitutes as grave a threat as can be imagined. The risks of inaction are far greater than the risks of action."

After an ominous silence lasting much of the summer, a debate about U.S. policy toward Iraq has finally begun. Remarkably, Democratic elected officials are not party to it. Some agree with Bush administration hawks; others have been intimidated into acquiescence or silence. The Senate Foreign Relations Committee hearings yielded questions rather than answers and failed to prod Democratic leaders into declaring their position. Meanwhile, Democratic political consultants are advising their clients to avoid foreign policy and to wage their campaigns on the more hospitable turf of corporate fraud and prescription drugs. The memory of the Gulf War a decade ago, when the vast majority of Democrats ended up on the wrong side of the debate, deters many from re-entering the fray today.

The Democratic Party's abdication has left the field to Republican combatants—unilateralists versus multilateralists, ideologues versus "realists." The resulting debate has been intense but narrow, focused primarily on issues of prudence rather than principle.

5   This is not to suggest that the prudential issues are unimportant, or that the intra-Republican discord has been less than illuminating. Glib analogies between Iraq and Afghanistan and cocky talk about a military cakewalk have given way to more sober assessments. President Bush's oft-repeated goal of "regime change" would likely require 150,000 to 200,000 U.S. troops, allies in the region willing to allow us to pre-position and supply those forces and bloody street battles in downtown Baghdad. With little left to lose, Saddam Hussein might carry out a "Samson scenario" by equipping his Scud missiles with chemical or biological agents and firing them at Tel Aviv. Senior Israeli military and intelligence officials doubt that Israeli Prime Minister Ariel Sharon would de-

fer to U.S. calls for restraint, as Yitzhak Shamir's government did during the Gulf War. Israeli retaliation could spark a wider regional conflagration.

Assume that we can surmount these difficulties. The Bush administration's goal of regime change is the equivalent of our World War II aim of unconditional surrender, and it would have similar postwar consequences. We would assume total responsibility for Iraq's territorial integrity, for the security and basic needs of its population, and for the reconstruction of its system of governance and political culture. This would require an occupation measured in years or even decades. Whatever our intentions, nations in the region (and elsewhere) would view our continuing presence through the historical prism of colonialism. *The Economist*, which favors a U.S. invasion of Iraq, nonetheless speaks of the "imperial flavour" of such a potential occupation.

But the risks would not end there. The Bush administration and its supporters argue that the overthrow of Saddam Hussein would shift the political balance in our favor throughout the Middle East (including among the Palestinians). Henry Kissinger is not alone in arguing that the road to solving the Israeli-Palestinian conflict leads through Baghdad, not the other way around. More broadly, say the optimists, governments in the region would see that opposing the United States carries serious risk, and that there is more to be gained from cooperating with us. Rather than rising up in injured pride, the Arab "street" would respect our resolve and move toward moderation, as would Arab leaders.

Perhaps so. But it does not take much imagination to conjure a darker picture, and the performance of our intelligence services in the region does not inspire confidence in the factual basis of the optimists' views. If a wave of public anger helped Islamic radicals unseat Pakistan's General Pervez Musharraf, for example, we would have exchanged a dangerous regime seeking nuclear weapons for an even more dangerous regime that possesses them.

All this, and I have not yet mentioned potential economic and diplomatic consequences. Even a relatively short war would likely produce an oil-price spike that could tip the fragile global economy into recession. Moreover, unlike the Gulf War, which the Japanese and Saudis largely financed, the United States would have to go it alone this time, with an estimated price tag of $60 billion for the war and $15 billion to $20 billion per year for the occupation.

Our closest allies have spoken out against an invasion of Iraq. 10
Gerhard Schröder, leading a usually complaisant Germany but

locked in a tough re-election fight, has gone so far as to label this possibility an "adventure," sparking a protest from our ambassador. Some Bush administration officials seem not to believe that our allies' views matter all that much. Others argue, more temperately, that the Europeans and other protesters will swallow their reservations after the fact, when they can see the military success of our action and its positive consequences. They may be right. But it is at least as likely that this disagreement will widen the already sizeable gap between European and American worldviews. Generations of young people could grow up resenting and resisting America, as they did after the Vietnam War. Whether or not these trends in the long run undermine our alliances, they could have a range of negative short-term consequences, including diminished intelligence sharing and cooperation.

Republicans have at least raised these prudential issues. For the most part, however, they have ignored broader questions of principle. But these questions cannot be evaded. An invasion of Iraq would be one of the most fateful deployments of American power since World War II. A global strategy based on the new Bush doctrine of preemption means the end of the system of international institutions, laws and norms that we have worked to build for more than half a century. To his credit, Kissinger recognizes this; he labels Bush's new approach "revolutionary" and declares, "Regime change as a goal for military intervention challenges the international system." The question is whether this revolution in international doctrine is justified and wise.

I think not. What is at stake is nothing less than a fundamental shift in America's place in the world. Rather than continuing to serve as first among equals in the postwar international system, the United States would act as a law unto itself, creating new rules of international engagement without the consent of other nations. In my judgment, this new stance would ill serve the long-term interests of the United States.

There is a reason why President Bush could build on the world's sympathy in framing the U.S. response to al-Qaeda after September 11, and why his father was able to sustain such a broad coalition to reverse Saddam Hussein's invasion of Kuwait. In those cases our policy fit squarely within established doctrines of self-defense. By contrast, if we seek to overthrow Saddam Hussein, we will act outside the framework of global security that we have helped create.

In the first place, we are a signatory to (indeed, the principal drafter of) the United Nations Charter, which explicitly reserves to sovereign nations "the inherent right of individual or collective self-defense," but only in the event of armed attack. Unless the administration establishes Iraqi complicity in the terrorism of 9-11, it cannot invoke self-defense, as defined by the charter, as the justification for attacking Iraq. And if evidence of Iraqi involvement exists, the administration has a responsibility to present it to Congress, the American people and the world, much as John F. Kennedy and Adlai Stevenson did to justify the U.S. naval blockade of Cuba during the 1962 missile crisis.

The broader structure of international law creates additional 15 obstacles to an invasion of Iraq. To be sure, such law contains a doctrine of "anticipatory self-defense," and there is an ongoing argument concerning its scope. Daniel Webster, then secretary of state, offered the single most influential statement of the doctrine in 1837: There must be shown "a necessity of self-defense . . . instant, overwhelming, leaving no choice of means, and no moment for deliberation." Some contemporary scholars adopt a more permissive view. But even if that debate were resolved in the manner most favorable to the Bush administration, the concept of anticipatory self-defense would still be too narrow to support an attack on Iraq: The threat to the United States from Iraq is not sufficiently specific, clearly enough established or shown to be imminent.

The Bush doctrine of preemption goes well beyond the established bounds of anticipatory self-defense, as many supporters of the administration's Iraq policy privately concede. (They argue that the United States needs to make new law, using Iraq as a precedent.) If the administration wishes to argue that terrorism renders the imminence criterion obsolete, it must do what it has thus far failed to do—namely, to show that Iraq has both the capability of harming us and a serious intent to do so. The abstract logical possibility that Saddam Hussein could transfer weapons of mass destruction to stateless terrorists is not enough. If we cannot make our case, the world will see anticipatory self-defense as an international hunting license.

Finally, we can examine the proposed invasion of Iraq through the prism of just war theories developed by philosophers and theologians over a period of centuries. One of its most distinguished contemporary exponents, Michael Walzer, puts it this way: First strikes can occasionally be justified before the moment of imminent attack, if we have reached the point of "sufficient threat." This concept has three dimensions: "a manifest intent to injure, a degree of active preparation that makes that intent a positive danger, and a general situation in which waiting, or doing anything other than fighting, greatly magnifies the risk." The potential injury, moreover, must be of the gravest possible nature: the loss of territorial integrity or political independence.

Saddam Hussein may well endanger the survival of his neighbors, but he poses no such risk to the United States. And he knows full well that complicity in a 9-11–style terrorist attack on the United States would justify, and swiftly evoke, a regime-ending response. During the Gulf War, we invoked this threat to deter him from using weapons of mass destruction against our troops, and there is no reason to believe that this strategy would be less effective today. Dictators have much more to lose than do stateless terrorists; that's why deterrence directed against them has a good chance of working.

In its segue from al-Qaeda to Saddam Hussein, and from defense to preemption, the Bush administration has shifted its focus from stateless foes to state-based adversaries, and from terrorism in the precise sense to the possession of weapons of mass destruction. Each constitutes a threat. But they are not the same threat and do not warrant the same response. It serves no useful purpose to pretend that they are seamlessly connected, let alone one and the same.

20 The United Nations, international law, just-war theory—it is not hard to imagine the impatience with which policy makers will greet arguments made on these bases. The first duty of every government, they will say, is to defend the lives and security of its citizens. The elimination of Saddam Hussein and, by extension, every regime that threatens to share weapons of mass destruction with anti-American terrorists, comports with this duty. To invoke international norms designed for a different world is to blind ourselves to the harsh necessities of international action in this new era of terrorism. Now that we have faced the facts about the axis of evil, it would be a dereliction of duty to shrink from their consequences for policy. Even if no other nation agrees, we have a duty to the American people to go it alone. The end justifies—indeed requires—the means.

These are powerful claims, not easily dismissed. But even if an invasion of Iraq succeeds in removing a threat here and now, it is not clear whether a policy of preemption would make us safer in the long run. Specifically, we must ask how the new norms of international action we employ would play out as nations around the world adopt them and shape them to their own purposes. (And they *will;* witness the instant appropriation of the United States' antiterrorism rhetoric by Russia and India, among others.) It is an illusion to believe that the United States can employ new norms of action while denying the rights of others to do so as well.

Also at stake are competing understandings of the international system and of our role within it. Some administration officials appear to believe that alliances and treaties are in the main counterproductive, constraining us from most effectively pursuing our national interest. Because the United States enjoys unprecedented military, economic and technological preeminence, we can do best by going it alone. The response to these unilateralists is that that there are many goals that we cannot hope to achieve without the cooperation of others. To pretend otherwise is to exchange short-term gains for long-term risks.

Even after we acknowledge the important distinctions between domestic and international politics, the fact remains: No push for international cooperation can succeed without international law and, therefore, without treaties that build the institutions for administering that law. This is one more reason, if one were needed, why the United States must resist the temptation to set itself apart from the system of international law. It will serve us poorly in the long run if we offer public justifications for an invasion of Iraq that we cannot square with established international legal norms.

We are the most powerful nation on earth, but we must remember we are not invulnerable. To safeguard our own security, we need the assistance of the allies whose doubts we scorn, and the protection of the international restraints against which we chafe. We must therefore resist the easy seduction of unilateral action. In the long run, our interests will best be served by an international system that is as lawlike and collaborative as possible, given the reality that we live in a world of sovereign states.

Starting Points

1. William Galston discusses the doctrine of "anticipatory self-defense," which allows nations to strike first under certain prescribed conditions. Research this doctrine and determine whether you believe the war in Iraq met the requirements for such an action.

2. Read additional articles on pre-emptive war and argue for or against Galston's view that the war in Iraq did not warrant a first strike.

3. Will the pre-emptive war in Iraq make the world safer by creating democracy in that region, or will it open the door for any nation to justify a first strike based solely on intelligence reports?

U.S. Use of Preemptive Military Force: The Historical Record

Richard F. Grimmett

What is the record of the U.S. military in the use of pre-emptive force? Richard F. Grimmett, a national defense specialist in the foreign affairs, defense, and trade division of the U.S. Congressional Research Service, reviews the history of U.S. military actions that might be interpreted as pre-emption.

———————— ✦ ————————

BACKGROUND

In recent months the question of the possible use of "preemptive" military force by the United States to defend its security has been raised by President Bush and members of his administration, including possible use of such force against Iraq.[1] This analysis reviews the historical record regarding the uses of U.S. military force in a "preemptive" manner. It examines and comments on military actions taken by the United States that could be reasonably interpreted as "preemptive" in nature. For purposes of this analysis we consider a "preemptive" use of military force to be the taking of military action by the United States against another nation so as to prevent or mitigate a presumed military attack or use of force by that nation against the United States. The discussion below is based upon our review of all noteworthy uses of military force by the United States since establishment of the republic.

HISTORICAL OVERVIEW

The historical record indicates that the United States has never, to date, engaged in a "preemptive" military attack against another nation. Nor has the United States ever attacked another nation militarily prior to its first having been attacked or prior to U.S. citizens or interests first having been attacked, with the singular exception of the Spanish-American War. The Spanish-American War is unique in that the principal goal of United States military action was to compel Spain to grant Cuba its political independence. An act of Congress passed just prior to the U.S. declaration of war against Spain explicitly declared Cuba to be independent of Spain, demanded that Spain withdraw its military forces from the island, and authorized the president to use U.S. military force to achieve these ends.[2] Spain rejected these demands, and an exchange of declarations of war by both countries soon followed.[3] Various instances of the use of force are discussed below that could, using a less stringent definition, be argued by some as historic examples of preemption by the United States. The final case, the Cuban missile crisis of 1962, represents a threat situation which some may argue had elements more parallel to those presented by Iraq today—but it was resolved without a "preemptive" military attack by the United States.

The circumstances surrounding the origins of the Mexican War are somewhat controversial in nature—but the term "preemptive" attack by the United States does not apply to this conflict. During, and immediately following the First World War, the United States, as part of allied military operations, sent military forces into parts of Russia to protect its interests, and to render limited aid to anti-Bolshevik forces during the Russian civil war. In major military actions since the Second World War, the President has either obtained congressional authorization for use of military force against other nations, in advance of using it, or has directed military actions abroad on his own initiative in support of multinational operations such as those of the United Nations or of mutual security arrangements like the North Atlantic Treaty Organization (NATO). Examples of these actions include participation in the Korean War, the 1990–1991 Persian Gulf War, and the Bosnian and Kosovo operations in the 1990s. Yet in all of these varied instances of the use of military force by the United States, such military action was a "response," after the fact, and was not "preemptive" in nature.

CENTRAL AMERICAN AND CARIBBEAN INTERVENTIONS

This is not to say that the United States has not used its military to intervene in other nations in support of its foreign policy interests. However, U.S. military interventions, particularly a number of unilateral uses of force in the Central America and Caribbean areas throughout the 20th century, were not "preemptive" in nature. What led the United States to intervene militarily in nations in these areas was not the view that the individual nations were likely to attack the United States militarily. Rather, these U.S. military interventions were grounded in the view that they would support the Monroe Doctrine, which opposed interference in the Western hemisphere by outside nations. U.S. policy was driven by the belief that if stable governments existed in Caribbean states and Central America, then it was less likely that foreign countries would attempt to protect their nationals or their economic interests through their use of military force against one or more of these nations.

5   Consequently, the United States, in the early part of the 20th century, established through treaties with the Dominican Republic, in 1907,[4] and with Haiti, in 1915,[5] the right for the United States to collect and disperse customs income received by these nations, as well as the right to protect the receiver general of customs and his assistants in the performance of his duties. This effectively created U.S. protectorates for these countries until these arrangements were terminated during the administration of President Franklin D. Roosevelt. Intermittent domestic insurrections against the national governments in both countries led the U.S. to utilize American military forces to restore order in Haiti from 1915–1934 and in the Dominican Republic from 1916–1924. But the purpose of these interventions, buttressed by the treaties with the United States, was to help maintain or restore political stability, and thus eliminate the potential for foreign military intervention in contravention of the principles of the Monroe Doctrine.

Similar concerns about foreign intervention in a politically unstable Nicaragua led the United States in 1912 to accept the request of its then-President Adolfo Diaz to intervene militarily to restore political order there. Through the Bryan-Chamorro treaty with Nicaragua in 1914, the United States obtained the right to protect the Panama Canal, and its proprietary rights to any future canal through Nicaragua as well as islands leased from Nicaragua for use as military installations. This treaty also granted to the United States the right to take any measure needed to carry out the treaty's purposes.[6] This treaty had the effect of making Nicaragua a quasi-protectorate of the United States. Since political turmoil in the country might threaten the Panama Canal or U.S. proprietary rights to build another canal, the United States employed that rationale to justify the intervention and long-term presence of American military forces in Nicaragua to maintain political stability in the country. U.S. military forces were permanently withdrawn from Nicaragua in 1933. Apart from the above cases, U.S. military interventions in the Dominican Republic in 1965, Grenada in 1983, and in Panama in 1989 were based upon concerns that U.S. citizens or other U.S. interests were being harmed by the political instability in these countries at the time U.S. intervention occurred. While U.S. military interventions in

Central America and Caribbean nations were controversial, after reviewing the context in which they occurred, it is fair to say that none of them involved the use of "preemptive" military force by the United States.[7]

COVERT ACTION

Although the use of "preemptive" force by the United States is generally associated with the overt use of U.S. military forces, it is important to note that the United States has also utilized "covert action" by U.S. government personnel in efforts to influence political and military outcomes in other nations. The public record indicates that the United States has used this form of intervention to prevent some groups or political figures from gaining or maintaining political power to the detriment of U.S. interests and those of friendly nations. For example, the use of "covert action" was widely reported to have been successfully employed to effect changes in the governments of Iran in 1953, and in Guatemala in 1954. Its use failed in the case of Cuba in 1961. The general approach in the use of a "covert action" is reportedly to support local political and military/paramilitary forces in gaining or maintaining political control in a nation, so that U.S. or its allies' interests will not be threatened. None of these activities has reportedly involved significant numbers of U.S. military forces because, by their very nature, "covert actions" are efforts to advance an outcome without drawing direct attention to the United States in the process of doing so.[8] Such previous clandestine operations by U.S. personnel could arguably have constituted efforts at "preemptive" action to forestall unwanted political or military developments in other nations. But given their presumptive limited scale compared to those of major conventional military operations, it seems more appropriate to view U.S. "covert actions" as adjuncts to more extensive U.S. military actions. As such, prior U.S. "covert actions" do not appear to be true case examples of the use of "preemptive" military force by the United States.

CUBAN MISSILE CRISIS OF 1962

The one significant, well documented, case of note, where "preemptive" military action was seriously contemplated by the United States, but ultimately not used, was the Cuban missile crisis of October 1962. When the United States learned from spy-plane photographs that the Soviet Union was secretly introducing nuclear-capable, intermediate-range ballistic missiles into Cuba, missiles that could threaten a large portion of the Eastern United States, President John F. Kennedy had to determine if the prudent course of action was to use U.S. military air strikes in an effort to destroy the missile sites before they became operational, and before the Soviets or the Cubans became aware that the U.S. knew they were being installed. While the military "preemption" option was considered, after extensive debate among his advisors on the implications of such an action, President Kennedy undertook a measured but firm approach to the crisis that utilized a U.S. military "quarantine" of the island of Cuba to prevent further shipments from the Soviet Union of military supplies and material for the missile sites, while a diplomatic solution was aggressively pursued. This approach was successful, and the crisis was peacefully resolved.[9]

The opinions expressed in this article are those of the author and do not necessarily reflect the views or policies of the U.S. Government.

Endnotes

1. See speeches of President George W. Bush at West Point on June 1, 2002 at http://www.whitehouse.gov/news/releases/2002/06/20020601-3.html; and the President's United Nations speech of September 12, 2002, at http://www.whitehouse.gov/news/releases/2002/09/20020912-I.html; *Washington Post*, June 2, 2002, p. A1; *Washington Post*, September 13, 2002, p.Al.

2. Joint Resolution of April 20, 1898 [Res. 241 30 Stat. 738].

3. There was no direct military attack by Spain against the United States prior to the exchange of declarations of war by the nations, and initiation of hostilities by the United States in 1898. See "Declarations of War and Authorizations for the Use of Military Force: Background and Legal Implications," CRS Report RL31133, by David M. Ackerman and Richard F. Grimmett. A notable event, the sinking of the U.S.S. Maine in Havana harbor, provided an additional argument for war against Spain for those advocating it in the United States. The actual cause of the sinking of the U.S.S. Maine in Havana harbor, even today, has not been definitively established. More recent scholarship argues that it was most likely not due to an external attack on the ship, such as the use of a mine by an outside party, but due to an internal explosion.

4. 7 UST 196.

5. 8 UST 660.

6. 10 UST 379.

7. For an excellent background discussion of U.S. policy toward the Caribbean and Central American nations during the first half of the 20th century see: Samuel Flagg Bemis, *A Diplomatic History of the United States* (New York, Holt, Rinehart and Winston, Inc., 1965), pp. 519–538. For a detailed historical study that provides valuable insights and commentary on U.S. actions taken toward Caribbean and Central American countries see chapters 9, 11, and 12 in Samuel Flagg Bemis, *The Latin American Policy of the United States* (New York, Harcourt, Brace & World), 1943. (Reprinted in paperback, New York, by W. W. Norton & Company, Inc., 1967.)

8. Section 503(e) of the National Security Act of 1947, as amended, defines covert action as "An activity or activities of the United States Government to influence political, economic, or military conditions abroad, where it is intended that the role of the United States Government will not be apparent or acknowledged publicly."

9. For detailed background regarding the issues surrounding the possible use of "preemptive" military force against the Soviet missile sites being established in Cuba, and the deliberative process engaged in by President Kennedy and his key advisors, see the published transcripts of tape recordings made during their White House meetings in *The Kennedy Tapes: Inside the White House During the Cuban Missile Crisis*, Ernest R. May and Philip D. Zelikow (eds.) (Cambridge, Massachusetts, Harvard University Press, 1997).

Starting Points

1. According to the author, how does the Spanish-American War of 1898 differ from other military actions undertaken by the United States? Is it similar in any way to the war in Iraq?

2. Does this text, written by an analyst within the government, support or undermine the stated rationale for pre-emptive war? What is the tone of this piece? Is it partisan—that is, weighted to one side or another—or measured and neutral? Identify specific elements or parts of this that support your analysis.

3. Read the disclaimer at the end of the article. Why is it necessary? Is history fact or interpretation? Closely read the article again, and find words that might reveal the author's personal position on preemptive force. (This will be your conclusion, and may or may not actually represent the personal view of Richard Grimmett.)

Possible War with Iraq
WILLIAM P. SAUNDERS

The Augustinian concept of "just war"—a theory that has often been cited and often ignored—has been an operating principle of Western warfare since the 5th century. This theory has been called into question with the arrival of "stateless" warfare and access to powerful weapons of mass destruction. William Saunders, who holds a PhD., a Catholic clergyman, writing in The Arlington (Va.) Catholic Herald *on October 17, 2002, explains the Augustinian theory of just war. Saunders is pastor of Our Lady of Hope Catholic Church and Dean Emeritus and Professor of Catechetics and Theology at the Notre Dame Graduate School of Christendom College. After reading the piece that follows, it might be useful to also read the explanation of jihad by Abdulaziz Sachedina in Chapter 5 and the fatwa of Osama bin Laden in Chapter 1.*

───────────── ✦ ─────────────

I have a question about the possible war with Iraq. Several leaders of our Church have spoken out on this issue, including Cardinal Theodore McCarrick and Bishop Wilton Gregory. What would be the moral teaching of our Church concerning war?

A READER IN ALEXANDRIA

In His Sermon on the Mount, Our Lord taught, "Blessed are the peacemakers." Real peace must be built upon love, truth, justice and mercy. In fact, sacred Scripture teaches that God is love, truth, justice and mercy. As faithful disciples, Christians and members of the Catholic Church, we strive to base our lives on that love, truth, justice and mercy, as has been revealed by our Savior, Jesus Christ.

What opposes God and those values is what we call "evil," and we have the duty to confront evil. Jesus did—He confronted demons who possessed people and exorcized them. He confronted the sinner, called him to repentance, and forgave him. He confronted the dishonest money changers in the Temple, and expelled them. He confronted His enemies, but never returned hatred. On the cross, Jesus forgave those saying, "Father, forgive them for they do not know what they are doing." While they thought His death was their victory, it was their defeat. In the vision of faith, Jesus conquered, offering the sacrifice for sin and rising to give us everlasting life. In all of these instances, Our

Lord confronted and conquered evil, including sin and death, and made peace.

To have peace means a person or even a country must confront the forces of evil which seek to destroy peace. Therefore, making peace entails legitimate acts of self-defense, which may even result in the taking of the life of an unjust aggressor.

At first hearing, such language seems antithetical to Christianity since the Fifth Commandment states, "Thou shalt not kill." However, the intent of the precept forbids the purposeful taking of human life (*Catechism*, no. 2307). Each person has a duty to preserve his life, and therefore has a right to legitimate self-defense. Although an act of self-defense may have a two-fold effect—the preservation of the person's life and the unfortunate taking of the aggressor's life—the first effect is intended while the second is not (*Catechism*, no. 2263).

A country also has the right to self-defense. In preserving its own life, a state—citizens and their governments—must strive to avoid war and settle disputes peacefully and justly. Nevertheless, "governments cannot be denied the right of lawful self-defense, once all peace efforts have failed" (Vatican II, *Gaudium et Spes*, no. 79). Such a right does not entail a *carte blanche* permission for any and all acts of war. Rather, just war theory establishes moral parameters for the declaration and waging of war.

St. Augustine (d. 430) was the originator of the just war theory, which St. Thomas Aquinas (d. 1274) later adapted and explicated in his *Summa Theologiae*. Since the Middle Ages, warfare has changed dramatically, as witnessed by World War II and the conflicts which have followed it. Therefore, we can expand St. Thomas' and St. Augustine's theory to the following principles: In preparing to wage a just war (*ius ad bellum*), a country must meet the following criteria:

1. Just cause—The war must confront an unquestioned danger. St. Augustine, quoted by St. Thomas, said, "A just war is apt to be described as one that avenges wrongs, when a nation or state has to be punished, for refusing to make amends for the wrongs inflicted by its subjects, or to restore what it has seized unjustly." Moreover, "the damage inflicted by the aggressor on the nation or community of nations must be lasting, grave, and certain," asserts the *Catechism* (no. 2309).

    The criterion of just cause, however, has been complicated with the availability of weapons of mass destruction. Some moral theologians posit that if a country has such weapons, and has made known its intent to use such weapons, not for defense but in an act of aggression or terrorism, and such an intent is serious, then a pre-emptive strike by the threatened nation may be justified. With weapons of mass destruction, the attacked country may not be able to defend itself and correct the wrong after the fact; a pre-emptive strike may be the only way to stop the unjust aggressor or terrorist. This qualification of the just cause criterion is still debated.

2. Proper authority—The legitimate authority must declare the war and must be acting on behalf of the people. In our system of government, Congress must empower the President with the authority to wage war on behalf of the American people.

10   3. Right Intention—The reasons for declaring the war must actually be based on just objectives and not a masking of ulterior motives. St. Thomas taught that the right intention is essential "so that they intend the advancement of good or the avoidance of evil." St. Augustine also noted, "True religion looks upon as peaceful those wars that are waged not for motives of aggrandizement or cruelty, but with the object of securing peace or punishing evil-doers, and of uplifting the good." An evil intention, such as to destroy a race or to absorb another nation, turns a legitimately declared war waged for just cause into a wrongful act. A war waged for a just cause but with the underlying intent of economic gain may be less than just.

4. Last resort—All reasonable peaceful alternatives must have been exhausted or have been deemed impractical or ineffective. The contentious parties must strive to resolve their differences peacefully before engaging in war, e.g., through negotiation, mediation, or even embargoes. Here too we see the importance of an international mediating body, such as the United Nations, to pressure the contentious nations into peacefully resolving their differences. Here all parties must be forthright in their negotiations and desire peace.

5. Proportionality—The good that is achieved by waging war must not be outweighed by the harm. What good is it to wage war if it leaves the country in total devastation with no one really being the "winner?" Modern means of warfare give great weight to this criterion.

6. Probability of success—The achievement of the war's purpose must have a reasonable chance of success.

If a country can meet these criteria, then it may justly enter war. Moreover, a country could come to the assistance of another country who is not able to defend itself as long as these criteria are met.

However, the event of war does not entail that all means of waging war are licit; essentially, the "all is fair in love and war" rule is flawed. During war, the country must also meet criteria to insure justice is preserved (*ius in bello*):

1. Discrimination—Armed forces ought to fight armed forces, and should strive not to harm noncombatants purposefully. Sadly, innocent people will always suffer and die in war because of mistake or accident. Moreover, armed forces should not wantonly destroy the enemy's countryside, cities, or economy simply for the sake of punishment, retaliation, or vengeance. This criterion is increasingly important with the development of nuclear, chemical, and biological weaponry. Responding to the horrors witnessed in World War II, Vatican II stated, "The development of armaments by modern science has immeasurably magnified the horrors and wickedness of war. Warfare conducted with these weapons can inflict immense and indiscriminate havoc which goes far beyond the bounds of legitimate defense. . . . Every act of war directed to the indiscriminate destruction of whole cities or vast areas with their inhabitants is a crime against God and man, which merits firm and unequivocal condemnation" (*Gaudium et Spes*, no. 80).

2. Due Proportion—Combatants must use only those means necessary to achieve their objectives. For example, no one needs to use nuclear missiles to settle a territorial fishing problem. Due proportion also involves mercy—towards civilians in general, towards combatants when the resistance stops (as in the case of surrender and prisoners of war), and towards all parties when the war is finished. Moreover, the victors must help the vanquished to rebuild with a stable government and economy so as to ensure a lasting peace.

These are the criteria for declaring and waging a just war. Given the present situation with Iraq, we need to ask the following questions: Is there a just cause, especially when considering a pre-emptive strike? Is the intention based on the actual objectives or is there an underlying intention, such as economic gain? Is this war a last resort, e.g., should the weapons inspectors be allowed to investigate first, should the United Nations apply greater pressure, should there first be a consensus with America's allies? Can negotiations succeed when the leadership of Iraq has in the past thwarted weapons inspections and defied UN resolutions? Will the war result in a power vacuum with an even worse destabilized Mideast and with an even greater terrorist threat? These are legitimate questions that ought to be answered. Keep in mind that this author, who is neither working for the White House nor any intelligence or defense agency, in no way suggests answers to these questions and in no way draws a conclusion to this matter.

While these may be the "just criteria" for declaring and waging war, they still are wrenching. No good person wants war. Yet we—as an individual, community or nations—must confront and stop an evil. Only by confronting evil will there be peace. We need to pray that the Holy Spirit will guide the leaders of nations in this very difficult time to make decisions that will lead to a just and lasting peace.

Starting Points

1. Carefully reread William Saunders's list of criteria for waging war under the Augustinian theory of just war. Write an essay analyzing the U.S. wars in Iraq and Afghanistan. Do these wars, together or individually, meet the criteria in your view?

2. In what ways have the terrorist attacks of September 11th altered the centuries-old Augustinian theory? Has it rendered this theory obsolete? Reinforced its necessity? Include, of course, the elements of WMD, instant communications, and stateless violence.

3. How would you respond to someone who states that the Augustinian theory of just war is incompatible with the historic separation of church and state in the United States?

The Immorality of Preemptive War

ARTHUR SCHLESINGER, JR.

Arthur Schlesinger, Jr., is a historian, former aide to President John F. Kennedy, and a Pulitzer Prize–winning author. In this piece, he attacks the idea of pre-emptive war as immoral and opposed to historical American foreign policy and to future American interests. This article first appeared in the New Perspectives Quarterly *(Fall 2002) and is available online at http://www.digitalnpq.org.*

--- ✦ ---

One of the astonishing events of present months is the presentation of preventive war as a legitimate and moral instrument of United States foreign policy.

This has not always been the case. Dec. 7, 1941, on which day the Japanese launched a preventative strike against the U.S. Navy, has gone down in history as a date that will live in infamy. During the Cold War, advocates of preventive war were dismissed as a bunch of loonies. When Robert Kennedy called the notion of a preventive attack on the Cuban missile sites "Pearl Harbor in reverse," and added, "For 175 years we have not been that kind of country," he swung the ExCom—President Kennedy's special group of advisors—from an airstrike to a blockade.

The policy of containment plus deterrence won the Cold War. After the collapse of the Soviet Union, everyone thanked heaven that the preventive-war loonies had never got into power in any major country.

Today, alas, they appear to be in power in the U.S. Rebaptizing preventive war as preemptive war doesn't change its character. Preventive war is based on the proposition that it is possible to foretell with certainty what is to come.

The Bush administration hawks just know, if we do not act today, that something horrible will happen to us tomorrow. Vice President Dick Cheney and Secretary of Defense Donald Rumsfeld evidently see themselves as Steven Spielberg's "precogs" in *Minority Report,* who are psychically equipped to avert crimes that are about to be committed.

Certainty about prediction is an illusion. One thing that history keeps teaching us is that the future is full of surprises and outwits all our certitudes.

What is it that Pentagon precogs know he is planning? What is the clear and present danger, the direct and immediate threat, to justify sending the Army into Iraq?

Do the administration's precogs expect that he will use his mass-destruction arsenal against Kuwait? Against Israel? Against the U.S.?

Since Hussein is not interested in suicide, he is unlikely to do any of these things. Aggression would play into American hands. By using his weaponry, Hussein would give the U.S. president his heart's desire—a reason the world would accept for invading Iraq and enforcing regime change.

The one thing that would very probably lead Hussein to resort to his ghastly weapons would be just this invasion of Iraq by the U.S.

Meanwhile, the containment policy seems to be working. If it doesn't work, war is always an option. And Hussein, after all, is mortal. He is sure to be gone one of these days. What is so vital about getting rid of him next week or next month? Consider the

5

10

instant case: Iraq. The policy of containment plus deterrence has kept Saddam Hussein behind his own frontiers for the last decade.

The possibilities of history are far richer and more various than the human mind is likely to conceive—and the arrogance of leaders who are sure they can predict the future invites retribution.

"The hardest strokes of heaven," the English historian Sir Herbert Butterfield has written, "fall in history upon those who imagine that they can control things in a sovereign manner, playing providence not only for themselves but for the far future—reaching out into the future with the wrong kind of farsightedness, and gambling on a lot of risky calculations in which there must never be a single mistake."

Unilateral preventive war is neither legitimate nor moral. It is illegitimate and immoral. For more than 200 years we have not been that kind of country.

Starting Points

1. What examples does Schlesinger present in arguing against pre-emptive war? Do you believe these examples are parallel and relevant ones?

2. In this and other articles in this chapter, distinctions have been made between preventive and pre-emptive wars. Are these distinctions without a difference, or is there a real and substantive difference between the two concepts?

3. Schlesinger obliquely makes the point that American foreign policy changes with each administration. Make a case that these policy changes are either (a) inconsistent and confusing for our allies and others, or (b) necessary for evolving philosophies and changing conditions in the world.

Doctrine of Preemptive War Has Its Roots in Early 1990s
STEVEN R. WEISMAN

Much of the debate on pre-emptive war has focused on its use in Iraq by the Bush administration. In the following article, Steven R. Weisman of the New York Times, *writing in the* International Herald Tribune, *redirects that focus to a decade earlier. In 1992, in a document called the Defense Planning Guidance and prepared for then Defense Secretary Dick Cheney, there were suggestions that the*

United States should use armed force to prevent the spread of nuclear weapons. This article first appeared in the Paris-based International Herald Tribune *in March 24, 2003.*

————————— ✦ —————————

In January 1998, a lineup of conservative policy advocates warned President Bill Clinton in an open letter that the "containment" of Iraq was a failure and that removing Saddam Hussein from power "now needs to become the aim of American foreign policy."

Among the 18 signers were Donald Rumsfeld, Paul Wolfowitz, Richard Armitage and Richard Perle, all former officials in Republican administrations. At the time, the men were affiliated with academic centers and policy institutes, with no particular expectation that they would, within five years, be in a position to turn their ideas into policy.

The second U.S.-led war in the Gulf represents far more than simply a triumph for Rumsfeld, the secretary of defense, and Wolfowitz, his deputy, or for Armitage, the deputy secretary of state, and Perle, chairman of the Defense Policy Board, a Pentagon advisory panel, not to mention their colleagues in the conservative press.

It also reflects, at least in the view of some, the ascendance under President George W. Bush of the conservatives' idea that chemical, biological and nuclear weapons programs of "rogue states" must be confronted with preemptive action before an imminent threat materializes.

The origins of the current war are, in fact, rooted in a series 5 of policy pronouncements by these and other conservative intellectuals that date from the early 1990s, after the end of the Cold War and the inconclusive end of the Gulf War in 1991, which left Saddam in power.

During the Clinton years, when many of these conservative intellectuals lost their perches inside the government and Iraq faded as a central foreign policy concern, they kept alive the cause of deposing the Iraqi leader in foreign policy magazines, conferences and other political forums.

Then, when Bush began filling the top layers of his administration, many of these ardently anti-Saddam intellectuals returned to power, including Douglas Feith, the undersecretary of defense for policy, and I. Lewis Libby, Vice President Dick Cheney's chief of staff.

Even as they gained influence within the new administration, however, it was not until after Sept. 11, 2001, that they succeeded in making Iraq Bush's top foreign policy priority. It was then that the president came to share their deep concern that Iraq might give unconventional weapons to terrorist groups.

"Without Sept. 11, we never would have been able to put Iraq at the top of our agenda," a senior administration official said. "It was only then that this president was willing to worry about the unthinkable—that the next attack could be with weapons of mass destruction supplied by Saddam Hussein."

10   Not everyone around Bush is comfortable with the Iraq war being seen as a symbol of a new doctrine.

"The battle over the direction of American policy will continue," said another senior administration official, adding that the debate about how to neutralize threats from Iran and North Korea—the other two nations in the "axis of evil" cited by Bush—would begin even before the fighting in Iraq ended.

But ever since Bush and his team started talking about the need to deal preemptively with foreign threats, Secretary of State Colin Powell and some others in the administration have emphasized that such actions are only a part of the large set of options available to the United States.

Asked the other day whether the Iraq war reflected a broader doctrine of preemptive attacks on enemies, Powell replied, "No, no, no." He said Iraq was being attacked because it had violated its "international obligations" under its 1991 surrender agreement, which required the disclosure and disarmament of its dangerous weapons.

In an interview, Powell said Friday (March 21, 2003) that the publicity over the doctrine of preemption, enshrined in the administration's National Security Strategy published last year, overlooked the fact that preemption was only one tool among many.

15   "I think it's a bit of an overstatement to say that, now this one's pocketed, on to the next place," Powell said.

The doctrine of preemption, especially with respect to Iraq, has been floating around conservative policy circles since at least the presidency of Bush's father, when it was embraced by conservative intellectuals like Wolfowitz, then a policy aide to Cheney, who was then defense secretary. In 1992, Cheney's aides—including Wolfowitz, Libby and Zalmay Khalilzad, the administration's envoy to Iraq—prepared a document known as the Defense Planning Guidance, which argued that the United States should be prepared to use force to prevent the spread of nuclear weapons. The document also suggested that the United States should be "postured to act independently when collective action cannot be orchestrated." But when drafts of the document were leaked, just as the first President Bush's re-election campaign was heating up, it embarrassed the administration as being too hawkish and was shelved.

The principle of preemptive action was picked up in 1996 in an influential article in the journal *Foreign Affairs* by Robert Kagan and William Kristol, the editor of *The Weekly Standard* and the former chief of staff to Vice President Dan Quayle, titled "Toward a Neo-Reaganite Foreign Policy."

Kristol and Kagan wrote that the 1990s under Clinton were a time of passivity toward the threat of terrorism comparable to that of the 1970s, when Ronald Reagan felt the same way about American attitudes toward the threat of communism.

Kristol now notes that Clinton himself had begun embracing many of the ideas of preemptive action while still in office. In a speech on Feb. 17, 1998, at the Pentagon, Clinton said the United States "simply cannot allow" Saddam to acquire nuclear, chemical and biological weapons arsenals.

In a foreshadowing of what the younger Bush president   20
would say a few years later, Clinton spoke of "an unholy axis" of terrorists and the "outlaw nations" that harbor them. At the end of 1998, Clinton authorized bombing raids on Iraq, prompted by Saddam's refusal to cooperate with weapons inspectors.

Policy analysts inside and outside the administration are now asking whether a successful campaign in Iraq would encourage the administration to apply the principle of preemption to Iran and North Korea, both of which are further along in their nuclear weapons programs than Iraq. Administration officials who advocate military preemption say that such an approach will not necessarily apply to those countries, in part because North Korea could retaliate and because Iran, even if there is a change in government, will not be likely to abandon its nuclear program. But there is little doubt that the fundamental debate will continue.

"This is just the beginning," an administration official said. "I would not rule out the same sequence of events for Iran and North Korea as for Iraq, but circumstances do not compel you to end up in the same place."

Starting Points

1. This article might be viewed as background information on the history of pre-emptive action. List three things from this piece that bolstered your view of supporting or decrying pre-emptive war.

2. Count the number of times the term "conservative" is used in this article. Is the term neutral to you, or does it contain positive or negative connotations? Write a short essay in which you define the term and give specific examples of beliefs or actions that might cause someone to be termed "conservative."

3. Weisman is affiliated with the *New York Times,* a newspaper that has often been called "liberal." Does the use of terms such as "liberal" and "conservative" sway your thinking when you consider serious issues such as preemption? What is gained and what is lost by the use of such appellations?

Preemptive War and International Law
STEVEN C. WELSH

Before and after the invasion of Iraq in March 2003, there was considerable debate about the legality of such a first-strike war. Steven C. Welsh, a lawyer and research analyst with the Center for Defense Information, looks at the conditions under international law that would allow a pre-emptive war.

✦

The Bush National Security Strategy has prompted continuing discussion over the legal and policy implications of preemptive military action and its impact on the future of the global security system. This backgrounder examines some of the international legal standards and related policy considerations forming the context of that debate.

A strategy of addressing an emerging threat with a range of options including force was envisioned by the UN Charter. While traditional international law emphasized respect for state sovereignty by placing greater restrictions on the use of force, the literal language of the UN Charter has a more liberal standard when force is used under the auspices of the Security Council. For cases where force is used outside of the Security Council framework, it is not definitively clear whether under the UN Charter a state retains a traditional right of self-defense, including a right of anticipatory self-defense against an imminent threat, or if that right is curtailed to not include anticipatory self-defense. Some commentators argue that the UN Charter itself is no longer a

valid source of international law, in which case a right of anticipatory self-defense would exist regardless and traditionally be
limited to cases in which there is a threat of imminent attack.

Given the UN Charter's authorization of preemptive acts by
the Security Council, ultimately the real division over preemption
is not necessarily over preemption itself but over the multilateral
framework under which it is carried out, who holds decision-
making authority, and the extent to which those arrangements
are codified and therefore rendered more stable and predictable.
If the original concept of the Security Council was that the ad hoc
coalition which won World War II would remain intact to stamp
out future Hitlers before they reached a critical level of strength,
historical changes such as the Cold War may have altered the
course of that plan.

The right and obligation of a governing authority to use force
to defend its citizens against an aggressor predates by centuries
modern nation-states and modern international law. Christian
just war theory, upon which the modern laws of armed conflict
are based, recognized such a duty as early as the 4th Century.
Since their emergence in the 16th Century, modern nation-states
have been believed to hold such a right. While aggression is traditionally considered unlawful, and self-defense lawful, more problematic is the question of whether a first-strike could ever be considered a defensive act rather than an act of aggression. The right
of anticipatory self-defense assumes that an aggressor is poised to
strike, and that one acts defensively in anticipation of the attack
rather than waiting for the attack to occur. Traditionally, it was
deemed theoretically possible that even a first-strike could be
deemed defensive in nature, and lawful, if it was to forestall an attack that was imminent.

The most widely accepted modern standard for anticipatory
self-defense was articulated by U.S. Secretary of State Daniel
Webster in diplomatic correspondence with his British counter-
part over the *Caroline* incident (often mischaracterized as the
Caroline "case") and consisted of two prongs. One was that the
need to use force in anticipatory self-defense must first rise to the
level of being a necessity, and one that is instant, overwhelming,
and leaving no choice of means and no moment for deliberation.
The other requirement was that the action taken must be proportionate to the threat and not be excessive.

Debate continues over the impact of the UN Charter on this
area of international law. The UN Charter has a general prohibition against the use of force, but authorizes the Security Council

to use force even in the absence of an act of aggression by the target, and permits unilateral and non-UN multilateral acts of self-defense under certain constraints.

With respect to the Security Council, the literal language of the UN Charter, in Articles 39, 41, and 42, envisions the use of a range of options, such as economic sanctions and varying degrees of force (e.g., blockades as well as all-out war) in response to acts of aggression, breaches of the peace, and threats to the peace. As a result, under the Charter force may be used against even a mere threat when authorized by the Security Council.

For unilateral acts and the multilateral use of force outside of the UN framework, Article 51 of the UN Charter refers to an inherent right of self-defense against armed attack, permitting defensive actions until the Security Council addresses the matter, and requires that such a defensive use of force be reported to the Security Council. The literal language of Article 51 seems to roll back the traditional right of self-defense, requiring that an armed attack have occurred before self-defense can be exercised, and implying that unilateral self-defense is an interim measure until the Security Council addresses the situation. Some commentators argue, however, that by referring to an "inherent" right of self-defense the UN Charter simply retains pre-existing international law regarding self-defense, including anticipatory self-defense. While it is not necessarily clear what role he plays in the matter, it appears that Secretary General Koffi Annan might hold the latter view, referring to states "retain[ing]" the inherent right of self-defense under the Charter.

To the extent the UN Charter can be deemed a relevant source of international law then some right of self-defense remains, which very well may include a right of anticipatory self-defense. At the same time, in international law, if a consistent pattern of state practice demonstrates a departure from preexisting norms, it can be argued that international law has changed. Some commentators suggest that state practice has indicated that with respect to the use of force the UN Charter no longer is a part of international law. If that is the case, then presumably international law would revert to the standard of anticipatory self-defense articulated by Webster.

10   The bottom line, then, is that with respect to anticipatory force exercised without Security Council authorization, either the UN Charter is essentially defunct with respect to the laws of armed conflict and the Webster standard continues, or the UN Charter is not defunct but retains the Webster standard, or that the Webster standard is displaced by a stricter standard requiring

an armed attack to have occurred before one may invoke a right of self-defense. The prevailing view probably is that, one way or another, anticipatory self-defense is permissible but traditionally has required the existence of an imminent threat.

Another aspect of the UN framework, emphasized during the Cuban missile crisis, is that the UN Charter does permit regional security arrangements as long as they are consistent with the purposes and principles of the United Nations. However, the literal language of Article 53 requires that enforcement actions taken under regional arrangements not be initiated without Security Council authorization.

With respect to preemption, the National Security Strategy (NSS) issued by U.S. President George W. Bush itself does not necessarily significantly challenge prevailing international law. It rests upon a standard doctrine of anticipatory self-defense, and explores the question of when an attack is imminent. On its face it does not seek to overturn the rule, but to explore how the rule and its underlying purpose could be applied in particular situations not existing in the past.

One could argue that the rule does not actually require an attack to be imminent to act, but rather permits defensive measures to be taken before one passes a point in time when it is too late to prevent catastrophe.

The NSS focuses on several major considerations, one being that the imminence of a terrorist attack is much harder to detect, another being the fact that innocents are often targeted, and the third being the devastating impact of weapons of mass destruction (WMD). While the text in the NSS relating to preemption does not necessarily limit its scope to WMD, it comes in a section dedicated to WMD.

Some commentators have suggested that WMD, and WMD 15 proliferation, might be carved out as a special category under anticipatory self-defense. They argue that the right implied by anticipatory self-defense to act against a threat before it is "too late" may require setting a threshold in the context of WMD at some earlier point in the proliferation process, with that earlier point serving as the equivalent of the imminence of a threat. Such a point, it is argued, could represent the presence of a danger justifying a "defensive" first-strike, perhaps when accompanied by other factors such as a history of aggression, ties to terrorism, or certain criminal activities by the target regime.

Even if an exception were limited to WMD, or rogue state WMD, however, there still would remain the problem of setting a new and potentially destabilizing precedent, with the U.S. pre-emption policy serving as a basis for other countries initiating or threatening conflicts they might not otherwise have been embold-ened to undertake.

Concerns over precedent highlight the fact that international law does in fact mean something, and serves more than simply a cosmetic role providing a rhetorical backdrop for actions taken for entirely different reasons. Whether in a local domestic context or the international arena, law and security go hand-in-hand to the extent that assumptions about reliable rules limit and guide conduct, if only by making more predictable its consequences. Countries do seem to care about what kind of reaction a particu-lar course of conduct will bring. In two major wars, Korea and Gulf War I, the United States in hindsight was accused of having overlooked hints by the aggressors of their intentions, failing to respond strongly enough to the hints. International law can help serve to warn state actors what other states would think of partic-ular courses of action, by clearly articulating norms of conduct and by drawing up more clearly defined parameters for joint ac-tion in response to unlawful or otherwise dangerous situations.

The Bush administration therefore faces an important chal-lenge to articulate its own policies clearly and carefully, deter-mine the extent to which the United States is willing to help con-tribute to the establishment of clear international norms, and explain whether and in what manner an international framework for decision-making will be honored. Concerns expressed by al-lies over the shaping of preemption do not necessarily evidence an unwillingness to adapt shared understandings of law and secu-rity to changing circumstances. Rather, they reflect a fundamen-tal appreciation for the prospect of a stable, effective and sustain-able global security system in which the sole superpower ideally provides leadership that is clearly articulated, predictable, rea-sonable and promotes respect for the law.

The National Security Strategy calls for accurate, honest, and timely threat-assessments and coordination with allies, wisdom reinforced by the Iraq war. One of the biggest lessons from the Iraq conflict might not center around what to call it (*i.e.,* preemp-tion or something else) but rather the weaknesses inherent in re-lying on potentially flawed intelligence and the difficulties that could be posed in the future if a U.S. administration once again seeks to convince the citizenry and the world community to trust undisclosed information, or disclosed allegations resting on simi-lar intelligence-gathering. Another lesson is that even the United

States needs help dealing with a large and complicated problem, whether it is before, during, or after a conflict addressing what the Bush administration deems a grave and gathering threat.

In the past, Bush has been somewhat reserved with respect to his own presentation of a preemption doctrine, and his decision to lead a multilateral coalition against Saddam Hussein was presented with a tapestry of arguments among which were references to Security Council resolutions, the ongoing situation since the previous Gulf War, Saddam's ties to terrorists, and humanitarian concerns. Secretary of State Colin Powell also has adopted a multifaceted and internationalist approach, and recently articulated a view of preemption that was closely akin to traditional anticipatory self-defense, referring to taking action when "see[ing] . . . a danger coming at you. . . ." Vice President Dick Cheney until recently adopted a more aggressive posture reminiscent of a Cold War ideology—"us good, them bad"—and the United States needing an unfettered capacity to take action anywhere at any time. Publicly, Cheney's focus seems to have shifted away from open support for preemption to the engagement of terrorists in an ongoing series of hostilities, the need to appraise the future of the system of global security, and the importance of democracy.

Important questions that must be answered include whether the world is safer with or without a strengthening of international law and carefully crafted international institutions restricting the use of force, and whether the United States is willing to provide the leadership it has demonstrated in the past in these areas.

At the same time, an examination of the global system of sovereign states might not be complete without a consideration of the rightful purpose of sovereignty itself, taken together with the more broad-based views of security expressed by the National Security Strategy, and Bush's decision to draw greater attention to the need to create a safer and more just world by promoting freedom and democracy.

Sovereignty was never appropriately meant to sanctify the frontiers of tyrants and prevent outside intervention against their crimes, but truly *is* meant to serve the cause of peace. The theoretical basis for having nation-states in the first place was the idea that power would be concentrated in the hands of the sovereign, rather than private armies, local warlords, and armed bands, and that sovereigns themselves would be limited with respect to the instances in which they would attack each other, with the overall effect of reducing the incidence of war and violence and thereby protecting innocent lives (see e.g., Cusimano Love,

"09.11.01: Globalization, Ethics, and the War on Terrorism," *Notre Dame Journal of Ethics & Public Policy*, Vol. 16, 2002, pp. 65–80). This system has been challenged by the nexus of modern technology with the reemergence of warlords and private armies, but it also has been challenged wherever sovereignty rests on oppression rather than democratic legitimacy.

Security and the diverse realities impacting it encompass a growing range of concerns. The National Security Strategy with its consideration of the importance of development and trade relationships, the president's renewed focus on democratization, and an appraisal of the forces of globalization and the connection between terrorism and poverty all point to a new direction in security that is not simply based on force but most definitely is based on prevention. The key, however, will be to not simply be preventive, but to be proactive. To not simply put out fires and react to events, but to invest in human potential and human freedom, to promote respect for human life and the dignity of the human person, and to sign on for the long haul to create a world that is more free, more just, and therefore decidedly more secure.

ADDENDUM

25   Since the drafting of this article, President George W. Bush delivered his London address of Nov. 19, 2003, in which he refrained from openly rearticulating a policy of preemption but did, in his second "pillar," voice the need for free nations to be willing as a last resort to use force to restrain "aggression and evil." While force employed in response to "aggression" could fall into the category of defense against an actual attack, using force to restrain "evil" seems a somewhat more nebulous concept, and Bush did not elaborate as to timing and circumstance. By referring to "free nations" in the plural, Bush did seem to continue a theme of multilateral action.

Efforts at multilateralism would be consistent with his first pillar, the need for international organizations to be effective at meeting today's challenges, with effectiveness measured by results and not just procedure. Bush recognized that global problems such as terrorism do require a global response. He pointed to the need for the United Nations to adequately address threats while also citing an American commitment to NATO, the need for security cooperation between the United States and the European Union, his multilateral approach to North Korea, and the importance of the International Atomic Energy Agency adequately addressing concerns over Iranian nuclear technology.

The question of "where to go from here" would seem to center around working to build greater effectiveness for international institutions and frameworks for multilateral action, but the third pillar, the president's call for democratization, especially in the Middle East, also is noteworthy. The United States appears to be expressing contrition for past policies of building ties with regimes of less than stellar democratic credentials, and even more importantly to be focusing on policy directions which are not simply preemptive or preventive, but actually proactive. Just as at the conclusion of World War II the United States learned from the mistakes of the Treaty of Versailles, it appears that the United States once again is endeavoring to learn from past mistakes by focusing on longer-term goals, addressing the sources of instability and aggression, and aspiring to unite values with practical action by investing in human potential and cultivating the foundations of true peace. As Pope John Paul II cautioned in Coventry in 1982, peace is more than just the absence of war, and must be built thoughtfully and patiently over time. A sincere and farsighted approach to that principle, grounded in freedom, justice, and the rule of law, would appear to be the rightful mission of a United States that assumes a position of global partnership with other free nations.

Sources and Additional Reading

Bruce Ackerman, "But What's the Legal Case for Preemption?" *Washington Post*, Aug. 18, 2002, republished at http://www.law.yale.edu/outside/html/Public_Affairs/282/yls_article.htm.

U.N. Secretary-General Kofi Annan, Address to the General Assembly, Sept. 23, 2003, http://www.un.org/webcast/ga/58/statements/sg2eng030923.htm.

Anthony Clark Arend, "International Law and the Preemptive Use of Military Force," *The Washington Quarterly*, Spring 2003, pp. 89–103, http://www.cfr.org/pdf/highlight/03spring_arend.pdf.

Anthony Clark Arend, "Anticipatory Self-Defense and International Law," American Society of International Law Briefing (live presentation), Washington, D.C., Aug. 2, 2002, http://www.asil.org/briefing.htm#selfdefense.

President George W. Bush, "President Bush Discusses Iraq Policy at Whitehall Palace in London: Remarks by the President at Whitehall Palace, Royal Banqueting House-Whitehall Palace, London, England," Nov. 19, 2003, http://www.whitehouse.gov/news/releases/2003/11/20031119-1.html.

President George W. Bush, "President Bush Discusses Freedom in Iraq and Middle East: Remarks by the President at the 20th Anniversary of the National Endowment for Democracy," United States Chamber of Commerce, Washington, D.C, Nov. 6, 2003, http://www.whitehouse.gov/news/releases/2003/11/20031106-2.html.

President George W. Bush, Commencement Address at the United States Military Academy in West Point, New York, June 7, 2002, Weekly Compilation of President Documents, pp. 943–975, at 946; text: http://frwebgate.access.gpo.gov/cgi-bin/getdoc.cgi?dbname=2002_presidential_documents&docid=pd10jn02_txt-5; PDF: http://frwebgate.access.gpo.gov/cgi-bin/getdoc.cgi?dbname=2002_presidential_documents&docid=pd10jn02_txt-5.pdf.

Vice President Richard B. Cheney, "VP Remarks at Southwest Florida Dinner," Nov. 3, 2003, http://www.whitehouse.gov/news/releases/2003/11/20031103-20.html.

Vice President Richard B. Cheney, "Remarks by the Vice President at the James A. Baker III Institute for Public Policy," Oct. 17, 2003, http://www.whitehouse.gov/news/releases/2003/10/20031017-11.html.

Vice President Richard B. Cheney, "Vice President's Remarks at 2003 Air Force Convention," Sept. 17, 2003, http://www.whitehouse.gov/news/releases/2003/09/20030917-3.html.

Charter of the United Nations, http://www.un.org/aboutun/charter/; PDF: http://www.unhchr.ch/pdf/UNcharter.pdf.

Michael J. Glennon, "Why the Security Council Failed," Foreign Affairs, May/June 2003, http://www.foreignaffairs.org/20030501 faessay11217/michael-j-glennon/why-the-security-council-failed.html.

Amb. Thomas Graham, Jr., "Is International Law Relevant to Arms Control? National Self-Defense, International Law, and Weapons of Mass Destruction," University of Chicago Journal of International Law, Spring 2003, pp. 1–17.

George E. Lopez, "Perils of Bush's Pre-emptive War Doctrine," Indianapolis Star, Oct. 3, 2003, http://www.indystar.com/print/articles/4/079947-6994-P.html.

Maryann Cusimano Love, "09.11.01: Globalization, Ethics, and the War on Terrorism," Notre Dame Journal of Ethics & Public Policy, Vol. 16, 2002, pp. 65–80.

The National Security Strategy of the United States of America, http://www.whitehouse.gov/nsc/nss5.html, PDF: http://www.whitehouse.gov/nsc/nss.pdf.

U.S. Secretary of State Colin Powell, "Remarks at the Elliot School of International Affairs," Sept. 5, 2003, http://www.state.gov/secretary/rm/2003/23836.htm.

Mary Ellen O'Connell, "The Myth of Preemptive Self-Defense," American Society of International Law, Task Force on Terrorism Essay, August 2002, http://www.asil.org/taskforce/oconnell.pdf.

W. Michael Reisman, "Assessing Claims to Revise the Laws of War," *The American Journal of International Law,* January, 2003, pp. 82–90.

Col. Guy B. Roberts, USMC, "The Counterproliferation Self-Help Paradigm: A Legal Regime For Enforcing the Norm Prohibiting The Proliferation of Weapons of Mass Destruction," *Denver Journal of International Law and Policy,* Vol. 27, No. 3, pp. 483–http://www.law.du.edu/ilj/online_issues_folder/robertsmacro.pdf.

Remarks by a Senior Administration Official in Briefing to the Travel Pool, Sept. 23, 2003, http://www.whitehouse.gov/news/releases/2-003/09/20030923-7.html.

David Sloss, "Is International Law Relevant to Arms Control? Forcible Control: Preemptive Attacks on Nuclear Facilities," *University of Chicago Journal of International Law,* Spring 2003, pp. 39–57.

Abraham D. Sofaer, "On the Legality of Preemption," *Hoover Digest,* 2003, No. 2, http://www-hoover.stanford.edu/publications/digest/032/sofaer.html.

U.S. Secretary of State Daniel Webster, diplomatic correspondence, republished in: Hunter Miller, editor, author of introductory notes, "Webster-Ashburton Treaty—The Caroline Case," http://www.yale.edu/lawweb/avalon/diplomacy/britian/br-1842d.htm, excerpt from *Treaties and Other International Acts of the United States of America,* Hunter Miller, editor, Vol. 4, Documents 80–121: 1836–1846, Washington, Government Printing Office, 1934.

United States Conference of Catholic Bishops, *The Challenge of Peace: God's Promise and Our Response: A Pastoral Letter on War and Peace by the National Conference of Catholic Bishops,* 1983 (quoting Pope John Paul II, address in Coventry, England, 1982).

Starting Points

1. Consider Steven Welsh's thesis that nation-states arose out of the imperative for controlling private armies and warlords, and thereby limiting the use of violence. Research the rise of nation-states and argue for or against this conclusion.

2. In a time of global terrorism, is it time for a reappraisal of international law regarding the rights of nations to defend themselves? Or would such an undertaking take decades without providing answers?

3. Is the goal of "democratization" a viable one, or is democracy a product of a unique set of historical circumstances that cannot be easily replicated? How should a democracy begin?

Preventive War or Preemptive War
ULRICH ARNSWALD

America's war in Iraq in 2003 was fiercely debated in the interna-
tional community as well as in the United States. Ulrich Arnswald,
a German professor of political philosophy and founding director of
the European Institute for International Affairs (in Heidelberg), at-
tacks the reasons cited for a pre-emptive war in Iraq. This article
was first published in Freitag *on August 22, 2003, and can be*
found online at la.indymedia.org.

─────────── ✦ ───────────

The Iraq war did not fulfill the criteria of a preventive war.
America carried out a preemptive war, not a preventive war.
What is the difference? Astonishingly one reads nothing about
this. However a preventive war is obviously not a preemptive war.

While a preventive war requires the fulfillment of criteria on
the immediate danger of the intentional aggression of a state, criteria for a preemptive strike or preemptive war are absolutely unknown. A war would be legitimated as a preventive war if "preventive self-defense" occurred according to the Caroline proviso
that no other choice of means existed or the possibility of negotiations was exhausted. A preventive war is only conceivable measured by such criteria. There can be no talk of the Iraq war as a
preventive war since an armed attack on the United States or on a
bordering state of Iraq was not immediately imminent.

An aggression must occur or be imminent for a preventive war.
Violence may not be practiced in the international community under any other signs, not even on account of differences in political
or religious viewpoints or to overthrow an unpopular dictator
through an intervention from the outside. Belligerent acts against a
state are illegitimate per se if no immediate danger of war is
demonstrated. In general, three basic conditions must be met to
speak of an immediate threat: an active war preparation, a manifest intention of inflicting damage on another state, and a situation
where waiting instead of fighting increases the risk of becoming a
victim of an aggression. A preventive war or preventive strike can
only be legitimated when these three criteria are satisfied.

In contrast, a "preemptive war," a war to nip possible dangers
in the bud, is not included and thus is rejected in international
law. In a word, international law doesn't know either preemptive
wars or preemptive strikes. "Preemptive military strike" is a new

concept that Americans have sought to enforce in international groups since 2002 with the Bush doctrine (National Security Strategy). The 1995 report of the strategic command of the U.S. (STRATCOM) already provided that "reaction" to a threat could be preemptive. However this policy could not be put in effect.

"Preemptive strikes" occurred in the past. An attempted con-   5
ceptual legitimating followed the Israeli attack on an Iraqi nuclear reactor and the bombardment of a suspected poison gas factory in the Sudan in 1998. While the UN condemned Israel's attack by resolution and the military-strategic highhandedness of Americans with an unknown number of Sudanese dead needs no further comment. The analogous attempt at justifying the Iraq war is very problematic. The war-mongering powers seek to derive a justification for their action relevant to international law from the doctrine of "preemptive strikes."

The argument of many military personnel that the idea of preemptive war is justified by the immediacy—or rapid deployment—of modern weapon delivery systems is controversial in politics. The question is raised how these operations can be legitimated. While border violations, general mobilizations, military alliances or marine blockades can be regarded as threats for preventive wars, justifying reasons for war are not clear for preemptive wars. Rather preemptive strikes are based on potential or presumed dangers.

Intentions and undocumented presumptions of aggression should legitimate preemptive wars, not evidence based on facts. Diffuse reasons can always be misused to wage preventive wars for power interests. No criteria catalogues are known to question and examine the cited reasons for war. Whether and when weapons could be deployed and a preemptive response justified cannot be shown. The Iraq campaign was an example.

The question of the proportionality of means should be decisive for the West in the presentation of evidence. The German standpoint was consistent. Whoever wants to pass from threat to war confrontation owes the Security Council and the world public evidence that all political efforts failed or were hopeless. Iraq seemed less capable of attack before the war than ever. The danger scenarios spread by the secret services of the belligerent governments are still unverified today.

The preemptive war against Iraq broke the norms of the community of states. International law was demonstratively degraded in its importance. What can replace international law is unclear. The preemptive war against Iraq was primarily an attempt of the U.S. to triumph over the sovereignty of the international community. This disempowerment (*Enthegung*) of international law is a unique dangerous mega-political experiment with unforeseeable consequences that could inflict great damage to U.S. interests. The Iraq war could serve as a precedent for further wars that cannot be legitimated.

Starting Points

1. Ulrich Arnswald argues that the war in Iraq "demonstratively degraded in its importance" international law and "broke the norms of the community of states." Of what importance is international opinion?
2. How have events in Iraq since the U.S. invasion affected your reading of Arnswald's article?
3. Regardless of whether you believe the war in Iraq was necessary, do you think that the American first-strike policy will open the door to other nations with grievances against their neighbors? Or was the war in Iraq an obvious, one-time exception?

Other Journeys: Suggestions for Further Writing and Research

1. After reading the selections in this chapter on pre-emptive war, write a position paper in which you argue for or against a first strike. How does the age of terrorism, or the possibility of WMD, affect your view?
2. Make notes of the key points in the articles in this chapter and in your research on the subject of pre-emptive war. Have the students in your classroom debate both sides of the issue, on the following proposition: "In an age of terrorism and weapons of mass destruction, international rules regarding pre-emptive war must be rewritten."
3. Conduct a poll on campus, in a local shopping mall, or other public location to determine views on pre-emptive war. Your questions should be carefully worded to avoid leading those responding and should include one or two open questions in which the respondents are asked to expand on their answers. Keep track of age, gender, party affiliation, education, religious affiliation, or other such demographic information. Then write a paper in which you report and analyze your findings.
4. Write a letter to the editor of your local or regional newspaper in which you cogently express your views on the subject of pre-emption. Keep the letter short, but display your knowledge of the issues.
5. Read further on the topic of a "just war." What do the precepts of the tradition dictate in terms of first strike, appropriate response to aggression, and duration of a war? Is the concept of a "just war," as laid out by St. Augustine, still a viable yardstick for ethical, legal, or moral approbation?

The Homefront
and Terrorism

All wars result in a variety of changes at home. Some are obvious, government-directed programs that affect everyone—the rationing of food and gasoline, for example, in World War II. Some affect us indirectly, such as when President Abraham Lincoln ordered several northern newspaper editors jailed on charges of sedition. Still others are less obvious—restrictions on travel, or expanded government powers to eavesdrop on conversations, intercept mail, or check our bank accounts.

In a democracy, there are always tensions between license and liberty, rights and responsibilities, security and freedom. A war setting highlights those tensions, making us more aware of the delicate balance required for the defense of a free society. A second area of tension arises in information about the war: who will provide that information, the government or a free press? Citizens of a democracy must be informed about the activities of their government, but are there occasions when the news media should not report everything they know? What information should a government legitimately keep secret? What prevents government officials from misleading the public if they classify important documents? And then there is the role of the individual in a democracy when soldiers are in harm's way. Is the right course of action to support our leaders' policies until the shooting stops, or to question decisions that result in troops being sent into combat?

One of the most visible—and controversial—actions of the federal government following the attacks of September 11th was the passage (with little opposition in Congress at the time) of the USA Patriot Act. An acronym for the unwieldy Uniting and Strengthening America by Providing Appropriate Tools Required to Intercept and Obstruct Terrorism, the act either (a) gives the government sweeping new powers that threaten civil liberties, or (b) grants much-needed

95

latitude to those charged with defending the United States, with appropriate oversight. In this chapter you will read articles by Attorney General John Ashcroft, who defends the necessity for the act, and an assessment by a law professor who questions its appropriateness and effectiveness. (The text of the act itself is available from a variety of sources, and therefore is not included here.)

Also in this chapter two writers from the Foreign Policy Research Institute, Stephen Gale and Lawrence Husick, argue that the end goal of the new terrorism is not individual targets but rather the faith of Westerners in our "common assets." They call for a risk-management approach to homeland security, which would include security impact statements (SIS) in the manner of environmental impact statements.

A little discussed aspect of American homeland security is the U.S. government's bid to make ports secure. As much as 90 to 95 percent of goods imported into this country arrive by ship, so the government will require that all vessels arriving at U.S. ports must have departed from a secure port, with specific requirements for ensuring that safety. Tim Weiner of the *New York Times* explores this issue in this chapter.

Finally, several articles are included that explore the roles of both citizens and a free press. The news media often come under attack for biased reporting, but how then should the citizens of a free society learn about wars in which their country is involved? What should be the stance of news organizations when a country readies for war? Leading up to the Spanish-American War, newspapers played a pivotal role in mustering up support for war, but during the war in Vietnam, televised images of the horror of combat were nightly fare in American living rooms, and were blamed by many (despite the U.S. Army's official history of the Vietnam war) for the defeat there. What was the role of news media here before the invasion of Iraq?

USA Patriot Act "Honors" Liberty and Freedom

JOHN ASHCROFT

U.S. Attorney General John Ashcroft, formerly a senator from Missouri, is a staunch defender of the USA Patriot Act. In a speech to the Federalist Society in November 2003, he assailed the notion that the Act erodes American freedoms, and asserted that it actually defends liberty by honoring the Constitution, and that "ordered liberty" is the goal of law.

◆

Thank you for the invitation to join you here this morning. I would like to know when the Federalist Society began keeping farmers' hours. I mean, a speech at 8 AM on a Saturday?

When your friends at the American Constitution Society for Law and Policy held their inaugural event, they let Janet Reno speak at a far more civilized hour. How do you expect me to do this and be fresh for tonight's John Ashcroft Dance Party?

I do appreciate your invitation to speak to you this morning. The Federalist Society and its membership have been resolute defenders of our nation's founding ideals: liberty, the rule of law, limited government. It is in this capacity that the Federalist Society is so necessary today.

America has an honored tradition of debate and dissent under the First Amendment. It is an essential piece of our constitutional and cultural fabric. As a former politician, I have heard a few dissents in my time, and even expressed a couple of my own.

The Founders believed debate should enlighten, not just enliven. It should reveal truth, not obscure it. The future of freedom demands that our discourse be based on a solid foundation of facts and a sincere desire for truth. As we consider the direction and destiny of our nation, the friends of freedom must practice for themselves . . . and demand from others . . . a debate informed by fact and directed toward truth. 5

Take away all the bells and whistles . . . the rhetorical flourishes and occasional vitriol . . . and the current debate about liberty is about the rule of law and the role of law.

The notion that the law can enhance, not diminish, freedom is an old one. John Locke said the end of law is, quote, ". . . not to abolish or restrain but to preserve and enlarge freedom." George Washington called this, "ordered liberty."

There are some voices in this discussion of how best to preserve freedom that reject the idea that law can enhance freedom. They think that passage and enforcement of any law is necessarily an infringement of liberty.

Ordered liberty is the reason that we are the most open and the most secure society in the world. Ordered liberty is a guiding principle, not a stumbling block to security.

10   When the first societies passed and enforced the first laws against murder, theft and rape, the men and women of those societies unquestionably were made more free.

A test of a law, then, is this: does it honor or degrade liberty? Does it enhance or diminish freedom?

The Founders provided the mechanism to protect our liberties and preserve the safety and security of the Republic: the Constitution. It is a document that safeguards security, but not at the expense of freedom. It celebrates freedom, but not at the expense of security. It protects us and our way of life.

Since September 11, 2001, the Department of Justice has fought for, Congress has created, and the judiciary has upheld, legal tools that honor the Constitution . . . legal tools that are making America safer while enhancing American freedom.

It is a compliment to all who worked on the Patriot Act to say that it is not constitutionally innovative. The Act uses court-tested safeguards and time-honored ideas to aid the war against terrorism, while protecting the rights and lives of citizens.

15   [James] Madison noted in 1792 that the greatest threat to our liberty was centralized power. Such focused power, he wrote, is liable to abuse. That is why he concluded a distribution of power into separate departments is a first principle of free governments.

The Patriot Act honors Madison's "first principles" . . . giving each branch of government a role in ensuring both the lives and liberties of our citizens are protected. The Patriot Act grants the executive branch critical tools in the war on terrorism. It provides the legislative branch extensive oversight. It honors the judicial branch with court supervision over the Act's most important powers.

First, the executive branch.

At the Department of Justice, we are dedicated to detecting, disrupting, and dismantling the networks of terror before they can strike at our nation. In the past two years, no major terrorist attack has been perpetrated on our soil.

Consider the bloodshed by terrorism elsewhere in that time:

- Women and children slaughtered in Jerusalem;
- Innocent, young lives snuffed out in Indonesia;
- Saudi citizens savaged in Riyadh;
- Churchgoers in Pakistan murdered by the hands of hate.

20   We are using the tough tools provided in the USA Patriot Act to defend American lives and liberty from those who have shed blood and decimated lives in other parts of the world.

The Patriot Act does three things:

First, it closes the gaping holes in law enforcement's ability to collect vital intelligence information on terrorist enterprises. It allows law enforcement to use proven tactics long used in the fight against organized crime and drug dealers.

Second, the Patriot Act updates our anti-terrorism laws to meet the challenges of new technology and new threats.

Third, with these critical new investigative tools provided by the Patriot Act, law enforcement can share information and cooperate better with each other. From prosecutors to intelligence agents, the Act allows law enforcement to "connect the dots" and uncover terrorist plots before they are launched.

Here is an example of how we use the Act. Some of you are   25
familiar with the Iyman Faris case. He is a naturalized American citizen who worked as a truck driver out of Columbus, Ohio.

Using information sharing allowed under the Patriot Act, law enforcement pieced together Faris's activities:

- How Faris met senior Al Qaeda operatives in a training camp in Afghanistan.
- How he was asked to procure equipment that might cause train derailments and sever suspension systems of bridges.
- How he traveled to New York to scout a potential terrorist target.

Faris pleaded guilty on May 1, 2003, and on October 28, he was sentenced under the Patriot Act's tough sentences. He will serve 20 years in prison for providing material support to Al Qaeda and conspiracy for providing the terrorist organization with information about possible U.S. targets for attack.

The Faris case illustrates what the Patriot Act does. One thing the Patriot Act does not do is allow the investigation of individuals, ". . . solely upon the basis of activities protected by the first amendment to the Constitution of the United States."

Even if the law did not prohibit it, the Justice Department has neither the time nor the inclination to delve into the reading habits or other First Amendment activities of our citizens.

Despite all the hoopla to the contrary, for example, the Patriot   30
Act . . . which allows for court-approved requests for business records, including library records . . . has never been used to obtain records from a library. Not once.

Senator Dianne Feinstein recently said, "I have never had a single abuse of the Patriot Act reported to me. My staff e-mailed the ACLU and asked them for instances of actual abuses. They e-mailed back and said they had none."

The Patriot Act has enabled us to make quiet, steady progress in the war on terror.

Since September 11, we have dismantled terrorist cells in Detroit, Seattle, Portland, Tampa, Northern Virginia, and Buffalo.

We have disrupted weapons procurement plots in Miami, San Diego, Newark, and Houston.

35 We have shut down terrorist-affiliated charities in Chicago, Dallas and Syracuse.

We have brought criminal charges against 286 individuals. We have secured convictions or guilty pleas from 155 people.

Terrorists who are incarcerated, deported or otherwise neutralized threaten fewer American lives. For two years, our citizens have been safe. There have been no major terrorist attacks on our soil. American freedom has been enhanced, not diminished. The Constitution has been honored, not degraded.

Second, the role Congress plays.

In six weeks of debate in September and October of 2001, both the House of Representatives and the Senate examined studiously and debated vigorously the merits of the Patriot Act. In the end, both houses supported overwhelmingly its passage.

40 Congress built into the Patriot Act strict and structured oversight of the Executive Branch. Every six months, the Justice Department provides Congress with reports of its activities under the Patriot Act.

Since September 24, 2001, Justice Department officials, myself included, have testified on the Patriot Act and other homeland security issues more than 115 times. We have responded to hundreds of written and oral questions and provided reams of written responses.

To date, no congressional committee has found any evidence that law enforcement has abused the powers provided by the Patriot Act.

Legislative oversight of the executive branch is critical to "ordered liberty." It ensures that laws and those who administer them respect the rights and liberties of the citizens.

There has not been a major terrorist attack within our borders in the past two years. Time and again, Congress has found the Patriot Act to be effective against terrorist threats, and respectful and protective of citizens' liberties. The Constitution has been honored, not degraded.

45 Finally, the judiciary.

The Patriot Act provides for close judicial supervision of the executive branch's use of Patriot Act authorities.

The Act allows the government to utilize many long-standing, well-accepted law enforcement tools in the fight against terror. These tools include delayed notification, judicially-supervised searches, and so-called roving wiretaps, which have long been used in combating organized crime and in the war on drugs.

In using these tactics to fight terrorism, the Patriot Act includes an additional layer of protection for individual liberty. A federal judge supervises the use of each of these tactics.

Were we to seek an order to request business records, that order would need the approval of a federal judge. Grand jury subpoenas issued for similar requests by police in standard criminal investigations are issued without judicial oversight.

Throughout the Patriot Act, tools provided to fight terrorism 50 require that the same predication be established before a federal judge as with similar tools provided to fight other crime.

In addition, the Patriot Act includes yet another layer of judicial scrutiny by providing a civil remedy in the event of abuse. Section 223 of the Patriot Act allows citizens to seek monetary damages for willful violations of the Patriot Act. This civil remedy serves as a further deterrent against infringement upon individual liberties.

Given our overly litigious society, you are probably wondering how many such civil cases have been filed to date. It is a figure as astronomical as the library searches. Zero.

There is a simple reason for this . . . the Patriot Act has not been used to infringe upon individual liberty.

Many of you have heard the hue and cry from critics of the Patriot Act who allege that liberty has been eroded. But more telling is what you have not heard. You have not heard of one single case in which a judge has found an abuse of the Patriot Act because, again, there have been no abuses.

It is also important to consider what we have not seen . . . no 55 major terrorist attacks on our soil over the past two years.

The Patriot Act's record demonstrates that we are protecting the American people while honoring the Constitution and preserving the liberties we hold dear.

While we are discussing the judiciary, allow me to add one more point. To be at its best, the judiciary requires a full bench. This is not like football or basketball, where the bench consists of reserves who might not see action. The judicial bench, to operate best for the people, must be at full strength.

Let me say this . . . President Bush has performed his duties admirably in selecting and nominating highly qualified jurists to serve.

The language in a judge's commission reads, and I quote, "George W. Bush, President of the United States of America . . . to all who shall see this, presents greeting: Know ye that reposing special confidence and trust in the wisdom, uprightness and learning, I have nominated . . .," you can fill in the blank, with the name Janice Rogers Brown, or Bill Pryor, or Priscilla Owen, or Carolyn Kuhl [Cool].

60   The commission's language may seem anachronistic. The ideals the men and women of the bench must uphold are not: Wisdom. Uprightness. Learning.

The president's nominees personify those noble ideals. They are proven defenders of the rule of law. They should be treated fairly. They deserve to be treated with the dignity that befits the position to which they seek to serve our country and its citizens.

You may think that some of the best of the president's nominees are being treated unfairly. In that case, you may want to exercise your right to dissent. The future of freedom and the rule of law depend on citizens informed by fact and directed toward truth.

To be sure, the law depends on the integrity of those who make it, enforce it, and apply it. It depends on the moral courage of lawyers like you . . . and our citizens . . . to insist on being heard, whether in town hall meetings, county council meetings, or the Senate.

There is nothing more noble than fighting to preserve our God-given rights. Our proven tactics against the terrorist threat are helping to do just that.

65   For more than two years, we have protected the lives of our citizens here at home. Again and again, Congress has determined and the courts have determined that our citizens' rights have been respected.

Twenty-six months ago, terrorists attacked our nation thinking our liberties were our weakness. They were wrong. The American people have fulfilled the destiny shaped by our forefathers and founders, and revealed the power of freedom.

Time and again, the spirit of our nation has been renewed and our greatness as a people has been strengthened by our dedication to the cause of liberty, the rule of law and the primacy and dignity of the individual.

I know we will keep alive these noble aspirations that lie in the hearts of all our fellow citizens, and for which our young men and women are at this moment fighting and making the ultimate sacrifice. What we are defending is what generations before us fought for and defended: a nation that is a standard, a beacon, to all who desire a land that promises to uphold the best hopes of all mankind. A land of justice. A land of liberty.

Starting Points

1. John Ashcroft talks about "ordered liberty," asserting that it is "a guiding principle, not a stumbling block to security." Consider whether you believe that laws, in theory, make us more or less free. If you believe they make us more free, then consider whether all laws are equal in doing so.
2. The first few paragraphs of this text are not particularly germane to the thesis of the speech. Where does the real text begin? What purpose is served in the first three or four paragraphs? Why is this more acceptable in a speech than in a magazine article or journal essay?
3. Carefully consider whether you are willing to give up a degree of freedom for increased security. Then write an essay in which you detail the extent of your support or opposition to the USA Patriot Act.

The USA Patriot Act and the U.S. Department of Justice: Losing Our Balances?

SUSAN HERMAN

Not everyone agrees with Attorney General John Ashcroft on whether the USA Patriot Act is a needed tool in the fight against terrorism. Susan Herman is a professor at the Brooklyn Law School, where she teaches criminal and Constitutional law. Her article appeared in the December 3, 2001, issue of Jurist, *the journal of the University of Pittsburgh School of Law.*

------------------ ✦ ------------------

WARS, FOREIGN AND DOMESTIC

Until Attorney General Ashcroft finally agreed to appear before Congress this week to report on the status of the domestic war against terrorism, rumors flew. Various reporters speculated about how many people were in detention, how many as material witnesses, and how many for immigration violations. There have been rumors about deplorable conditions, coercive tactics, and failure to report the detention of certain foreign nationals to their consulates. Formal Freedom of Information Act requests for information were denied.

Ashcroft has now provided some information about numbers of detainees, but not names, and not the quality of evidence in the individual cases. He has confirmed the rumor that some suspects, in New York, are being held under seal. He has also affirmed that the detentions are of people suspected of being terrorists, and that the detentions have prevented terrorist acts. At least one federal judge in New York, looking at the evidence in a particular case, ordered that one of the detainees be released on bail, given that the evidence against him tended to show not that he was a terrorist, but that he had lied to a grand jury. To expressions of doubt, or requests for additional information, Ashcroft reaffirms more loudly that he is detaining terrorists, that those detained would otherwise have committed terrorist acts, and that to share any more information than he has already shared with us or with Congress would aid Osama bin Laden in his anti-American campaign. The message is simple: we must stop asking questions and just trust the Department of Justice to do the right thing.

Being asked to have blind faith in the Attorney General is a difficult message for a child of the Vietnam Era. I am troubled by the fact that I know so little about the conduct of our domestic war against terrorism, for the same reason that I dislike knowing so little, except through government accounts, about the war in Afghanistan. It is difficult not to be able to judge what is being done in my name and with my tax dollars, and it is difficult not to be able to do what I understand to be my job as a citizen—to hold our elected officials accountable.

Partly because of the most recent spate of anti-terrorism legislation, two out of three branches of the federal government are also being left out of the loop in a growing number of circumstances. In its October USA Patriot Act (an eye-popping acronym for "Uniting and Strengthening America by Providing Appropriate Tools Required to Intercept and Obstruct Terrorism"), as in its September Use of Military Force Authorization, Congress has been consistently funneling power to the President and his Executive branch subordinates, while minimizing its own role, as well as the role of the judiciary, in the decisions that are to be made about the conduct of our foreign as well as our domestic war. The depth and breadth of the delegation of war powers is apparent on the face of the September 18 enactment, authorizing the President to "use all necessary and appropriate force against those nations, organizations, or persons he determines planned, authorized, committed, or aided the terrorist attacks that occurred on September 11, 2001, or harbored such organizations or persons. . . ." [Text available at the Library of Congress website.] Under this authorization, could the President simply decide to extend the war from Afghanistan to Iraq, Saudi Arabia, or even Germany without any further input from Congress? If Congress does not maintain an active role (as it reserves some option to do under the War Powers Resolution), the judiciary is unlikely to intervene, and the voting public only knows what the government tells us, where is the check?

It is less obvious how the balance of power has been shifted 5 in the domestic war against terrorism because the provisions of the enormous USA Patriot Act are only the tip of an iceberg of amended legislation. Most of its provisions amend previous law by adding or deleting words, paragraphs, or sections, forcing people reading the legislation to embark on an elaborate treasure hunt, tracking each amendment back to try to determine its impact on the previous law. In addition, it is difficult to comprehend the new changes if one is not already conversant with labyrinthine webs of law in many different areas.

Here are a few examples of how the new legislation continues to force feed power to the executive branch, while limiting the judiciary, and keeping Congress in the dark.

SURVEILLANCE PROVISIONS

The thrust of the USA Patriot Act surveillance provisions is to provide federal agencies with more surveillance options, and less judicial supervision. The principal statute governing electronic surveillance in criminal investigations, Title III of the Crime Control and Safe Streets Act of 1968, tried to meet concerns the Supreme Court had expressed about the constitutionality of electronic surveillance under Fourth Amendment, by providing standards to limit the scope of surveillance and by providing a judicial check. Except in certain cases deemed emergencies, applicants must persuade a judicial officer that they have probable cause that the interception they seek may provide evidence of one of a number of listed offenses. The court order permitting surveillance, like the statute, will require investigators to submit to various forms of limitations and judicial supervision. Evidence intercepted in violation of Title III's central provisions, which include a requirement that intrusions into conversations be "minimized," is made inadmissible in judicial and other proceedings. Cases decided in response to defendants' motions to suppress evidence seized then flesh out the nature of judicial participation.

The Foreign Intelligence Surveillance Act of 1978 (FISA), on the other hand, was aimed not at gathering evidence for a criminal prosecution, but at gathering information about the activities of foreign persons and agents (as opposed to "U.S. persons"). Judicial involvement in deciding whether to issue orders permitting this type of surveillance is both covert and minimal. Instead of requiring probable cause, surveillance orders are issued on a certification by the Attorney General that has nothing to do with probable cause. Between 1996 and 2000, out of 4,275 applications for FISA warrants, 4,275 were granted. Because the point is to gather intelligence rather than evidence, challenges to the legality of surveillance aren't likely to arise. The subjects may never even know that they have been under surveillance.

The USA Patriot Act allows surveillance of U.S. citizens under standards more like FISA than Title III, and allows powers permitted under Title III to be employed even where there is no probable cause and minimal judicial involvement, as in FISA. FISA warrants may now be used even if intelligence is not the primary purpose of an investigation. "Roving wiretaps" are a good example of how the powers under Title III have been extended. The Department of Justice argued to the public that revision of existing wiretap law was necessary to keep up with modern technology—to allow a roving wiretap that would allow a person's conversations to be intercepted even if the person carried a cell phone, or moved from phone to phone. Why should an investigation be limited to wiretapping one particular telephone, the argument ran, when modern telephone users frequently have access to several phones? The authority to issue an order for a roving wiretap already existed under Title III, for investigations where probable cause has been demonstrated. (The Supreme Court has not yet decided whether this blanket permission to intercept a person's conversations on any telephone is a refreshing modernization of an antiquated notion that a telephone is a physical place, or a violation of the Fourth Amendment's requirement that any warrant describe the "place to be searched" with particularity.) The USA Patriot Act extends the roving wiretap authority to intelligence wiretaps, which are authorized secretly and are not based on probable cause. The authorization may be nation-wide. Once additional telephones that a target uses (perhaps in someone else's home) are being monitored, other users of that telephone will also be subject to continuing surveillance.

Authority already existed for the government to order a tele- 10 phone company to turn over a list of the numbers being dialed to and from a particular telephone, on a standard less than probable cause. If the government certifies that the information sought is "relevant to an ongoing criminal investigation," a judge "must" grant the order, regardless of whether or not the judge agrees with the government's conclusion, and even if the judge thinks the government is fishing. This ample authority, on the same un-examined certification, is now extended to trap and trace orders providing access to "dialing, routing and signaling information" in connection with computers. These terms are not defined (and are certainly not clear to a technologically challenged person like me), but seem to allow the government access to lists of e-mails sent and received, as well as a list of the websites visited on a par-ticular computer. In the telephone context, getting a "pen regis-ter," with its list of telephone numbers to and from which calls were made on a particular phone, offered no opportunity to hear the contents of those conversations. In the computer context, the information about e-mail addresses and websites evidently trav-els with its content. The Department of Justice promises to sepa-rate the two, and not pry into content. There seems to be no way of supervising whether this promise is kept. In addition, it seems that if a target uses a computer in a cyber café or the public li-brary to check e-mail or visit a website, surveillance of that com-puter may simply continue, giving the government access to the e-mail and Internet activities of a multitude of non-targets.

Most of the new surveillance powers granted will expire after four years pursuant to the statute's sunset provisions. Most of the powers are not confined to investigations concerning terrorism, but apply to any criminal investigations. If there is to be any check on the Attorney General's use of these powers, it will have to come from congressional oversight. Will Congress be able to muster the political will to hold effective hearings, and to over-come the Bush Administration's reluctance to share what it claims as executive prerogative?

IMMIGRATION

The USA Patriot Act also further increases the authority of the Attorney General to detain and deport non-citizens with little or no judicial review. The Attorney General may certify that he has "reasonable grounds to believe" that a non-citizen endangers national security. The Attorney General and Secretary of State are also given the authority to designate domestic groups as terrorist organizations, and deport any non-citizen who belongs to them.

Like the Anti-Terrorism and Effective Death Penalty Act of 1996, the Illegal Immigration Reform and Immigrants' Responsibility Act of 1996 had sharply curtailed judicial review of the Attorney General's actions in a variety of circumstances. Last term, the Supreme Court interpreted some of those provisions as allowing more judicial supervision than Congress probably intended, on the theory that the alternative interpretation might leave the provisions in question open to constitutional challenge. This year, Congress has resumed its campaign to enhance executive prerogative and minimize judicial review. The Supreme Court could, as it did last year, resist some of these instances of court-stripping. Are the Justices likely to throw themselves in front of this year's train if Congress, the President, and we the people are not expressing any dissatisfaction, or was judicial supremacy just last year's fashion?

THE EXECUTIVE BRANCH ADDITIONS

In addition to collecting the various powers described above, the Attorney General announced that he intends to eavesdrop on inmates' attorney-client conversations. He also announced plans to have state and local law enforcement officials cooperate in questioning 5,000 people, who appear to have been selected according to their ethnicity or religion. He acted to expand his power to detain immigrants, and to contract the information available under the Freedom of Information Act.

15   The President issued an Executive Order declaring that he will decide when trials will take place before military commissions rather than in civilian courts, under his Commander-in-Chief powers. This decision cuts out the Article III courts, as well as Congress, which has constitutional authority to "define and punish Piracies and Felonies committed on the high Seas, and Offenses against the Law of Nations." [Article I, section 8, cl. 10]

Evidently, the powers conferred by the USA Patriot Act were just an appetizer.

CHECKS AND BALANCES

Of course, I know the arguments in favor of granting the Attorney General and President the powers said to be necessary to keep us safe. Some of the more vocal members of Congress have been congratulating themselves for having struck an appropriate balance between our need for security and our need for civil liberties. But their balance was struck on the face of the legislation by confiding the critical decisions to the President, the Attorney General, and other Executive Branch officials. The avidity with which the Attorney General and President have shown themselves willing to make dramatic unilateral decisions does not reassure me about the existence of balance, or of checks. And how will we ever be able to evaluate whether or not the powers now wielded by the Executive Branch are, as the legislation asserts, "required" to combat terrorism? We may be selling our birthright for a mess of pottage.

My general level of trust in the government is conditioned on the existence of the Constitution's elaborate structure of checks and balances: the hydraulic pressures among the three branches of the federal government, the dialectic of federalism, and the ultimate political power of an informed electorate. Now, there increasingly often seems to be only one locus of power. Increasingly often, the other two branches, the other axis of government (the states), and the electorate, including me, are asked not to know, but just to trust.

I have found myself thinking often lately about the world of George Orwell's *1984*, and not only because Orwell's "Big Brother" has become such a pervasive metaphor for expansive governmental surveillance. The people in Orwell's totalitarian state, Oceania (Orwell's prescient amalgam of Britain and America?), knew that their state was engaged in a murky foreign war, against some enemy or other—either Eastasia or Eurasia. The war had become wallpaper, and there wasn't much point in trying to understand what the war was about, or evaluating the government's claims of victory. Information about the war was no more specific and no more reliable than the Newspeak about domestic affairs.

I don't know whether we have lost our balance, but I do know   20
that power is careening in one direction. That, combined with the extent of what I don't know, is reason enough to worry.

Starting Points

1. Susun Herman is concerned about the concentration of power in the Executive Branch that she believes is embedded within the USA Patriot Act. Research the act (the entire text may be found at http://Thomas.loc.gov), read Attorney General Ashcroft's speech preceding this article, and write an essay with an arguable thesis supporting either one.
2. Little information is available about many of the detainees held after 9/11, and this is one of the causes for Herman's lack of enthusiasm for the USA

Patriot Act. Does Herman take an overly legalistic view, in your opinion, or does she speak for average Americans here? Should the government have the power thus enacted, or should all citizens be concerned about the possible misuse of the power of detention?

3. "Being asked to have blind faith in the Attorney General is a difficult message for a child of the Vietnam Era," writes Herman in the third paragraph. Learn more about the Tonkin Gulf Resolution and the Pentagon Papers. What does Vietnam have to do with trusting the attorney general and the government in general?

John Ashcroft, Maligned Again
The New York Times Tells More Whoppers about the Patriot Act
DAVID TELL

Newspaper, journals, and magazines often have a particular political or philosophical stance. David Tell, opinion page editor of the Weekly Standard, *takes the* New York Times *to task for what he construes as misleading news articles about the Bush Administration as it relates to the war on terror. This article was published in the August 4/August 11, 2003, issue (Vol. 8, issue 45)*

———————— ✦ ————————

Report on U.S. Antiterrorism Law Alleges Violations of Civil Rights"—so read the headline on the July 21 front page of the *New York Times*. It was a scoop of sorts: The report in question, prepared by the office of Justice Department inspector general Glenn A. Fine, hadn't yet been released. It had, however, been delivered to the department's congressional overseers, one of whom, ranking House Judiciary Committee Democrat John Conyers of Michigan, arranged for a copy to be "made available" to *Times* correspondent Philip Shenon. Conyers also provided Shenon with a written statement helpfully highlighting the document's significance: "This report shows that we have only begun to scratch the surface with respect to the Justice Department's disregard of constitutional rights and civil liberties." And Shenon repaid Conyers's courtesy with a 1,200-word piece more or less explicitly concluding that, yup, that's what the IG report does, all right.

Thus, the *Times* story's lead: "A report by internal investigators at the Justice Department has identified dozens of recent
cases in which department employees have been accused of serious civil rights and civil liberties violations involving enforcement
of the sweeping federal antiterrorism law known as the USA Patriot Act." And, later, the scene-setting back-story: "The report is
the second in recent weeks from the inspector general to focus on
the way the Justice Department is carrying out the broad new
surveillance and detention powers it gained under the Patriot
Act"—the first report's findings having generated "widespread, bi-
partisan criticism" of the Bush administration.

And, later still, at the very end, Shenon's account of the fresh,
purportedly damning details in Report Number Two: The IG's office appears to have been "overwhelmed by accusations of abuse,
many filed by Muslim or Arab inmates in federal detention centers"—1,073 such accusations during the six months ending June
15, to be precise. Each of them " 'suggesting a Patriot Act-related'
abuse of civil rights or civil liberties." And 34 of them raising
what the IG's report called "credible Patriot Act violations on
their face."

Is 34 a frightening lot? The *Times* gave its readers no means to
judge this obvious question, apparently believing it self-evident that
the answer was "yes." And similarly automatic thinking characterized most of the catch-up coverage published by competing major
papers the following day; with a few notable exceptions, even the
best of these stories generally tracked the *Times* version. This, even
though these better stories, many of them, were sprinkled through
with quotations and information hinting—correctly—that the *New
York Times*'s original report was dead wrong: crippled by a fundamental factual error and, therefore, thoroughly misleading.

For example: Three-quarters of the way down Toni Locy's   5
USA Today dispatch ("Report Outlines Rights Violations in Sept.
11 Act"), we learned that . . . well, actually, "The report does not
cite any examples of alleged abuse of the powers provided by the
Patriot Act." Moreover, three-quarters of the way down Susan
Schmidt's *Washington Post* story, the best of the bunch, we saw
quoted the inspector general's principal deputy, a man named
Paul Martin, explaining that the report wasn't really "about" the
Patriot Act at all. "This report is not an assessment of the Patriot
Act as a piece of legislation," Martin said. And "[i]t doesn't exam-
ine the department's use of Patriot Act authorities," either.

What the report does do, instead, is comply with a provision
of the Patriot Act, Section 1001, requiring the inspector general to

make semi-annual submissions to Congress concerning his re-
ceipt and review of "complaints alleging abuses of civil rights and
civil liberties by employees and officials of the Department of Justice." Notice: that's *all* alleged civil rights abuses, not just those
that might arise as a consequence of the Patriot Act or in connection with the war on terrorism.

Indeed, the inspector general's office has since made clear
that only a "tiny fraction" of the complaints at issue in his latest
report have even the remotest connection to the exercise of law
enforcement powers granted by the Patriot Act. And none of this
tiny fraction is among the 34 allegations the report deems "credible . . . on their face." In other words: The only thing "Patriot Act-
related" about the vast majority of the complaints discussed in
the IG's report is the fact that it's the Patriot Act which obliges
him to discuss them in the first place. Just the same, the overall
numbers involved are interesting. And they do suggest something
meaningful about the Ashcroft Justice Department's reputation
for "disregard of constitutional and civil rights"—something an
innocent *New York Times* subscriber would never expect.

Whether or not it's fair to say that the IG's office has been
"overwhelmed" by the resulting workload, it's certainly the case
that civil rights protests lodged against Justice employees are
sharply on the rise. During the previous six-month reporting period, June through December 2002, Glenn A. Fine and his staff received 783 complaints "in which the complainant makes any
mention of a civil rights or civil liberties violation, even if the allegation is not within the [inspector general's] or the [department's]
jurisdiction, or the allegation appears unsupported on its face."
Those 1,073 total complaints the IG has more recently tabulated,
then, represent a 37 percent upward spike.

And yet the absolute number of complaints judged "credible
on their face" has remained almost perfectly flat: 34 this time, 33
the time before. The other 1,039 are either misdirected, involving
gripes against people who don't work at the Justice Department;
or not stuff properly considered a "civil rights" issue ("e-mails
from individuals asking about the status of immigration paper-
work they had submitted to the INS," for instance); or altogether
"unrelated," as the IG report gently puts it ("individuals who
claim they are under 24-hour surveillance by the CIA" and "non-
detained individuals who claim they are being tortured by the
government"—that kind of thing).

10   Bottom line: People are more and more likely to accuse the
Justice Department of doing them wrong—which only stands to

reason, since the *New York Times* and its hundreds of imitators have spent the past two years telling them that John Ashcroft is raping the Constitution. But it's less and less likely that those accusations are "credible."

And "credible" is not the same thing as "true," incidentally. A fair bit of last week's IG report was devoted to the disposition of "credible" allegations first identified in earlier reports. Most remain unsubstantiated. And all the worst of them—like the American-Arab Anti-Discrimination Committee's claim that an INS detainee in Texas was forced to eat pork, beaten, "had six teeth extracted against his will," and was then denied medical treatment—turned out to be false.

Starting Points

1. David Tell raises some important concerns about the relationship between headlines—read by many—and news articles, which might be read by fewer subscribers. Study your local newspaper and determine whether headlines accurately reflect the content of news stories.

2. Consider how you reach conclusions regarding items of political give and take. Do you get your news from a single source or from a variety of viewpoints and political perspectives? How should citizens in a free society approach information, especially regarding a war or legislation concerning civil liberties, when there often are conflicting interpretations?

3. Closely study two sources of news for two weeks and analyze their reporting on the same topic. Are the facts identical? Why do their interpretations differ? What is responsible for the differing slants on the same subject? And how should responsible readers arrive at their informed conclusions?

From MAD (Mutual Assured Destruction) to MUD (Multilateral Unconstrained Disruption): Dealing with the New Terrorism

STEPHEN GALE AND LAWRENCE HUSICK

During the Cold War, which began shortly after World War II and ended with the breakup of the Soviet Union in 1989, a kind of nuclear stand-off ensued. Mutually Assured Destruction (MAD) was

*the theory that in a potential nuclear war both sides would be oblit-
erated and in knowing that would seek alternatives to war at almost
any cost. In the following article from the* Foreign Policy Research
Institute Journal *(February 2003), Stephen Gale and Lawrence
Husick call for a new approach to the new reality of terrorism,
which they characterize as MUD (Multilateral Unconstrained
Disruption).*

◆

Al Qaeda's actions on September 11, 2001, demonstrated the
use of a new form of warfare, requiring relatively modest resources and aimed at achieving maximum disruption of the
morale and the economic core of Western society. Unlike the attacks Cold War strategists feared and planned for, however, these
actions do not envision mass destruction. Rather, the terrorists'
targets are Western society's economic foundations and its supporting political infrastructure (the nation's "commons").
Security in this new age will not be achieved by a policy that seeks
to safeguard an almost infinite number of individual targets at all
times. Instead, we must protect these foundations by developing
public and, equally important, private-sector measures that deny
the terrorists the leverage they seek in disrupting our societies.

RISK MANAGEMENT AND SECURITY

Virtually every current method of risk management begins with
the assumption that individual assets (e.g., buildings, aircraft,
people) are the proper focus for investments in security. Even
where the characteristics of an asset (or of its environment) are
dynamic—for example, a presidential motorcade—risk management focuses on the methods for protecting against threats such
as theft or destruction. Indeed, both our legal system and insur-
ance (and reinsurance) industries—the institutional foundations
of risk management in Western society—base their policies and
procedures on calculations of the risk-adjusted value of specific
identified assets.

In the face of the potential for ongoing terrorist attacks from
al Qaeda (and potentially others), the objective of risk management must now be shifted to a focus on protection from the leverage that attacks on assets can achieve with respect to the continued functioning of our society. Assets of any type may be the
specific targets—they are the concrete focus of terrorist actions

that provide the leverage needed to cause "unconstrained disruption"—but it is the ability of Western society to continue to rely on the vitality and utility of these functions and systems that is really in al Qaeda's sights.

Al Qaeda's actions on September 11 were certainly horrific, but they were not catastrophic. The destruction of what risk managers would regard as the targeted assets—the four airplanes, the passengers and crew, the three major buildings, the occupants of the buildings, and so on—was the source of the horror. But even the number of deaths (exceeding the strike on Pearl Harbor), the destruction of the World Trade Center and airplanes, and the damage to the Pentagon were not catastrophic for the nation or for the West. And as difficult as it is for us to comprehend, the death and destruction were, in fact, incidental to the terrorists' goals. Al Qaeda's objective was simply to use the attacks on those assets as the means to gain the leverage needed to disrupt and destabilize the governments, economies, and social structure of the West. Aside from al Qaeda's interest in retribution through death and destruction, the assets employed and destroyed were merely the means to pursue the broader goal of neutralizing the West.

Osama bin Laden has been extraordinarily clear about the goals of al Qaeda: restructuring—and purifying—Islam and creating a modern version of a caliphate. To achieve this goal, al Qaeda's leadership recognizes that the West must be neutralized in the role it plays in the world—and the Middle East in particular. Or, in bin Laden's words (from his 1998 fatwah): 5

> The ruling to kill the Americans and their allies—civilians and military—is an individual duty for every Muslim who can do it in any country in which it is possible to do it, in order to liberate the al-Aqsa Mosque and the holy mosque from their grip, and in order for their armies to move out of all the lands of Islam, defeated and unable to threaten any Muslim. This is in accordance with the words of Almighty God, "and fight the pagans all together as they fight you all together," and "fight them until there is no more tumult or oppression, and there prevail justice and faith in God."

Seen through this new lens, the actions on September 11 were only marginal tactical successes. As was the case after the failure of the first attack on the World Trade Center in 1993, however, al Qaeda has not changed its ultimate goals. The leadership and member cells of al Qaeda may bide their time before initiating new major attacks, but they certainly have not been eliminated as a threat. We must therefore begin to work on protecting the West and our global partners from the potential threat to the "commons"—to society's commonly held assets—by redirecting the focus of risk management so that it can, in fact, offer standards and guidelines in the face of the this new form of terrorism. Rather than focusing on the management of risks to specific assets, we must now ask "How can we restructure risk management (and counterterrorism and homeland security) procedures, standards, and methods to account for leverage protection? How can the methods of risk management be extended to supply estimates of the relative value of security investments aimed at mitigating the effects of the leverage provided by attacks on assets?" Put another way, the assets that are the focus of virtually all current risk management methods are, in effect, simply a means to an end with respect to terrorism. The real targets of the type of terrorism that we face today are the derivative values of these assets: the systems of production and government, the means of economic exchange, and the vitality of and confidence in our social organizations and institutions.

THE TRAGEDY OF THE COMMONS, REDUX

Although often forgotten in the face of its message about the disastrous condition of the world's rivers and air, Garrett Hardin's now classic call-to-arms for the environmental movement, *The Tragedy of the Commons,* opens with a quotation from Wiesner and York on the dilemma of national security in the nuclear age:

> Both sides in the arms race are . . . confronted by the dilemma of steadily increasing military power and steadily decreasing national security. It is our considered professional judgment that this dilemma has no technical solution. If the great powers continue to look for solutions in the area of science and technology only, the result will be to worsen the situation. (Wiesner and York[1] in Hardin[2])

Both Hardin's analogy and his conclusions about the need for a better means for making choices where there are common critical interests have been given new life by changes in international terrorism. Hardin's "commons," a shared town pasture used by all farmers to graze their livestock, but owned and cared for by no one, finds its analogue in our shared infrastructure and the core critical functions necessary to the operation of Western society. In most cases, such commons—the electric grid, water systems, transportation networks—are privately owned and geographically dispersed, but are nonetheless essential to our ability to function as a society.

In Hardin's example, with an openly available common asset and an absence of institutional measures to ensure that there is a focus of responsibility for the maintenance of that asset, the result is the destruction of the commons. Our commons, our systems of production and government, the means of economic exchange, and our social organizations and institutions, while not a single physical asset, are nonetheless commonly held and valuable property without a proprietor, with the potential to be ruined by terrorist actions.

In the face of terrorist threats, traditional risk management seems counterproductive in much the same way as would be a letter to each of the farmers who use Hardin's commons requesting that they reduce the size of their herds. From the perspective of the individual farmers who use the field for grazing, the objective is simply to get the best source of feed at the lowest possible price and, short of some sort of regulatory constraints and/or externally imposed fee structure aimed at preserving the value of the common asset, there is simply no reason for any individual to do other than that which is personally best. Similarly, in the case of the potential targets of terrorism, there is no rationale for any individual or organization to make investments in security measures that benefit the U.S. economy and society as a whole (the "commons")—at least in the short-term. And clearly this type of approach to risk management creates problems in a world where terrorists have the reach and capabilities of al Qaeda.

Attacks on specific assets, as horrific as they may be, are in fact interchangeable from the perspective of al Qaeda and other terrorist groups that are seeking to disrupt and defeat the U.S. and the West. Seen in this light, the problem of protecting the electrical grid, for example, from a devastating attack is not a risk management problem for the electric utility industry alone—although the utilities and independent system operators would undoubtedly be involved in the design and implementation of the protective measures. However, it is an attack that would ultimately result in the destruction of the "commons." Similarly, managing the risks to the nation's rail system is not solely a problem for the various railroad companies. Rail transport provides the mission-critical links in the nation's manufacturing and distribution processes and is therefore at the core of our ability to maintain the "commons."

Private companies—even individuals—may own these critical assets, but the management of the risks must ultimately account for the value—and even the relative value—of these "commons" to the U.S. and our global partners.

ENVIRONMENTAL RISK MANAGEMENT AND HOMELAND SECURITY

Our methods for management of risks from threats to the environment provide an example of one way to manage homeland security. Although often seen as more of a political bludgeon than a management tool, the most effective technique for protecting our environmental commons has proven to be requiring (and setting standards and priorities for) a full accounting of actions—private and public—that would affect the environment. If, for example, a factory is free to pollute a river and that pollution will have adverse consequences such as destroying fisheries or reducing tourism, the account of the full range of expected economic losses caused by the pollution provides the basis for society's determination of the relative value of investments in preventing pollution. When all the current and future costs and benefits of the actions affecting the commons are tallied up, a large social cost may prompt society to pass laws and regulations aimed at reducing or eliminating pollution. In other cases, the cost/benefit balance may result in the opposite conclusion: given the cost of, say, measures to control effluents and the projected benefits of pollution control, the proposed project may fail to meet the standards of economic viability. In effect, it is the use of clear assessments of the costs and benefits to society that is at the heart of a democracy's determination of the value of its investments in protecting and securing its commonly held assets.

Of course, where the issues at stake are complex (e.g., large-scale dredging projects, dams, construction of canals) economists and environmentalists have used more sophisticated methods than a mere summing of readily observable costs and benefits. In the case of the use of the pesticide DDT, for instance, one of the limitations of simple economic measures is that, in environmental terms, the benefits of increased agricultural productivity are often easier to quantify than the long-term and often unknown costs of using chemical herbicides and pesticides. As we now know, many environmental costs are extremely difficult to value, due, for example, to the absence of a functioning market to set the value of effects that impact the commons. Valuations are also made more difficult in those many cases where people hold substantially conflicting visions of the desired future.

15   In order to satisfy the variety of interests in environmental decisions under current U.S. regulations, major actions signifi-

cantly affecting the quality of the environment may only proceed after preparation of an Environmental Impact Statement (EIS). Under current federal law (see, for example, Sec. 102, National Environmental Policy Act, Public Law 91-190, 1970) this statement must provide a description and assessment of:

1. The environmental impacts of the proposed action;
2. Any adverse environmental effects that cannot be avoided should the proposal be implemented;
3. Alternatives to the proposed action;
4. The relationship between local short-term uses of the environment and the maintenance and enhancement of long-term productivity; and
5. The irreversible and irretrievable commitments of resources that would be involved in the proposed action should it be implemented.

Of course, an EIS does not legally require federal agencies to take any particular action. An agency may even decide to implement the most environmentally damaging alternative if the agency can demonstrate compelling reasons (e.g., national security)—and has the political will to justify its decision to the nation's legislators, courts, and public. But the EIS process provides society a means of assessing the value and priorities of alternative environmental actions.

With this in mind, let us examine the objectives of the new Department of Homeland Security (DHS). At least as it is currently organized, the Department's mandate is described largely in terms of improvements in communications among the government agencies having functional responsibilities associated with responses to terrorist attacks. However, while such coordination among first responders is certainly valuable, it does little to help prevent or deter future terrorist acts. The nation would be best served if, in addition to its responsibilities for the coordination among first responders, the DHS focused on security measures that offer "leverage protection."

We believe that the DHS must focus directly on the management of risks to our commonly held assets. This is a two-part process: (1) the Department should take the lead in setting standards for societal investments in securing our "commons," and (2) it should work with private sector groups (industry trade associations, standards bodies, financial markets) and other government agencies (the national laboratories, the National Institute for Standards and Technology) to render a full accounting of investment decisions that affect homeland security.

A "Security Impact Statement" (SIS), an analogy to the EIS, should serve as the operational heart of the DHS; the SIS should, at a minimum, provide a description and assessment of:

1. The impacts on security of both the proposed action and the failure to act;
2. Any adverse security effects that would be avoided should the proposal be implemented, as well as those that are unavoidable;
3. Alternatives to the proposed action, the expected criteria for decision making, and analysis of why the proposed action is preferred under those criteria;
4. The costs of the proposed action (including the expected costs to the nation as a whole) of a successful attack, and an estimate of the net present value of the investment required to take the proposed action; and
5. An estimate of the expenditures involved in implementing the proposed action.

20   Using the SIS process as its organizational and operational methodology, the DHS will be able to provide both the leadership and coordination necessary for the protection of our "commons" in a manner that is fully consistent with both the core values of our democracy and the prerogatives of ownership in a market economy. More important, the SIS process may permit the Department to act for the common good without resorting to outright federal management of critical infrastructure assets, the likely result in the aftermath of a true catastrophe. And, most important, the Department will thus be able to serve its true purpose—enhancing the security of the U.S. homeland by protecting that which is essential to our national interests rather than by simply coordinating and facilitating post-attack responses in order to minimize the cost in lives and property. Hardin's *The Tragedy of the Commons* served as the intellectual backbone of a rational approach to environmental protection. Its translation into the management of risks resulting from potential acts of terrorism could well serve as the motivating force for a rational approach to the management of homeland security. Failures in the environmental field led to Rachel Carson's famous *Silent Spring*.[3] It should be our goal to avoid failures in homeland security that lead, tragically, to a "Dark Winter."[4]

Endnotes

1. J. B. Wiesner and H. F. York, *Scientific American* 211 (No. 4) (1964), p. 27.
2. "The Tragedy of the Commons," Garrett Hardin, *Science* 162 (1968), pp. 1243–48 (http://www.constitution.org/cmt/tragcomm.htm).

3. Rachel Carson, *Silent Spring* (Houghton Mifflin Co., Boston, 1962).
4. Peter J. Roman, "The Dark Winter of Biological Terrorism," *Orbis* Summer 2002, p. 469.

Starting Points

1. Stephen Gale and Lawrence Husick write about the "commons," that is, systems so vital to the lifeblood of the nation that, even though they might be privately owned, must be protected by the nation against disruption or destruction. Brainstorm with others in your class and compile a list of what you believe are systems that fall into this category. Then discuss what should be done in a free society to protect, to the extent possible, those national assets.

2. Choose a particular "commons" system and write a SIS (Security Impact Statement) as discussed by the authors that would lead to maximum protection of your chosen asset in an age of terrorism.

3. The analogy of the authors of environmental concerns to homeland security is predicated on a cost/benefits ratio. Are there other possible paradigms for assessing the value of a particular action regarding protection from terrorism? In a collaborative group, discuss this. (You might consider historical value—how much should be spent to safeguard the original copy of the Constitution for example—or ethical or religious considerations, elements that have no clear monetary value.) List your results and discuss them in class.

Terrorism and Economic Security
ROBERT L. HUTCHINGS

The impact of the ongoing war on terror, and the reverberations of the attacks of September 11th, are being felt in ways that most of us do not routinely consider. Robert L. Hutchings, chair of the National Intelligence Council (NIC), addresses security managers about ways that national and international economic security has been affected by terrorism. The NIC is a U.S. government body that provides analyses of foreign policy issues for the President, the Director of Central Intelligence, and major policy makers. This text is from a speech to the International Security Management Association in Scottsdale, Arizona, on January 14, 2004.

———————— ✦ ————————

We live in turbulent and complex times. We possess unrivaled power, yet we remain vulnerable—as the terrorist attacks of 9/11 demonstrated so tragically.

The breakdown of the Cold War order thawed out historical problems that had been frozen over for decades. Globalization has brought with it enormous benefits, but it has also led to sharpened polarization between the haves and have-nots. Also, the very success of Western values has threatened in an existential way those who seek to preserve traditional ways of life in the face of modernity—ushering in a new era of asymmetrical warfare in which adversaries compensate for their relative military weakness by devising new strategies and adapting new technologies to exploit U.S. vulnerabilities—the vulnerabilities of an open society.

These trends have imposed new challenges on the U.S. Intelligence Community. And they have imposed new challenges on security professionals in American businesses to help keep U.S. citizens abroad safe and our economy growing. Effective security management—on either the national or corporate levels—clearly hinges on our ability to identify, understand, and counter threats to our people, facilities, and interests. In some cases, these threats are all too visible—as demonstrated by our recent experiences with elevated homeland security threat levels and "orange-alerts." In other cases, they are more subtle but no less ominous.

I would like to focus my remarks today on international terrorism, which I know is a preoccupation for all of you. I will begin with a "status report" in the war against terrorism, from the perspective of the U.S. Government. Then I will offer some thoughts about the implications of terrorist dangers for American economic interests at home and abroad.

TERRORISM—A STATUS REPORT

5 First, a status report: we have made great progress in the war against terrorism since September 11 . . . progress that has prevented the loss of many lives but that is causing dramatic changes in the nature of the challenges we face.

- We have disrupted scores of plots at home and abroad—plots that were audacious in terms of the numbers of attacks under consideration and their global scope.
- Al-Qa'ida is in disarray. More than two-thirds of its senior leaders, operatives, and facilitators are dead or in long-term custody. Those remaining are in hiding, their ability to function constrained by physical isolation, disrupted communications, and reduced access to funds.

To put this in business terms, imagine that you are trying to lead a multinational enterprise. Almost all of your senior leadership is gone. You have no one you trust who can fill in. You cannot communicate with your subordinates. Your ability to conduct business is suffering and your shareholders are beginning to question whether their investments will ever pay dividends.

Despite this progress, the global war on terrorism will be a long fight and other organizations are increasingly adopting al-Qa'ida's ideology to attract new, young recruits. As we adapt our tactics, the terrorists are adapting theirs. They are trying to find new ways to share information and get funds. They understand that small ad hoc networks can still inflict significant damage.

Bin Ladin and many other al-Qa'ida terrorists see attacks that weaken our economy as key to undermining our strength and morale. In video statements after 9/11 we saw Bin Ladin marveling at the economic impact of the attacks, claiming New York lost over $1 trillion.

- Soft targets, including the U.S. stock market, banks, major companies, and tall buildings are a primary focus of active al-Qa'ida planning. These softer targets are seen as easier to hit than other high-priority targets, such as U.S. Government buildings and major infrastructure targets, which have higher security postures.
- Targets such as nuclear power plants, water treatment facilities, and other public utilities are high on al-Qa'ida's targeting list as a way to sow panic and hurt our economy.

The group has continued to hone its use of transportation assets as weapons. We have found several examples of al-Qa'ida adjusting its tactics to circumvent enhanced airline security. Although we have disrupted several airline plots, we have not eliminated the threat to airplanes. There are still al-Qa'ida operatives who we believe have been deployed to hijack planes and fly them into key targets.

- Just this past year, al-Qa'ida attacks in Kenya, Saudi Arabia, and Turkey have demonstrated the group's impressive expertise to build truck bombs, and we are concerned it will try to marry this capability to toxic or radioactive material to increase the damage and psychological impact of an attack.
- We know the group has looked at derailing trains—perhaps carrying HAZMAT—to attack us.

- Al-Qa'ida has demonstrated a keen ability to use maritime assets to attack ships at berth as well as at sea. We are concerned that al-Qa'ida might employee these techniques to attack U.S. ships, ports, and coastal infrastructure targets such as chemical and oil facilities.
- My biggest worry, however, is how far al-Qa'ida might have progressed in being able to deploy a chemical, nuclear, or biological weapon against the United States or its allies.

10   We have been able to uncover important and complicated plotlines across all these disciplines and have been able to disrupt and capture key individuals involved. But al-Qa'ida is a many-headed Hydra: regional nodes remain active—and fully capable of mounting large-scale plots, as we have seen. The terrorists we face are patient, resilient, and sophisticated. The fact that we have not seen a successful major attack against the U.S. Homeland since 9/11 should not cause us to relax our vigilance. Today we have an important responsibility not only to continue to educate the American people, but to put a program of security in place that is agile, seamless, and reduces our vulnerabilities without panicking our people.

- Despite our successes in stopping or disrupting attacks, the exact date, time, and place of an attack will always be elusive.
- Al Qa'ida's intent is clear. Its capabilities are circumscribed but still substantial. And our vulnerabilities are still great. Thus, in the Intelligence Community, we have to assume that more attacks will be attempted, and we have to reckon with the possibility that one of these may eventually be successfully carried out.

WHAT THIS MEANS TO YOU

Let me now turn to how these trends in the war against terrorism affect your business interests and our economic security more generally. I do so with some trepidation, knowing that in most of these areas the expertise is in the audience rather than on the podium.

As you well know, the risks and challenges faced by corporate security officers have only multiplied in the post 9/11 security environment. Undoubtedly much of your immediate focus post 9/11 has been on physical security as you endeavored to assure corporate boards, personnel, and shareholders that terror-related risks to personnel and facilities—at home and abroad—were identified and that actions had been taken to mitigate those risks. Yet even before 9/11, corporate risks were mounting as globalization, deregulation, outsourcing, just-in-time inventory practices, and increasing use of information technology and the Internet brought greater openness and efficiency, along with new vulnerabilities.

- The change in priority security concerns is illustrated by a Pinkerton survey of the largest U.S. firms. In 2001 firms ranked workplace violence as the main security threat, followed by Internet security and employee screening, while terrorism ranked a lowly 17th. In 2003, terrorism jumped to third place as the most pressing concern for the largest U.S. corporations, although workplace violence remains the leading worry.
- The President's Council of Economic Advisers has estimated that private business spent an estimated $55 billion a year on private security before Sept. 11th; since then some experts forecast that corporate America may have to increase that spending by 50 to 100 percent.
- In the global economy, a security vulnerability could be a headquarters office or a factory gate, but also a computer network connection that could be a gateway to exploit a firm's databases, product designs, financial information, or personal information for identity fraud.

I have already detailed the terrorist threat and feel it is important to point out that according to State Department statistics, more businesses are targeted in terrorist attacks than all other types of facilities combined. U.S. interests both abroad and at home, as well as U.S. citizens working abroad, are prime targets for terrorist groups seeking to damage the U.S. economy and affect our way of life. High-profile facilities such as nuclear power plants, oil and gas production, and export and receiving facilities remain at risk; moreover al-Qa'ida and other terrorist groups' targets and methods may be evolving.

- Private sector cooperation is essential to protecting U.S. critical infrastructure because nearly 90 percent is privately owned—from shipping and banking to nuclear power production, food processing, and chemical manufacturing.
- The increased number of kidnappings in the Middle East attributed to terrorist groups—a long established tactic in Latin America—may point to a new strategy to ransom the release of captured foreign combatants in U.S. custody. U.S. engineers working in foreign oilfields and other industrial projects could be particularly at risk.

- Shipping experts suggest that ports and maritime industries worldwide are increasingly at risk. Evidence indicates that terrorist groups have taken note of the value and vulnerability of the maritime sector, including the cruise ship industry.

At the same time the costs of mitigating these risks have skyrocketed, particularly for large multinational companies.

- The September 11th attacks inflicted the biggest single loss— currently estimated at $50 billion—ever sustained by the global insurance industry. A survey conducted by the Conference Board after September 11th found that insurance costs had risen on average 33 percent since 2001, while costs for 20 percent of companies surveyed had doubled.

FINANCIAL THREATS

15   We have heard a lot about terrorists' financial networks since 9/11, but there are other financial threats that should concern us. Money laundering may not be much in the news these days, but narcotraffickers, organized criminal gangs, and corrupt leaders from around the world continue to move tens of billions of dollars into the international and U.S. banking systems and securities markets every year. Not only does money laundering make crime profitable, the huge flows of illicit funds can undermine the integrity of individual banks, distort economies, and fuel insurgencies, such as the Revolutionary Armed Forces of Colombia (FARC).

Rogue states also engage in a wide array of illicit financial activity. They use financial cutouts to covertly acquire the goods and services needed to build weapons of mass destruction. They hide money abroad; they use front companies to beat UN sanctions with surprising ease.

Saddam Hussayn's regime amassed one of the most sophisticated illicit financial networks. It earned several billion dollars from oil smuggling and in kickbacks paid by companies that participated in the UN's "oil-for-food" program. It had covert bank accounts, front companies, and investments scattered throughout the Mideast and as far afield as East Asia, Europe, and possibly South America.

We know that the wide extent of Saddam's network, and of the networks controlled by Iran, North Korea, and other rogues, means that numerous legitimate firms become unwittingly involved in supplying these states. The components of the network may look innocuous—a European bank or a firm run by a Singaporean businessman. In fact, increasingly they do, which can make it tough to spot the purchaser who's really helping Kim Chong-il buy a proscribed good, or the investment advisor who wants to hide Kim's nest egg.

It should also be apparent that illicit financial activity can threaten the integrity of the global financial and business system. We've seen major banks collapse because their officials were involved in money laundering, theft, and other crimes. BCCI—the Bank of Credit and Commerce International—is the "poster child," but we've seen a number of smaller banks fail for similar reasons, and several Chinese banks have suffered huge losses because of corrupt "sweetheart" loans. Cleaning up bad banks is a major goal of the U.S.-led Financial Action Task Force. As the world grows more interconnected, the ripple effect from problems in traditional havens for illicit finance is becoming of increasing concern.

We are particularly concerned about the security of rapidly   20
spreading electronic financial activity. The Internet has spawned a host of on-line gambling systems, banks, and other businesses that can facilitate money laundering and covert movement of money. We've already seen a pioneer Internet bank in Aruba collapse, after it was determined to be a front for money launderers and embezzlers. We're also seeing on-line casinos set up in money laundering hubs.

Not all the threats to corporate interests are linked to terrorism or illicit finance. Intellectual property rights protection is another concern. Strong, effective IPR protection is critical to innovation, investment, and the long-term growth of the U.S. and global economy. Unfortunately, enforcement of IPR rules around the world is lacking, particularly in developing countries. As a result, the risk of theft of intellectual property or proprietary information continues to be a large and growing problem for multinational corporations. The U.S. Trade Representative has identified counterfeiting of trademarked goods as an increasing problem in many countries, including China, Paraguay, Poland, the Philippines, Russia, Vietnam, and Turkey.

Likewise, while outsourcing of business functions is a growing trend that helps firms cut costs, it also brings potential security risks—particularly when outsourcing involves entities owned and operated abroad.

- As many as 3 million software industry jobs could move offshore by 2015, with 70 percent of these jobs moving to India, 20 percent to the Philippines, and 10 percent to China.

- Corporate leaders need to be on guard and know who their business partners are and what security measures they have in place to protect against loss, whether through unintended leakage of proprietary business information, deliberate theft of intellectual property, or outright economic espionage.
- Technology now allows companies to have their most sensitive proprietary computer code written overseas. The inability of companies to sufficiently vet the personnel involved in these activities can create a significant vulnerability.

U.S. openness to foreign trade and investment and our commitment to global information sharing through academic and scientific exchange unfortunately also leave our technologies highly exposed to foreign exploitation.

- Collectors last year employed a wide variety of techniques in their quest to circumvent U.S. restrictions in the acquisition of sensitive technologies—not only militarily critical technologies but manufacturing processes, biometrics, and pharmaceuticals, to name just a few.
- Naturally, the simplest, safest, and least expensive methods were the ones most widely used. In a surprising number of cases, foreigners—often through middlemen—acquired sensitive U.S. technologies simply by requesting them via e-mail, faxes or telephones.

CYBER THREATS

Globally networked information systems also present vulnerabilities, and even the simplest computer threats pose real risks for your companies' business interests and proprietary knowledge. Some of you may even have personal experience with these threats from your international travels and business dealings: a laptop computer or Palm Pilot stolen at a conference, in an airport, or from your hotel room.

- We have seen foreign intelligence services make use of many such venues, sometimes more subtly than outright theft: Hard disks, CDs, and other media can be copied and then quickly returned. The hacker underground studies the art of computer intrusions with no physical tethers at all, scanning computers with wireless network capabilities for access holes to slip through.

No country in the world rivals the United States in its re- 25
liance, dependence, and dominance of information systems. The
great advantage we derive from this also presents us with unique
vulnerabilities. Rapid changes in technology, the integration of
telecommunications and computer networks, and increasing de-
pendencies of traditional infrastructure elements on digital networks create avenues for access that attackers can exploit before
defensive measures can be devised. At the same time, Internet-
available hacker tools, now more sophisticated and accessible,
have matured from being a source of nuisance to a credible and
serious attack threat.

The vulnerabilities to U.S. national and economic security as
a result of increasing U.S. dependency on foreign IT hardware
and software design and manufacture, outsourcing, knowledge
transfer and globalization, are significant.

- Information technology has become as important to the U.S.
  economy as oil, and the growing dependency of the U.S. on
  foreign IT raises concerns for corporate as well as national
  security. For example, half of the world's laptops, one quarter
  of all desktop computers, and half of all PC motherboards are
  now assembled in China. Taiwan is now responsible for
  about 70 percent of all semiconductor production for hire—
  producing chips designed and marketed by others.
- This growing U.S. dependence makes U.S. IT firms vulnerable to interruptions of foreign-built critical components,
  whether intentional or accidental. Foreign supply disruptions
  could suspend U.S. firms' deliveries of finished systems
  within only a few days as most carry limited inventories.

Advanced technologies and tools for computer network operations are becoming more widely available, resulting in basic,
but operationally significant, technical cyber capability for U.S.
adversaries.

The majority of malicious software that has caused some
damage and disruption to U.S. infrastructure has not used the
most advanced or targeted techniques. In most cases, the malicious software takes advantage of vulnerabilities that have simply gone unpatched. A couple of the most significant recent examples include:

- *Slammer—Winter 2003.* Slammer worm's rapid propagation
  resulted in a flood of spurious network traffic and many reports of disruptions. According to industry experts, within

the first 10 minutes, Slammer had infected 90 percent of all vulnerable computers worldwide. At its peak, Slammer displaced 20 percent of Internet traffic—an impact that matches the most disruptive viruses and worms to date.

- *Bugbear—Spring 2003.* Bugbear—one of the first worms to target a specific group—is designed to extract information from victims' computers that may be used for future theft, extortion, and disruption. It attempts to steal passwords from bank employees associated with a pre-composed list of 1,200 financial institutions, and its targeting may result in back-office operations access, where more valuable transactions occur.

Whatever direction the cyber threat takes, the United States will be confronting an increasingly interconnected world in the years ahead. As a recent CIA report points out, a major drawback of the global diffusion of information technology is our heightened vulnerability. Our "wired" society puts all of us—U.S. businesses, in particular, because you must maintain an open exchange with customers—at higher risk from enemies. In general, IT's spread and the growth of worldwide digital networks mean that we are challenged to think more broadly about national security. We should think in terms of global security, to include the dawning reality that freedom and prosperity in other parts of the world are inextricably bound to U.S. domestic interests.

TERRORISM'S ROOT CAUSES

30   I referred earlier to the "war on terror," but war is a poor metaphor, or at least an incomplete one. In some respects this surely is a war. But the struggle against terrorism, as I have outlined it today, has many facets. Some dimensions can only be addressed by governments; others fall to the private sector.

If this is a war, it is a war that cannot be "won" in any final sense, but only attenuated, contained, managed. Terror is the tactic, not the adversary itself. To deal with these threats over the longer-term we have to deal with underlying causes: . . . like the numbers of societies and peoples excluded from the benefits of an expanding global economy, places where autocratic rulers rig politics and economies for their own benefit, where the daily lot may be hunger, disease, displacement, where young people grow increasingly disaffected and believe that radical solutions are the last remaining choice.

- Large areas of the world are becoming hard-to-govern lawless zones—veritable no man's lands—where extremist movements may find the breathing space to grow and new safe-havens are created.

Let me explain this in more detail.

Imagine a large map of the world. Let's say we stick a map pin in every country that had a low per capita income. And another for a high rate of infant mortality. Another for a sizable "youth bulge"—what Robert Kaplan calls "unemployed young guys walking around"—a strong indicator of social volatility. And another pin to mark an absence of political freedoms and participatory government.

- At the end of this exercise, we would have marked out a large number of vulnerable states—many in the Muslim world.

We could go on to mark out another set of what we could call "beleaguered states"—states unable to control their own borders and internal territory, that lack the capacity to govern, educate their peoples, or provide fundamental social services.

We end up with a map full of pins and many states with more 35 than one. We know from experience that states struggling with these problems are the natural targets of the terrorists. We've seen—in places like Afghanistan—terrorists gaining a foothold and turning them into terrorist havens.

Now consider this:

An estimated *1 billion* people worldwide remain chronically malnourished today. The vast majority live in 70 low-income food-deficit countries.

- This is despite an improved global food picture—steady increases in world grain production, falling real food prices, and rising incomes in key developing countries, such as China and India.

Meanwhile, during the last year 3 million people died of AIDS.

- By 2010, as many as 100 million HIV-infected people will reside outside of Africa. China could have 15 million cases and India between 20 and 25 million—more than any other country in the world.
- AIDS encourages the spread of tuberculosis, including drug-resistant strains. And malaria kills almost a million Africans per year, mostly children.

- The national security implications are staggering. Disease honors no border, will undermine economic growth, diminish military readiness, and further weaken beleaguered states—creating great opportunities for extremists to exploit. And, it will affect the multinational work forces you will need to hire to run your businesses.

By 2007, *for the first time in human history*, a majority of the world's population will live in cities. High urban population densities in economies that are not growing go hand-in-hand with acute problems of governance, highly uneven income distribution, and ethnic and religious tensions.

- In the next 15 years, the global population will grow by 1.5 billion people, mostly in Asia and Sub-Saharan Africa.

40   As for the destabilizing "youth bulge," of the 54 countries with large Muslim populations, 21 are currently contending with large numbers of unemployed young people.

- Half the Saudi population is under the age of 15.

"Globalization," which brings tremendous benefits to societies able to participate, is nevertheless creating new classes of haves and have nots. For all its advantages, globalization can also contribute to unequal growth and highly skewed income distributions. According to the World Bank:

- In Honduras, the richest fifth of the population receive about 38 times as much as the poorest quintile. In Bolivia, the top quintile receive 32 times the lowest.

Contrast these to Japan or Austria, in which the top fifth earns just about three times more than the lowest. (In our own country, the ratio is about 14/1.)

If you want a recent dramatic example of the potentially destabilizing effects of widespread poverty amid a high concentration of wealth, look no further than Bolivia and the forced resignation of former President Sanchez de Lozada. (I might add that the mobilization of the Inca population is itself a phenomenon that would have been hard to imagine just a few years ago, before globalization took hold.)

We also have to reckon with reactions to U.S. preeminence around the world—as other countries and peoples adjust to a world with a single superpower—and with a sharp rise in anti-Americanism, especially (but not only) in the Arab Middle East.

We are already seeing some backlash against the U.S. eco- 45
nomic model that will surely complicate business relations. Indeed, many accuse the United States of defining the rules in the
international system to favor its own cultural propensity. The situation can become particularly dangerous for U.S. business when
cultural resentments against the United States are used to legiti-
matize economic resentments.

- The United States' "pure" form of capitalism—allowing companies to die and then reallocating capital to more "efficient"
  organizations—already is creating a perception of U.S. cal-
  lousness that enhances tensions between the United States
  and other cultures. For many, equality, distributive justice,
  and social harmony are just as important as how politics and
  society are organized.

Animosity against the United States and U.S. interests is unlikely to dissipate over time. For example, the emerging generation in many countries has a stronger sense of nationalism than
predecessor generations; this trend, even in democracies, could
unleash xenophobic policies harmful to U.S. interests.

AN AGENDA FOR THE FUTURE

Let me mention a few ways in which we are trying to address these
new strategic challenges. Within the NIC, we have just created a
new NIO account to deal with transnational threats, including terrorism—not to duplicate the work of the many organizations dealing with day-to-day counter-terrorist work, but to look over the
horizon at broader trends that day-to-day operators may miss.

- For example, we know that failed states can offer safe havens
  for terrorists. But which states will fail, and which of those
  will in fact be attractive sites for terrorists?
- Also, we need to monitor global trends in political Islam—not
  all of which are associated with terrorism, let me hasten to add.
- What about other sources of global terrorism? Will Leftist
  terrorism, which virtually disappeared from Europe after the
  disbanding of the Red Brigades and the Bader-Meinhof gang,
  make a comeback? Will class-based terrorism make a revival
  in Latin America?

On these and many other issues, we must look outside government to find the expertise on which we must draw. Here the NIC
can play a critical bridging role between outside experts and policymakers. Having spent a career going back and forth between
these two worlds, I see this as one of the principal roles I can play.

Toward that end, the NIC just launched an ambitious, year-long project called NIC 2020, which will explore the forces that will shape the world of 2020 through a series of dialogues and conferences with experts from around the world. For our inaugural conference, we invited 25 experts from a wide variety of backgrounds to join us in a broad-gauged exploration of key trends.

- These included prominent "futurists"—the longtime head of Shell's scenarios project, the head of the UN's millennium project, and the director of RAND's center for the study of the future.
- Beyond that, we had experts on biotechnology, information technology, demography, ethnicity, economic development, and energy, as well as more traditional regional specialists.

50   Later on we will be organizing conferences on five continents and drawing on experts from academia, business, government, foundations, and the scientific community, so that this effort will be truly global and interdisciplinary. We will commission local partners to convene these affairs and help set them up, but then we will get out of the way so that regional experts may speak for themselves in identifying key "drivers" of change and a range of future scenarios.

- As the 2020 project unfolds, we will be posting discussion papers, conference reports, and other material on our unclassified Web site, so I encourage you to follow the project as it unfolds over the coming year.

It may seem somewhat self-indulgent to engage in such futurology at a time of acute security challenges, but I see this as integral to our work. If we are entering a period of major flux in the international system, as I believe we are, it is important to take a longer-term strategic review.

We are accustomed to seeing linear change, but sometimes change is logarithmic: it builds up gradually, with nothing much seeming to happen, but then major change occurs suddenly and unexpectedly.

- The collapse of the Soviet empire is one example.
- The growing pressures on China may also produce a sudden, dramatic transformation that cannot be understood by linear analysis.

As I used to say to my students, linear analysis will get you a much-changed caterpillar, but it won't get you a butterfly. For that, you need a leap of imagination. I hope that the 2020 project will help us make that leap, not to predict the world of 2020—that is clearly beyond our capacity—but to prepare for the kinds of changes that may lie ahead.

I have said a few words about our agenda. But let me add that we have a lot to learn from you. So while I have enjoyed this opportunity to speak and look forward to your questions and comments, I hope the dialogue between business and government will be ongoing—through national and international organizations like ISMA and the State Department's Overseas Security Advisory Council, in local contacts with the Joint Terrorism Task Forces, and in regular contacts at all levels.

Thank you for your attention. I look forward to your comments.   55

Starting Points

1. After close reading of Robert Hutchings's speech, what do you consider the most potentially dangerous threat to the national or global economy of the post-9/11 climate? What should be done to reduce the threat level to average citizens?
2. In paragraph 2, the author discusses "asymmetrical warfare"—warfare in which adversaries exploit the vulnerabilities of a free society. What do you believe are the chief areas of vulnerability? What would you be willing to risk to avoid our becoming an armed camp?
3. In discussing the causes of terrorism, what do you believe is the responsibility of informed persons in terms of inequality and injustice in the world? Write an essay in which you articulate a plan that would result in the elimination of the causes of terrorism.

In a Time of Terror, Protest Is Patriotism
Jim Hightower

Jim Hightower, who bills himself as "America's Number One Populist," is a columnist, author, and radio commentator. The following column was posted at AlterNet.org on November 14, 2001.

───────────── ✦ ─────────────

I'm flying a flag these days. The Stars and Stripes, Old Glory, America's flag—OUR flag! I've strapped it to my '97 made-in-the-USA Ford Escort, and I'm zipping around town as proudly as anyone else in the red, white and blue, like some modern-day Patrick Henry on wheels.

As with so many others, I'm flying our flag out of an assertive, perhaps defiant pride—for I am proud, damned proud, to be an American citizen, and, in this time of true woe and deep national trauma, I'll be damned to hell before I meekly sit by and allow this symbol of our nation's founding ideals—"liberty and justice for all"—to be captured and defiled by reactionary autocrats, theocrats, xenophobic haters, warmongers, America-firsters, corporatists, militarists, fearmongers, political weasels, and other rank opportunists.

Our flag is no piece of sheeting for authoritarians to hide behind as they rend our hard-won liberties in the name of "protecting" us from a dangerous world. We Americans are not that frightened. Nor is our flag some bloody rag to be waved by politicians hoping to whip us into such a lust for vengeance that they can turn our people's republic into a garrisoned state, armed to the teeth and mired in a quasi-religious war that George W. defines as "this crusade" to "rid the world of the evildoers." We Americans are not that blind.

Our flag is the banner of freedom seekers, risk takers, democracy builders, rebels, pioneers, mavericks, barnraisers, and hellraisers—a liberty-loving people who are naturally suspicious of authority and able to detect that the real threat to our land of the free comes not from afar, but from within.

5   Our flag is made of strong democratic cloth, artfully designed and painstakingly stitched together over 225 years—liberty by individual liberty, people's movement by people's movement. Our flag embodies a democratic continuum that connects us today to the pamphleteers and Sons of Liberty, the Declaration of Independence and the Bill of Rights, the abolitionists and the suffragists, Sojourner Truth and Frederick Douglass, the populists and Wobblies, Mother Jones and Joe Hill, Martin Luther King Jr. and Cesar Chavez.

"The first job of a citizen is to keep your mouth open," wrote German Nobel Prize winner Gunther Grass. The Powers That Be are not interested in having a national conversation, but I believe we must push for one from the grassroots up. Open your mouth—"Hey, I'm an American, red-blooded and true, and here's what that means to me; what do you think?"

Americans desperately need to talk—about what our society is, where we're headed, what kind of future we're creating for the next generation. Our fellow citizens are eager to engage. Early one morning, as I sat in a coffee shop writing two days after the terrorist assault, a fellow in a suit and tie stepped over to me. I didn't know him, but he said that he occasionally read my weekly columns and felt the need to acknowledge something: "I mostly don't agree with you," he blurted, "but I guess today, we're all Americans."

Indeed. Let's talk.

What astonishes me is not that the Powers That Be would want to stifle any talk that doesn't assert lock-step "patriotism," but that so many weak-kneed progressive leaders have counseled hiding our light under a bushel and withdrawing from the noble field of protest.

For example, an internal memo to Sierra Club leaders   10
mewed, "We strongly need to avoid any perceptions that we are being disrespectful to President Bush." Hello? Protest is not disrespectful. It is the essence of American democracy, of America itself, and it is especially essential when a muddleheaded guy like George W. sits in the President's chair, totally dependent on the military establishment and corporate elite, thrusting our sons and daughters (theirs won't have to go) into an unlimited and secretive world war against terrorists supposedly entrenched in 60 nations, while simultaneously rushing to Congress with a package of 51 "emergency" antiterrorism bills to put some convenient crimps and cuts in America's Bill of Rights.

If we don't protest now, when will it matter? Yet the Sierra Club's memo-writer urges that we shut our mouths for fear of being deemed unpopular: "Now is the time for rallying together as a nation," he whimpered. Excuse me, but rally together for what, exactly?

HOW TO DESTROY DEMOCRACY

Terrorists have no ability to destroy our democracy—but we do, simply by surrendering it, by keeping our mouths shut while it is dismantled by the authorities.

"America is being tested," bellowed the political and media establishments after September 11. True, but the test is not merely of whether the military has the brute force to smite our enemies, though this will certainly continue to be mightily tested in the far-flung, open-ended offensive drawn up by the Bushites. The real test is going to be of our democratic resolve. Will we citizens settle for life in a guarded and gated corporate empire?

"Everything has changed," we're told. No, it hasn't.

This pitiful wail by politicians and pundits went up as quickly   15
as the Trade Center towers fell, and now it's the prevailing excuse

used by those who tell us that to defend freedom we must surrender freedoms, to stop terrorist assaults on our democracy we must militarize our society.

Republicans are the harshest of the newly assertive autocrats in Washington, but Democrats, too, were quick to accept the post-September 11 conventional wisdom that liberties now must be set aside: "We need to find a new balance between freedom and security," asserted House Democratic leader Dick Gephardt just days after the attack, adding ominously: "We are in a new world."

No, we're not. We're in the exact same world. It has just come a lot closer to us, that's all, introducing itself to us in a terrible and personal way that we've basically been uninformed about until now. Yet we are not some backward, powerless people who must flee to our caves.

The adjustment we most need to make is not in our freedoms, but in our understanding of who else is in this big world with us and what it will take for all of us to get along. At a minimum, getting along will require that our nation's political and economic policies begin to reflect our people's democratic values—economic fairness, social justice, equal opportunity for all.

In practical terms, this means putting America on the side of the poor and repressed people of the world, rather than continuing to stand alongside the thugs, dictators, corporatists, and monarchists who prosper on the misery of an increasingly angry Third World majority.

20   Far from building on these strengths, however, the Powers That Be are appealing solely to our nativism and pessimism, demanding that we withdraw into Fortress America and meekly allow them to deal secretively, paternalistically, and cataclysmically with an uppity world.

But it's our world, too, that they plan to up-end. The same old pols like Dick Cheney, Trent Lott, and Denny Hastert—who built their political careers on the hackneyed line that the ten scariest words in the English language are "I'm from the government and I'm here to help you"—are now squinting into the TV cameras and, with tight-lipped greasy smiles, saying, "We're here to protect you."

A mess of the "protection" they have in mind is collected into a hellish handbasket that they've labeled the "Provide Appropriate Tools Required to Intercept and Obstruct Terrorism Act." Yes, believe it or not, they've cynically constructed an acronym that spells: PATRIOT.

Clever, what? T.J., Jimmy Madison, Old Ben, Tom Paine, the original George W., and all the other founding patriots would gag on this piece of privacy-invading, liberty-denying nastiness. It brings back racial profiling with a vengeance; it makes wiretapping and Internet surveillance a free-for-all; it authorizes the indefinite detention of anyone "suspected" of any terrorist connection, without the nicety of charging them with anything, and denies them any appeal; it requires your bank to spy on you and to report to federal agents any "unusual transaction" (such as depositing or withdrawing as little as $5,000); it leaves it to the FBI, CIA, and other bastions of authoritarianism to define terrorist activity (protest at a WTO meeting?) . . . and so much more.

If only that were the end of it. They also propose to "unleash" the CIA. (When, exactly, was it leashed, and to what?) They want our super-snoop agency to be officially authorized to assassinate people—just like the terrorists do. They want it to return to what George Bush the Elder calls the "dirty business" of espionage, which is to say hiring "unsavory people" as CIA agents to do what needs to be done (Daddy Bush would know about unsavory, for he was V.P. when our CIA financed Osama bin Laden).

Now along comes Bush the Younger with a dream-come-true 25 for those who yearn for more police power in our lives. It's called the Office of Homeland Security, and he's given it powers to match the National Security Agency and a vague mandate that he glibly defines as "to make sure that anybody who wants to harm America will have a hard time doing so."

The OHS was created by executive fiat to be a White House agency. It will have no congressional oversight of its activities or budget. In addition, Bush has unilaterally decided to establish a "Homeland Defense Command" within the Pentagon, empowering the military to gain a foothold over civilian authority and to act against U.S. citizens at home.

If this is not enough democracy-quashing firepower, Congress is also contemplating approval of a longtime civil-liberties no-no: the national ID card. Welcome to your "new world." It's really no big deal, says Republican subcommittee chairman George Gekas, who notes that something already exists that you might not know about: the National Standard for the Driver's License/Identification Card.

It might be one thing if any or all of these measures would actually stop terrorism, but even their proponents won't make such a claim.

It's being done not because it makes sense, but simply because there is an urgency to "do something," or at least appear to do something, and the easiest thing to do in a national crisis is always to reach for the hammer and cuffs to shut down everything from people's movements to their mouths. Well, after all, say the politicians and media with near unanimity, we're at war.

30   No, we're not. Yes, our forces are in "hot pursuit" of the maniacal fiends who, in a grotesque perversion of Islam (practicing a violent, puritanical, fringe version called Wahhabism), have exploded our buildings, our people, and our comforting sense of isolation from an unsettled world's religious wars. And yes, George W. has declared us to be "at war" with these murderous zealots.

Good for him—except, of course, that a president has no authority to declare war. This is more than a Constitutional nicety; it is basic to the rule of law, which in turn is an absolutely essential underpinning of democracy—in fact, the founders took on King George III in the Revolutionary War so we'd be governed by law, not kings.

Attorney General John Ashcroft, never one to contend for a civil-liberties award, has been especially pushy in his assertion of martial-law-style executive power, stamping his tiny feet and demanding at one point that Congress pass his police-powers package "by next week."

Likewise, the media, Congress, and the White House have clamored to censor those who have dared to dissent or diverge from the orthodox line. For example, when comedian Bill Maher expressed some unapproved thoughts on television, President Bush's mouthpiece Ari Fleischer said: "Americans . . . need to watch what they say, watch what they do."

Any time the authorities lock arms and assert that "everything has changed," grab your copy of the Bill of Rights and rush to the barricades.

SO WHAT CAN WE DO?

35 What should we ask our government to do?

On the military front, the United States has no choice but to go after the bastards. Terrorism ain't beanbags. The ruthless mass murderers smacked our nation and all of civilization right in the face, and turning the other cheek only means we'll get smacked again.

There's no subtlety to their agenda. However, there must subtlety be to ours. The trick in smacking back is in knowing who "they" are, where they are, and particularly in smacking them without slaughtering the innocents they hide among. This requires a scalpel, not a sledgehammer, and it requires a long, patient siege (years) that is dependent more on creative diplomacy and old-fashioned gumshoe espionage than on high-tech, made-for-CNN missile shots. Bringing them to justice in a court of law would be ideal, and we should seek their capture, but these are suicidal, doctrinaire diehards, so blood will flow.

With blood and billions of our dollars involved, we have a right to demand a new honesty from Washington. For starters, they should start telling us the truth about the elites of Saudi Arabia, Egypt, and the United Arab Emirates, who are the primary source of brains, money, and recruits for this Wahhabi jihad.

Leaders of these nations, however, are the oil buddies, business partners, and longtime Middle Eastern enforcers of America's corporate empire, so Bush, Cheney & Co. won't cop to the fact that the murderous theocratic movement now tormenting us is based in the very nest where their corporate chums have found such comfort and profit. Will Bush go there to "smoke 'em out of their holes"?

How about a little honesty, too, on money laundering? Bush has pointed furiously at foreign banks, but how about the multi-billion-dollar networks of secret accounts in the "private banking" departments of such U.S. giants as Citigroup (a major Bush campaign contributor)?

It's on the home front, however, where we citizens must be most forceful in holding Washington accountable. The looters are loose. Not common looters rampaging through the streets, but corporate looters rampaging through the Congress.

They are grabbing for bills and billions that have zero to do with combating terrorism or rebuilding our economy—the Star Wars missile-defense shield, for example, was zapped through a week after the attack, even though a box-cutter defense shield would be much more useful. Then came "fast track" authority to ram more global trade deals down the throats of the world's people—pushed by lobbyists and Bush's odious trade chief in the name of patriotism!

The looters also want huge bailouts, massive corporate tax cuts, oil drilling in the Arctic National Wildlife Refuge, slashing-capital gains taxes (80 percent of this break goes to the wealthiest 2 percent of Americans), and a host of other thefts.

Instead of aiding the looters, Washington should launch a major reinvestment in grassroots America. First, stop the firing. Why should airlines get $15 billion from taxpayers while axing 100,000 employees? The same with hotel chains, car-rental corporations, and other industries that now demand bailouts. Yes, these corporations are hard-hit, but so is America. To stimulate the economy, put these bailout funds into the hands of working families all across America.

45   Second, strengthen our national security by making major, long-overdue public investments in our infrastructure—schoolhouses, hospitals, roads and bridges, parks, etc. Add to this a new nationwide project to reconnect our population corridors with high-speed passenger trains. This makes so much sense that even the tightly bowtied, right-wing, anti-government scribe George Will has embraced it. Then it's way past time we expanded renewable energy sources to wean us off oil, which weds the Bush-Cheney crowd to the Saudi royal family and their ilk.

Third, to deal with the recession: Instead of cutting income taxes, cut payroll taxes; raise the minimum wage; extend health care, unemployment benefits, and day care. All of this spreads money, like fertilizer, to the grassroots economy, rather than piling it up inside global banks.

Finally, we must demand openness and full public discussion on everything from war and peace to restrictions on our liberties.

Since September 11, I find a deep hunger among most Americans for serious discussion (including hearing dissent). This gives me great hope in such a horrible time. Contrary to the media's portrayal of Bellicose America, the people I've encountered in meetings, in cafes and bars, and elsewhere (including the majority of people writing letters-to-the-editor in papers from coast to coast) are expressing anger, grief, and shock—but they oppose the hush-hush and rush-rush we're getting, and they want us to talk and think as a democratic community.

The better part of patriotism is for us to raise hard questions, put out inconvenient information, assert our values, and appeal to what Lincoln called "the better angels of our nature."

Starting Points

1. Part of Jim Hightower's appeal to his regular audience is his bluntness. Putting aside questions of style, do you agree or disagree with his contention that the "Powers That Be are not interested in having a national conversation" (paragraph 6)? Write an essay in which you agree or disagree with the quotation from Gunther Grass: "The first job of a citizen is to keep your mouth open" (paragraph 6).

2. The greatest threat to democracy is not terrorists, Hightower says, but silence in the face of its dismantling by authorities (paragraph 12). Make a case for either terrorism or complacency as the ultimate threat to democracy.

3. Consider Hightower's style. Is it refreshing, a needed antidote to conservative commentators, or does his take-no-prisoners approach discourage meaningful dialogue?

U.S. Law Puts World Ports on Notice

TIM WEINER

Many of the effects of U.S. legislation and other acts promulgated since 9/11 will extend far beyond our own borders. Tim Weiner of the New York Times *looks at the effects of efforts to improve port security outside of the United States, and the possible consequences of both enforcing and failing to enforce the measures. This news article first appeared on March 24, 2004.*

───────────── ✦ ─────────────

Right there," said Manuel Pereira, a security guard here at the largest shipping port in the Caribbean, pointing to the ground beneath his feet. "That's the new border of the United States."

Since the Sept. 11 attacks in the United States, American officials have spoken of "pushing back the borders" of the United States in the name of national security. Now they are doing it across the seas.

The threat they envision is a catastrophic attack on a major American port by a ship bearing a bomb. Al Qaeda has sought for seven years to use commercial ships to attack the United States at home and abroad, public records show.

A seaborne terrorist attack could cost thousands of lives and inflict billions of dollars in damage, maritime security experts say, while closing major American ports at a cost to world trade measured in tens or hundreds of billions of dollars.

"Their ultimate goal is attacking our economy," said Adm. 5 James M. Loy, deputy secretary of homeland security and retired commandant of the Coast Guard. "Our link to the global economy is by water—95 percent of what comes and goes to this country comes and goes by ships."

The response to this threat is a new law of the sea, spurred by Admiral Loy, passed by Congress and signed by President Bush 16 months ago. A parallel global code was adopted days later under American pressure by the United Nations's International Maritime Organization.

The law and the code set a July 1 deadline for all of the world's ships and ports to create counterterrorism systems—computers, communications gear, surveillance cameras, security patrols—to help secure America against an attack.

The cost of compliance at home and abroad will be many billions of dollars. Many American and foreign ports lack the funds to comply. But the cost of not complying could be steeper still. The law's demands create a stark confrontation between world trade and national security.

If a ship, or any one of the last 10 ports it visited, does not meet the new security standards, it can be turned away from American waters. If a port falls short, no ship leaving it can enter American harbors. That means ports, and their nations, can be barred from trading with the United States.

10 "We're dead serious about this," said Rear Adm. Larry L. Hereth, director of port security for the Coast Guard. The law holds "some very harsh economic consequences," he said, like banning ships and blacklisting ports, "and we're prepared to do that." Enforcement will largely fall to the United States.

The high costs and the tight deadline have created a scramble in the world's major ports—especially in poor ones like Puerto Cortés, a sprawling, run-down harbor crucial to the livelihood of Honduras and its neighbors in Central America.

Some say the price is too high, the task too huge and the time too short to comply.

"The developing world is saying that the wealthiest, most powerful nation in the world is exporting the cost of protecting itself onto some of the world's poorest countries," said Stephen E. Flynn, a retired Coast Guard commander and a maritime security expert at the Council on Foreign Relations.

American officials contend that the costs are outweighed by the benefits: higher security against terrorism will also cut cargo thefts and the smuggling of drugs, guns and people. But if the United States cannot balance the competing demands of national security and global trade, "we are playing with fire," Mr. Flynn said. "If the U.S. locks down its ports for more than two weeks, the entire global trade system crashes."

15 Policing the sea is daunting: the maritime system is bigger, more complex and far less controlled than international aviation. Ninety percent of world commerce moves on water, though, in 46,000 ships plying 3,000 ports. They carry millions of containers with billions of tons of goods. Roughly half of all international

shipping is carried out under "flags of convenience"—registries based in countries like Liberia, often intended to disguise a vessel's true ownership.

Here in Honduras, one of the poorest countries in the Western Hemisphere, the economy depends on Puerto Cortés, which is about 350 miles south of Cancún, Mexico. More than 100 ships a month leave the port for the United States, carrying everything from bluejeans to bananas, returning with American exports.

If the United States were to bar ships from the port for even a week, "our national economy would collapse," said Mauro Membreño, chief of Honduras's new National Commission on Port Security.

The port was a wide-open place, protected mainly by a rusting five-foot-high chain-link fence and a poorly paid police force, until the Honduran government began trying to secure it three months ago. Under an emergency decree, Honduras is spending $4 million to buy computer systems, patrol boats, police cars, cameras and other security gear for Puerto Cortés. "We have gotten moral support from the United States," said the national port director, Fernando Álvarez. "Nothing concrete."

A United States official in Honduras says American pressure to secure Puerto Cortés is intense, but notes that the United States is not paying for security, as it did when it gave Honduras more than $250 million during Central America's anti-communist campaigns in the 1980's.

"We've got a gun to their heads," the official said. "If this is the war on terrorism—well, this is not how we fought the war on Communism."

Dennis Chinchilla, Honduras's new national port security officer, said "the people who work in Puerto Cortés will have to completely change their way of life" to adapt to the American law. Once the commercial harbor is secured, he said, the law demands that Honduras fix its main tourist port, on the island of Roatán, where 250,000 travelers a year disembark from cruise ships. The security there today is a dollar-an-hour guard in a shack without a phone.

In the United States, many ports and ships missed a Dec. 31 deadline for submitting security plans. Port authorities note that President Bush's budget for port security in the coming year is $46 million, while the costs of compliance in the United States alone will reach $7 billion.

The Coast Guard, which must enforce the law, has three people assigned to international compliance, Mr. Flynn said. They confront a tradition of secrecy and deception that makes the maritime trade a tempting target for terrorists.

Roughly half of the world's commercial ships fly flags of convenience registered in more than two dozen nations, including tiny tax havens and money-laundering centers like the Cayman Islands and Vanuatu. The tradition, which began with United Fruit Company vessels in Honduras in the 1920's, was devised to cut costs and, in many cases, evade taxes.

25   "It's a bit like Swiss banks," Mr. Flynn said.

Flags of convenience "allow shippers to function with a high degree of anonymity," said Rupert Herbert Burns, a senior analyst at the Maritime Intelligence Group, a security firm in Washington.

Maritime security officials say an American port could be struck in several ways. A cargo ship filled with fuel oil and ammonium nitrate fertilizer could become a waterborne fireball; a ship could carry a radiological "dirty bomb" into a harbor; a speedboat carrying explosives could blow up a tanker laden with oil or delivering liquefied natural gas.

Admiral Loy, citing court testimony and government reports, warned two years ago in the military journal Defense Horizons that Osama bin Laden, through associates using flags of convenience, controlled a fleet of cargo ships, including the vessel that delivered the explosives that blew up American Embassies in Kenya and Tanzania in 1998.

He noted that a month after the Sept. 11 attacks, Italian inspectors found an Egyptian on a ship bound for Canada. The Egyptian, hiding in a shipping container, had a false Canadian passport, a satellite phone, two computers, forged security passes for airports in three countries and papers identifying him as an aircraft mechanic.

30   Uncovering such a suspect is like finding a particular shark in a boundless sea. United States officials say the threat of an attack demands that nations like Honduras do their part. But Carl Bentzel, a Democratic counsel to the Senate Commerce Committee, said most of the world's ships and ports "have so far to go and the costs are so high that most will not be in compliance" by July 1.

If that happens, the United States has three choices, maritime security experts say. It can enforce the law, creating potential economic chaos abroad; bend the law, saying economic imperatives make full enforcement impossible; or apply the law selectively, creating a two-tier system in which rich ports in Europe and Asia trump poor Caribbean ones like Puerto Cortés.

At Puerto Cortés, Fermin Chong Wong, an American-educated computer expert working for the national port authority, is trying to track 400,000 containers and more than 2,000 ships a year.

"I don't think there will be enough time to meet the United States requirements everywhere in the world," he said. "I don't think U.S. ports can meet them. Here, we are going to try—and we might. But the time's too short and the money's too scarce to do all this."

"We want to protect our borders," said Kim Petersen, who runs one of the world's biggest maritime consultancies, SeaSecure. "But what happens when we cripple the economy of a developing country and create a breeding ground for the very problems we're trying to prevent?"

Starting Points

1. Tim Weiner's introduction acquaints the reader with a security guard in Honduras, who alleges that the new border of the United States is his guard post. Why does the reporter begin with an unknown person in a foreign place? What is gained by the reader in seeing the issue through the guard's eyes?

2. Port security—that is, ensuring that illegal persons, weapons, or technology do not enter the country by way of ocean-going vessels—seems to be a monumental task (2,000 ships a year; 400,000 containers). Is it reasonable to try to police such venues, when the borders with Canada or Mexico are so easily crossed?

3. Read the last paragraph of Weiner's article again. Weigh carefully the benefits and drawbacks to a protection measure that enhances our security while possibly crippling the economy of another country. What is the solution to such a conundrum?

The Unchallenged "Evidence" for War
JOHN R. MACARTHUR

The Columbia Journalism Review, *centered in the Columbia University School of Journalism, is a watchdog and critic of national news media. It often takes the Fourth Estate to task for failing in what it views as the primary task of the press: to inform citizens about events which affect them. In this piece from the May/June issue of 2003, John R. Macarthur chastises journalists for failing to question President George W. Bush and others in his administration on their decision to pursue war in Iraq.*

———————— ✦ ————————

Shortly before American military forces invaded Iraq, a troubled Ellen Goodman raised a singularly important question about the Bush administration's propaganda campaign for war— "How we got from there to here."

There, according to Goodman, was innocent 9/11 victimhood at the hands of religious fanatics; here, was bullying superpower bent on destroying a secular dictator. I assumed that someone as astute as Goodman would reveal at least part of the answer—that the American media provided free transportation to get the White House from there to here. But nowhere in her nationally syndicated column did she state the obvious—that the success of "Bush's PR War" (the headline on the piece) was largely dependent on a compliant press that uncritically repeated almost every fraudulent administration claim about the threat posed to America by Saddam Hussein.

The few corrections and refutations of the White House line were too little and too late for American democracy.

Late as she was, Goodman was better than most in even recognizing that there was a disinformation campaign aimed at the people and Congress. Just a few columnists seriously challenged the White House advertising assault. Looking back over the debris of half-truths and lies, I can't help but ask my own question of Goodman: Where was she—indeed, where was the American press—on September 7, 2002, a day when we were sorely in need of reporters?

5   It was then that the White House propaganda drive began in earnest, with the appearance before television cameras of George Bush and Tony Blair at Camp David. Between them, the two politicians cited a "new" report from the UN's International Atomic Energy Agency that allegedly stated that Iraq was "six months away" from building a nuclear weapon. "I don't know what more evidence we need," declared the president.

For public relations purposes, it hardly mattered that no such IAEA report existed, because almost no one in the media bothered to check out the story. (In the twenty-first paragraph of her story on the press conference, *The Washington Post*'s Karen De-Young did quote an IAEA spokesman saying, in DeYoung's words, "that the agency has issued no new report," but she didn't confront the White House with this terribly interesting fact.) What mattered was the unencumbered rollout of a commercial for war—the one that the White House chief of staff and former General Motors executive Andrew Card had famously withheld earlier

in the summer: "From a marketing point of view, you don't introduce new products in August."

Millions of people saw Bush tieless, casually inarticulate, but
determined-looking and self-confident, making a completely un-
corroborated (and, at that point, uncontradicted) case for preemptive war. While we contemplate the irony of Bush quoting a
UN weapons inspection agency that he would later dismiss, we
might ask ourselves why no more evidence was needed than the
president's say-so—and why no reporters asked for any. But the
next day, more "evidence" suddenly appeared, on the front page
of the *Sunday New York Times*. In a disgraceful piece of stenography, Michael Gordon and Judith Miller inflated an administration
leak into something resembling imminent Armageddon: "More
than a decade after Saddam Hussein agreed to give up weapons
of mass destruction, Iraq has stepped up its quest for nuclear
weapons and has embarked on a worldwide hunt for materials to
make an atomic bomb, Bush administration officials said today."

The key to this A-bomb program was the attempted purchase
of "specially designed aluminum tubes, which American officials
believe were intended as components of centrifuges to enrich uranium." Mysteriously, none of those tubes had reached Iraq, but
"American officials" wouldn't say why, "citing the sensitivity of
the intelligence." Disgraceful pieces of stenography suddenly appeared on the front page of the *New York Times*.

Gordon and Miller were mostly careful to attribute their information to anonymous "administration officials," but at one
point they couldn't restrain themselves and crossed the line into
commentary. After nodding to administration "critics" who fa-
vored containment of Hussein, they wrote this astonishing paragraph: "Still, Mr. Hussein's dogged insistence on pursuing his nuclear ambitions, along with what defectors described in
interviews as Iraq's push to improve and expand Baghdad's chemical and biological arsenals, have brought Iraq and the United
States to the brink of war."

That Sunday, Card's new-product introduction moved into
high gear when Vice President Dick Cheney appeared on NBC's
"Meet the Press" to brandish Saddam's supposed nuclear threat.
Prompted by a helpful Tim Russert, Cheney cited the aluminum
tubes story in that morning's *New York Times*—a story leaked by
Cheney's White House colleagues. Russert: "Aluminum tubes."
Cheney: "Specifically aluminum tubes." This gave the "six months
away" canard a certain ring of independent confirmation: "There's
a story in *The New York Times* this morning," said Cheney. "And I

10

want to attribute the *Times.*" Does it matter that, in the months that followed, aluminum tubes as weapons of mass destruction were discredited time and again? Does it matter that the former U.S. weapons inspector David Albright (not the usual suspect Scott Ritter) told "60 Minutes," in an interview broadcast on December 8 (a program in which I participated) that "people who understood gas centrifuges almost uniformly felt that these tubes were not specific to gas centrifuge" for production of enriched uranium—that the administration was "selectively picking information to bolster a case that the Iraqi nuclear threat was more imminent than it is, and in essence, scare people"? Will the *Times* ever publish a clarification (à la Wen Ho Lee) based on IAEA chief Mohammed el-Baradei's January 9 and March 7 reports insisting that there was "no evidence" that the 81 mm tubes were intended for anything other than conventional rocket production?

As for the "defectors" with special knowledge of Saddam's elusive chemical weapons stockpile, did Miller and Gordon—did anyone in the mainstream U.S. press—take proper note of *Newsweek*'s exclusive on March 3? In it, John Barry reported that Iraq's most important defector, Hussein Kamel, who had run Saddam's nuclear and biological weapons program, told the CIA and UN weapons inspectors in the summer of 1995 "that after the gulf war, Iraq destroyed all its chemical and biological weapons stocks and the missiles to deliver them."

And what of Saddam's overall nuclear procurement program? When el-Baradei told the UN Security Council on March 7 that supporting documents of alleged attempts to buy uranium from Niger were forged, no clarification of the Gordon-Miller report appeared in the Grey Lady. Perhaps *Times* people still believed their own scare story from all those months before: "Hard-liners are alarmed that American intelligence underestimated the pace and scale of Iraq's nuclear program before Baghdad's defeat in the gulf war," the September 8 piece reported. "The first sign of a 'smoking gun,' they argue, may be a mushroom cloud."

The few corrections and refutations of the White House line were too little and too late for American democracy. Enterprising reporting was needed from the moment of the Bush-Blair p.r. gambit to October 10, the day Congress abdicated its war-making power to the president. During that crucial period, I was able to find only one newspaper story that straightforwardly countered the White House nuclear threat propaganda; it appeared, of all places, in the right-wing, Sun Myung Moon–owned *Washington Times*. On September 27, a very competent piece by Joseph Curl (unfortunately buried on page 16) pointed out not only that there was no "new report" by the IAEA saying Saddam was six months away from the A-bomb, but also that the agency had never issued a report predicting any time frame. Indeed, when IAEA inspectors pulled out of Iraq in December 1998, spokesman Mark Gwozdecky told Curl, "We had concluded that we had neutralized their nuclear-weapons program. We had confiscated their fissile material. We had destroyed all their key buildings and equipment."

The American media failed the country badly these past eight months. As journalists, what can we do about it? Perhaps we need to adopt the rapid-response techniques used in public relations, something akin to James Carville's and George Stephanopoulos's famous "War Room" ethos: never leave an accusation unanswered before the end of a news cycle.

Unfortunately, the politicians and their p.r. people know all too well the propaganda dictum related nearly twenty years ago by Peter Teeley, press secretary to then Vice President George H.W. Bush. Teeley was responding to complaints that the elder Bush, during a televised debate, had grossly distorted the words of his and Ronald Reagan's opponents, the Democratic candidates Walter Mondale and Geraldine Ferraro. As Teeley explained it to *The New York Times* in October 1984, "You can say anything you want during a debate, and 80 million people hear it." If "anything" turns out to be false and journalists correct it, "So what. Maybe 200 people read it, or 2,000 or 20,000."

15

Starting Points

1. Not everything that appears in a newspaper, news magazine, or a news media-centered journal is objective reporting. Editorials, letters to the editor, and op-ed (opposite editorial page) opinion columns are regular features of most vehicles for news. Carefully reread this article and determine in which category this falls. How does that affect its impact on you as a reader?

2. Observe the use of adjectives and adverbs in this piece (as in paragraph 7, "disgraceful stenography"). In what way do such qualifiers affect your reading of a text? If you remove all such words from this piece, how does it change the tone, and perhaps, the effectiveness?

3. Choose a topic relating to peace, war, or terrorism, and write your own opinion piece.

Other Journeys: Suggestions for Further Writing and Research

1. Locate two news sources generally considered to be at opposite ends of the political spectrum and analyze their coverage of the same issue over several releases (daily, weekly, monthly, etc.). What specific clues in the texts of their reporting do you find indicate a bias or an inclination one way or the other? How do we as readers make informed decisions if we obtain our information only from sources that may be slanted?

2. Establish within your school a public debate between supporters and opponents of the USA Patriot Act. Write a news account of the debate, attempting to be objective and unbiased.

3. Interview someone who lived through World War II on the homefront to learn more about public sacrifices made during that war. Compare or contrast the effect on daily lives of the present War on Terror with this conflict of the 1940s.

4. Research the effects of the War on Terror on different segments of the population or economy. What is the history of government regulations during wartime? In what ways has the economy been affected? What are the psychological effects of violence and war? What ethical or religious considerations does war impact? What happens in the movie industry, the publishing field, and/or in journalism, during wartime?

5. What impact has the War on Terror had on popular culture? Consider song lyrics, what is played on radio, sale of CDs, and the popularity or castigation of performers. How has the war affected television series, late night talk shows, or running skits? Bumper stickers? Message t-shirts? Talk radio? Is pop culture an effective gauge of the support or opposition to a war by a country's citizens?

6. What is people's perception regarding the news media in wartime? Consider studying the 1988 official U.S. Army history of the Vietnam war (*U.S. Army in Vietnam*, published by the U.S. Army Center of Military History), in which military historians dispel the notion that the news media "lost the war." What was different about the position and freedom of journalists in Vietnam, the first Gulf War, the war in Iraq? Does "embedding" journalists affect objectivity or the freedom to report?

Weapons
and Terror

A s bad as the attacks of September 11, 2001 were, what would it have been like had the hijackers possessed nuclear weapons? And what if the phalanx of suicide bombers gains access to miniature nuclear devices?

The resulting catastrophe is nearly unthinkable and unfathomable, yet in an age of a variety of weapons that can deal wholesale death, we must confront the possibility that such an event could happen.

WMD—weapons of mass destruction—have received a great deal of attention since the War on Terror became America's war. They were cited, correctly or not, as a major reason for going to war with Iraq. They have been the focus of scrutiny as North Korea and Iran tout their nuclear programs. There have been attacks in the 1990s using chemical weapons—in Japan with the agent Sarin, in northern Iraq against the Kurds—and, of course, the fear as American troops marched toward Baghdad of the unleashing of more. Biological agents have been the subject of news and frantic efforts to curb them, most tellingly in Washington, D.C., when anthrax killed several people, closed post offices, and emptied the Capitol Building.

How do we prevent the proliferation of such weapons? Can we, in fact, halt the use of such lethal means of killing wholesale numbers of people? How can we prevent someone such as Timothy McVeigh, who used fertilizer to fuel a bomb that killed 168 persons in the Murrah government building in Oklahoma.

There are currently a number of initiatives to halt the spread of WMD. The UN has proposed several steps to combat the proliferation of nuclear weapons, as well as to control chemical and biological agents that could become weapons. Treaties designed to

153

stop additional nations from acquiring nuclear weapons have been around for years, and more are being proposed.

Are such efforts feasible? Do they miss more quotidian weapons? A report by Amnesty International and Oxfam suggests that since 9/11, worldwide sales of conventional arms have skyrocketed and have resulted in the deaths of a half-million people each year—one a minute. Those human rights organizations have launched a global campaign to regulate the arms trade, but it remains to be seen how effective such an initiative will be.

The increasing numbers of suicide bombers also makes the jobs of those in charge of security here and abroad much tougher. It is likely that such tactics will be used in the United States and Europe, according to intelligence reports. The carnage caused by conventional high explosives is massive; if miniaturized nuclear devices were to be used, the results might well be described as catastrophic.

Following the breakup of the Soviet Union in the 1990s, there was a great deal of fear expressed regarding the security of the vast array of weapons in the hands of various small republics. Osama bin Laden's terrorist group al-Qaida has claimed that it now possesses suitcase-sized nuclear devices, and although many counterterrorism experts discount the claim, such a possibility is a frightening one. What then is the state of weapons in an age of terror? Is true security of existing WMD—nuclear, biological, and chemical—chimerical, a goal beyond achieving? Should we steel ourselves to the probability of watching—endlessly on television news—a mushroom cloud marking the former site of one of our large cities?

This chapter makes no claim for being a complete primer on WMD. Rather, it should be viewed as a starting point for further, more extensive research into one of the most troubling issues of the modern age: the abundance of weapons that can kill thousands of people, and the abundance of those willing to use them.

New Measures to Counter the Threat of WMD

GEORGE W. BUSH

President George W. Bush addressed the National Defense University on February 11, 2004, and discussed new measures to counter the threat of weapons of mass destruction. The National

Defense University, located at Fort Lesley J. McNair in Washington, D.C., is a military school for senior officers.

———————————— ✦ ————————————

On September the 11th, 2001, America and the world witnessed a new kind of war. We saw the great harm that a stateless network could inflict upon our country, killers armed with box cutters, mace, and 19 airline tickets. Those attacks also raised the prospect of even worse dangers—of other weapons in the hands of other men. The greatest threat before humanity today is the possibility of secret and sudden attack with chemical or biological or radiological or nuclear weapons.

In the past, enemies of America required massed armies, and great navies, powerful air forces to put our nation, our people, our friends and allies at risk. In the Cold War, Americans lived under the threat of weapons of mass destruction, but believed that deterrents made those weapons a last resort. What has changed in the 21st century is that, in the hands of terrorists, weapons of mass destruction would be a first resort—the preferred means to further their ideology of suicide and random murder. These terrible weapons are becoming easier to acquire, build, hide, and transport. Armed with a single vial of a biological agent or a single nuclear weapon, small groups of fanatics, or failing states, could gain the power to threaten great nations, threaten the world peace.

America, and the entire civilized world, will face this threat for decades to come. We must confront the danger with open eyes, and unbending purpose. I have made clear to all the policy of this nation: America will not permit terrorists and dangerous regimes to threaten us with the world's most deadly weapons.

Meeting this duty has required changes in thinking and strategy. Doctrines designed to contain empires, deter aggressive states, and defeat massed armies cannot fully protect us from this new threat. America faces the possibility of catastrophic attack from ballistic missiles armed with weapons of mass destruction. So that is why we are developing and deploying missile defenses to guard our people. The best intelligence is necessary to win the war on terror and to stop proliferation. So that is why I have established a commission that will examine our intelligence capabilities and recommend ways to improve and adapt them to detect new and emerging threats.

We're determined to confront those threats at the source. We will stop these weapons from being acquired or built. We'll block

5

them from being transferred. We'll prevent them from ever being used. One source of these weapons is dangerous and secretive regimes that build weapons of mass destruction to intimidate their neighbors and force their influence upon the world. These nations pose different challenges; they require different strategies.

The former dictator of Iraq possessed and used weapons of mass destruction against his own people. For 12 years, he defied the will of the international community. He refused to disarm or account for his illegal weapons and programs. He doubted our resolve to enforce our word—and now he sits in a prison cell, while his country moves toward a democratic future.

To Iraq's east, the government of Iran is unwilling to abandon a uranium enrichment program capable of producing material for nuclear weapons. The United States is working with our allies and the International Atomic Energy Agency to ensure that Iran meets its commitments and does not develop nuclear weapons.

In the Pacific, North Korea has defied the world, has tested long-range ballistic missiles, admitted its possession of nuclear weapons, and now threatens to build more. Together with our partners in Asia, America is insisting that North Korea completely, verifiably, and irreversibly dismantle its nuclear programs.

America has consistently brought these threats to the attention of international organizations. We're using every means of diplomacy to answer them. As for my part, I will continue to speak clearly on these threats. I will continue to call upon the world to confront these dangers, and to end them.

10   In recent years, another path of proliferation has become clear, as well. America and other nations are learning more about black-market operatives who deal in equipment and expertise related to weapons of mass destruction. These dealers are motivated by greed, or fanaticism, or both. They find eager customers in outlaw regimes, which pay millions for the parts and plans they need to speed up their weapons programs. And with deadly technology and expertise going on the market, there's the terrible possibility that terrorists groups could obtain the ultimate weapons they desire most.

The extent and sophistication of such networks can be seen in the case of a man named Abdul Qadeer Khan. This is the story as we know it so far.

A. Q. Khan is known throughout the world as the father of Pakistan's nuclear weapons program. What was not publicly known, until recently, is that he also led an extensive international network for the proliferation of nuclear technology and know-how.

For decades, Mr. Khan remained on the Pakistani government payroll, earning a modest salary. Yet, he and his associates financed lavish lifestyles through the sale of nuclear technologies and equipment to outlaw regimes stretching from North Africa to the Korean Peninsula.

A. Q. Khan, himself, operated mostly out of Pakistan. He served as director of the network, its leading scientific mind, as well as its primary salesman. Over the past decade, he made frequent trips to consult with his clients and to sell his expertise. He and his associates sold the blueprints for centrifuges to enrich uranium, as well as a nuclear design stolen from the Pakistani government. The network sold uranium hexafluoride, the gas that the centrifuge process can transform into enriched uranium for nuclear bombs. Khan and his associates provided Iran and Libya and North Korea with designs for Pakistan's older centrifuges, as well as designs for more advanced and efficient models. The network also provided these countries with components, and in some cases, with complete centrifuges.

To increase their profits, Khan and his associates used a factory in Malaysia to manufacture key parts for centrifuges. Other necessary parts were purchased through network operatives based in Europe, the Middle East, and Africa. These procurement agents saw the trade in nuclear technologies as a shortcut to personal wealth, and they set up front companies to deceive legitimate firms into selling them tightly controlled materials.

Khan's deputy—a man named B. S. A. Tahir—ran SMB computers, a business in Dubai. Tahir used that computer company as a front for the proliferation activities of the A. Q. Khan network. Tahir acted as both the network's chief financial officer and money launderer. He was also its shipping agent, using his computer firm as cover for the movement of centrifuge parts to various clients. Tahir directed the Malaysia facility to produce these parts based on Pakistani designs, and then ordered the facility to ship the components to Dubai. Tahir also arranged for parts acquired by other European procurement agents to transit through Dubai for shipment to other customers.

This picture of the Khan network was pieced together over several years by American and British intelligence officers. Our intelligence services gradually uncovered this network's reach, and identified its key experts and agents and money men. Operatives followed its transactions, mapped the extent of its operations. They monitored the travel of A. Q. Khan and senior associates. They shadowed members of the network around the world, they recorded their conversations, they penetrated their operations, we've uncovered their secrets. This work involved high risk, and all Americans can be grateful for the hard work and the dedication of our fine intelligence professionals.

Governments around the world worked closely with us to unravel the Khan network, and to put an end to his criminal enterprise. A. Q. Khan has confessed his crimes, and his top associates are out of business. The government of Pakistan is interrogating the network's members, learning critical details that will help them prevent it from ever operating again. President Musharraf has promised to share all the information he learns about the Khan network, and has assured us that his country will never again be a source of proliferation.

Mr. Tahir is in Malaysia, where authorities are investigating his activities. Malaysian authorities have assured us that the factory the network used is no longer producing centrifuge parts. Other members of the network remain at large. One by one, they will be found, and their careers in the weapons trade will be ended.

20   As a result of our penetration of the network, American and the British intelligence identified a shipment of advanced centrifuge parts manufactured at the Malaysia facility. We followed the shipment of these parts to Dubai, and watched as they were transferred to the BBC China, a German-owned ship. After the ship passed through the Suez Canal, bound for Libya, it was stopped by German and Italian authorities. They found several containers, each forty feet in length, listed on the ship's manifest as full of "used machine parts." In fact, these containers were filled with parts of sophisticated centrifuges.

The interception of the BBC China came as Libyan and British and American officials were discussing the possibility of Libya ending its WMD programs. The United States and Britain confronted Libyan officials with this evidence of an active and illegal nuclear program. About two months ago, Libya's leader voluntarily agreed to end his nuclear and chemical weapons programs, not to pursue biological weapons, and to permit thorough inspections by the International Atomic Energy Agency and the Organization for the Prohibition of Chemical Weapons. We're now working in partnership with these organizations and with the United Kingdom to help the government of Libya dismantle those programs and eliminate all dangerous materials.

Colonel Ghadafi made the right decision, and the world will be safer once his commitment is fulfilled. We expect other regimes to follow his example. Abandoning the pursuit of illegal weapons can lead to better relations with the United States, and other free nations. Continuing to seek those weapons will not bring security or international prestige, but only political isolation, economic hardship, and other unwelcome consequences.

We know that Libya was not the only customer of the Khan network. Other countries expressed great interest in their services. These regimes and other proliferators like Khan should know: We and our friends are determined to protect our people and the world from proliferation.

Breaking this network is one major success in a broad-based effort to stop the spread of terrible weapons. We're adjusting our strategies to the threats of a new era. America and the nations of Australia, France and Germany, Italy and Japan, the Netherlands, Poland, Portugal, Spain and the United Kingdom have launched the Proliferation Security Initiative to interdict lethal materials in transit. Our nations are sharing intelligence information, tracking suspect international cargo, conducting joint military exercises. We're prepared to search planes and ships, to seize weapons and missiles and equipment that raise proliferation concerns, just as we did in stopping the dangerous cargo on the BBC China before it reached Libya. Three more governments—Canada and Singapore and Norway—will be participating in this initiative. We'll continue to expand the core group of PSI countries. And as PSI grows, proliferators will find it harder than ever to trade in illicit weapons.

There is a consensus among nations that proliferation cannot be tolerated. Yet this consensus means little unless it is translated into action. Every civilized nation has a stake in preventing the spread of weapons of mass destruction. These materials and technologies, and the people who traffic in them, cross many borders. To stop this trade, the nations of the world must be strong and determined. We must work together, we must act effectively. Today, I announce seven proposals to strengthen the world's efforts to stop the spread of deadly weapons.

First, I propose that the work of the Proliferation Security Initiative be expanded to address more than shipments and transfers. Building on the tools we've developed to fight terrorists, we can take direct action against proliferation networks. We need greater cooperation not just among intelligence and military services, but in law enforcement, as well. PSI participants and other willing nations should use the Interpol and all other means to bring to justice those who traffic in deadly weapons, to shut down their labs, to seize their materials, to freeze their assets. We must act on every lead. We will find the middlemen, the suppliers and the buyers. Our message to proliferators must be consistent and it must be clear: We will find you, and we're not going to rest until you are stopped.

Second, I call on all nations to strengthen the laws and international controls that govern proliferation. At the U.N. last fall, I proposed a new Security Council resolution requiring all states to criminalize proliferation, enact strict export controls, and secure all sensitive materials within their borders. The Security Council should pass this proposal quickly. And when they do, America stands ready to help other governments to draft and enforce the new laws that will help us deal with proliferation.

Third, I propose to expand our efforts to keep weapons from the Cold War and other dangerous materials out of the wrong hands. In 1991, Congress passed the Nunn-Lugar legislation. Senator Lugar had a clear vision, along with Senator Nunn, about what to do with the old Soviet Union. Under this program, we're helping former Soviet states find productive employment for former weapons scientists. We're dismantling, destroying and securing weapons and materials left over from the Soviet WMD arsenal. We have more work to do there.

And as a result of the G-8 Summit in 2002, we agreed to provide $20 billion over 10 years—half of it from the United States— to support such programs. We should expand this cooperation elsewhere in the world. We will retain [*sic*] WMD scientists and technicians in countries like Iraq and Libya. We will help nations end the use of weapons-grade uranium in research reactors. I urge more nations to contribute to these efforts. The nations of the world must do all we can to secure and eliminate nuclear and chemical and biological and radiological materials.

30   As we track and destroy these networks, we must also prevent governments from developing nuclear weapons under false pretenses. The Nuclear Non-Proliferation Treaty was designed more than 30 years ago to prevent the spread of nuclear weapons beyond those states which already possessed them. Under this treaty, nuclear states agreed to help non-nuclear states develop peaceful atomic energy if they renounced the pursuit of nuclear weapons. But the treaty has a loophole which has been exploited by nations such as North Korea and Iran. These regimes are al-

lowed to produce nuclear material that can be used to build bombs under the cover of civilian nuclear programs.

So today, as a fourth step, I propose a way to close the loophole. The world must create a safe, orderly system to field civilian nuclear plants without adding to the danger of weapons proliferation. The world's leading nuclear exporters should ensure that states have reliable access at reasonable cost to fuel for civilian reactors, so long as those states renounce enrichment and reprocessing. Enrichment and reprocessing are not necessary for nations seeking to harness nuclear energy for peaceful purposes.

The 40 nations of the Nuclear Suppliers Group should refuse to sell enrichment and reprocessing equipment and technologies to any state that does not already possess full-scale, functioning enrichment and reprocessing plants. This step will prevent new states from developing the means to produce fissile material for nuclear bombs. Proliferators must not be allowed to cynically manipulate the NPT to acquire the material and infrastructure necessary for manufacturing illegal weapons.

For international norms to be effective, they must be enforced. It is the charge of the International Atomic Energy Agency to uncover banned nuclear activity around the world and report those violations to the U.N. Security Council. We must ensure that the IAEA has all the tools it needs to fulfill its essential mandate. America and other nations support what is called the Additional Protocol, which requires states to declare a broad range of nuclear activities and facilities, and allow the IAEA to inspect those facilities.

As a fifth step, I propose that by next year, only states that have signed the Additional Protocol be allowed to import equipment for their civilian nuclear programs. Nations that are serious about fighting proliferation will approve and implement the Additional Protocol. I've submitted the Additional Protocol to the Senate. I urge the Senate to consent immediately to its ratification.

We must also ensure that IAEA is organized to take action   35
when action is required. So, as a sixth step, I propose the creation of a special committee of the IAEA Board which will focus intensively on safeguards and verification. This committee, made up of governments in good standing with the IAEA, will strengthen the capability of the IAEA to ensure that nations comply with their international obligations.

And, finally, countries under investigation for violating nuclear non-proliferation obligations are currently allowed to serve on the IAEA Board of Governors. For instance, Iran—a country suspected of maintaining an extensive nuclear weapons program—recently completed a two-year term on the Board. Allowing potential violators to serve on the Board creates an unacceptable barrier to effective action. No state under investigation for proliferation violations should be allowed to serve on the IAEA Board of Governors—or on the new special committee. And any state currently on the Board that comes under investigation should be suspended from the Board. The integrity and mission of the IAEA depends on this simple principle: Those actively breaking the rules should not be entrusted with enforcing the rules.

As we move forward to address these challenges we will consult with our friends and allies on all these new measures. We will listen to their ideas. Together we will defend the safety of all nations and preserve the peace of the world.

Over the last two years, a great coalition has come together to defeat terrorism and to oppose the spread of weapons of mass destruction—the inseparable commitments of the war on terror. We've shown that proliferators can be discovered and can be stopped. We've shown that for regimes that choose defiance, there are serious consequences. The way ahead is not easy, but it is clear. We will proceed as if the lives of our citizens depend on our vigilance, because they do. Terrorists and terror states are in a race for weapons of mass murder, a race they must lose. Terrorists are resourceful; we're more resourceful. They're determined; we must be more determined. We will never lose focus or resolve. We'll be unrelenting in the defense of free nations, and rise to the hard demands of dangerous times.

Starting Points

1. Summarize the seven steps that President George W. Bush says are necessary to stopping the spread of WMDs. Will these steps work? What, if anything, is missing from this plan? How would these initiatives have stopped the hijackers of 9/11?

2. Consider the audience for this speech, including their probable knowledge of the various programs discussed by the President. How would you change this address for a general audience?

3. Learn more about "black market operatives" (paragraph 10) who deal in nuclear and other WMD components. Are they a major threat to nations, or are they confidence men selling sleight-of-hand tricks?

War on Terror Fuels Small Arms Trade

OWEN BOWCOTT AND RICHARD NORTON-TAYLOR

Oxfam, Amnesty International, and the International Network on Small Arms issued a joint report in 2003 that outlined an unforeseen result of the international campaign against terrorism: an exponential increase in the sales of small arms, with a corresponding spike in the number of people killed around the globe. The news summary of the report that follows first appeared in the British newspaper The Guardian *on October 10, 2003. The entire report can be found on the web sites of any of the three organizations noted above.*

◆

The "war on terror" has weakened national arms controls and fuelled the proliferation of conventional weapons, a coalition of leading human rights charities warned yesterday. Launching a global campaign to regulate the arms trade, Amnesty International, Oxfam, and the International Network on Small Arms said that on average 500,000 people were killed each year by armed violence—roughly one victim a minute.

Existing arms control laws, including those in Britain, are riddled with loopholes, the agencies claim, and what is needed is a common approach similar to the initiative that produced the 1997 Ottawa treaty banning landmines.

The charities' proposed international arms trade treaty would outlaw weapons sales involving exportation for use entailing "violations of international human rights or humanitarian law." The plan will be presented to a United Nations conference on small arms in 2006.

"A new urgency has been created by the so-called war on terror," said Irene Khan, secretary general of Amnesty. "This is fuelling the proliferation of weapons rather than combating it. Many countries, including the U.S., have relaxed controls on sales of arms to allies known to have appalling human rights records.

"In the past two years, the U.S. has increased arms sales to [such states] and Britain has followed suit. British arms sales to Indonesia [the second highest recipient of UK overseas aid] rose from £2m in 2000 to £40m in 2002." 5

Shipments of arms had been delivered on the basis that "the enemy of my enemy is my friend," despite knowing that allies could become future dangers, said the charities. In June 2003, there were thought to be 24m guns in Iraq—enough to arm every man, woman and child. The charities term small arms the true "weapons of mass destruction," which claim hundreds of thousands of lives, destabilising countries and prolonging conflicts.

Britain, the second largest exporter of arms, is urged, in a 100-page report entitled *Shattered Lives*, to sign up to the arms trade treaty. It is criticised for military aid and arms sales to Pakistan and Uzbekistan, which soared after the September 11 attacks on the U.S.

Shipments of weapons to Saudi Arabia, where thousands of people are detained arbitrarily, and Jamaica, where the police have killed more than 600 people in the past four years, are also highlighted.

Britain's recently introduced arms control legislation is blamed for failing to outlaw the activity of British arms brokers who work outside the UK, despite an earlier manifesto commitment.

10   The report notes that in 2002 the G8 group of industrialised countries allocated $20bn (£12.5bn) to a programme designed to prevent terrorists acquiring nuclear, chemical and biological weapons. But "the G8 failed to address the proliferation of conventional weapons, including small arms, to states and armed groups that they know will abuse such weapons to terrorise [civilians]."

Kofi Annan, UN secretary general, has said the death toll from small arms "dwarfs that of all other weapons systems, and in most years greatly exceeds the toll of the Hiroshima and Nagasaki atomic bombs. In terms of the carnage they cause, small arms could well be described as weapons of mass destruction—yet there is still no global non-proliferation regime to limit their spread."

The small arms trade has widespread repercussions, especially in poor countries, Amnesty and Oxfam say. Weapons in the wrong hands prevent access to hospitals, markets, schools, and productive land. Poverty fuels conflict and vice versa, and the problem is compounded by corrupt, and often scarce, official security forces. Weapons have permeated daily life to such an extent that in northern Uganda AK-47s are replacing spears; in Somalia some children are now named AK.

Most of the estimated 639m small arms in the world are in private hands. And the problems facing countries after an armed conflict often overwhelm them. "Half of newly pacified countries revert to war within a decade," adds the report.

The campaign follows concern also about Britain, where use of firearms in violent crime grew by 35% last year.

Yesterday, the campaign also launched a petition to gather a   15 million signatures supporting the draft arms treaty. Showing the cost in human lives, 300 model gravestones were erected in Trafalgar Square, London, each with the slogan "One person every minute killed by arms".

Mike O'Brien, the Foreign Office minister, yesterday welcomed the report, but added: "Britain has been in the forefront of efforts to improve arms controls and we have one of the toughest export control systems in the world."

COUNTING COST

- 500,000 people, one a minute, killed by conventional arms every year.
- 639m small arms circulating in world today, produced by more than 1,135 companies in 98 countries.
- In June there were 24m guns in Iraq, enough to arm every man, woman, and child. They could be bought for $10.
- Over 59% of small arms are privately owned, 38% are in hands of government forces, less than 3% held by police.
- Nearly 8m small arms made a year.
- Up to 100m Kalashnikov rifles have been produced.
- 300,000 children are fighting in conflicts around world. As many as 70,000 boys serve in Burma's national army.

Starting Points

1. What should the United States and other nations do to curb the sales of small arms? Are small arms truly the weapons of mass destruction, or should nations continue to focus on controlling weapons such as nuclear, chemical, and biological devices?
2. Discuss the ways in which the money spent on small arms, as well as the resulting use of those arms, has a particularly deleterious effect on developing nations.
3. Select one developing nation that is experiencing violence and research the root causes of the strife as well as the impact of small arms on the lives of its citizens and the economy of the state.

Al-Qaida Leader Says They Have Briefcase Nukes

THE ASSOCIATED PRESS

The first atomic bombs dropped on Japan were the size of industrial boilers, and required the largest airplane in the world at the time to carry them. Miniaturization of virtually all business and manufacturing technology has also included military hardware and all manner of lethal weapons. In this Associated Press article from March 21, 2004, a top al-Qaida leader claims the terrorist organization now possesses suitcase-size nuclear devices. If true, it would mean a new era of mass terror.

———————————— ✦ ————————————

Osama bin Laden's terror network claims to have bought ready-made nuclear weapons on the black market in central Asia, the biographer of al-Qaida's No. 2 leader was quoted as telling an Australian television station.

In an interview scheduled to be televised on Monday, Pakistani journalist Hamid Mir said Ayman al-Zawahri claimed that "smart briefcase bombs" were available on the black market.

It was not clear when the interview between Mir and al-Zawahri took place.

U.S. intelligence agencies have long believed that al-Qaida attempted to acquire a nuclear device on the black market, but say there is no evidence it was successful.

5   In the interview with Australian Broadcasting Corp. television, parts of which were released Sunday, Mir recalled telling al-Zawahri it was difficult to believe that al-Qaida had nuclear weapons when the terror network didn't have the equipment to maintain or use them.

"Dr. Ayman al-Zawahri laughed and he said 'Mr. Mir, if you have $30 million, go to the black market in central Asia, contact any disgruntled Soviet scientist, and a lot of . . . smart briefcase bombs are available,' " Mir said in the interview.

"They have contacted us, we sent our people to Moscow, to Tashkent, to other central Asian states and they negotiated, and we purchased some suitcase bombs," Mir quoted al-Zawahri as saying.

Al-Qaida has never hidden its interest in acquiring nuclear weapons.

The U.S. federal indictment of bin Laden charges that as far back as 1992 he "and others known and unknown, made efforts to obtain the components of nuclear weapons."

Bin Laden, in a November 2001 interview with a Pakistani journalist, boasted having hidden such components "as a deterrent." And in 1998, a Russian nuclear weapons design expert was investigated for allegedly working with bin Laden's Taliban allies. 10

It was revealed last month that Pakistan's top nuclear scientist had sold sensitive equipment and nuclear technology to Iran, Libya and North Korea, fueling fears the information could have also fallen into the hands of terrorists.

Earlier, Mir told Australian media that al-Zawahri also claimed to have visited Australia to recruit militants and collect funds.

"In those days, in early 1996, he was on a mission to organize his network all over the world," Mir was quoted as saying. "He told me he stopped for a while in Darwin (in northern Australia), he was . . . looking for help and collecting funds."

Australia's Attorney-General Philip Ruddock said the government could not rule out the possibility that al-Zawahri visited Australia in the 1990s under a different name.

"Under his own name or any known alias he hasn't traveled to Australia," Ruddock told reporters Saturday. "That doesn't mean to say that he may not have come under some other false documentation, or some other alias that's not known to us." 15

Mir describe al-Zawahri as "the real brain behind Osama bin Laden."

"He is the real strategist, Osama bin Laden is only a front man," Mir was quoted as saying during the interview. "I think he is more dangerous than bin Laden."

Al-Zawahri—an Egyptian surgeon—is believed to be hiding in the rugged region around the Pakistan-Afghan border where U.S. and Pakistani troops are conducting a major operation against Taliban and al-Qaida forces.

He is said to have played a leading role in orchestrating the Sept. 11, 2001, attacks on the United States.

Starting Points

1. Write an essay in which you envision the effect upon an urban population if a terrorist nuclear device is exploded. How would life be different? What changes in daily routines would be required?

2. Argue for or against the claim of whether al-Qaida possesses suitcase nukes. Is the claim credible? Why would they say they have such

weapons if they do not? If they have them, why have they not used them yet?

3. Research the availability of miniaturized nuclear devices. What is the source? What steps have been taken to prevent their purchase by terrorist organizations? How effective have international agencies been in keeping track of weapons-grade nuclear material?

Overview of the Terrorist Threat to International Peace and Security

PAUL WILKINSON

Six weeks after the terrorist attacks of September 11, 2001, the United Nations held a symposium on terrorism and disarmament. Paul Wilkinson, a professor at the University of St. Andrews, Scotland, is also director of the Center for the Study of Terrorism and Political Violence, the co-editor of the Journal on Terrorism and Political Violence, *and the author of several books on the topic of terrorism. This overview was given at the UN symposium in New York City on October 25, 2001.*

———————— ✦ ————————

"MASS TERRORISM"

I have been asked to deal with the implications of terrorism for international peace and security, and I am going to deal first with the escalation to mass terrorism. It is clear in the events of 11 September that we have crossed a terrible watershed for terrorism, which has been largely seen as a form of low-intensity conflict, very often of main concern to the governments of a particular country, as a relatively routine problem of security and law and order.

We are now dealing with cases of sub-State groups inflicting death on such a scale that we cannot describe it in any other way than by the description "mass terrorism." More civilians died in one day on 11 September than died in 25 years of sub-State terrorism in Northern Ireland and Spain.

The statistics should give you some sense of the dramatic escalation in lethality that we are dealing with in the atrocities in the United States. To put another figure to you, which, I think, dramatizes the increase in the lethality of terrorism, the figure of total deaths in the American atrocities exceeds the total deaths through international terrorism recorded in the major academic chronologies over a 20-year period, that is, incidents of terrorism involving the citizens of more than one country.

We are dealing with a much more strategic level of threat. Indeed, it is a strategic threat, not simply to the United States, but to the international community. It is clearly a step towards the kind of terrorism that has been constantly discussed in the special academic fora in which students of violence have exchanged views, that is, the possibilities of terrorists using chemical, biological and nuclear weapons. It has made that kind of mass lethality terrorism far more likely.

It is, in fact, worth reminding ourselves that the airline suicide hijackings are themselves a form of mass destruction terrorism, and that that threat is something which our aviation security was totally inadequate to prevent, and this is not simply a feature of aviation security in America. It is, sadly, characteristic of aviation security in general around the world. I am sorry to say that that threat is still a real one. It would be dishonest of me as a person who specialized in the problems of aviation terrorism and aviation security for many years to pretend that we had already taken the necessary measures to ensure that this kind of mass terrorist attack will not happen again. Sadly, I have flown in recent weeks many thousands of miles in aircraft in which it was perfectly easy to move from the passenger cabin into the cockpit. I have flown in aircraft where there was no form of sky marshal protection. Yet, against the suicide hijacking threat, given the inadequate level of ground airport security that exists in many airports in the world, in-flight security is clearly absolutely vital. So, when we talk about escalation to mass terrorism, we should not simply be thinking of the more exotic unconventional weapons that we have always feared might be used by terrorists. We should be thinking of some of the adaptations of traditional techniques, such as hijacking of airliners, turning commercial airplanes into weapons of mass destruction, and we should be trying to take comprehensive steps to protect our communities against that type of attack.

IMPACT ON THE UNITED STATES

What is the impact of this latest development on the United States itself?

Clearly, grief, shock, a sense of the vulnerability of the United States' own territory to the phenomenon of terrorism. But, on the other side of the picture, an inspiring strength of purpose, of courage, in the American democracy, a determination not to be intimidated by the cowardly evil of those who were responsible for those devastating attacks. America has not been cowered by those attacks into retreating from its foreign policy responsibilities in the wider world. On the contrary, the United States has shown an energetic global activism, maintaining its interest in the Middle East peace process, maintaining its humanitarian effort in aid to those areas of the world that are in so desperate need of it and, of course, sustaining its interest in increasing peace and stability in other parts of the world. And so, those who assume that terror, even on a mass scale, will automatically cower a country into retreating from its responsibilities and changing its political system or its foreign policy behavior, are once again, I am glad to say, shown to be totally deluded.

IMPACT ON THE INTERNATIONAL COMMUNITY

The impact on the international community is one of genuine outrage and heartfelt sympathy—a tremendous upsurge of sympathy—for America, for the victims and the bereaved, the realization that this is a threat to us all. It has also meant the swift emergence of an extraordinarily wide global coalition against terrorism, an intensive global criminal justice investigation, involving cooperation with a remarkable range of countries, a global intelligence effort, sharing intelligence on a scale not seen since the early 1990s in the crisis when Iraq invaded Kuwait.

Other important consequences for the international community are the military operations in Afghanistan; sadly, a humanitarian crisis in Afghanistan which already existed on account of the poverty and enormous hardship suffered by that long-suffering people, spilling over into the refugee camps on the Pakistan side of the border; disruption and damage not only to the United States economy but to the global economy; and, of course, the plight of the aviation industry has been one that has been most immediately noticed. The attacks have been felt in the aerospace industry, in tourism, in the financial sector, in the confidence in the stock markets, and so on. One should not underestimate the disrupting effect of mass terrorism on the general well-being of the global economy, though I, for one, fully believe that confidence will be restored—**is** being restored—and that economic stability and growth can be achieved by ensuring that we tackle this problem of international terrorism with urgency and calm determination.

10   Positive developments are also worth noting. As Lech Walesa, the Polish President has remarked, what this crisis has brought

forward is "a new era of global cooperation." And I believe we really are seeing that. I noticed in my recent travels to Greece and in my discussions with colleagues in Asia and in Africa a change in the climate of public opinion regarding terrorism, even in countries traditionally reluctant to view it as a problem, or to take any significant action against it. Interesting too are the various terrorist groups around the world who have been put on the defensive by the enormous upsurge of international determination to tackle terrorism. I am sure that the improved situation of the peace process in Northern Ireland is not unconnected with this hardening of international resolve and determination to resist terrorism in all its various manifestations. It is interesting too that the Spanish government is now, I think, in a stronger position to exert pressure to bring an end to ETA's murderous terrorist campaign that has been going on within their borders in recent months.

It is also important to remember that we have many Islamic countries in the coalition against terrorism. I found it very difficult to understand why a well-known commentator on international affairs has suggested in a news broadcast that the structure of the coalition did not matter, that it did not matter whether there were Muslim countries in that international coalition or not. I think that showed a total misunderstanding of what this campaign about terrorism is really concerned with. This is not a coalition against any particular ethnic or religious group. It is a coalition against terrorism, a method of violence that law-abiding people and law-abiding countries in the world have come to recognize as simply unacceptable, because it is a massive violation of human rights. It is essentially a human rights problem, just in the same way that war crimes by States are human rights problems. It is not something we can afford to tolerate and regard with complacency, as something we do not need to act on. Therefore, it is very significant that Muslim countries, such as Pakistan, have made clear their determination to be part of this coalition and to try to cooperate as well as they can, and often, as we see in the case of Pakistan, in very difficult circumstances, to try to tackle this threat. It is also important to note that countries that perhaps, previously, were not so willing to cooperate with the United States, have joined the United States with great determination to try to bring an end to this challenge to human rights.

ILLEGITIMACY OF TERRORISM

I would argue that what the latest development in mass terrorism has shown is that the big fault line in the international system is not actually between civilizations in some terrible confrontation, not a clash of religions—thank goodness—the last thing we want is some terrible renewal of religious wars of the kind that we had in earlier historical periods. That would be a disaster for humanity, a disaster for peace and security. What we have is a fault line, in the case of this campaign against terrorism, between those who believe that terrorism is a perfectly legitimate, acceptable means of fighting for a political or religious cause, and those who would argue that, as a method, because it is inherently a threat to the most fundamental human right, it is unacceptable and must be curbed and the international community must seek to eradicate it.

NEED FOR GLOBAL ACTION

This particular problem that we face in relation to the attacks in America, the Al Qaeda network which masterminded those attacks, is an illustration of the complex and transnational nature of this phenomenon. It is a hydra. It is true that if the action by the coalition allies succeeds in capturing and bringing Osama bin Laden to justice, it will certainly inflict major damage on Al Qaeda and, hopefully, a psychological blow to the organization to bring the organization to its decline. But, I fear that will not be by itself enough to dismantle this transnational network.

We are beginning to see in Europe and elsewhere how well-entrenched this network has become, with many support networks as well as operational cells working for Al Qaeda in many countries, and we still are unable to unravel all the links between those various branches of the network. We, therefore, need to remember that globalization, which is particularly evident in the Al Qaeda network, has affected the whole phenomenon of terrorism. Even those groups which we tend to think of as internal or domestic terrorist groups have a geographically dispersed network of supporters managing to pump in considerable finances as well as propaganda and armament support through their causes.

15   We have to remember that those networks, in the case of all protracted terrorist campaigns, are an essential part of keeping those campaigns going. They would not be able to carry out murder and destruction so effectively if we were able to eradicate these support networks in countries where they have operated in virtual safe havens. In order to dismantle this hydra's tentacles of international support networks, we need global cooperation. It is, therefore, a global strategy that is needed. There is no way that a superpower or a coalition of major powers alone can really hope

to succeed in this longterm battle to eradicate the terrorist threat to human rights. It has to be a multilateral effort involving the world organizations in a prime role.

ROLE OF THE UNITED NATIONS

There is a key role for the United Nations here, and it is very heartening to see in the strong Security Council resolution, in the work of the committee to counter terrorism and in the work of the Department for Disarmament Affairs, a high priority given to combating this terrorist threat. The United Nations has a number of important roles to play. It has, in its conventions, set very important standards for national governments and their law enforcement agencies to achieve, and we should not underestimate the importance of that standard setting.

We know that in some countries who have failed to fully implement those conventions or to consistently uphold them, the standard setting itself places a pressure on national governments to conform to standards of lawful behavior that are important to a civilized international community. And it is interesting that in countries which are now considering their national legislation, reviewing it to address loopholes in their handling of laws on terrorism, time and again, the existence of the UN conventions is being utilized as a means of both defining the nature of the threat and, of course, of achieving a certain model of response which is inherent in the United Nations approach.

It is also important to notice the work of the United Nations at the humanitarian level, seeking to assist in those conflict situations that spawn terrorist violence—the work of the UN in Afghanistan is a dramatic illustration of this. I also share the view that has been expressed by many academic observers and international diplomats that the United Nations must have a leading role—indeed a key role in guiding the international community in the aftermath of this effort to track down bin Laden and his key lieutenants and to bring them to justice, because the Afghan people, after years of suffering civil conflict in that country, deserve a chance to recover the means of subsistence, the means of reconstructing their country, which only the many-sided technical capabilities and expertise of the UN can help to bring about. I think the UN is the right agency, the right mechanism to assist in that process.

COUNTER-PROLIFERATION

There is also an absolutely crucial role for disarmament and counter-proliferation activities, especially in finding means of enhancing the security of materials that could so easily be used for WMD terrorism. Sadly, there are many countries where there are great deficiencies in the protection of chemical and biological materials which can be used for terrorist purposes. We have already heard allegations that the materials that are being used in the campaign in America were obtained through a relatively easy transaction, from the stockpiles that have been accumulated in other countries. That is still to be confirmed, but it seems likely, if one is dealing with a very high grade of biological weapon, that that happened, in which case the Biological Weapons Convention, so heavily criticized by many, should be revisited. Moreover, I hope that those countries that have become disappointed or disillusioned with the effort at arms control and disarmament in that field, would revisit that problem and attempt to adapt this international legislation more strongly to the prevention of the proliferation of these materials into the hands of terrorists. There are pitfalls in this global strategy; allowing, for example, the campaign against terrorism to turn into some wider conflict or deflecting attention from the task of bringing the terrorists to justice would spell disaster. A wider war would be an evil greater than the evil that terrorism presents, and which we are trying to eliminate. I am, therefore, a strong supporter of maintaining a considered, precise and proportionate level of violence to bring the perpetrators of terrorism to justice, making sure that the violence used in order to do that does not threaten the well-being of a whole civilian population.

PURSUIT OF JUSTICE

20   I think another final point is the pitfall that many fall into of thinking that there is a simple political solution to every terrorist threat. There are many situations—South Africa, Nicaragua, Northern Ireland, East Timor—where peace processes can succeed in ending conflict, and conflict resolution techniques are clearly appropriate. I strongly support them, and I am a strong supporter of the peace process method.

But for fanatical and incorrigible murderers who are not interested in bargaining, or in re-associating with rational politics, groups like the Aum Shinrikyo in Japan, which was responsible for the sarin nerve gas attack, or the Osama bin Laden Al Qaeda network, I think the only sensible course is to tackle such challenges to human rights and the rule of law by the firm application of a criminal justice response from the international community. We must suppress those who are committed to murdering the innocent.

I believe that we should revisit the international criminal court statute and consider extending it to include international terrorism of the sort we have seen in New York and Washington. I do not see any moral difference between those responsible for such massive violations of human rights and those who are before the Human Rights tribunal for war crimes in the former Yugoslavia. Morally, they are all in the same level of massive violations of human rights, and the International Criminal Court (ICC) should be able to deal with that. I am sure that will have a wide support from the international community.

Starting Points

1. In the last two paragraphs, Paul Wilkinson writes that there are many different terrorists driven by a variety of agendas. The most destructive attacks by terrorists in recent years occurred in New York City on September 11th, and he brands the al-Qaida network as "fanatical and incorrigible murderers." There have always been murders. Does this mean that the War on Terror will never be over, akin to the war on crime?

2. The author distinguishes between the old terrorism and the rise of "mass terrorism," and uses the phrase "fault line" (paragraph 12) to describe the differences between those who view terrorism as a legitimate means of resistence or intent to change and those who see it as absolutely illegitimate. Americans in the War for Independence might have been termed terrorists. What is different today?

3. Conduct further research (including other readings here) and consider whether the bombings of civilian population centers in World War II was different from the attacks on civilians on 9/11. Why are the deaths caused by "sub-State" groups (paragraph 2) less acceptable than state-sponsored violence?

Mission of Suicide Bombers Is Martyrdom, Retribution

Desperation, Faith Seen as Driving Forces

Joyce M. Davis

Suicide bombings in Israel and Iraq have become a fact of life for those who live there, and U.S. intelligence agencies have begun to issue warnings that such tactics will soon be used here in America.

*Are such tactics legitimate in any circumstances? What are the mo-
tivating factors in the recruitment of suicide bombers? Joyce M.
Davis of the* Detroit Free Press *presents a look at suicide bombers
in Israel. This article first appeared on April 8, 2002.*

———————————— ✦ ————————————

It has become a ghastly routine: an explosion. Glass, metal, wood,
blood and body parts fly everywhere. Shocked survivors stumble
into the street, blood running from wounds. Rescue workers race
to the scene, pushing gurneys, gesturing frantically for more help.

This routine is the work of suicide bombers, claiming to be
striking a blow for Islam and Palestinian liberation. More than 50,
many of them teenagers, some women, have killed more than 200
people during the past 18 months. Some of the victims have been
soldiers. Most were civilians; men, women and children, Jews and
Arabs. The day Izzidene al Masri blew himself up last August inside the Sbarro pizzeria in Jerusalem, killing 15 other people, six
of them children, and wounding 130, his neighbors in the West
Bank town of Jenin danced in the streets and sang his praises.

They see al Masri as a soldier who sacrificed his life to strike
deep into the heart of the enemy, Israel. They say he is not unlike
the biblical Samson, who used his body to bring a temple down
on himself and his enemies.

Millions of other people consider him a fanatic and a mur-
derer. What drives people such as al Masri to strap explosives to
their bodies and seek out crowded places to blow themselves—
and others—into bits?

5   The answer is not simple. Here are the general views based
on interviews with Palestinian militants and experts on Islam and
the Mideast:

People who make that drastic choice often grow up hearing
their religious leaders promising martyrdom and everlasting life
in heaven to people who die killing Israelis.

They believe interpretations of Islam that encourage martyrdom as the ultimate act of sacrifice and bravery.

They believe that Muslims in general, and Palestinians in particular, have been victimized by more powerful nations, particularly the United States.

They nurture a hatred of Israel so powerful that they see Jews
only as enemies who must die.

10   They say suicide bombers are their best weapons against the
Israelis, striking them where it hurts, inside their shopping centers, markets and restaurants.

THE BOMBERS' PSYCHE

Certainly not every Muslim agrees that suicide bombers should be revered. Even al Masri's mother is not so sure:

"I think someone put into his head that this was the way to go to paradise," said Um Iyad, 46.

"What prompts a 20-year-old to blow himself up and kill as many Israelis in the process?" asked Labib Kamhawi, a political analyst in Amman, Jordan, who has studied the phenomenon. "It definitely takes more than belief in God to turn a boy into a martyr. It takes desperation, anger, loss of hope. It's believing that your life is not worth living anymore."

The source of that desperation, Kamhawi said, is evident in places such as al Masri's hometown of Jenin.

Soot stains the blown-out windows of buildings newly 15
bombed by the Israeli armed forces in the town of cinder block houses. Its pockmarked roads and dirt streets turn muddy and black when it rains.

Israeli officials say they believe Jenin is a virtual factory for suicide bombers. Israeli tanks, towers of sandbags and barbed wire greet everyone who enters or leaves, a futile effort to seal the town and provide Israelis a degree of security.

The young men of Jenin also have grown up listening to Muslim clergy rail against the new Israeli settlements perched near what once were Palestinian villages and olive groves. And they have heard the singing and dancing that envelop the town when a young man such as al Masri dies in a battle or a suicide bombing against the Israelis.

ROLE OF RELIGION

Many Palestinians see their struggle with Israel as a holy war. They say their religion compels them to fight until they regain control of Muslim holy land, which they consider to be the part of east Jerusalem that holds the Al Aqsa Mosque, the site where Muslims believe the Prophet Mohammed ascended to heaven and then returned with God's rules for Islam.

But the same land is also holy to Jews, who call the area Temple Mount. It is the site of the remains of Solomon's Temple, whose Western Wall is Judaism's holiest site.

The quest for martyrdom by some Palestinians is not just 20
about religion, although religion is used, or misused, to justify the suicide bombings.

It is also about what Arabs say is the daily misery that has made fanatics of young men such as al Masri.

"What we have now in the Middle East are people who feel they are fighting at a disadvantage, who do not have weaponry or troops or forces equal to their adversaries," said John Kelsay, a professor of religion at Florida State University in Tallahassee and author of *Islam and War*. "They feel they are justified in taking irregular actions."

But many Muslims feel greatly conflicted about suicide bombings and question whether they are sullying the teachings of Islam and are used as a justification for murder and terrorism.

"What you call suicide bombings in my view are illegitimate and have nothing to do with jihad in the cause of God," Abdulaziz bin Abdallah al Sheikh, the leading Islamic scholar in Saudi Arabia, told Arab journalists a year ago.

25   As the leading religious authority in Islam's holiest land, al Sheikh is a powerful figure who has great influence among the world's 1 billion Muslims. But he's also a Sunni Muslim. While about 85 percent of Muslims are Sunnis, some members of the groups waging a terror war against Israel are from the other sect, the Shiites. Because there is no one authority in Islam who can rule whether Islam approves suicide bombings, Muslims look to scholars for guidance in interpreting the Koran. Yet Muslim scholars often disagree on the details of Islam's teachings, especially on the question of jihad and suicide bombings.

"Everyone who dies in war or is killed by the enemy is considered a martyr," said Sheikh Ahmed Yassin, the spiritual leader of Hamas, the militant group that has vowed to fight the Israeli occupation of the West Bank and Gaza, which are predominantly Palestinian areas adjacent to Israel.

Yassin, who's under house arrest after his organization claimed responsibility for recent bombings in Jerusalem and Haifa, said he believes Islam condones suicide bombings. "Anybody who dies in battle, even those who blow themselves up, are martyrs," he said during a recent interview at his offices in Gaza City.

Yassin said the targets of suicide bombers should be the Israeli military and government, not civilians. Yet his organization claims responsibility for numerous suicide bombings that have killed civilians, including the Sbarro pizzeria bombing and the March 27 suicide bombing that killed at least 20 people who were sitting down to a Passover meal at a hotel restaurant in Netanya.

It's the children her son killed in that pizza parlor that haunt Um Iyad.

"I have to say it was not a good thing that he did. There were   30
many innocents there. So many children.

"We don't support it when the Israelis kill our people, so we can't support when their innocent people are killed. We just can't condone that kind of martyrdom," she said.

Starting Points

1. Americans have faced suicide bombers only in other theaters of war—the Pacific in World War II, and now in the Mideast. How does this article affect your understanding of this fact of war? Does giving bombers names, families, or personalities in any way alter your view of the tactic?

2. What is the cause and the effect of a suicide bombing? In what ways does this journalist link the two?

3. Consider three or four other readings in this text and compare with this one. How is Joyce Davis's approach different? Rate the effectiveness in contributing to an understanding of the issue of a narrative journalistic style to a government report or a scholarly journal article.

"Smarter" Bombs Still Hit Civilians

In Every War since Iraq, the U.S. Used More "Smart" Bombs. So Why Do Civilian Casualty Rates Keep Rising?

Scott Peterson

Despite increasingly high-tech weaponry, with resulting higher costs, contemporary wars still result in higher numbers of civilian casualties. Here, Scott Peterson, writing in the Christian Science Monitor, *explores the reasons for this. This article first appeared in the* Monitor *on October 22, 2002.*

◆

The two American "smart" bombs worked perfectly, striking what the Pentagon had identified as an Iraqi command and control center during the 1991 Gulf War.

The 2,000-pound laser-guided bombs burrowed through 10 feet of hardened concrete and detonated, punching a gaping hole in the Amiriyah bomb shelter—and incinerating 408 Iraqi civilians. It is considered the single most lethal incident for civilians in modern air warfare.

As U.S. military planners prepare for another battle with Iraq, the Amiriyah bunker bombing illustrates a conundrum that has grown during the Yugoslav and Afghan air campaigns: more accurate bombs aren't necessarily reducing civilian casualty rates.

In the Gulf War, just 3 percent of bombs were precision-guided. That figure jumped to 30 percent in the 1999 bombing of Yugoslavia, and to nearly 70 percent during the Afghan air campaign last year.

5   Yet in each case, the ratio of civilian casualties to bombs dropped has grown. Technology, say analysts, isn't the key issue. In Afghanistan, tough terrain, inability to discern combatants from civilians, and paucity of fixed military targets led to estimates of 850 to 1,300 civilian deaths. Red Cross food depots were hit twice, as well as some mosques, and so was a wedding party of mostly pro-U.S. civilians last July.

By one estimate, the number of civilians killed per bomb dropped may have been four times as high in Afghanistan as in Yugoslavia.

A number of factors contribute to this trend, including the changing nature of combat. The U.S. is relying more on air power, in part to protect American lives. Its foes, aware of the propaganda power of civilian deaths, are hiding military equipment and troops in civilian areas. The Amiriyah bunker bombing illustrates some of the problems, including the lack of good intelligence on the ground.

The Pentagon targeted Amiriyah because it picked up electronic signals coming from the site, and spy satellites could see a lot of people and vehicles moving in and out of the bunker. It fit the profile of a military command center, says Charles Heyman, the London-based editor of Jane's World Armies. The Pentagon didn't find out until much later, says Mr. Heyman, that the Iraqis had put an aerial antenna on top of the bunker. The antenna was connected by cable to a communications center safely 300 yards away.

Of the 250,000 bombs and missiles dropped on Iraq in 1991, only two impacted here at the bunker, on Feb. 13. But those two bombs defined the war for many Iraqis, and, six weeks into the air campaign, prompted Washington to curtail further attacks on downtown Baghdad. "I want the Americans to come here to see what happened, because this place bears witness, because the

U.S. is talking about a new war," says Intesar Ahmed Hassan, as she takes a visitor on a tour of the blackened Amiriyah bunker—today a shrine to the victims—which still smells of smoke. "Maybe they won't do it again, if they see that this is the result."

PROPAGANDA WAR

But Heyman predicts that if the U.S. launches another air war on Iraq, "[Hussein] is going to make sure that civilians get killed. And he's going to make sure that all over the world, there are pictures of weeping Iraqi mothers and dead babies. That is part and parcel of the game."

Earlier this month, the Brookings Institution in Washington estimated the "Iraqi civilian deaths could number in the tens of thousands. . . . "Even careful bombing by the U.S. would produce large numbers of civilian casualties, given Saddam's likely decision to hole up in cities, using civilian populations as shields for his military forces."

Military experts say with the shift from trench warfare, the aversion of military losses, and the rise of long-distance high-tech weapons, the proportion of civilian casualties to military in war has grown from 10 percent a century ago, to about 90 percent on modern battlefields.

BETTER TECHNOLOGY

"Smart" bombs have advanced by magnitudes since 1991. But war takes place under imperfect conditions. Targeting data may be faulty, computer chips can fail, and greater accuracy can breed overconfidence.

The air campaign to free Kosovo of Serbian control in 1998 underscores the point, according to Fred Kaplan, author of *The Wizards of Armageddon*. "Ton for ton, the bombing killed civilians at the same rate as the [Rolling Thunder] air campaign over Vietnam," Mr. Kaplan wrote. One reason was that the improved accuracy of "smart" bombs "emboldened commanders to aim more bombs at targets than required it," he says—leading to more frequent misses. William Arkin, an air war expert and military commentator who visited Iraq after the Gulf War as part of a Harvard University study team sent to assess battle damage, has seen the Iraqi hospital records that confirm the Amiriyah casualty count. The bombing was the "single largest incident of collateral damage that has ever occurred in modern warfare," he says, and it impacted both sides in the war. "All of a sudden, after six weeks of there being bloodless conflict, there was blood," Mr. Arkin says. Orders went out that subsequent downtown targets would require approval from Washington. "It had as big an impact on [then Chairman of the Joint Chiefs of Staff] Colin Powell's psychology, as it did on the Iraqi people's psychology."

15   But Arkin doesn't see the Amiriyah bombing as a warning of the risks of air warfare. Rather, he sees it as an example of how efficient smart bomb targeting had become, even then.

"More than 10 percent of all civilians who died in the air war, died in that single incident," says Arkin, who notes that nearly 50,000 allied sorties flown only produced a half dozen cases of numerous civilian dead in Baghdad. But he doesn't expect there to be a greater number of casualties in another Gulf war.

That's because Iraq has the largest conventional army in the Mideast, with a vast array of installations and bases. Targeting will be simpler than in previous conflicts. This "new era of warfare" translates into minimizing casualties, Arkin says—a feat the military can pull off. Civilian casualties in Iraq may instead depend on the length of the war, U.S. and Iraqi strategies in the cities, and Iraq's possible use of chemical weapons.

U.S. planners are putting their faith in better bombs. Laser-guided munitions that can cost $250,000 each have given way to the Joint Direct Attack Munition, or JDAM, which is a $20,000 technical kit that can turn many types of bombs into "smart" ones that navigate by satellite. In Afghanistan, the mix was about half and half. Traditional laser-guided bombs were often used on mobile, short notice targets called in—and sometimes "painted" with a laser—by U.S. Special Forces units on the ground. The JDAM was used mostly for fixed targets. In anticipation of war in Iraq, the Pentagon is boosting their production.

"When laser-guided bombs fail, they tend to fail spectacularly," says Arkin. "They could go a mile or more off target, because if a laser fails to lock, if the laser is impacted by weather, if the pilot makes an error, that bomb does not know where to go."

20   But if the JDAM's satellite system fails, its inertial system kicks in, usually bringing it to within 50 yards of the target.

The advice given after the Amiriyah incident by the Pentagon was that "the safest place for an Iraqi civilian is at home in his bed." But that was little solace to Iraqis who were near the Amiriyah shelter when it was hit by "smart" bombs that worked flawlessly.

Hussein Abdallah still lives in the house across from the shelter, and was asleep in his bed at 4:30 a.m. when the bombs dropped, blasting out the windows of his house, splitting still-visible cracks along grey plastered foundations, and sending a chunk of hot shrapnel the size of his thick forearm hurtling in a wall just 1.5 feet from his head. "We fell down because of fear of the explosion. Our bodies were trembling," recalls Mr. Abdallah, a portly truck driver whose toes protrude from worn plastic sandals.

His children were affected most, when they saw rescue workers pull the dead from the bunker. "In every war there are civilian casualties," Abdallah says. "They will throw rockets, not stones. Always, innocent people will die."

Starting Points

1. Consider the lead or introduction to this article (paragraphs 1–3). How effective is it? Read the text closely, and try to write a new and equally compelling introduction to this article. What is the purpose of using an incident from more than a decade ago?

2. Scott Peterson shifts, in the last paragraphs, from statistics and officials to a "portly truck driver whose toes protrude from worn plastic sandals." What does this do in terms of effectiveness? Does humanizing the conflict make the text more or less effective?

3. What does the author list as obstacles to minimizing civilian casualties in an age of high-tech warfare? Are civilians destined to die so that soldiers are more protected, or will improvements in future weaponry reduce casualties to non-combatants?

The International Aspects of Terrorism and Weapons of Mass Destruction

JOHN R. BOLTON

The proliferation of weapons of mass destruction has changed the landscape of national and international security. John R. Bolton, Under Secretary for Arms Control and International Security for the U.S. State Department, discusses how the United States is responding to possible threats posed by both terrorist groups and rogue nations. This speech was addressed to the Second Global Conference on Nuclear, Biological, and Chemical Terrorism: Mitigation and Response at the Hudson Institute in Washington, D.C., on November 1, 2002.

───────────── ✦ ─────────────

When the United States and other nations began working together on the problem of proliferation of weapons of mass destruction over thirty years ago, the world was a very different place, where the largest source of the most dangerous materials was contained within two superpowers. Weapons of mass destruction (WMD) were considered weapons of last resort. Non-state actors were not yet considered to pose a meaningful threat, since they were not linked to abundant sources of supply. With the end of the Cold War, however, the international security environment changed and the proliferation problem increased. Now, more states are seeking increasingly advanced WMD capabilities; more states are entering the supply market; and all of this is compounded by the fact that terrorists are also seeking weapons of mass destruction. When the world witnessed the destructive potential of terrorism on September 11, [2001,] we were reminded of the need to remain steadfast in recognizing emerging threats to our security, and to think one step ahead of those who wish to do us harm.

Today, the United States believes that the greatest threat to international peace and stability comes from rogue states and transnational terrorist groups that are unrestrained in their choice of weapon and undeterred by conventional means. The September 11th attacks showed that terrorist groups were much better organized, much more sophisticated, and much more capable of acting globally than we had assumed possible. Our concept of what terrorists are able to do to harm innocent civilians has changed fundamentally. There can be no doubt that, if given the opportunity, terrorist groups such as Al-Qaeda would not hesitate to use disease as a weapon against the unprotected; to spread chemical agents to inflict pain and death on the innocent; or to send suicide-bound adherents armed with radiological explosives on missions of murder.

A CONFLUENCE OF NEFARIOUS MOTIVES

Terrorist groups seek to acquire chemical, biological, or nuclear weapons any way they can; state sponsors of terrorism are actively working to acquire weapons of mass destruction and their missile delivery systems. Here lies a dangerous confluence of nefarious motives, and we must prevent the one from abetting the other. As President [George W.] Bush said in September, "In cells, in camps, terrorists are plotting further destruction and building new bases for their war against civilization. And our greatest fear is that terrorists will find a shortcut to their mad ambitions when an outlaw regime supplies them with the technologies to kill on a massive scale."

To ensure that terrorist groups and their state sponsors are never able to gain access to chemical, biological, or nuclear weapons, or the means to deliver them via missile, the United States is employing a variety of methods to combat the spread of weapons of mass destruction, including multilateral agreements, diplomacy, arms control, threat reduction assistance, export control, and other means where necessary. Most importantly, we must maintain an unvarnished view of the proliferators and disrupt their supply of sensitive goods and technology before it contributes to an increased WMD capability or falls into the hands of terrorists or other rogue states.

Without question, the states most aggressively seeking to acquire WMD and their means of delivery are Iran, Iraq, and North Korea, followed by Libya and Syria. It is no coincidence that these states, which are uniformly hostile to the United States, as well as to many of our friends and allies, are among the ones we identify as state sponsors of terrorism.

Iran, one of the most egregious state sponsors of terror, is known to be seeking dual-use materials, technology, and expertise for its offensive biological and chemical weapons programs from entities in Russia, China, and Western Europe. It is also seeking to upgrade its large ballistic missile force with the help of Russian, North Korean, and Chinese firms. Our intelligence clearly shows that Iran seeks to acquire a nuclear weapons capability, and thus we are extremely concerned about transfers to Iran of dual-use materials. Once a rogue state's intentions become apparent, we should assume that the dual-use technologies it acquires will be used for illegitimate purposes.

Iraq, despite UN sanctions, maintains an aggressive program to rebuild the infrastructure for its nuclear, chemical, biological, and missile programs. In each instance, Iraq's procurement agents are actively working to obtain both weapons-specific and dual-use materials and technologies critical to their rebuilding and expansion efforts, using front companies and whatever illicit means are at hand. We estimate that once Iraq acquires fissile material—whether from a foreign source or by securing the materials to build an indigenous fissile material capability—it could fabricate a nuclear weapon within one year. It has rebuilt its civilian chemical infrastructure and renewed production of chemical warfare agents, probably including mustard, sarin, and VX. It actively maintains all key aspects of its offensive BW (biological weapons) program. And in terms of its support for terrorism, we have established that Iraq has permitted Al-Qaeda to operate within its territory. As the President said recently, "The regime has long-standing and continuing ties to terrorist organizations. And there are Al-Qaeda terrorists inside Iraq." The President has made his position on Iraq eminently clear, and in the coming weeks and months we shall see what we shall see.

Now let us turn to North Korea.

As you know, last month during official talks between the United States and North Korea, North Korean officials acknowledged that they have a program to enrich uranium for nuclear weapons. This constitutes a violation of the 1994 Agreed Framework, the Nonproliferation Treaty, North Korea's International Atomic Energy Agency safeguards agreement, and the Joint North-South Declaration on the Denuclearization of the Korean Peninsula. In the course of this brazen admission, the North Koreans declared the Agreed Framework nullified. As Secretary [Colin] Powell later said, "When we have an agreement between two parties and one says it's nullified, then it looks like it's nullified." The fact that the North Koreans are seeking a production scale capability to produce weapons-grade uranium is a cause of grave concern to us, to the states in the region, and to the world as a whole. The U.S. Intelligence Community already assesses that "North Korea has produced enough plutonium for at least one, and possibly two, nuclear weapons." In consultation with the other four nuclear powers, our allies in the region, and other interested states, we are now considering what our next steps will be. President Bush has made it very clear that the North Koreans must comply with its commitments under the Nonproliferation Treaty and eliminate its nuclear weapons program immediately in a verifiable manner. He has also stated that he wants to resolve this matter peacefully and through the exertion of maximum diplomatic pressure on North Korea. We want to emphasize that this is a global problem, not simply a regional one. The security of all nations, as well as the continued credibility of the Nonproliferation Treaty, hinge on the successful resolution of this problem.

10   North Korea poses other dangers. We have long been aware of North Korea's role as the world's number one exporter of mis-

sile technology and equipment. These sales are one of its major sources of hard currency, which in turn allow continued missile development and production. As the CIA publicly reports: "North Korea has assumed the role as the missile and manufacturing technology source for many programs. North Korean willingness to sell complete systems and components has enabled other states to acquire longer-range capabilities."

With regard to chemical weapons, there is little doubt that North Korea has an active program. Despite efforts to get North Korea to become a party to the Chemical Weapons Convention, it has refused to do so. In a recent report to Congress, the U.S. Government declared that North Korea "is capable of producing and delivering via missile warheads or other munitions a wide variety of chemical agents."

The news on the biological weapons front is equally disturbing. The U.S. Government believes that North Korea has one of the most mature offensive bioweapons programs on earth. North Korea to date is in stark violation of the Biological Weapons Convention (BWC). Indeed, at times North Korea has flouted it. In the 1980s, the North Korean military intensified this effort as instructed by then-President Kim Il-sung, who declared that, "poisonous gas and bacteria can be used effectively in war." The United States believes North Korea has a dedicated, national-level effort to achieve a BW capability and that it has developed and produced, and may have weaponized, BW agents in violation of the BWC. North Korea likely has the capability to produce sufficient quantities of biological agents within weeks of a decision to do so.

Finally, North Korea has one of the world's largest armies—nearly one million men under arms. This force has over 10,000 artillery tubes, many of which can reach Seoul and surrounding areas south of the Demilitarized Zone. Such a force, far larger than needed for legitimate defense needs, is capable of inflicting massive damage, as it would most likely be charged with deploying chemical and biological weapons during the course of an attack.

In addition to Iran, Iraq, and North Korea, other rogue states that concern us include Libya and Syria. Libya continues to pursue an indigenous chemical warfare production capability, relying heavily on foreign suppliers for precursor chemicals, technical expertise, and other key chemical warfare-related equipment. Moreover, the United States believes that Libya has an offensive BW program in the research and development stage, and it may currently be capable of producing small quantities of biological agent. It continues efforts to obtain ballistic missile-related equipment, materials, technology, and expertise from foreign sources. Further, we are persuaded that Libya is continuing its longstanding pursuit of nuclear weapons, and the suspension of UN sanctions against it has increased its access to nuclear-related materials and equipment.

15   Syria, through foreign assistance, is seeking to expand its chemical weapons program, which includes a stockpile of nerve agent. We believe that it is developing biological weapons and is able to produce at least small amounts of biological warfare agents. Syria is also pursuing assistance from North Korea and firms in Russia for its missile development programs. The country has become a major transshipment point for goods and technology going to Iraq.

Among these regimes flow dangerous weapons and dangerous technology. States such as these rely heavily on front companies and illicit arms traders to seek out arms, equipment, sensitive technology, and dual-use goods for the benefit of their WMD programs. A growing concern is that cooperation among proliferators is increasing, recipients have become suppliers, and this "onward proliferation" presents yet another difficult problem. It is on these rogue regimes in particular that the United States and its partners in multilateral nonproliferation agreements must focus a watchful eye.

AN EMPHASIS ON COMPLIANCE

To this end, we have placed much weight in our arms control policy on strict compliance with existing multilateral treaties and agreements. This Administration strongly supports treaties such as the Nonproliferation Treaty, the Chemical Weapons Convention, and the Biological Weapons Convention. But in order to be effective and provide the assurances they purport to bring, they must be carefully and universally enforced among all signatories. It is for this reason that we are reinvigorating the Department of State's Verification and Compliance Bureau. The United States must do its utmost to be forthright in letting the public know when states violate their commitment not to acquire or transfer the tools and materials necessary for making weapons of mass destruction. This has been our aim in particular with the Biological Weapons Convention. This international treaty, signed by more than 140 countries, prohibits the production, use, and stockpiling of biological weapons. While the vast majority of the BWC's parties have conscientiously met their commitments, the

United States is extremely concerned that some states are conducting offensive biological weapons programs while publicly avowing compliance with the agreement. To expose some of these violators to the international community, a year ago I named publicly several states the U.S. Government knows to be pursuing the production of biological warfare agents in violation of the BWC—including Iraq, North Korea, Iran, and Libya. Later in the year I named Cuba, which we believe has at least a limited, developmental offensive biological warfare R&D effort, and which has provided dual-use biotechnology to other rogue states. Such states will not be given a pass on their violations simply because they are signatories to the treaty. We are also concerned about the activities of some states not party to the treaty including Syria and Sudan. The Administration believes it is critical to put such states on notice. Should they choose to ignore the norms of civilized society and pursue biological weapons, their actions will not go unnoticed.

The United States last fall proposed several important measures to combat the BW threat. In the past year great progress has been made to combat the threat posed by biological weapons. National, bilateral, and multilateral efforts have made it more difficult for those pursuing biological weapons to obtain the necessary ingredients and made it easier to detect and counter any attack.

CONCLUSION

The Bush Administration firmly believes that, as the President said, "Almost every state that actively sponsors terror is known to be seeking weapons of mass destruction and the missiles to deliver them at longer and longer ranges." It is not simply coincidence that those states we know to be seeking chemical, biological, or nuclear weapons are also the states designated as sponsors of global terrorism.

In the past, the proliferation and acquisition of weapons of mass destruction fell outside the definition of "terrorism." But we are in a new era. We must be very clear: the U.S. Government believes that the threat of terrorism, the actions of state sponsors of terrorism, and the proliferation and potential use of weapons of mass destruction are inextricably linked. As President Bush said last month, "Terror cells, and outlaw regimes building weapons of mass destruction, are different faces of the same evil. Our security requires that we confront both. And the United States Military is capable of confronting both."

20

America is determined to prevent the next wave of terror. This means directing firm international condemnation toward states that shelter—and in some cases directly sponsor—terrorists within their borders. It means uncovering their activities that may be in violation of international treaties. And it means having a direct dialogue with the rest of the world about what is at stake.

Starting Points

1. This speech was written before the start of the Iraq war. John Bolton represents the State Department's official view that Iraq had significant stockpiles of WMD, or ongoing programs to develop them. Does the failure to find WMD there following the fall of Baghdad invalidate this entire speech, or does the author present a strong case for concern about other nations (e.g., Korea, Iran, Libya, Syria)?
2. Search carefully for modifiers in this text. How do they affect the tone of the speech? Try substituting different modifiers. How does the tone change?
3. Consider the level of language employed in Bolton's speech. Was it appropriate for the intended audience? What words were new to you? How do we make meaning from words from context? List the words about which you are uncertain, and write what you believe to be their definition from contextual clues. Then consult a dictionary to confirm. Consider keeping a journal of new and effective words which you can employ to make your own writing more interesting.

Other Journeys: Suggestions for Further Writing and Research

1. Consider the rise in casualties of non-combatants in 20th and 21st century warfare. Is today any different from ancient times when all the inhabitants of a city might be put to the sword by a conquering army? In what ways are civilian deaths today viewed differently than during World War II, where massive aerial bombing campaigns were directed against enemy cities? Is there a difference between "innocent civilians" and non-combatants?
2. Should all nuclear weapons in all countries be eliminated and banned from future development? Will that keep WMD from the hands of terrorists, or simply make the world safer from accidents or rogue nations?
3. Research further the report from Oxfam and Amnesty International on the increased global trade in small arms. Using what you learn from that report and other sources, argue for or against an International Small Arms Treaty.

4. Access the United Nations web site and read the various resolutions and initiatives that the world community has agreed to in order to control nuclear weapons and WMD, particularly those regarding terrorism. Are these moves, in addition to numerous treaties, going to be effective, or will nationalistic concerns render these efforts sterile?

5. How is the security of nuclear weaponry assured in the United States? Research the various departments, administrations, committees, and organizations with some oversight over nuclear power or weapons. Do you believe it is overly complicated, or that such an organization chart provides needed redundancy in the management of such potentially dangerous technology? Have there been major lapses in security? How serious were they?

6. With a collaborative group, propose and write a model global treaty governing the production, distribution, and use of weapons designed to kill. Would you ban all such weapons? Allow weapons for self-defense to nations? For individuals? How would you decide which weapons were legitimate? For example, is a single-shot rifle allowable? A machine gun? How would you monitor the use of weapons? What sanctions could be applied?

7. We have heard a great deal about WMD, including biological and chemical agents. What is the history of such weapons? Do stockpiles still exist in the world? In the United States? How easy is it to manufacture such weapons? How lethal are they? What steps should be taken to safeguard against them?

8. Does the threat of suicide bombers in the United States change the War on Terror for you in any way? How would your life be affected if suicide bombers become a fact of life for those living in the United States?

Ethics, Peace,
and Tomorrow

Much of the attention to the War on Terrorism came to be focused on the continuing violence in Iraq. Each month following the toppling of the statue of Saddam Hussein in Baghdad seemed to bring with it new horrors, new debates, and new forms of violence. The search for weapons of mass destruction, touted originally as the main reason for the invasion, yielded nothing. Instead of a peaceful capitulation and the building of a democratic nation, U.S. troops faced a guerilla-style urban war in which hundreds of Americans and thousands of Iraqis have died. The oil and gas pipelines that were the lifeblood of a new Iraqi economy were regularly bombed. Foreign workers were kidnapped by insurgents and several were beheaded, with grisly videos offered up on the Internet. American soldiers were accused of torture and war crimes at the prison Abu Ghraib. Congressional investigations slammed U.S. intelligence as totally inadequate in their assessments of the threat posed by Iraq and its connection to al-Qaida and international terrorism.

Thus, this last chapter, originally envisioned as a series of closing thoughts on ways to achieve global peace and security, now must lose some of that sharp focus and attempt to address a broad spectrum of troubling and perplexing issues. Despite bromides to the contrary, all is not fair in love and war—or, at least, in war. A series of treaties and conventions, many signed more than a half-century ago in Geneva, were designed to regulate the behavior of combatant nations and their individual soldiers. Included here are the articles of the Geneva Convention that apply to the treatment of POWs, and a memo from the legal counsel to the president of the United States that suggests that such accords do not apply to detainees in the War on Terror.

192

Beyond the formal and legalistic language of such documents is the reaction of the world community to alleged violations of the norms of war. While the enforcement of international treaties might be difficult, the reaction of nations, communities, and individuals to the abrogation of limitations on the conduct of warring states and their troops can be ignored only at extreme cost and peril.

Yet even here, we find upon looking deeply that it can be difficult to make sweeping statements. Much of the world, including the United States, reacted with disgust and stunned disbelief when hundreds of photographs surfaced that showed smiling American soldiers, male and female, brutalizing Iraqi detainees at Abu Ghraib prison in Baghdad. Was it a result of a few renegade lower-echelon soldiers, or part of a policy that was intended to "soften up" prisoners who might have valuable information? Does the War on Terror mean all the old rules should be scrapped, since in many cases terrorists are not soldiers as traditionally defined? Is torture justified if it means preventing another 9/11-style attack? Does America lose its claim to moral authority by resorting—on whatever scale is ultimately revealed—to the tactics of its enemies?

Another abiding issue is that of the role of religion in the current crisis of terrorism. Regularly, U.S. leaders characterize the perpetrators of violence as "Islamist extremists," and just as regularly Islamic and other religious leaders decry the defamation of one of the largest religions in the world. Yet al-Qaida and other terrorist groups have identified themselves as religious warriors. What is the truth? Some of the articles in this chapter attempt to shed light on that question.

And finally, it is hoped, you will find here articles that will provide new opportunities for thought, for analysis, and ultimately for ideas and dedication that will lead to peace and justice in the world.

Memorandum for the President
ALBERTO R. GONZALES

During the war in Afghanistan against the Taliban and al-Qaida, there was a flurry of legal memoranda regarding the treatment of prisoners taken there, including the use of torture. What follows is a memo by Alberto R. Gonzales, counsel to the President, that fol-

lowed the protest of Secretary of State Colin Powell to suggestions that the Geneva Conventions did not apply. Later, in hearings before the 9/11 commission, after the Abu Ghraib photos were discovered and released to the public, Attorney General John Ashcroft refused to release the memos regarding policy on torture. The White House later released the documents. The Gonzales memo was written January 25, 2002.

———————— ✦ ————————

SUBJECT: DECISION RE APPLICATION OF THE GENEVA CONVENTION ON PRISONERS OF WAR TO THE CONFLICT WITH AL QUEDA AND THE TALIBAN

Purpose

On January 18, I advised you that the Department of Justice had issued a formal legal opinion concluding that the Geneva Convention III on the Treatment of Prisoners of War (GPW) does not apply to the conflict with al Queda. I also advised you that DOJ's opinion concludes that there are reasonable grounds for you to conclude that GPW does not apply with respect to the conflict with the Taliban. I understand that you decided that GPW does not apply and, accordingly, that al Queda and Taliban detainees are not prisoners of war under the GPW.

The Secretary of State has requested that you reconsider that decision. Specifically, he has asked that you conclude that GPW does apply to both al Queda and the Taliban. I understand, however, that he would agree that al Queda and Taliban fighters could be determined not to be prisoners of war (POWs) but only on a case-by-case basis following individual hearings before a military board.

This memorandum outlines the ramifications of your decision and the Secretary's request for reconsideration.

Legal Background

As an initial matter, I note that you have the constitutional authority to make the determination you made on January 18 that the GPW does not apply to al Queda and the Taliban. (Of course, you nevertheless, as a matter of policy, decide to apply the principles of GPW to the conflict with al Queda and the Taliban.) The Office of Legal Counsel of the Department of Justice has opined that, as a matter of international and domestic law, GPW does not apply to the conflict with al Queda. OLC has further opined that you have the authority to determine that GPW does not apply to the Taliban. As I discussed with you, the grounds for such a determination may include:

- A determination that Afghanistan was a failed state because the Taliban did not exercise full control over the territory and people, was not recognized by the international community, and was not capable of fulfilling its international obligations (e.g., was in widespread material breach of its international obligations).
- A determination that the Taliban and its forces were, in fact, not a government, but a militant, terrorist-like group.

OLC's interpretation of this legal issue is definitive. The Attorney General is charged by statute with interpreting the law for the Executive Branch. This interpretive authority extends to both domestic and international law. He has, in turn, delegated this role to OLC. Nevertheless, you should be aware that the Legal Adviser to the Secretary of State has expressed a different view. 5

Ramifications of Determination that GPW Does Not Apply

The consequences of a decision to adhere to what I understand to be your earlier determination that the GPW does not apply to the Taliban include the following:

POSITIVE:

Preserves flexibility:

- As you have said, the war against terrorism is a new kind of war. It is not the traditional clash between nations adhering to the laws of war that formed the backdrop for GPW. The nature of the new war places a high premium on other factors, such as the ability to quickly obtain information from captured terrorists and their sponsors in order to avoid further atrocities against American civilians, and the need to try terrorists for war crimes such as wantonly killing civilians. In my judgment, this new paradigm renders obsolete Geneva's strict limitations on questioning of enemy prisoners and renders quaint some of its provisions requiring that captured enemy be afforded such things as commissary privileges, scrip (i.e., advances of monthly pay), athletic uniforms, and scientific instruments.
- Although some of these provisions do not apply to detainees who are not POWs, a determination that GPW does not apply

to al Queda and the Taliban eliminates any argument regarding the need for case-by-case determinations of POW status. It also holds open options for the future conflicts in which it may be more difficult to determine whether an enemy force as a whole meets the standard for POW status.
- By concluding that GPW does not apply to al Queda and the Taliban, we avoid foreclosing options for the future, particularly against nonstate actors.

Substantially reduces the threat of domestic criminal prosecution under the War Crimes Act (18 U.S.C. 2441).

- That stature, enacted in 1996, prohibits the commission of a "war crime" by or against a U.S. person, including U.S. officials. "War crime" for these purposes is defined to include any grave breach of GPW or any violation of common Article 3 thereof (such as "outrages against personal dignity"). Some of these provisions apply (if the GPW applies) regardless of whether the individual being detained qualifies as a POW. Punishments for violations of Section 2441 include the death penalty. A determination that the GPW is not applicable to the Taliban would mean that Section 2441 would not apply to actions taken with respect to the Taliban.
- Adhering to your determination that GPW does not apply would guard effectively against misconstruction or misapplication of Section 2441 for several reasons.
- First, some of the language of the GPW is undefined (it prohibits, for example, "outrages upon personal dignity" and "inhuman treatment"), and it is difficult to predict with confidence what actions might be deemed to constitute violations of the relevant provisions of GPW.
- Second, it is difficult to predict the needs and circumstances that could arise in the course of the war on terrorism.
- Third, it is difficult to predict the motives of prosecutors and independent counsels who may in the future decide to pursue unwarranted charges based on Section 2441. Your determination would create a reasonable basis in law that Section 2441 does not apply, which would provide a solid defense to any future prosecution.

NEGATIVE:

On the other hand, the following arguments would support reconsideration and reversal of your decision that the GPW does not apply to either al Qaeda or the Taliban:

- Since the Geneva Conventions were concluded in 1949, the United States has never denied their applicability to either U.S. or opposing forces engaged in armed conflict, despite several opportunities to do so. During the last Bush Administration, the United States stated that it "has a policy of applying the Geneva Conventions of 1949 whenever armed hostilities occur with regular foreign armed forces, even if arguments could be made that the threshold standards for the applicability of the Conventions . . . are not met."
- The United States could not invoke the GPW if enemy forces threatened to mistreat or mistreated U.S. coalition forces captured during operations in Afghanistan, or if they denied Red Cross access or other POW privileges.
- The War Crimes Act could not be used against the enemy, although other criminal statutes and the customary law of war would still be available.
- Our position would likely provoke widespread condemnation among our allies and in some domestic quarters, even if we make clear that we will comply with the core humanitarian principles of the treaty as a matter of policy.
- Concluding that the Geneva Convention does not apply may encourage other countries to look for technical "loopholes" in future conflicts to conclude that they are not bound by GPW either.
- Other countries may be less inclined to turn over terrorists or provide legal assistance to us if we do not recognize a legal obligation to comply with the GPW.
- A determination that GPW does not apply to al Qaeda and the Taliban could undermine U.S. military culture which emphasizes maintaining the highest standards of conduct in combat, and could introduce an element of uncertainty in the status of adversaries.

Response to Arguments for Applying GPW to the [sic] al Qaeda and the Taliban

On balance, I believe that the arguments for reconsideration and reversal are unpersuasive. 10

- The argument that the U.S. has never determined that GPW did not apply is incorrect. In at least one case (Panama in 1989) the U.S. determined that GPW did not apply even though it determined for policy reasons to adhere to the convention. More importantly, as noted above, this is a new type of warfare—one not contemplated in 1949 when the GPW was framed—and requires a new approach in our actions toward captured terrorists. Indeed, as the statement quoted from the administration of President George Bush makes clear, the U.S. will apply GPW "whenever hostilities occur *with regular armed forces.*" By its terms, therefore, the policy does not apply to a conflict with terrorists, or with irregular forces, like the Taliban, who are armed militants that oppressed and terrorized the people of Afghanistan.

- In response to the argument that we should decide to apply GPW to the Taliban in order to encourage other countries to treat captured U.S. military personnel in accordance with the GPW, it should be noted that your policy of providing humane treatment to enemy detainees gives us the credibility to insist on like treatment for our soldiers. Moreover, even if GPW is not applicable, we can still bring war crimes charges against anyone who mistreats U.S. personnel. Finally, I note that our adversaries in several recent conflicts have not been deterred by GPW in their mistreatment of captured U.S. personnel, and terrorists will not follow GPW rules in any event.
- The statement that other nations would criticize the U.S. because we have determined that GPW does not apply is undoubtedly true. It is even possible that some nations would point to that determination as a basis for failing to cooperate with us on specific matters in the war against terrorism. On the other hand, some international and domestic criticism is already likely to flow from your previous decision not to treat the detainees as POWs. And we can facilitate cooperation with other nations by reassuring them that we fully support GPW where it is applicable and by acknowledging that in this conflict the U.S. continues to respect other recognized standards.
- In the treatment of detainees, the U.S. will continue to be constrained by, (i) its commitment to treat the detainees humanely and, to the extent appropriate and consistent with military necessity, in a manner consistent with the principles of GPW, (ii) its applicable treaty obligations, (iii) minimum standards of treatment universally recognized by the nations of the world, and (iv) applicable military regulations regarding the treatment of detainees.
- Similarly, the argument based on military culture fails to recognize that our military remain bound to apply the principles of GPW because that is what you have directed them to do.

Starting Points

1. Characterize the tone of this memorandum. Does the use of legal language and the citation of legal precedents contribute to the tone?
2. Alberto Gonzales lists objections to the suspension of GPW for al Qaeda and Taliban detainees, most of which were realized when abuse became widely known: American soldiers have been mistreated when captured, the United States was widely condemned around the world for abuse of detainees, and consternation and conflict within the U.S. military about proper treatment of prisoners. Why does Gonzales believe that the negative consequences are outweighed by other considerations?
3. Many of the points detailed by Gonzales appear to be worth debate by informed people of good will. Write a persuasive essay on either side of the issue, using as a starting point Gonzales's memorandum.

Ethical Issues in Counterterrorism Warfare

MARTIN L. COOK

Martin L. Cook is Professor of Philosophy at the U.S. Air Force Academy in Colorado Springs, Colorado, and has written extensively on ethics and morality involving war and military service. Shortly after the attacks on the Pentagon and the World Trade Center, he wrote the following article while at the time teaching at the U.S. Army War College.

✦

INTRODUCTION

Much has been said and written in recent weeks about the changed nature of "warfare" as it pertains to responding to the attacks on the Pentagon and the World Trade Center. The fact that attacks of such vast scale are made directly on U.S. soil by non-state actors poses important new questions for military leaders and planners charged with conceiving an appropriate and effective response.

The established moral and legal traditions of just war are similarly challenged. Forged almost entirely in the context of interstate war, those traditions are also pressed to adapt to the new and unforeseen character of a "war against terrorism." This paper is a preliminary effort to extrapolate and apply existing fundamental moral principles of just war theory to this novel military and political terrain.

FUNDAMENTAL MORAL PRINCIPLES

The theoretical framework of the just war tradition provides two separate moral assessments of uses of military force. The first, *jus ad bellum* (right or justice *toward* war) attempts to determine which sets of political and military circumstances are sufficiently grave to warrant a military response. It focuses on the "just cause" element of war, and attempts to determine whether use of force to redress a given wrong has a reasonable hope of success and whether non-violent alternatives have been attempted (the "last resort" criterion) to redress the grievance. Given the horrendous loss of innocent American (and other) life in these recent attacks, it is without serious question that a just cause exists to use military force in response to those attacks. However, legitimate questions remain regarding reasonable hope of success given the difficult and diffuse nature of the perpetrators of these events. Indeed, the very definition of success in conflict of this sort is to some degree ambiguous.

The second body of assessments concerns *jus in bello*, right conduct of military operations. The central ideas here concern *discrimination* (using force against those who are morally and legally responsible for the attack and not deliberately against others) and *proportionality* (a reasonable balance between the damage done in the responding attack and the military value of the targets destroyed).

5   These fundamental moral principles continue to have force, even in the quite different "war" in which we are now engaged.

Jus ad Bellum *Considerations*

The scale and nature of the terrorist attacks on the U.S. without question warrant a military response. The important questions about *jus ad bellum* are confined to the other questions the just war tradition requires us to ask regarding the ability to respond to those attacks with military force that will, in fact, respond to the attackers themselves and be effective in responding to the wrong received.

Just cause requires that we identify with accuracy those responsible and hold them to be the sole objects of legitimate attack. Who are those agents? In the first instance, those directly responsible for funding and directing the activities of the now-deceased hijackers. There is a tremendous intelligence demand to identify those agents correctly. But, having identified them to a moral certainty (a standard far short of what would be required by legal criteria of proof, it should be noted) there is no moral objection to targeting them. Indeed, one of the benefits of framing these operations as "war" rather than "law enforcement" is that it does not require the ideal outcome to be the apprehension and trial of the perpetrators. Instead, it countenances their direct elimination by military means if possible.

What of the claim that we may legitimately attack those who harbor terrorists, even if they are not directly involved in authorizing their activities? The justification for attacking them has two aspects: first, it holds them accountable for activities which they knew, or should have known, were being conducted in their territories and did nothing to stop; second, it serves as a deterrent to motivate other states and sponsors to be more vigilant and aware of the activities of such groups on their soil.

How far ought the moral permission to attack parties not directly involved extend? I would propose application of a standard from American civil law: the "reasonable person" (or "reasonable man") standard of proof. This standard asks not what an individual knew, as a matter of fact, about a given situation or set of facts. Instead, it asks what a reasonable and prudent person in a similar situation should know. Thus, even if a person or government truthfully asserts that they were unaware of the activities of a terrorist cell in their territory, this does not provide moral immunity from attack. This standard asks not what they *did* know, but what they *ought to have known* had they exercised the diligence and degree of inquiry a reasonable person in their circumstance would have exercised.

Also, legitimate targets include more than those who have carried out or are actively engaged in preparing to carry out attacks against U.S. citizens and forces. There will presumably be numerous individuals who, in various ways, assisted or harbored attackers, or who possessed knowledge of planned attacks. From a moral perspective, the circle of legitimate targets surely includes at least these individuals. A rough analog for the principle here is the civil law standard for criminal conspiracy: all those within the circle of the conspiracy are legitimate targets. The analogy is not

10

perfect, but in general it justifies attacks on those who possessed information about the contemplated terrorist activity or who supplied weapons, training, funding or safe harbor to the actors, even if they did not possess full knowledge of their intent.

Jus in Bello *Considerations*

How do ethical considerations constrain the manner of attack against legitimate adversaries? The traditional requirements of just war continue to have application in this kind of war. Attacks must be *discriminate* and they must be *proportionate*. Discrimination requires that attacks be made on persons and military objects in ways that permit successful attack on them with a minimum of damage to innocent persons and objects. In practical terms, this requires as much precision as possible in determination of the location and nature of targets. Further, it requires choice of weapons and tactics that are most likely accurately to hit the object of the attack with a minimum of damage to surrounding areas and personnel.

Proportionality imposes an essentially common-sense requirement that the damage done in the attack is in some reasonable relation to the value and nature of the target. To use a simple example: if the target is a small cell of individuals in a single building, the obliteration of the entire town in which the structure sits would be disproportionate.

There are two important real world considerations that bear on this discussion. The first is military necessity. Military necessity permits actions that might otherwise be ethically questionable. For example, if there simply is no practical alternative means of attacking a legitimate target, weapons and tactics that are less than ideal in terms of their discrimination and proportionality may be acceptable. It is important not to confuse military *necessity* with military *convenience*. It is the obligation of military personnel to assume some risk in the effort to protect innocents. However, situations can certainly arise in which there simply is not time or any alternative means of attacking in a given situation. There, military necessity generates the permission to proceed with the attack.

The other consideration is the tendency of adversaries of this type to co-locate themselves and their military resources with civilians and civilian structures in order to gain some sense of protection from such human shields. Obviously, when possible, every effort should be made to separate legitimate targets from such shields. But when that is not possible, it is acceptable to proceed with the attack, foreseeing that innocent persons and property will be destroyed. The moral principle underlying this judgment is known as "double effect," and permits such actions insofar as the agent sincerely can claim (as would be the case here) that the destruction of the innocents was no part of the plan or intention, but merely an unavoidable by-product of legitimate military action.

It is important to note, however, that there can be no just war   15
justification for a response to these attacks with attacks of a similar character on other societies. Not only would this constitute an unethical and illegal attack on innocent parties, it would almost certainly erode the moral "high ground" and widespread political support the U.S. currently enjoys.

The Moral Status of the Adversary

The individuals who initiated the terror attacks are clearly not "soldiers" in any moral or legal sense. They, and others who operate as they did from the cover of civilian identities, are not entitled to any of the protections of the war convention. This means that, if captured, they are not entitled to the benevolent quarantine of the POW convention or of domestic criminal law. For the purposes of effective response to these individuals, as well as future deterrence, it may be highly undesirable even if they are captured to carry out the extensive due process of criminal proceedings. If we can identify culpable individuals to a moral certainty, their swift and direct elimination by military means is morally acceptable and probably preferable in terms of the goals of the policy.

However, as this conflict proceeds, especially if ground operations commence against fixed targets, one may foresee that individuals and groups may come to operate against U.S. forces as organized military units. It is important to keep in mind that, no matter how horrific the origins of this conflict, if and when this occurs and such groups begin to behave as organized units, to carry weapons openly, and to wear some kind of distinctive dress or badge, they become assimilated to the war convention. At that point, close moral and legal analysis will be required to determine the degree to which they become entitled to the status of "combatant" and are given the Geneva Convention protection that status provides. The previous permission for swift elimination applies to the period in which they operate with civilian "cover."

Should elements of the adversary force eventually choose to operate as an organized military force, the long-term importance of universal respect for the Geneva Convention's provision would make our treating them at that point as soldiers under the law the preferred course of action.

Starting Points

1. Martin Cook discusses the just war concepts of last resort, discrimination, and proportionality. Respond to his analysis of these concepts as they relate to the U.S. response in Afghanistan and Iraq to the September 11th attacks. Do you agree or disagree with the author's treatment of these issues, and, depending on your stand, agree or disagree with the U.S. response?

2. The audience for this essay originally was the U.S. military. Analyze the content of this essay in light of that audience (one example is in paragraph 13, "real world" considerations). How would you frame this argument for a different audience, such as a church congregation, a high school history class, or even a kindergarten class?

3. Read William Saunders' "Possible War With Iraq" in Chapter 2, which details the theory of just war. Using Saunders and Cook's readings, write an essay that compares or contrasts the views of a clergyman and a scholar working for a U.S. military academy.

The Road to Abu Ghraib: A Policy to Evade International Law

HUMAN RIGHTS WATCH

Human Rights Watch, a non-governmental organization that monitors human rights abuses around the world, began in 1978 as Helsinki Watch to track Soviet bloc countries for compliance with the Helsinki Accords. In the 1980s, it expanded to Americas Watch, primarily to track abuses in Latin America. In 1988, all the "Watch" committees around the globe were united under the umbrella Human Rights Watch, now based in New York City. This report, from its web site at www.hrw.org, was issued in June 2004. It is highly critical of U.S. treatment of detainees from the conflicts in Iraq and Afghanistan, including those held at Guantanamo Bay, Cuba. In July 2004, the U.S. Supreme Court held that those prison-

ers were entitled to have their cases heard in American courts, chal-
lenging their detention and their status as "enemy combatants."

———————————— ✦ ————————————

In the aftermath of the September 11 attacks on the United States, the Bush administration seemingly determined that winning the war on terror required that the United States circumvent international law. "There was a before-9/11 and an after-9/11," said Cofer Black, former director of the CIA's counterterrorist unit, in testimony to Congress. "After 9/11 the gloves came off."[1]

The first public manifestation of a policy to circumvent normal detention rules came in January 2002, when the United States began sending persons picked up during the armed conflict in Afghanistan to its naval base at Guantánamo Bay, Cuba. Ultimately Guantánamo would hold more than 700 detainees from forty-four countries, many apprehended far from any conflict zone. Guantánamo was deliberately chosen in an attempt to put the detainees beyond the jurisdiction of the U.S. courts. Indeed, in response to a legal challenge by several detainees, the U.S. government later argued that U.S. courts would not have jurisdiction over these detainees even if they were being tortured or summarily executed.[2]

CIRCUMVENTING THE GENEVA CONVENTIONS

Ignoring the deeply rooted U.S. military practice of applying the Geneva Conventions broadly, U.S. Defense Secretary Donald H. Rumsfeld labeled the first detainees to arrive at Guantánamo on January 11, 2002 as "unlawful combatants," automatically denying them possible status as prisoners of war (POWs). "Unlawful combatants do not have any rights under the Geneva Convention," Mr. Rumsfeld said, overlooking that the Geneva Conventions provide explicit protections to all persons captured in an international armed conflict, even if they are not entitled to POW status. Rumsfeld signaled a casual approach to U.S. compliance with international law by saying that government would "for the most part, treat them in a manner that is reasonably consistent with the Geneva Conventions, to the extent they are appropriate."[3] On February 7, Rumsfeld questioned the relevance of the Geneva Conventions to current U.S. military operations: "The reality is the set of facts that exist today with the al-Qaeda and the Taliban were not necessarily the set of facts that were considered when the Geneva Convention was fashioned."[4]

At the same time, a series of legal memoranda written in late 2001 and early 2002 by the Justice Department helped build the framework for circumventing international law restraints on prisoner interrogation. These memos argued that the Geneva Conventions did not apply to detainees from the Afghanistan war.

5 Alberto R. Gonzales, the White House counsel, in a January 25, 2002 memorandum to President Bush, endorsed the Justice Department's (and Rumsfeld's) approach and urged the president to declare the Taliban forces in Afghanistan as well as al-Qaeda outside the coverage of the Geneva Conventions. This, he said, would preserve the U.S.'s "flexibility" in the war against terrorism. Mr. Gonzales wrote that the war against terrorism, "in my judgment renders obsolete Geneva's strict limitations on questioning of enemy prisoners." Gonzales also warned that U.S. officials involved in harsh interrogation techniques could potentially be prosecuted for war crimes under U.S. law if the Conventions applied.[5] Gonzales said that "it was difficult to predict with confidence" how prosecutors might apply the Geneva Conventions' strictures against "outrages against personal dignity" and "inhuman treatment" in the future, and argued that declaring that Taliban and al-Qaeda fighters did not have Geneva Convention protections "substantially reduces the threat of domestic criminal prosecution."[6]

Gonzales did convey to President Bush the worries of military leaders that these policies might "undermine U.S. military culture which emphasizes maintaining the highest standards of conduct in combat and could introduce an element of uncertainty in the status of adversaries."[7]

The Gonzales memorandum drew a strong objection the next day from Secretary of State Colin L. Powell. Powell argued that declaring the conventions inapplicable would "reverse over a century of U.S. policy and practice in supporting the Geneva Conventions and undermine the protections of the law of war for our troops, both in this specific conflict and in general."[8]

On February 7, 2002, in the face of growing international criticism,[9] President Bush announced that the U.S. government would apply the "principles of the Third Geneva Convention" to captured members of the Taliban, but would not consider any of them to be POWs because, in the U.S. view, they did not meet the requirements of an armed force under that Convention. As for captured members of al-Qaeda, he said that the U.S. government considered the Geneva Conventions inapplicable but would nonetheless treat the detainees "humanely."

These decisions essentially reinterpreted the Geneva Conventions to suit the administration's purposes. Belligerents captured in the conflict in Afghanistan should have been treated as POWs unless and until a competent tribunal individually determined that they were not eligible for POW status. Taliban soldiers should have been accorded POW status because they openly fought for the armed forces of a state party to the Convention. Al-Qaeda detainees would likely not be accorded POW status, but the Conventions still provide explicit protections to all persons held in an international armed conflict, even if they are not entitled to POW status. Such protections include the right to be free from coercive interrogation, to receive a fair trial if charged with a criminal offense, and, in the case of detained civilians, to be able to appeal periodically the security rationale for continued detention.

Even after the Abu Ghraib scandal broke, Secretary Rumsfeld continued to take a loose view of the applicability of the Geneva Conventions. On May 5, 2004, he told a television interviewer the Geneva Conventions "did not apply precisely" in Iraq but were "basic rules" for handling prisoners.[10] Visiting Abu Ghraib on May 14, Rumsfeld remarked, "Geneva doesn't say what you do when you get up in the morning." In fact, the U.S. armed forces have devoted considerable energy over the years to making the Geneva Conventions fully operational by military personnel in the field. Various U.S. military operational handbooks and manuals provide the means for implementing Geneva Convention provisions, even where those provisions are vague. Decisions by foreign and international criminal courts and interpretations of customary international law provide other means for clarifying Geneva Convention requirements.

UNDERMINING THE RULES AGAINST TORTURE

All the while, the Bush administration resisted publicly discussing the requirements for the treatment of detainees under international human rights law, in particular the U.N. Convention against Torture and Other Cruel, Inhuman, or Degrading Treatment or Punishment (the Convention Against Torture). That convention bars not only torture but "cruel, inhuman or degrading treatment or punishment which do not amount to torture."[11] After the first reports of so-called "stress and duress" tactics against detainees appeared in the *Washington Post* in December 2002,[12] Human Rights Watch called on President Bush to investi-

gate and condemn allegations of torture and other cruel and inhuman treatment.[13] In response, Department of Defense General
Counsel William J. Haynes II stated that "United States policy
condemns torture," but he did not acknowledge that the United
States also had a legal obligation to refrain from cruel, inhuman
or degrading treatment. He also failed to address whether the
United States was using the "stress and duress" techniques reported in the press.[14] In June 2003, Senator Patrick Leahy wrote
to National Security Advisor Condoleezza Rice asking if "stress
and duress" techniques were being employed and urging the administration to issue a clear statement that cruel, inhuman, or degrading treatment of detainees will not be tolerated. Finally, in
June 2003, in response to the Leahy letter, Haynes stated, correctly, that the Convention Against Torture prohibits (at the very
least) interrogators overseas from using any technique that would
be unconstitutional if employed in the United States.[15] There is
no evidence, however, that this message was ever conveyed to
U.S. commanders in the field.

Rather, at the same time that the administration was publicly
rejecting the use of torture or cruel, inhuman, or degrading treatment, it was apparently laying the legal groundwork for the use of
just such tactics. The *Washington Post* has reported that in August
2002, the Justice Department advised Gonzales, in response to a
CIA request for guidance, that torturing al-Qaeda detainees in
captivity abroad "may be justified," and that international laws
against torture "may be unconstitutional if applied to interrogations" conducted in the war on terrorism.[16] The memo added the
doctrines of "necessity and self-defense could provide justifications that would eliminate any criminal liability" on the part of
officials who tortured al-Qaeda detainees. The memo also took an
extremely narrow view of which acts might constitute torture. It
referred to seven practices that U.S. courts have ruled to constitute torture: severe beatings with truncheons and clubs, threats of
imminent death, burning with cigarettes, electric shocks to geni-
talia, rape or sexual assault, and forcing a prisoner to watch the
torture of another person. It then advised that "interrogation
techniques would have to be similar to these in their extreme nature and in the type of harm caused to violate law." The memo
suggested that "mental torture" only included acts that resulted in
"significant psychological harm of significant duration, e.g., lasting for months or even years."

The legal reasoning of the Justice Department memo reappeared in an April 2003 memorandum from a working group

appointed by Pentagon legal counsel Haynes that was headed by Air Force General Counsel Mary Walker and included senior civilian and uniformed lawyers from each military branch, and which consulted the Justice Department, the Joint Chiefs of Staff, the Defense Intelligence Agency and other intelligence agencies, according to the *Wall Street Journal.*[17] They contended that the president was not bound by the laws banning torture. According to a draft of the classified memo, the lawyers argued that the president had the authority as commander in chief of the armed forces to approve almost any physical or psychological actions during interrogation, up to and including torture, in order to obtain "intelligence vital to the protection of untold thousands of American citizens." The memo presented a number of legal doctrines, including the principles of "necessity" and "self-defense," and the inherent powers of the president which could be used to evade the prohibition on torture. The memo advised that the president issue a "presidential directive or other writing" that subordinates charged with torture could use as evidence that their actions were authorized, since authority to set aside the laws in wartime is "inherent in the president."

The Convention Against Torture provides, however, that "[n]o exceptional circumstances whatsoever, whether a state of war or a threat or war, internal political instability or any other public emergency, may be invoked as a justification of torture."[18] The International Covenant on Civil and Political Rights, which also bans torture and other mistreatment, considers the right to be free from torture and other cruel, inhuman or degrading treatment as nonderogable, meaning that it can never be suspended by a state, including during periods of public emergency.

And, according to media accounts and Human Rights Watch interviews, senior officials in the Defense and Justice Departments and the Central Intelligence Agency approved a set of coercive interrogation techniques for use in Afghanistan and Iraq that violate the prohibition of cruel, inhuman, or degrading treatment and can amount to torture.[19] These techniques apparently include stripping detainees naked during interrogation, subjecting them to extremes of heat, cold, noise, and light, hooding them, depriving them of sleep, and keeping them in painful positions.[20]

The *New York Times*, citing current and former counterterrorism officials, reported that in one case CIA interrogators used graduated levels of force against Khalid Sheikh Mohammed, a detainee held in an "undisclosed location" (see *infra*), including a technique known as "water boarding," in which a prisoner is

15

strapped down, forcibly pushed under water and made to believe he might drown. According to the *Times*, "these techniques were authorized by a set of secret rules for the interrogation of some 12 to 20 high-level al-Qaeda prisoners that were endorsed by the Justice Department and the CIA."[21]

RENDITIONS

The Bush administration facilitated or participated directly in the transfer of an unknown number of persons without extradition proceedings, a practice known as "irregular rendition," to countries in the Middle East known to practice torture routinely. The *Washington Post* in December 2002 described the rendition of captured al-Qaeda suspects from U.S. custody to other countries, such as Syria, Uzbekistan, Pakistan, Egypt, Jordan, Saudi Arabia, and Morocco, where they were tortured or otherwise mistreated. Unnamed U.S. officials suggested that detainees were deliberately moved to countries known for their use of torture to ease constraints on their interrogations. One official was quoted as saying, "We don't kick the [expletive] out of them. We send them to other countries so they can kick the [expletive] out of them." An official who had supervised the capture and transfer of accused terrorists said, "If you don't violate someone's human rights some of the time, you probably aren't doing your job . . . I don't think we want to be promoting a view of zero tolerance on this."[22]

Tarek Dergoul, a Briton released from Guantánamo in March 2004, said that during interrogation there he was threatened with being sent to Morocco or Egypt, "where I would be tortured."

In one case, Maher Arar, a Syrian-born Canadian in transit from a family vacation through John F. Kennedy airport in New York, was detained by U.S. authorities. After holding him for nearly two weeks, U.S. authorities flew him to Jordan, where he was driven across the border and handed over to Syrian authorities, despite his repeated statements to U.S. officials that he would be tortured in Syria and his repeated requests to be sent home to Canada. Mr. Arar, whom the United States asserts has links to al-Qaeda, was released without charge from Syrian custody ten months later and has described repeated torture, often with cables and electrical cords, during his confinement in a Syrian prison.

In another case, Swedish television reported in May 2004 that in December 2001 a U.S. government-leased Gulfstream 5 jet airplane transported two Egyptian terrorism suspects who were

blindfolded, hooded, drugged, and diapered by hooded operatives, from Sweden to Egypt. There the two men were tortured,
including in Cairo's notorious Tora prison.[23] The plane was apparently the same one that had allegedly been used two months earlier to transport a Yemini suspect from Pakistan to Jordan.

In a third case, U.S. operatives reportedly managed the cap-   20
ture and transfer of Mohammed Haydar Zammar, a top al-Qaeda
suspect and dual German-Syrian national, to Syria in June 2002,
over the protests of the German government. The United States
has reportedly provided questions to Syrian interrogators.[24]

"DISAPPEARANCES"

Among the most disturbing cases, perhaps unprecedented in U.S.
history, are the detainees who have simply been "disappeared."[25]
Perhaps out of concern that Guantánamo will eventually be monitored by the U.S. courts, certainly to ensure even greater secrecy,
the Bush administration does not appear to hold its most sensitive and high-profile detainees there. Terrorism suspects like
Khalid Sheikh Mohammed, accused architect of the September
11 attacks, and Abu Zubaydah, a close aide of Osama bin Laden,
are detained by the United States instead in "undisclosed loca-
tions," presumably outside the United States, with no access to
the ICRC, no notification to families, no oversight of any sort of
their treatment, and in most cases no acknowledgement that they
are even being held. Human Rights Watch has pieced together information on 13 such detainees, apprehended in places such as
Pakistan, Indonesia, Thailand, Morocco, and the United Arab
Emirates, who have "disappeared" in U.S. custody.[26]

Endnotes

1. John Barry, Michael Hirsh and Michael Isikoff, "The Roots of
   Terror," *Newsweek,* May 24, 2004.
2. See *Gherebi v. Bush,* 9th Circuit, Dec. 18, 2003. The United States
   asserts the power "to do with [them] as it will, when it pleases, without any compliance with any rule of law of any kind, without permitting [them] to consult counsel, and without acknowledging any
   judicial forum in which its actions may be challenged. . . . Indeed,
   at oral argument, the government advised us that its position would
   be the same even if the claims were that it was engaging in acts of
   torture or that it was summarily executing the detainees. To our
   knowledge, prior to the current detention of prisoners at

Guantánamo, the U.S. government has never before asserted such a grave and startling proposition. . . . a position so extreme that it raises the gravest concerns under both American and international law."

3. "Geneva Convention doesn't cover detainees," Reuters, January 11, 2002.

4. See Jim Garamone, DefenseLink News (U.S. Military), American Forces Press Service, February 7, 2002.

5. Gonzales was referring to prosecution under the War Crimes Act of 1996 (18 U.S.C. Section 2441), which punishes the commission of a war crime, including torture and humiliating or degrading treatment, by or against a U.S. national, including members of the armed forces.

6. Memorandum from Alberto R. Gonzales to the President, January 25, 2002.

7. Ibid.

8. Memorandum from Colin L. Powell to Counsel to the President, January 26, 2002.

9. See, e.g., Statement of High Commissioner for Human Rights on Detention of Taliban and al-Qaeda Prisoners at U.S. Base in Guantanamo Bay, January 16, 2002; Kieran Murray, "EU, Latin America condemn U.S. prison abuse in Iraq," Reuters, May 28, 2004. Rumsfeld dismissed the criticism as "isolated pockets of international hyperventilation." See "High Taliban official in U.S. custody," Associated Press, February 9, 2002.

10. United States Department of Defense News Transcript, Secretary Rumsfeld Interview with Matt Lauer, NBC "Today," http://www.dod.gov/transcripts/2004/tr20040505-secdef1425.html.

11. Convention against Torture and Other Cruel, Inhuman or Degrading Treatment or Punishment, adopted and open for signature, ratification and accession by General Assembly resolution 39/46 of December 10, 1984, article 16.

12. Dana Priest and Barton Gellman, "U.S. decries abuse but defends interrogations," *Washington Post*, December 26, 2002; see discussion *infra*.

13. Human Rights Watch, "United States: Reports of Torture of Al-Qaeda Suspects," December 27, 2002, http://www.hrw.org/press/2002/12/us1227.htm.

14. http://www.hrw.org/press/2003/04/dodltr040203.pdf.

15. The Haynes letter to Leahy followed an earlier exchange with U.S.-based human rights groups, including Human Rights Watch, in which Haynes stated that "United States policy condemns torture," but did not acknowledge that the United States also had a legal obligation to refrain from cruel, inhuman or degrading treatment. See

Human Rights Watch, "U.S. Sidesteps Charges of Mistreating Detainees," http://www.hrw.org/press/2003/04/us041703.htm; "Timeline of Detainee Abuse Allegations and Responses," http://www.hrw.org/english/docs/2004/05/07/usint8556.htm.

16. Dana Priest and R. Jeffrey Smith, "Memo Offered Justification for Use of Torture," *Washington Post,* June 8, 2004.

17. Jess Bravin, "Pentagon Report Set Framework For Use of Torture," *Wall Street Journal,* June 7, 2004.

18. Convention against Torture and Other Cruel, Inhuman or Degrading Treatment or Punishment, adopted and open for signature, ratification and accession by General Assembly resolution 39/46 of December 10, 1984, article 16.

19. The *Washington Post* has reported that a "list of about 20 techniques was approved at the highest levels of the Pentagon and the Justice Department," techniques for use at the Guantánamo Bay prison. Dana Priest and Joe Stephens, "Pentagon Approved Tougher Interrogations," *Washington Post,* May 9, 2004. Senior government officials had earlier told Human Rights Watch of the approval of a "72-point matrix." It is possible that this 72-point list was reduced to 20 in the approval process.

20. According to Physicians for Human Rights: "Prolonged periods of sleep deprivation can result in confusion and psychosis, physical symptoms including headaches and dizziness, and chronic disruption of normal sleep patterns." Also, "deprivations or normal sensory stimulation (e.g., sound, light, sense of time, isolation, restrictions of sleep, food, water, toilet facilities, bathing, motor activity, medical care, and social contacts) serve to disorient victims, to induce exhaustion and debility, difficulty concentrating, impair memory and instill fear, helplessness, despair, and, in some cases, can result in severe anxiety and hallucinations and other psychotic reactions." Physicians for Human Rights, "Interrogations, Torture and Ill Treatment: Legal Requirements and Health Consequences," May 14, 2004, at pages 7–8, http://www.phrusa.org/research/pdf/iraq_medical_consequences.pdf.

21. James Risen, David Johnston and Neil A. Lewis, "Scrutiny Worries CIA Interrogators," *New York Times,* May 13, 2004.

22. Dana Priest and Barton Gellman, "U.S. Decries Abuse But Defends Interrogations," *Washington Post,* December 26, 2002.

23. Swedish TV4 Kalla Fakta Program: "The Broken Promise," May 17, 2004. See English Transcript at http://hrw.org/english/docs/2004/05/17/sweden8620.htm.

24. Murhaf Jouejati, Adjunct Professor at George Washington University, and an expert on Syria, told the National Commission on

Terrorist Attacks Upon the United States that "Although U.S. officials have not been able to interrogate Zammar, Americans have submitted questions to the Syrians." Statement of Murhaf Jouejati to the National Commission on Terrorist Attacks Upon the United States, July 9, 2003, http://www.9-11commission.gov/hearings/hearing3/witness_jouejati.htm.

25. According to the preamble of the Declaration on the Protection of all Persons from Enforced Disappearance, "enforced disappearances occur, in the sense that persons are arrested, detained or abducted against their will or otherwise deprived of their liberty by officials of different branches or levels of Government, . . . followed by a refusal to disclose the fate or whereabouts of the persons concerned or a refusal to acknowledge the deprivation of their liberty, which places such persons outside the protection of the law. . . ." [emphasis added]. General Assembly resolution 47/133 of December 18, 1992. "Enforced disappearance" has been defined by the Rome Statute of the International Criminal Court as the "arrest, detention or abduction of persons by, or with the authorization, support or acquiescence of, a State or a political organization, followed by a refusal to acknowledge that deprivation of freedom or to give information on the fate or whereabouts of those persons, with the intention of removing them from the protection of the law for a prolonged period of time." Article 7(2)(1).

26. They are: (1) Abdul Rahim al-Sharqawi (aka Riyadh the facilitator), arrested before April 2002, al-Qaeda member, allegedly coordinated logistics for attacks; (2) Ibn Al-Shaykh al-Libi, arrested before April 2002, allegedly al-Qaeda training camp commander; (3) Abd al-Hadi al-Iraqi, arrested before April 2002, allegedly al-Qaeda training camp commander; (4) Abu Zubaydah (aka Zubeida, aka Zain al-Abidin Muhahhad Husain), arrested in March 2002 in Faisalabad, Pakistan, al-Qaeda member, Palestinian (born in Saudi Arabia), allegedly senior al-Qaeda operational planner, potential heir to Bin Laden; (5) Omar al Faruq, arrested in June 2002 in Indonesia, al-Qaeda member, Kuwaiti, allegedly planned large-scale attacks against U.S. interests in Indonesia, Malaysia, the Philippines, etc.; (6) Abu Zubair al-Haili, arrested in June 2002 in Morocco, al-Qaeda member, Saudi, allegedly operational and military chief (deputy to Abu Zubaydah); (7) Ramzi bin al-Shibh, arrested in September 2002, al-Qaeda member, Yemeni, alleged conspirator in Sept. 11 attacks (former Atta roommate), meant to be 20th hijacker; (8) Abd al-Rahim al-Nashiri (aka Abu Bilal al-Makki), arrested in November 2002 in

the United Arab Emirates, al-Qaeda member, Saudi or Yemeni, allegedly chief of operations in Persian Gulf and mastermind of USS Cole bombing and recent attack on the French oil tanker Limburg; (9) Mustafa al-Hawsawi, arrested March 1, 2003 (together with Khalid Sheikh M.) in Rawalpindi, Pakistan, al-Qaeda member, Saudi, allegedly financier; (10) Khalid Sheikh Mohammed (aka Shaikh Mohammed), arrested March 1, 2003 in Rawalpindi, Pakistan, al-Qaeda member, Kuwaiti (Pakistani parents), alleged mastermind behind Sept. 11 attacks as well as [Daniel] Pearl killing, USS Cole attack, etc.; (11) Waleed Mohammed Bin Attash (aka Tawfiq bin Attash or Tawfiq Attash Khallad), arrested in late April 2003 in Karachi, Pakistan, al-Qaeda member, Saudi (of Yemeni descent), alleged "top al-Qaida operative suspected of playing crucial roles in both the bombing of the U.S. destroyer Cole in 2000 and the Sept. 11 terror attacks"; (12) Adil al-Jazeeri, arrested June 17, 2003 in Peshawar, Pakistan, al-Qaeda member, alleged "leading member"; (13) Hambali (aka Riduan Isamuddin), arrested August 11, 2003 in Aytthaya, Thailand, Jemaah Islamiyah (and al-Qaeda) member, Indonesian, allegedly organized/financed Bali nightclub bombing, Jakarta Marriot Hotel bombing, preparations for Sept. 11.

Starting Points

1. Write a letter to Human Rights Watch supporting or opposing their contention that the United States has sought to circumvent international law. You might consider this from the perspective that the War on Terror calls for (or does not) new rules, or perhaps from the point of view that as a civilian your rights to live outweigh the rights of terrorists to their day in court (or that such rights are the basis for a democratic people and must not be suborned.)
2. Interview a current or former soldier about their training regarding the treatment of detainees or prisoners of war. Are American military personnel briefed on the Geneva Conventions? Write a paper about your findings, including a conclusion on whether the soldiers at Abu Ghraib were acting alone or were encouraged in the treatment of the detainees there.
3. Read the Geneva Conventions regarding treatment of prisoners (in this chapter) or the entire Convention agreed upon in 1949 (available at the UN web site and other sources). Does the war on terror—including the possibility of the use of weapons of mass destruction, the lack of accountability of combatants to a state, and the failure to wear uniforms and openly carry arms—mean that a new set of rules should be considered? What should the new conventions include?

Geneva Convention Relative to the Treatment of Prisoners of War

Following World War II and the often horrific treatment of prisoners of war and of non-combatants during that six-year conflict, the international community convened in Geneva to establish conventions, or guidelines, for the humane treatment of victims of war. Much of the controversy that swirled around the alleged abuse of detainees in Iraq by the U.S. military focused on possible violations of the Geneva Convention, as it is known, particularly the following articles. Also at issue is whether the War against Terror exempts a nation from the strictures of the Convention when dealing with non-state violence.

—————————— ✦ ——————————

Adopted on 12 August 1949 by the Diplomatic Conference for the Establishment of International Conventions for the Protection of Victims of War, held in Geneva from 21 April to 12 August 1949. Enter into force 21 October 1950.

GENERAL PROTECTION OF PRISONERS OF WAR

Article 12

Prisoners of war are in the hands of the enemy Power, but not of the individuals or military units who have captured them. Irrespective of the individual responsibilities that may exist, the Detaining Power is responsible for the treatment given them.

Prisoners of war may only be transferred by the Detaining Power to a Power which is a party to the Convention and after the Detaining Power has satisfied itself of the willingness and ability of such transferee Power to apply the Convention. When prisoners of war are transferred under such circumstances, responsibility for the application of the Convention rests on the Power accepting them while they are in its custody.

5 　　Nevertheless if that Power fails to carry out the provisions of the Convention in any important respect, the Power by whom the prisoners of war were transferred shall, upon being notified by the Protecting Power, take effective measures to correct the situation or shall request the return of the prisoners of war. Such requests must be complied with.

Article 13

Prisoners of war must at all times be humanely treated. Any unlawful act or omission by the Detaining Power causing death or seriously endangering the health of a prisoner of war in its custody is prohibited, and will be regarded as a serious breach of the present Convention. In particular, no prisoner of war may be subjected to physical mutilation or to medical or scientific experiments of any kind which are not justified by the medical, dental or hospital treatment of the prisoner concerned and carried out in his interest.

Likewise, prisoners of war must at all times be protected, particularly against acts of violence or intimidation and against insults and public curiosity.

Measures of reprisal against prisoners of war are prohibited.

Article 14

Prisoners of war are entitled in all circumstances to respect for their persons and their honour. Women shall be treated with all the regard due to their sex and shall in all cases benefit by treatment as favourable as that granted to men. Prisoners of war shall retain the full civil capacity which they enjoyed at the time of their capture. The Detaining Power may not restrict the exercise, either within or without its own territory, of the rights such capacity confers except in so far as the captivity requires.

Article 15

The Power detaining prisoners of war shall be bound to provide free of charge for their maintenance and for the medical attention required by their state of health.

10

Article 16

Taking into consideration the provisions of the present Convention relating to rank and sex, and subject to any privileged treatment which may be accorded to them by reason of their state of health, age or professional qualifications, all prisoners of war shall be treated alike by the Detaining Power, without any adverse distinction based on race, nationality, religious belief or political opinions, or any other distinction founded on similar criteria.

PART III CAPTIVITY
SECTION I BEGINNING OF CAPTIVITY

Article 17

Every prisoner of war, when questioned on the subject, is bound to give only his surname, first names and rank, date of birth, and army, regimental, personal or serial number, or failing this, equivalent information. If he willfully infringes this rule, he may render himself liable to a restriction of the privileges accorded to his rank or status.

Each Party to a conflict is required to furnish the persons under its jurisdiction who are liable to become prisoners of war, with an identity card showing the owner's surname, first names, rank, army, regimental, personal or serial number or equivalent information, and date of birth. The identity card may, furthermore, bear the signature or the fingerprints, or both, of the owner, and may bear, as well, any other information the Party to the conflict may wish to add concerning persons belonging to its armed forces. As far as possible the card shall measure 6.5 × 10 cm. and shall be issued in duplicate. The identity card shall be shown by the prisoner of war upon demand, but may in no case be taken away from him.

No physical or mental torture, nor any other form of coercion, may be inflicted on prisoners of war to secure from them information of any kind whatever. Prisoners of war who refuse to answer may not be threatened, insulted, or exposed to any unpleasant or disadvantageous treatment of any kind.

15   Prisoners of war who, owing to their physical or mental condition, are unable to state their identity, shall be handed over to the medical service. The identity of such prisoners shall be established by all possible means, subject to the provisions of the preceding paragraph.

The questioning of prisoners of war shall be carried out in a language which they understand.

Starting Points

1. Article 17 specifically prohibits any form of torture, coercion, threats, insults, or unpleasant treatment directed against a prisoner of war. Some have argued that even with this specificity, the language might be vague (e.g., what does "unpleasant" mean?) enough to justify such things as "stress positions." Marshal your best arguments for either side, then conduct a debate on the issue of whether such provisions in the Convention are out of date in the age of terrorism, or that now, especially, the Convention should be followed scrupulously.

2. Exact definitions of terms are helpful in conversations, but are essential in legal documents. Compounding the vagueness of certain key words or terms is the additional difficulty that arises in translation to dozens of languages of the signatory nations to the Geneva Convention. Carefully read Articles 12 through 17 and note any terms that seem to you vague or possibly subject to several interpretations. Then in discussions with multilingual students, students from other cultures, or instructors of modern languages, determine if the problem is indeed compounded through translation.

3. Read Alberto Gonzales's memorandum and Martin Cook's article on ethics, and write an essay on the bromide "all's fair in love and war."

White House Should Clarify Torture Policy
E. Thomas McClanahan

When photos and stories began appearing in the summer of 2004 about alleged abuse of prisoners in Iraq by American troops, an avalanche of disapprobation around the globe was seen in demonstrations, news broadcasts, and newspaper editorials. Subsequently, the discovery of various memos from executive department lawyers that seemed to suggest torture might be acceptable in the war on terror caused a second uproar. E. Thomas McClanahan, a member of the editorial board of The Kansas City Star, *took a somewhat different approach, choosing to concentrate not on legal language or definitions contained in treaties but on what he calls "a hypothetical." His piece appeared on the op-ed page of* The Star *on June 22, 2004.*

◆

*S*ept. 11 revealed not only our vulnerability to terrorist acts, but how unprepared we were to deal with the unforeseen legal issues, including how to deal with the terrorists we capture and how hard to lean on them during interrogation.

A hypothetical: You're in charge of interrogating a detainee who knows the location of a ticking bomb or the location of hostages being tortured by terrorists.

Do you torture your prisoner to get him to talk? What if you have "credible evidence" the bomb is a nuke? Or: Would you torture someone to prevent another Sept. 11?

A few years ago, such questions seemed almost academic. In 1994, Congress passed a law making torture during interrogations a crime, but it generated almost no debate. What's to debate? Everyone knows the United States doesn't torture people, period.

5   Sept. 11 revealed not only our vulnerability to terrorist acts, but how unprepared we were to deal with the unforeseen legal issues, including how to deal with the terrorists we capture and how hard to lean on them during interrogation. The old "rules of war" seem increasingly out of sync with the threat posed by international terrorism.

The 1949 Geneva Conventions, for example, say prisoners may not "be threatened, insulted, or exposed to any unpleasant or disadvantageous treatment of any kind"—language that seems almost quaint. What does "unpleasant" mean, exactly? Kansas City in July is *unpleasant.*

Al-Qaida terrorists aren't eligible for prisoner-of-war status anyway. They don't wear uniforms, they aren't part of a military organization with a chain of command and they aren't directed by a recognizable government authority—all required by the Geneva Conventions. The main point of such rules is to protect civilians, who are easier to separate from combatants when people wear uniforms. Al-Qaida's goal, by contrast, is to *kill* civilians.

The Bush administration was on solid ground in classifying the Guantanamo detainees as illegal combatants, not POWs. But subsequent revelations have created an impression of complete confusion.

- The Pentagon says Guantanamo detainees will be treated in accord with the Geneva Conventions, but that's hard to believe in light of the prisoner-abuse revelations and the Pentagon's refusal to say what interrogation techniques are being used at Guantanamo.
- Some techniques deemed too rough for use against al-Qaida suspects at Guantanamo nevertheless found their way to Abu Ghraib prison in Iraq, where they were used with less supervision.
- Government lawyers have argued that no law—including the 1994 law against torture noted above—can limit a president's power to detain and interrogate enemy combatants.

To be sure, the so-called "torture memos" are not policy statements. Rather, they represent lawyers' opinions about what existing law might allow. But the conclusions are extreme, and the White House has not done enough to rebut the impression that the administration is laying the basis for a policy allowing torture.

One of President Bush's strengths is his ability to delegate, 10
which leaves him free to deal with big-picture issues. In his leadership since Sept. 11, he has displayed real boldness: He recognized the attack not as a crime but an act of war; he understood
the need to stay on offense; he carried the fight to the enemy in
Afghanistan and, in Iraq, he has planted the seed of democracy in
the Arab Middle East.

He recognized that to fully confront international terrorism,
he would have to put his presidency at risk. I believe history will
validate his major decisions, including the decision to invade Iraq.

But the administration has made mistakes. It was unprepared for the post-Saddam Hussein insurgency in Iraq, and it has
badly mishandled the prisoner/detainee issue.

When you see people farther down the chain of command essentially making it up as they go along, it's a sign of lack of direction from above. Recently, Bush was asked whether he would approve torture in a classic ticking time-bomb case. He replied that
what he's authorized "is that we stay within U.S. law."

That's not much of an answer, given that government lawyers
claim that in prisoner interrogation, a president's constitutional
commander-in-chief power can't be curbed by *any* law.

The administration is right in drawing a distinction between 15
prisoners of war and illegal combatants, but new policies are
needed to cover the latter and the White House should be doing
more to fill the vacuum in law and policy.

Israel's experience in dealing with terrorism is longer than
ours, and a decision by that country's Supreme Court could provide some guidance. In a 1999 ruling, the court banned all forms
of forceful interrogation, namely hooding, shaking, the use of
stress positions and the use of "powerfully loud music."

But it left open a potential loophole—the ticking-bomb scenario. If interrogators honestly and reasonably believed that using rough methods was necessary to prevent a devastating attack,
they might be able to rely on a "necessity" defense, meaning they
could argue that the methods used, however harsh, were justified
by the threat. After all, few rules in life have no exceptions—even
one banning torture.

Starting Points

1. Respond to E. Thomas McClanahan's "hypothetical"—under what condi-
    tions would you accede to the torture of a prisoner? If it might avert a
    9/11-type attack? To prevent the deaths of others? To prevent the deaths of
    your own family?

2. Analyze the content of this author's column. How balanced is his approach? What issues of government policy does he support, which does he say have been mishandled? Does he appear to take a measured, informed approach? On the political scale, where would you place McClanahan?
3. Study the entire text of the Geneva Convention on the treatment of prisoners of war and other victims of war (it can be found at the United Nations web site). Write an essay arguing for or against the application of the Geneva conventions to members of the al-Qaida network.

From Defensive to Offensive Warfare: The Use and Abuse of Jihad in the Muslim World

ABDULAZIZ SACHEDINA

Much debate across the globe has focused on the term "jihad," sometimes referred to as "holy war." Abdulaziz Sachedina, an Islamic scholar at the University of Virginia, explains the various categories of jihad and argues that the expropriation of the term by some global terrorists defames a religion. This article first appeared in Religion, Law, and Force, *published by Transnational Publishers in 2002.*

───────── ✦ ─────────

ABSTRACT

The purpose of this paper is to demonstrate that although one must avoid highly essentialist interpretations of the classical Muslim juristic formulations, so common in contemporary studies on jihad, one cannot ignore their systematic retrieval by extremist Muslims for justifying activist and even armed response to aggression and oppression by Muslim and non-Muslim forces. Numerous places and events have provided occasions when extremist Muslim groups have formed and called for jihad in tones, and often in terms, that have articulated rationales for greater violence against enemies than the language of classical juristic discourse and modern definitions of jihad would seem to sanction. The post-colonial conditions in the Muslim world have affected modern understandings of jihad, rendering it at times meaningless violence that achieves none of the goals of Islamic tradition in building an ideal just society. My central argument in this paper is that the Muslim legal-theological discourses were articulated in order to highlight the Qur'anic message about "islam" ('submission') being the only true religion with God" (3:19) and the only one desired by God (3:85) in the context of successful and dominant political and social position of the community. This interaction between the exclusivist idea of Islam being the religion for the entire humanity and the existing predominance of Muslim empire created the specific juridical-theological language that provided the normative justification to extend the notion of jihad beyond its strictly defensive meaning in the Qur'an to its being an offensive device for the hegemonic expansion of the Muslim empire.

INTRODUCTORY REMARKS

In this paper I use the word "Islam" in three senses. In the Western studies of Islam, the term "Islam" is primarily used in the meaning of a religious tradition with fundamental principles of the creed that provide authoritative perspectives for interpreting contradictions and tensions in human existence. I have retained this usage whenever I deal with normative sources for the derivation of justifications as well as criteria for jihad. But I also use the term "Islam" signifying an important ingredient in the internal structure of cultural values that permeate dispositions and practices connected with jihad among Muslims within a specific time and place. Finally, I use the term to convey an overarching ideological system related to the power in the name of a sacred authority that aims in providing justifications for the creation of the state as a means to promoting the common good. In a way, the three senses covering the beliefs, attitudes, and practices of the community demonstrate the intricate developing relationship within the context of sociopolitical history between the authoritative and determinative teachings of Islam and emerging power of the state that undertakes to implement these teachings for the creation of an ideal public order.

To be sure, belief about an ideal public order as much determines as it is determined by the way in which Muslims deal with the questions of resistance and opposition to the abuse of power or submission to it. The ultimate outcome of this historical interplay between Islam as a religion and Islam as a source of power is also reflected in the way the community has responded to the need to confront the obstacles to the realization of the idealized vision of a religious polity on earth. In other words, the idea of jihad (in its essential meaning of "'struggle" and "striving") as an instrument of realizing the Islamic ideal on earth has had to interact with the sociopolitical realities that confronted the Muslims when responding to its call to take arms in the name of a sacred authority. Like Judaism and Christianity, Islam emphasized concern for the ordinary moral needs and abilities of the common people to undertake to work for an ideal just society. This outlook stressed active involvement of the people in creating its own public order that would reflect the moral and social teachings of Islam. In this sense, Islam in its primary meaning of being a religious tradition, inherently functioned as an "activist" ideology within a specific social-political order that it evaluated, calling upon its followers to defend and preserve or to overthrow and transform it. However, in its third signification of being an important source of legitimate power, Islam was understood as a divine blueprint that awaits implementation to realize God's will on earth to the fullest extent possible and, if necessary, through force, that is, jihad.

Inasmuch as the Qur'an, the foundational source for Muslim social-political consciousness, introduced the injunction legitimizing the use of force through the instrumentality of jihad, it was responding to the pre-Islamic Arab tribal culture, which had institutionalized military power on which depended the security of a tribe and even its existence. Primacy among the tribes belonged to those that were able to protect all their clients and to avenge all insults, injuries, and deaths through their military strength. The Semitic system of retaliatory justice based on "a life for a life" in the circumstances of desert life could not always ensure that crime would not be committed lightly and irresponsibly. Against this background, the legitimate use of force prescribed by the Qur'an was merely to provide appropriate moral restrictions on the use of military power to resolve conflicts. Legitimation of jihad in the meaning of "fighting" appears in the context of defending the community and bringing the breakdown of the public order to a halt so that "there is no persecution and the religion be only for God" (K. 2:193).

5   This was a prescriptive measure to arrest the harm caused to the people at large and to redress the wrongs suffered by the weak at the hands of those who perpetrated immoralities in order to defeat the divine purposes on earth. The use of force, as far as the Qur'an is concerned, is defensive and limited to the violation of

interpersonal human conduct. For the Qur'an it is crucial to emphasize its defensive strategy in dealing with the problem of violence stemming from human rejection of faith. My categorization of the Qur'anic jihad as strictly defensive jihad is based on absolute absence of any reference to an offensive jihad in the Qur'an, that is, jihad, undertaken to convert all humanity to Islam. Nonetheless, as the historical development of the relationship between Islam and power progressed, Muslim jurists regarded this explicitly Qur'anic principle of defensive warfare as abrogated by the verse, which has been dubbed as "the sword verse" (Q. 9:5) that declares war on the unbelievers: ". . . slay them wherever you find them, and take them, and confine them, and lie in wait for them at every place of ambush." They maintained that fighting was obligatory for Muslims, even when the unbelievers had not begun hostilities. This accommodation with the historical practice of jihad is not uncommon in the works of the jurists. In the wake of the phenomenal conquests achieved by Muslim armies during the seventh century, the jurists began to apply the term jihad to military action and to efforts to expand the Muslim empire through the extension of the boundaries of the Islamic polity.

However, the Qur'an does not stop at this duty of self-defense against hostile forces. It leaves the possibility of offensive jihad when it requires the Prophet to strive to create an ideal public order. At this point, the jihad becomes an offensive struggle to bring about the kind of world order Islam envisions. The requirement of offensive jihad as a means in the creation of the Islamic world order gives rise to the tension between the tolerance advocated in matters relating to the religious destiny of human beings, and the active response required against those disbelievers who engage in persecution of Muslims. The development of Muslim political power provides a warrant for wars of expansion, depending upon how one interprets the passages of the Qur'an that speak about fighting the hostile unbelievers "until there is no persecution and the religion be only for God" (K. 2:191).

JIHAD IN MODERN TIMES

In the recent history the call for jihad has been heard coming from both religious as well as secular Muslim leaders, fighting sometimes external aggression or domination, and at other times internal enemies of the Muslim state. The use of the word jihad for these wars of national liberation or internal rebellion among

Muslim nations raises serious questions about inappropriate use of religiously sanctioned jihad. A number of Muslim scholars have questioned the pre-modern juridical formulations about jihad and declared them incompatible with the international norms that govern laws of war. At the same time, some Muslim scholars have argued that the antecedents for the just war tradition's concerns with proportionality and discrimination in war, which in turn contributed to the rise of humanitarian law, are embedded in Islamic conceptions of jihad. The focus of pre-modern juridical discussion of jihad was on *jus in bello*—concerns with the principles of discrimination (or non-combatant immunity) and proportionality in use of force in warfare. The legality—*jus ad bellum*—of engaging in warfare was taken as established through the historical precedents which showed jihad to be both a war of defense as well as a war for territorial expansion. The focus of modern writers, on the other hand, is on *jus ad bellum*, with little attention on the conduct of war. This lack of interest in *jus in bello* raises serious questions about the ethics of war in modern appropriation of jihad.

Today jihad as a divinely sanctioned means to combat the enemy provides justifications for going to war for reasons of realpolitik without concern for limitations upon the means. This means that overemphasis on the *jus ad bellum* criteria at the expense of undermining the *jus in bello*, which formed the major focus of the classic discussions of jihad and served to justify wars fought for advancing Muslim hegemony, has served to justify even the use of terrorism and individual acts of violence against those deemed "the enemy."

The term jihad, with its long and complex history in Islam as it interacted with political power, has been used and abused to justify endless violence that has plagued many of these countries in the Middle East. The frequent abuse of the term by the religious leaders has led many Western observers to treat jihad essentially in the meaning of "holy war," with an implication that Muslim international relations will continue to be conflict-ridden because, as a religious obligation to fight dark forces of disbelief and arrogance harb al-kuffar', jihad will continue to determine Muslim relations with the non-Muslim world. But jihad has also been used to speak about conflict among the "brother nation-states" in the "family" al-bughat, and certainly this jihad is not the same as the one fought against non-Muslims.

10   To add to this complexity of the term and the circumstances of different kinds of jihad in Muslim history are the preconceived and historically entrenched interpretations of wars between Mus-

lims and the Christian world which continue to loom large in Western understanding of jihad. Most Western attempts to explain the culture of violence in the Muslim world have connected this culture to the religious appropriation of the term jihad in the meaning of "holy war" and as such to a Muslim political goal of extending "the sphere of Islam" dar al-islam, that is, territories administered by the Muslim state, by obliterating "the sphere of war" dar al-harb, that is, territories to be subdued. The two phrases, as argued by these writers, highlight the theological foundation of Muslim religious convictions about forming a Muslim empire that must ultimately subdue and dominate non-Muslim world. Such an evaluation of jihad is essentialist and based entirely on a narrow range of theological-juridical sources that responded to the real as well as idealized history of the last fourteen centuries. The theological-juridical expression of the doctrine and the legal issues surrounding jihad, as well as modern interpretations required by such momentous changes for the Muslim world as colonialism and responses to modernity and the West, require us to be cautious in linking the past heritage to the contemporary Muslim responses to oppression and aggression by Muslim and non-Muslim forces.

Nevertheless, with the growing influence of the religious extremism in the last three decades it is possible to speak about the influence of a major article of faith in dealing with unjust rulers on the on-going conflicts in the Muslim world, whether that conflict involves non-Muslim or Muslim countries with illegitimate rulers in power. These rulers are perceived as the followers of the pre-Islamic system of the jahiliyya—the period that is regarded as ungodly by these ultra-pious Muslims. The belief that can be exploited to generate perpetual conflict is the one that maintains the superiority of Islam regards it as the final and perfected message that abrogated the pre-Qur'anic religions like Judaism and Christianity. This sense of spiritual-moral superiority also serves to instigate not only interfaith conflicts; it also provides with sufficient religiously crafted justifications for mutual condemnation and ensuing deadly conflict in the intra-faith relations between the Sunnites and the Shi'ites.

THE PERFECT RELIGION THAT WILL
REPLACE ALL OTHER RELIGIONS

The debate over the role of religious ideas in engendering deadly conflicts around the globe is still going on. In the Islamic context, my own observations lead me to affirm that religion and religious beliefs are a source of much activism in Muslim world. During the most recent conflicts, such as in Bosnia and Chechnya, the statements calling the people for jihad make frequent references about the world in which Muslims are increasingly under physical threat by non-Muslim governments and groups. Anti-modernism is prominent in the religious pronouncements. Closely related to discourses against modernity are theological arguments against the West, the U.S. in particular. According to John Kelsay, "The momentum of Islamic thinking about justice and war leads to an emphasis on such *jus ad bellum* concerns as right authority and just cause, and ultimately to a discussion of how conceptions of nature and destiny of human beings set a framework for discussions of war."

The importance of religious beliefs in spawning conflicts among the "peoples of the Book" cannot be underestimated. The source of many a deadly conflict among Muslims has been the belief that Islam is the only true religion which will dominate all other religions, superceding them. This confinement of salvation to only one religion rules out the plurality of faiths and communities and ensuing toleration founded upon the principle of coexistence. The exclusivist belief effectively rules out peaceful coexistence among different faith communities, and within the community itself. The establishment of Dar al-taqrib bayna al-madhahib (Reconciliation between various schools of thought) in Cairo, Egypt and Qumm, Iran have a single goal in mind: to understand the differences between various Muslim schools of thought, and generate a meaningful dialogue between the majority Sunnites and the minority Shi'ites. However, the extremists on both sides regard these attempts to reconcile the Shi'ites and the Sunnites as nothing less than a compromise on one's monopoly over the religious truth. When this exclusivist doctrine is applied to determine interfaith relations, then it has the potential to disrupt peaceful relations between different faith communities. Consequently, it is important to examine in some detail the idea of perfect religion abrogating all other religions—the idea that can be retrieved by the extremists in any tradition to dehumanize the religious "other."

The idea that Islam is the ultimate and perfect religion in the line of Abrahamic religions is derived from the Tradition (the Sunna). One might even suggest that the idea of Islam being the only monotheistic tradition that offers the indubitable guarantee of salvation in the hereafter is post-Qur'anic. For the Qur'an saw itself as confirming rather than altering the central message of the Abrahamic religions that preceded it chronologically. More importantly, it saw itself as a conclusive revelation in the ongoing process of divine guidance from the day the earth became inhabited by the first human couple, Adam and Eve. Consequently, the Qur'an does not take up the issue of abrogation or supersession of the previous Abrahamic religions of Christianity or Judaism and prescribe the forced conversion of the followers of these religions. Quite to the contrary, it recognizes the salvific efficacy of the Abrahamic faiths, whose central doctrines are shared by Islam.

In the light of growing tensions in inter- and intra-faith relations in countries like Sudan, Pakistan and Afghanistan, an extremely important question needs to be raised about the way religions respond to the plurality of human responses to the religious impulse. How does it treat those who do not share its salvation narrative? The question should also lead us to explore the ways in which public space is negotiated and controlled by the dominant faith community. Furthermore, it should reveal the strategies that were adopted in the power-faith tradition like Islam to regulate legal-ethical relations with its non-Muslim minorities at home and maintain its international relations abroad. Theological-juridical justifications for the jihad with non-Muslims were provided by the Muslim jurists who had hoped that the entire world would become the "sphere of Islam." My central thesis in this paper is that the Muslim juristic-theological discourses were articulated to justify the claim of conquering Muslim armies that "Islam as the only true religion with God" (Q. 3:19) and the only one desired by God (Q. 3:85) provided the divinely ordained mandate for the offensive jihad in the context of successful political and social domination of the community. This interaction between the idea of Islam being the universal religion for all humankind and the existing predominance of Muslim political power created the specific legal language that provided the justification to extend the notion of jihad beyond its strictly defensive meaning in the Qur'an to its being an offensive instrument for Muslim creation of a dominant political order.

Muslim juristic discourse in the area of jihad becomes a thoroughly legitimating discourse, justifying the undertaking of the jihad as a divinely ordained duty, with a prescription to expand the sphere of Muslim dominions, assuring the Muslim warriors their reward in this and the next world for fulfilling the duty of fighting in the path of God. And although one can observe the attempt to strike a balance between conservative legitimation and aspiration generated by simple fidelity to the inherited doctrines or precedents of a juristic culture, more than often this discourse tended to be based on imperfect understanding of a reality or a change of circumstances that required a practical or functional response. By "practical" I mean an outlook that tends to assess what is actually feasible, whereas by "functional" I mean an outlook oriented towards the potential function of maintaining an Islamic order. For instance, a Muslim jurist may write that a permanent state of peace may not exist between Muslims and non-Muslims, and that non-Muslims should be fought at least once a year. The jurist might believe that this describes an actual practice or that it responds to a practical concern. Yet, the jurist's imperfect understanding of reality or a change in circumstances might reveal that, more than anything else, this statement is prescriptive in nature, that is, it lays down what is desirable. However, if the ruling is based on a reading of a context suggesting a political and social reality then it is a functional ruling to accomplish a specific result. If non-Muslims will not contravene against Muslims, or if attacking non-Muslims once a year will not produce the desired effect of inspiring fear in non-Muslims, then the rule is simply in the books waiting to be implemented. On the other hand, if the statement is a moral prescription, then regardless of the consequences or results, the rule remains valid, and non-Muslims, as desired by the lawgiver, should be attacked at least once a year.

"A PROPHET FOR ALL HUMANITY"

The fatwas reminding Muslims about their religious duty to undertake jihad in the modern times shows an important shift from the way classical prescriptive rulings about engagement in the war against non-Muslims were prescribed. Whereas the classical juristic discourse reflected how Muslim jurists aspired to provide justifications for engaging in jihad with the non-Muslims as part of the divinely ordained activity to bring all of humanity under Islamic dominion, modern fatwas call for radical resistance to the Western aggression against Muslim peoples. The classical rulings were established when Muslims were in power and when emphasis on the exclusivist doctrine contrived from the Qur'anic verse was seen more in political terms: "We have sent you [o Muhammad] not, except to humankind entire kaffatun-nas, good tidings to bear, and warning" (Q. 34:27). Under the classical juristic discourse the limitations set upon the conduct of warfare against Muslims and non-Muslims were not the same. If Muslims fight other Muslims, there are binding regulations that do not necessarily apply to Muslims fighting non-Muslims. If Muslims fight one another, the fugitive and wounded may not be dispatched. Muslim prisoners may not be executed or enslaved. Children and women may not be intentionally killed or imprisoned. Imprisoned male Muslims must be released once the fighting, or the danger of continued fighting, ends. Even more, strategies of mass destruction may not be used unless absolutely necessary. In principle Muslims are prohibited from fighting each other; if they do, they are considered to have committed a grave sin. Muslim jurists in general cautioned against the evil of rash and violent rebellions against unjust rulers. It is important to emphasize that Muslim jurists hinged the treatment of Muslim combatants on a perceived moral culpability of those who were the cause of social unrest, but most of their efforts focused on the morality of conduct and not the morality of purpose. As for issues related to the fighting against non-Muslims its legality was not discussed because the doctrine of the finality of the Islamic revelation and its universality for all humankind was taken as a given. Muslim jurists conceded the authority to the ruler to negotiate relations with foreign powers, keeping in mind the protection of Muslims and Islam under their domain. However, the rules about the conduct of war were not very different from those that applied to the Muslim rebels engaged in fighting an unjust Muslims ruler. All proper limits that applied to the "in family" Muslims fighting Muslims were articulated for conducting war against non-Muslims to whom the jurists imputed a degree of moral culpability.

In comparison to these classical formulations, modern statements on jihad not only argue the justifications for going to war against Western enemies, but also justify terrorism and individual acts of violence against the enemy, civilian or otherwise, wherever they may be found in the world. Thus, Usama ben Laden, the Saudi rebel, in his fatwa of 1998 justified terrorist acts against the United States in terms of aggressive American policy towards Muslims in general, and its support of corrupt Saudi regime. He regards jihad an individual duty (fard ayn), which must be performed by all male, able-bodied Muslims, and not simply a collective one (fard kifaya), which, if performed by sufficient number, relieves others from performing it. Ben Laden goes even further to argue that terrorism is a legitimate and morally demanded duty so long as anti-Muslim forces are carrying arms in Muslim lands, especially Muslim holy places. This argument for terrorism as a legitimate means of conduct in war is a clear departure from the classical rulings which regard the ethics of war as important part of jihad.

THE CRISIS OF INTERPRETING ISLAMIC
JIHAD FOR WORLD PEACE

It is appropriate to speak about a crisis of retrieval and interpretation of the rulings about jihad today. In the world of nation-states where international relations are conducted without any reference to religious affiliation (or lack thereof) of the member states, the discourse about jihad among the extremist groups gives rise to uncompromising attitudes that render all chances of negotiated peace practically impossible. To elaborate on the seriousness of the crisis created by selective retrieval of past rulings on jihad and their interpretation by the leaders of radical movements, who lack the necessary training in contextualizing the past rulings to investigate their applicability in the modern times, has led to untold misery suffered by the innocent civilians caught up in the crossfire. Muslim jurists follow certain guidelines in their investigation whether rulings on an institution like jihad, which legitimized and provided moral limits on the conduct of war, can have relevance in the new world order. There are three basic steps that must be covered in order to derive fresh rulings on the subject of the "sphere of war" today:

a. Investigation in the usul-fundamental sources like the Qur'an and the Sunna (the Tradition) that provide direct or indirect statements describing or defining the "sphere of war" and its limits;
b. Investigation in the furu paradigm-cases that could guide the jurist to determine a legal-ethical outcome of the present case;
c. Investigation of the mawdu at—"objects" or "situations" that might share similarity or variations with paradigm cases in order to understand changed "situations" and the ordinances that could be based on them to decide whether the "sphere of war" today can be described the same way as it was done in the past.

20   The ah-kam rulings can be derived only after the above three steps have been followed in the investigation to guide the practice today.

This traditional method of deriving fresh decisions has given rise to several fundamental problems related to the determination of the "situational" context of jihad against Muslim rebels and non-Muslims. First of all, it is obvious to the jurists in the traditional centers (who are severely criticized by the radicals) that Muslims are not living under the universal caliphal state. Therefore, the legal terms used to divide the world between dar al-islam and dar al-harb are defunct in modern times. The use of dar al-islam for any Muslim country is legally problematic. Moreover, during the Iran-Iraq and the Gulf War Muslim countries were pitted against one another, and neither of these wars could be described as jihad, because in both cases the rhetorical use of jihad had rendered the term meaningless. Hence, the classical rulings and the terminology used there proved to be irrelevant in classification of the jihad. The requirement to investigate changed situation prior to issuing of the legal decision affecting the status of Muslim countries under consideration remains contentious even now. The role of Muslim jurists in ascertaining the legality of jihad in the "Family" was circumvented by the realities of public international order where Islam was no longer a determining factor in resolving the conflict peacefully. Neither the classical heritage nor the contemporary radical interpretations of jihad as a means to achieve political ends of extremist factions have proven capable of providing solutions to the concerns for peace among ordinary Muslim peoples in a given Muslim state.

The prerequisite of individual rational inquiry in the situational context in Islamic legal inquiry makes it necessary that people should be involved in representing their own concerns in all matters related to their social and political well being. Implicit in this prerequisite is that any legal decision affecting not only Muslims but also non-Muslim minorities living within Muslim territories should be made while allowing the people to exercise their right to determine their general well-being in the society.

However, the granting of the protected religious minority (ahl al-dhimma) status by the law, which accorded autonomous legal status to the minority, was deduced from an ideological standpoint of the superiority of the Muslim community. There was no acknowledgement of the Qur'anic monotheistic egalitarianism in dealing with the Christians and the Jews of the empire. Lurking behind the concept of the ahl al-dhimma was the supersessionist theology of the Muslim scholars in which the only form of monotheism was the religion of Islam. Moreover, because of this theological conviction, the institutional recognition of these subject peoples as spiritually and morally inferior religious communities became one of the major factors in obstructing the integrating objects and situations that would have gradually led to the creation of an egalitarian civil society in the Muslim world.

The majority of the discriminatory rulings against non-Muslims, it must be pointed out, were derived by reference to the juristic principle that "averting causes of corruption has prece-

dence over bringing about that which has benefit" (daru al-mafasid muqaddam ala jalb al-masalih). This and other similar juristic principles were designed to regulate inter-human relationships in the law and were more than often invoked to curb the rights of minorities to function as full citizens in Muslim societies.
25   The supersessionist theology notwithstanding, a cursory glance at the juridical decisions made in relation to the followers of other monotheistic faiths indicates that, relatively speaking, Muslim jurists succeeded in pursuing the Qur'anic impulse towards asserting individual rights of all the followers of the Abrahamic traditions on the basis of God-centered equality. And, although Muslims retained wide authority in the society laws were enacted to give minorities unprecedented respect and protection in the Muslim polity.

CONCLUDING REMARKS

Let me conclude by saying that Kitab al-jihad ("The Book on Jihad") section of the juridical corpus continues to exercise enormous influence in the way Muslim world conceives its relation with the non-Muslim "other." One can hardly ignore the implications of the religious statements contained in the legal rulings and the widely circulated traditions in the formulation of policies affecting Muslim–non-Muslim relations. Kitab al-jihad in any work on Islamic law is a key to our understanding of the way in which Muslim community related itself to the world at large, including to the tolerated minorities within its own borders. If anything, it is the rationalization of jihad in the jurisprudence that demonstrates the interaction between theology and politics in its most clear contours. In the final analysis, no comprehension of Christian-Muslim or Jewish-Muslim relations is possible without adequate understanding of the theology of supersession and its impact upon the Muslim treatment of its religious minorities. Recognition of religious pluralism in Islam has always been determined either by absolutist or relative claim of Islam being the "only" accepted way. And, it is the Muslim jurists who have allowed one or the other interpretation to prevail, depending on their evaluation of the perceived threat to Islam and its peoples.

Starting Points

1. Abdulaziz Sachedina is an academic, that is, he is a professional educator and writer. This essay is written in a style commonly called "academic." What are some characteristics of the style? What is the purpose of academic or scholarly writing? Is this essay effective in that purpose?

2. How does Sachedina's explanation of jihad as defensive and limited to "the violation of interpersonal human conduct" (paragraph 5) affect your own reading of the rest of this essay?

3. If you are not Muslim, some of the author's explanations may sound exotic or foreign when he details some specifics of Islamic religious law. Yet other religions have equally difficult precepts, such as the trinity or communion. In a collaborative group or in your classroom, discuss a variety of religions, and their differences or similarities, in an open and receptive atmosphere.

A Second Moment of Hope
MARY ELLEN McNISH

The American Friends Service Committee (AFSC), an organ of the Society of Friends (Quakers), has long worked for peace and justice issues here and abroad. Mary Ellen McNish, general secretary of the organization, delivered the following address to the Fourth World Summit of Nobel Peace Laureates in Rome in November 2003. The AFSC and the British Friends Service Council were awarded the Nobel Peace Prize in 1947.

◆

I would like to call my talk today "A Second Moment of Hope." I call it that because there was another moment of hope that we in the United States experienced. It was in the days following 9/11, when every country in the world stood shoulder to shoulder to support us. So many vigils were held in cities around the world; we were overwhelmed with gratitude and were very hopeful. That is why it was so hard for us to see that moment of hope squandered in the past two years—squandered through unilateral military action and a disregard for international opinion.

Many of you have heard the phrase, "A society is judged by how it treats its most vulnerable members." In the Torah, Israel is constantly reminded of its duty to the widow, the orphan, and the stranger. Jesus says that "whatever you do to the least of these, you do to me." Charity is one of the five pillars of Islam. Buddhism reminds us again and again of our duty to compassion. Many faiths and philosophies tell us that a society that tolerates disregard for the poor and the vulnerable will never be healthy, secure, or at peace. How will future generations judge us?

In too many places in the world today, prosperous and privileged individuals and nations are willing to sacrifice the vulnerable. Human beings are defined as collateral damage in war and as disposable in economic relationships. In Iraq, the American occupiers do not even report the number of civilian dead. What does this say about the value given to these lives? Trade pacts encourage the free movement of capital—but what about fairness to workers, environmental impacts and developing nations. International monetary institutions waffle between working for the good of the vulnerable and acquiescing to the wishes of the powerful nations that give them legitimacy.

All the world's spiritual traditions tell us that this cannot be allowed to stand, that we are embedding the seeds of war into the heart of the international system. If our international institutions speak beautiful words, but by their actions protect the status quo, the words are hypocrisy. If we champion the rights of the powerful over the rights of the poor, we create a debt, a moral debt, that will only compound over time.

5   Quakerism teaches that there is that of God in every person. This belief calls us to hold up the human face of war, to stand in support of those who suffer injustice, to be with those who live in the midst of poverty and disease.

Today in the United States, the world's wealthiest country, the American Friends Service Committee is lifting its voice, with others, to oppose and turn back the policies of military unilateralism that claim the right to invade other nations and to bypass international institutions in the name of security. We work to mobilize the American people to call on President Bush and his administration to honor nuclear non-proliferation agreements and to stop the development of small nuclear weapons. We are working in coalition with others to call for the UN to administer Iraq's reconstruction. We are calling for the U.S. and the United Kingdom to fulfill their obligations to compensate the Iraqi people for the damage those countries have caused.

We are speaking out against new policies that harass and imprison immigrants in our own country and that violate the ancient dictum to give especial care to the stranger in our midst. We are working for fair global trade policies that lift the standard of living for workers in developing countries. We labor for an end to capital punishment in our country, a stain that calls our entire justice system into question.

But these efforts in the U.S. will never be enough. As an American organization, we ask, in fact need, your help in holding our country accountable. We are working harder than we have ever worked to bring together new coalitions—coalitions who've never worked together before. We are reaching out to pull together poor and privileged, North and South, East and West to make those in power take note.

While the U.S. continues to use its disproportionate military and economic power to mute criticism by other governments, I am heartened by what I see happening around the world. Ten million people in cities across the globe took to the streets to oppose the invasion of Iraq last February. People around the world are uniting in the belief that an arrogant superpower is as much of a threat to global stability as any number of extremist groups.

It is no longer only religious leaders and secular visionaries who say that neither militarism nor terrorism will give us security, that economic structures that create a new form of colonialism will not give the world prosperity. The events of the last two years have made it clear that it is no longer enough for states to support international institutions. These institutions that will guide our future must be bolstered by the strength of tens of millions of voices. I believe that we are witnessing the birth of a global, grassroots movement uniting those who long for peace, those who know that our collective futures are intertwined and those who know in the deepest part of their soul—*there can be no peace without justice.*

As civil society within nations has been the mother of liberty and equality, a new global citizenship must now call the current world order to account for itself. As individuals and organizations honored by the Nobel Peace Prize, we have a special responsibility to call powerful institutions and nations to task, to remind them of their moral obligations.

The Peace Prize is given for the exercise of moral courage. People know moral hollowness when they see it. They respond when the prophetic voice names it. We who have been granted a moral platform must exercise that prophetic voice.

The world's people are beginning to speak in a common voice to say that peace will not come at the end of a gun, the tip of a warhead, or in a backpack of explosives. Peace will come with food and healthcare and education. Peace will come through the right-sharing of resources and through honoring the dignity and worth of every person.

As Nobel Peace Laureates, we must not shrink from speaking prophetically, from saying that the path being imposed on us leads not to peace and security, but to destruction, and the downward cycle of violence and conflict. As each of us travels in our own countries and around the world, we must redouble our efforts to build bridges across movements, among peoples, between North and South, East and West, so that the voices of the world's citizens can be heard.

15   This will be fluid movement of networks and groupings brought together by the threat of full spectrum dominance and all that is implied by that term. It will be messy and chaotic, but we cannot be daunted by the scope and audacity of the task.

As people of peace, our path is before us, though perhaps not as clearly marked as we would like. I think of the words of Chief Leon Shenandoah of the Onondaga people:

> *Everything is laid out for you.*
> *Your path is straight ahead of you.*
> *Sometimes it's invisible, but it's there.*
> *You may not know where it's going,*
> *but you have to follow that path.*
> *It's the path to the Creator.*
> *It's the only path there is.*

Starting Points:

1. The author makes references to a variety of religious views regarding protection of the most vulnerable members of society. Is her plea effective, and does the invocation of religious thinking in any way detract from her message? Is her message enhanced by such references? What do you believe should be the role of religions and affiliated organizations in the search for peaceful resolution of conflicts?

2. The American Friends Service Committee (with the British Friends Service Council) was awarded the Nobel Peace Prize in 1947. The author alludes to that honor in her address. Do such awards cause you as a reader to give more credence to what an author has to say? What other considerations, aside from the text itself, influence your reception of a written article or essay?

3. Write an essay in which you argue for or against the work of NGOs (non-governmental organizations) to influence the national policies of a political state. Do nation-states, prepared as they are for war, have the same impetus for peace as NGOs?

Ethics and Policy
4TH GLOBAL SUMMIT OF NOBEL PEACE LAUREATES

Nobel Peace Prize Laureates held a global summit in Rome in November 2003 to consider world-wide issues of peace and justice. What follows is the statement released by the Laureates—individuals and organizations—at the conclusion of the summit. Its vision is far-reaching and global in scope rather than national, and in regard to international terrorism, seeks both multilateral response and the promotion of human rights to combat the underlying causes of terrorism.

◆

FINAL STATEMENT

We are the first generation making decisions that will determine whether we will be the last generation. We have an ethical responsibility to future generations to ensure that we are not passing on a future of wars and ecological catastrophe. For policies to be in the interest of humanity, they must be based on ethical values.

We express our profound anxiety that current policies are not creating a sufficiently secure and stable world for all. For this reason, we need to reset our course based on strong ethical foundations.

Compassion and conscience are essential to our humanity and compel us to care for one another. Cooperation amongst nations, multilateralism, is the logical outgrowth of this principle. A more equitable international order based on the rule of law is its needed expression.

We reiterate our conviction that international politics need to be reformed to address effectively three critical challenges: ending wars and violence, eliminating poverty, and saving the environment.

We call upon everyone to join us in working to replace the 5 culture of war with a culture of peace. Let us ensure that no child is ever again exposed to the horrors of war.

Recent events, such as the escalation of the conflict in the Middle East, bloodshed in Afghanistan, Iraq and Chechnya, as well as in parts of Africa and Latin America, confirm that problems with deep economic, social, cultural or religious roots cannot be resolved unilaterally or by armed force.

International terrorism is a threat to peace. Multilateral co-operation and the promotion of human rights under the rule of law are essential to address terrorism and its underlying sources.

The threat of weapons of mass destruction remains with us. We call for an immediate end to the newly resurgent arms race, which is being fueled by a failure to universally ratify a treaty banning nuclear testing, and by doctrines that lower the threshold of use and promote the creation of new nuclear weapons. This is particularly dangerous when coupled with the doctrine of pre-emption.

For some to say that nuclear weapons are good for them but not for others is simply not sustainable. The failure of the nuclear weapons states to abide by their legal pledge to negotiate the elimination of nuclear weapons, contained in the Nuclear Nonproliferation Treaty, is the greatest stimulus to their proliferation.

10   Nuclear weapons are immoral and we call for their universal legal prohibition. They must be eliminated before they eliminate humanity.

We support the treaty to ban landmines and call for effective agreements to limit conventional weapons and arms trade.

Trillions of dollars have been spent since the end of the Cold War in developing military approaches to security. Yet, the daily lives of billions remain bereft of adequate health care, clean water, food and the benefits of education. These needs must be met.

Humanity has developed sophisticated technologies for destruction. Appropriate social and human technologies based on cooperation are needed for survival.

The international community has a proven tool, the universality of the United Nations. Its work can and must be improved and this can be done without undermining its core principles.

15   We assert that unconditional adherence to international law is essential. Of course, law is a living institution that can change and grow to meet new circumstances. But, the principles that govern international relations must not be ignored or violated.

Ethics in the relations between nations and in government policies is of paramount importance. Nations must treat other nations as they wish to be treated. The most powerful nations must remember that as they do, so shall others do.

Economic hardship is often the result of corruption and lack of business ethics, both internationally and locally.

Through utilizing more effective ethical codes of conduct the business community can contribute to protecting the environment and eliminating poverty. This is both a practical and moral necessity.

The scientific community could serve human interests more fully by affirmatively adopting the ethical principle of doing no harm.

The international community has recently recognized the importance of establishing an ethical framework. Leaders of States issued the Millennium Declaration at the United Nations and set forth common values of freedom, equality, solidarity, tolerance, respect for nature and shared responsibility. From these values, a plan to address sustainable development and poverty, the Millennium Development Goals, emerged. We urge all to join in implementation of these goals and prevent any retreat from specific commitments. Moreover, we share the principles of the Earth Charter and urge governments at all levels to support this important document.   20

For globalization to enhance sustainable development, the international community needs to establish more democratic, transparent, and accountable forms of governance. We advocate extending the benefits of democracy and self governance but this goal cannot be achieved through coercion or force.

After a special session, the Nobel Peace Prize Winners have agreed that the death penalty is a particularly cruel and unusual punishment that should be abolished. It is especially unconscionable when imposed on children.

We affirm the unity of the human family. Our diversity is an enrichment, not a danger. Through dialogue we gain appreciation of the value of our differences. Our capacity to work together as a community of peoples and nations is the strongest antidote to violence and our reason for hope.

Our commitment to serve the cause of peace compels us to continue working individually and together on this path. We urge you to join us.

Starting Points

1. Choose one specific issue addressed by the Nobel Peace Laureates and discuss in a collaborative group how to best resolve the problem, with specific goals and plans for proceeding. Who should lead the effort? What are the obstacles to success? What other issues are inter-related?

2. Audience is a factor often discussed in composition classes. But to what extent is author also a factor? Does the message of a Nobel laureate carry greater weight for you than the identical text with an anonymous author, or

someone with whom you are completely unfamiliar? Why do you think this is so? Should we as an audience valorize a text delivered by someone of high standing more than that of an unknown?
3. The selection of the recipient of the Nobel Peace Prize has sometimes been controversial. Research the process by which individuals and groups are nominated, and how the committee selects the eventual honoree. Do international politics affect the results? What are the perquisites following the bestowal of the honor? What have been some of the more controversial selections?

Other Journeys: Suggestions for Further Writing and Research

1. If you believe that the war on terror against stateless warriors calls for a new convention on treatment of prisoners or detainees, write your own Geneva policy, closely following the style and elements of the current Geneva Convention on Prisoners of War.
2. Study the Crusades of the Middle Ages in an effort to discern why "crusader" is such a negative term in Muslim countries. Is the current War on Terror a crusade, or simply a defensive war against violent attackers? Should the term "crusader" be dropped from the current lexicon of policymakers?
3. Create your own paradigm for peace with your classmates. If you were czar of the universe, what global changes would you effect regarding economics, education, armaments, justice, and the environment? Are these necessary changes to secure peace? Are they viable, or are they chimerical?
4. Choose a particular topic of peace, war, or terrorism and study the information available from government sources, from news media, and from scholarly journals. Which source gave you the most easily digestible information? Which source seemed to "spin" the issue? Which source treated it most thoroughly?
5. Consider the reports from international agencies or charities that are critical of U.S. actions and policies in the current War on Terror in Afghanistan and Iraq. What is your response to the criticism? If you agree with the conclusions, consider focusing on one issue (for example, torture, Abu Ghraib, the Gonzales memo and others, sending prisoners to countries where torture is used, or the increased global sale of small arms) and after additional research write a persuasive essay to change American policy. If you disagree, detail your argument against the international reports, explaining why such policies and/or actions are necessary for our national security.
6. Learn more about Islam and the current debate over jihad. Write a well-researched and documented essay on either side of the issue: Does Islam support a frame of mind that leads to fanaticism and terrorism?

Arnswald, Ulrich. "Preventive War or Preemptive War," from *Freitag* (August 22, 2003). Reprinted with permission of author.

Ashcroft, John. "Patriot Act Honors Liberty and Freedom," from a speech given to the Federalist Society National Convention, November 15, 2003.

Associated Press, "Al-Qaida Leader Says They Have Briefcase Nukes," from AOL News (March 21, 2004). Reprinted with permission of The Associated Press.

Benjamin, Daniel. "Two Years After 9/11: A Balance Sheet," from *United States Institute of Peace Special Report 111*, October 2003. Reprinted by permission of the author.

Bolton, John R. "The International Aspects of Terrorism and Weapons of Mass Destruction," from an address to the Second Global Conference on Nuclear, Biological, and Chemical Terrorism: Mitigation and Response, Hudson Institute, Washington, D.C., November 1, 2002.

Bowcott, Owen, and Richard Norton-Taylor, "War on Terror Fuels Small Arms Trade," from *The Guardian* (October 10, 2003). Copyright © the authors and *The Guardian*.

Bush, George W. "President Announces New Measures to Counter the Threat of WMD," from an address to the National Defense University, February 11, 2004, Fort Leslie J. McNair, Washington, D.C.

Cook, Martin L. "Ethical Issues in Counterterrorism Warfare," from *Defeating Terrorism: Strategic Issue Analysis* (U.S. Army, 2002). Reprinted with permission.

Davis, Joyce M. "Mission of Suicide Bombers Is Martyrdom, Retribution," from *Detroit Free Press* (April 8, 2002). Copyright © 2004 Detroit Free Press.

Engel, Richard. "Inside Al-Qaeda: A Window into the World of Militant Islam and the Afghani Alumni," from *Jane's.com* (September 28, 2001). Reproduced with permission of Jane's Information Group.

Gale, Stephen, and Lawrence Husick, "From MAD (Mutual Assured Destruction) to MUD (Multilateral Unconstrained Disruption): Dealing With the New Terrorism," from *Foreign Policy Research Institute* (online, vol. 11 no. 1, February 2003). Published with permission of the Foreign Policy Research Institute Wire.

Galston, William. "The Perils of Preemptive War," from *The American Prospect* (vol. 13 no. 7, September 23, 2002). Reprinted with permission from the *American Prospect*. All Rights Reserved.

Grimmett, Richard F. "U.S. Use of Preemptive Military Force: The Historical Record," from *U.S Foreign Policy Agenda* (vol. 7 no. 4, December 2002). Reprinted with permission.

Herman, Susan. "The USA Patriot Act and the US Department of Justice: Losing Our Balances?" from *Jurist* (December 3, 2001), a publication of the University of Pittsburgh School of Law online. Published with permission of the author and *Jurist*.

243

Hightower, Jim. "In a Time of Terror, Protest Is Patriotism," from *Independent Media Institute* (November 14, 2001). Reprinted with permission.

Human Rights Watch, "The Road to Abu Ghraib: A Policy to Evade International Law," from *Road to Abu Ghraib* (June 2004). Copyright © 2004 Human Rights Watch.

Hutchings, Robert L. "Terrorism and Economic Security," from a speech given to the International Security Management Association, January 14, 2004. Reprinted with permission of the International Security Management Association.

Macarthur, John R. "The Lies We Bought: The Unchallenged 'Evidence' for War," from the *Columbia Journalism Review* (May/June, 2003). Reprinted with permission.

McClanahan, E. Thomas. "White House Should Clarify Torture Policy," from *The Kansas City Star* (June 22, 2004). Copyright © Kansas City Star.

McNish, Mary Ellen. "A Second Moment of Hope," from an address to the 4th World Summit of Nobel Peace Laureates.

Meacher, Michael. "This War on Terrorism Is Bogus," from *The Guardian* (September 6, 2003). Copyright © Michael Meacher, *The Guardian*.

Nobel Peace Laureates, "Ethics and Policy," final statement of the 4th Global Summit of Nobel Peace Laureates, Rome, Italy, November 30, 2003.

Peterson, Scott. "'Smarter' Bombs Still Hit Civilians," from the *Christian Science Monitor* (October 22, 2002). Reprinted with permission of the *Christian Science Monitor*.

Rice, Condoleezza. "A Balance of Power that Favors Freedom," from *U.S. Foreign Policy Agenda* (vol. 7 no. 4). Adapted from 2002 Wriston Lecture delivered to the Manhattan Institute in New York, New York, October 1, 2002.

Sachedina, Abdulaziz. "From Defensive to Offensive Warfare: The Use and Abuse of Jihad in the Muslim World," from *Issues in Contemporary Islam: Religion, Law and Force* (Transnational Publishers, 2002). Reprinted with permission.

Saunders, William P. "Possible War With Iraq," from the *Arlington* (Va.) *Catholic Herald*, October 17, 2002. Reprinted with permission of the *Arlington Catholic Herald*.

Schlesinger, Arthur, Jr., "The Immorality of Preemptive War," from *New Perspectives Quarterly* (vol. 19 no. 4, Fall 2002).

Simpson, Peter. "The War on Terrorism: Its Moral Justification and Limits," from the website Ethics Updates, sponsored by the University of San Diego. Reprinted by permission of the author.

Tell, David. "John Ashcroft, Maligned Again," from *The Weekly Standard* (August 4 & 11, 2003). Published with permission of *The Weekly Standard*.

Weiner, Tim. "U.S. Law Puts World Ports on Notice," *New York Times* (March 24, 2004). Copyright © 2004 by the New York Times Co. Reprinted with permission.

Weissman, Steven R. "Doctrine of Preemptive War Has its Roots in Early 1990s," from the *International Herald Tribune* (March 24, 2003). Reprinted with permission of the author and the International Herald Tribune.

Welsh, Steven C. "Preemptive War and International Law," from *Center for Defense Information* (online) (December 5, 2003). Reprinted with permission of the author.

Wilkinson, Paul. "Overview of the Terrorist Threat to International Peace and Security," given at the UN Symposium on Terrorism and Disarmament, New York, New York, October 25, 2001. Reprinted with permission of the author.